A SKY
FULL
OF
LOVE

A SKY FULL OF LOVE

a novel

LORNA LEWIS

LAKE UNION
PUBLISHING

This is a work of fiction. Names, characters, organizations, places, events, and incidents are either products of the author's imagination or are used fictitiously. Otherwise, any resemblance to actual persons, living or dead, is purely coincidental.

Text copyright © 2025 by Lorna Lewis

All rights reserved.

No part of this book may be reproduced, or stored in a retrieval system, or transmitted in any form or by any means, electronic, mechanical, photocopying, recording, or otherwise, without express written permission of the publisher.

Published by Lake Union Publishing, Seattle

www.apub.com

Amazon, the Amazon logo, and Lake Union Publishing are trademarks of Amazon.com, Inc., or its affiliates.

EU product safety contact:
Amazon Media EU S. à r.l.
38, avenue John F. Kennedy, L-1855 Luxembourg
amazonpublishing-gpsr@amazon.com

ISBN-13: 9781662526947 (paperback)
ISBN-13: 9781662526930 (digital)

Cover design by Caroline Teagle Johnson
Cover image: © Christian Sanchez, © JamesBrey, © Troy Harrison, © Chetan Panchal / Getty
Interior image: © Pro_Art / Adobe Stock

Printed in the United States of America

This book is dedicated to my parents who, unbeknownst to them, were the inspiration behind this story.

CHAPTER 1

Nova

October 2018

"Something wrong?" His baritone voice overpowered the small space and pulled me back to the hell he'd created for me.

A space that could only be described as cluttered chaos. Adam tried to turn the bedroom into a living space but failed. The small card table, which we used as a dining table, was barely enough for one person, but night after night, we both sat and ate. Just like we did now. Against the wall, directly across from the table, was the bed.

"Nothing's wrong." I leaned back, causing the chair leg to rock, and crossed my arms over my chest. I stared over his shoulder at the faded pink and yellow flowers on the torn wallpaper. Those flowers were once bright and colorful.

Like I used to be.

"Ain't you gon' eat?" Adam pointed to the macaroni and cheese and smoked sausage that sat untouched on my paper plate.

"I'm not hungry."

I'd been burdened with a heaviness since that morning. It happened every year around this time when I looked out the window from the upper floor of this house and saw the leaves on the trees in the field across the street had sprinkles of red, orange, and yellow—the same as when he'd brought me here. Seeing them reminded me that another year had come and gone, and I was still trapped in this room.

A room I would never call mine, no matter how long I was forced to be here. It was high enough to give me a good view of the trees, but I couldn't jump without breaking something or worse. Not that I could've anyway, since the window was bolted shut.

A loud crash snapped me to attention. I straightened in my chair as a thousand horses raced through my chest. Adam's jar of lemonade shattered all over the wooden floor.

When he didn't order me to get up and clean that mess, I looked over at him. "What's the matter with you?" I asked, seeing the beads of sweat on his forehead. He'd lost weight, and his narrow eyes held a hint of yellowish tint.

He wasn't well. Hadn't been for weeks.

Adam fanned himself with his hands. There wasn't an air conditioner in the room, but it wasn't that hot. He stood. Without saying a word, he inched his way to the door.

I stood, too, the chain around my ankles clanking—a souvenir from my last escape mission. It had been a while since the previous time he'd put them on me. It probably would've been longer had I not had that dream—the one where my parents died. I knew I had to try to escape. I came close. I would've made it out if that old door hadn't creaked. I'd looked back at Adam, who had been in bed sleeping. When he heard the door, he jumped up. His clenched jaw showed the fury I later felt. That was over a week ago, and parts of me still ached from the aftermath of his rage.

"Maybe you should stay here so I can take care of you." I coated my words with an extra dose of sweetness. His chest rose and fell hard, his eyes stretched wide, and his breathing was the only sound in the room. What if something happened to him while I was locked in?

Adam's shaky hand fought to insert the key into the lock. After opening the door, he leaned against the doorframe. I could've overpowered him and run, but my chains were hooked to the bedpost. They were long enough for me to get to the bathroom and the small table, but they weren't long enough to reach across the room to the door.

The silence was louder and heavier than ever. I gasped for air that refused to fill my lungs.

Adam mustered the energy to push himself out.

The lock clicked so loudly that it was like the room vibrated.

Lifting my hand to my face, I realized it wasn't the lock. It was me. I was trembling. The knowledge I could die alone in this room, among the outdated furniture and stained carpet, had always been a reality, but it had never felt as real as it did at that moment.

"Adam!" I shouted, then stretched my hand toward the door, hoping with everything inside me that it would open again. "You can't leave me locked in here! You're sick! I could die!" I banged my foot against the floor as hard as I could, ignoring the pain of the chain as it scrubbed against my raw skin. Maybe the noise would make him angry enough to come running back. I knew my actions would come with repercussions, but every sting from his hand would be worth it if it meant him possibly dying in this room. His death and those keys were all I needed to take back the freedom he'd stolen so long ago. "Adam!" My voice echoed off the walls. I called for him until my words seared my throat and attempted to steal my voice, but as I had learned to do so many times before, I pushed past the pain and kept calling out for him. I called until my thunderous pleas became desperate cries. I fell to the floor, my body convulsing with sobs as I curled into a ball.

I didn't see Adam for days.

I had rationed the food from our dinner that night, taking it in and out of the dorm-size refrigerator that sat in the corner of the room, and ate small bites throughout the day. Some days, like today, I waited until I couldn't take it anymore. But now it was all gone.

Not even a crumb was left.

I didn't know how long I'd last without food. Maybe I'd be okay just drinking the water from the bathroom faucet. I didn't feel okay, though. I was weak. Too weak. I wouldn't make it much longer.

Tired from trying to pick the lock around my ankle, I lay in bed and stared at the ceiling. My thoughts bounced from how I could get out of there to *maybe death will be quick and painless.*

My family was heavy on my heart, so I reached over and grabbed the notebook from the food tray used as a nightstand. That tray, the card table, and most things in that room no longer served their real purpose. Just like me. My fingers trembled as I clutched the pen, trying to steady my breathing. Tears blurred my vision, and I wiped them away with the back of my hand, but not before some escaped onto the page, causing a visual imprint of all the pain I'd held inside.

The weight of loneliness settled like a stone in my chest. An emotion I'd fought for years not to feel came back, but I didn't have the strength to push it aside. This time, I didn't close my eyes and make myself go to another place when Mama's face appeared. Instead, I gave in to the vision and closed my eyes so I could fully submerge myself in the thought of Mama. This had to be a movie, and Mama was the star. I saw her moving around her kitchen, humming and smiling as she always did when she was cooking or baking, especially during the holidays. I heard the sound of one of her old songs playing through the small radio that sat in the kitchen window. I smelled the sweetness that flowed from the oven, and then I saw myself leaning my head on Mama's shoulder as she filled my mouth with a piece of her warm, buttery cake.

I saw Daddy, dancing into the room, grabbing Mama's hand and twirling her around as they often did. He told her that nothing in that kitchen was as sweet as she was. He'd then look over at me and mouth, "Except you," then wink. Daddy and I laughed every time he did that, and Mama would hit his shoulder, knowing he'd said something smart.

I didn't try to stop the tears as they flowed harder than ever. My mind drifted to Leah, and the ache that never left grew stronger. My

Leah. Mama said I'd called her that so much when we were younger that people thought that was her real name. I could hear Leah's loud laughter when we'd sneak away to our room and mock Mama and Daddy. There was so much I still had to tell her—so many dreams we were supposed to fulfill together. I couldn't help but wonder if she'd found a replacement sister. Was there someone else she told her secrets to? I exhaled at the thought.

I couldn't do it anymore—I needed to retreat to my cocoon of nothingness. The thought of my husband was so strong that I smelled the spicy cologne that he used to drown himself in. Did he move on with someone else? Was there another woman raising my . . . And then I couldn't think of anything except my baby girl. I often dreamed of her, at least, I thought it was her. The fact that I had no idea what my daughter looked like now was almost suffocating.

I'd leaned my head against the wall with the notebook and pen still on my lap. I opened my eyes and threw myself back into my world. A world where there was no Mama, no Daddy, no sister, no husband, and no daughter. And now, no Adam. In my world, there was only me. I picked up the pen again and stared down at the paper. My family may never read any of these entries I'd written over the years, but that didn't stop me from writing. In the closet were stacks of notebooks I'd filled. I kept them pushed behind the wool coats and boxes that held more women's clothes. I could only assume those things belonged to Adam's late wife. The closet, which smelled of mothballs and dust, was one place Adam never bothered. I'd hoped the notebooks would be safe there. In the beginning, Adam monitored everything I did and wrote. Back then, it was too painful to even think about my family, so writing about them was out of the question. Besides, I didn't want to share anything about my family with him. He didn't deserve to know about them. So, my earlier notebooks were filled with pictures that made me happy. A sun. A big house that reminded me of my parents. Rain. I loved the rain. I missed the rain. I'd forgotten how it was to stand outside and allow it to tap against my skin.

As the years passed, Adam was less interested in the notebooks. I never knew when I'd get one. Every now and then, he'd throw one on the bed and wait for my forced words of gratitude.

I was probably wasting my time on these messages anyway. But if my family ever got the chance to read them, I wanted them and everyone else to know that I never stopped fighting to get home.

CHAPTER 2
Leah

Leah promised herself that she wouldn't cry. Tears gave her the heebie-jeebies, and she avoided them as much as possible. For reasons she couldn't explain, today was hard for her. That wasn't true. She knew the reason behind the heaviness she'd carried around since this morning. When she decided to do something different with her hair, she hadn't expected to see her sister's face staring back at her. Leah ran her fingers through her newly straightened hair that hung past her shoulders and down her back. Usually, she wore it natural and curly, but tonight's occasion called for something different.

When Leah first saw her reflection in the salon's mirror, tears instantly sprang to her eyes. She looked like an older version of Nova. Or maybe it seemed that way because her sister had been on her mind lately. The anniversary of Nova's . . . Leah still had trouble saying *death* since Nova was never found. She usually resorted to *disappearance*. Not that it was any better, since it all meant Nova was gone.

After all these years, her heart still ached for one of their sister talks and to hear Nova's high-pitched laugh that used to annoy her. It sucked that it was hard for her to remember the sound of Nova's voice. It had been fifteen years, and the pain of losing Nova was just as present today as it was back then. Whoever said time healed all wounds obviously never had a sister like Nova. It was impossible not to feel that kind of loss for the rest of your life.

But in a few minutes, she'd have a houseful of guests to celebrate her husband's success.

Leah lifted her eyes and fanned away the tears that threatened to ruin hours of cosmetic magic. That couldn't happen because tonight had to be perfect. As a therapist and a realist, Leah didn't often look for perfection. However, if she had to sum up her life here lately, she'd say it was as close as it could get. She had a wonderful husband and great stepdaughter. The only things that could make her life better would be to have her sister and her dad, as well as the baby she wished she could give her husband. But, of course, none of that could happen.

"Nope! You're not going down that road tonight either. Tonight is all about Quinton and his success. No negative memories." She wagged her fingers at her reflection.

A tap on her bedroom door pulled Leah away from her pep talk and her vanity table. She stood in the bathroom doorway when her bedroom door, which was already cracked, opened wider. Leah gasped when her seventeen-year-old stepdaughter, Skye, stepped into the room. Leah couldn't stop the chuckle when Skye attempted to walk, holding out her arms like she was on a tightrope and trying to balance.

"Before you start . . . Don't," Skye warned. "And how am I supposed to walk in these things?" She pointed down to the kitten heels, which was a compromise between her and Leah. Skye wanted to wear her black-and-white Converse, but Leah shut that idea down real quick.

Leah couldn't stop staring at Skye. She covered her mouth with her hand and tried to conceal the squeal that was anxious to burst through.

Skye pursed her glossy lips. "I look ridiculous." She scowled down at the fitted black dress.

"What are you talking about? You look amazing," Leah gushed, closing the gap between her and Skye.

If Leah had Skye's athletic yet very shapely body, she'd barely wear clothes. However, Skye wasn't a dress kind of girl. She was a jeans-and-T-shirts-or-hoodie kind of girl.

"Why do I have to wear this?" Skye whined. "Tonight is about Dad. Not me. Who cares what I look like?"

Leah picked a piece of lint off Skye's dress. "I care what you look like, and so does your dad. And tonight, you look amazing." Leah tilted her head. "And you know I don't give out compliments all willy-nilly. Those must be earned."

Skye rolled her eyes. "Yes, I know." She lowered her head. "Can I at least put on my ballerina slippers? I'm not going to make it in these heels."

"I'm insulted that you called those heels, but, yes, you can wear the ballerina slippers."

Skye wasted no time holding on to the wall while bending and pulling off the shoes. "What time is Dad coming?" She arched her neck toward Leah.

Leah looked at the gold-and-diamond watch on her wrist. One of the many gifts that Quinton insisted she had to have. "In about forty-five minutes or so. Go put on your shoes so we can go down and entertain our guests."

Leah stuck her feet in her six-inch peep-toe stilettos and, for a second, thought about following Skye's idea of wearing ballerina slippers instead, but that wasn't going to happen because her man deserved to see her looking top-notch. Leah turned to the floor mirror that sat in the corner of their bedroom and assessed herself. When Quinton saw her, she needed him to be just as blown away as she had been with Skye. So, even with her toes throbbing, she plastered on a smile and hoped she looked more elegant than she felt. With each click of her stilettos on the hardwood floor, Leah felt a growing sense of achievement, her doubts melting away with the increasing sounds of muffled conversation and laughter from the living room where everyone had gathered.

Leah was in the middle of a conversation with Quinton's secretary, Ms. Janice, when her cell phone dinged.

"Okay, everyone, that's Mario. They'll be pulling up soon, so let's get ready," Leah announced to the room.

The air was thick with secrecy and excitement as they all waited for the door to open.

"Surprise!" the room erupted as soon as Quinton walked in. His wide eyes and open mouth were all the proof Leah needed to know she'd pulled it off. She'd managed to do the one thing she hadn't been able to do in the three years they'd been married: plan and execute a surprise party. Quinton claimed to be the know-it-all king. He bragged that nobody could pull anything over on him. And he had been right—until tonight. Leah finally got him.

Her husband was surrounded by a roomful of people, but all Leah saw was him. Six two and two hundred pounds of pure muscle. Who would've thought she'd one day refer to him as the man of her dreams? Certainly not her.

In high school, she couldn't stand him. The obnoxious football player who thought the world was created for him. Plus, he had been off-limits. Quinton's eyes and heart belonged to one girl back then, and it wasn't Leah.

She observed Quinton navigating through the crowd of enthusiastic well-wishers. He made his way to the center of the room where she stood, quietly appreciating the man who'd introduced her to true love.

"Honey." Quinton's deep voice sang through clenched pearly white teeth. His light-brown eyes, the same ones he'd passed on to Skye, burned into her.

"Surprised?" Leah asked, taking two glasses of champagne from the waiter who'd approached.

"This is too much."

"Too much? For the man who just won the Insurance Agency of the Year award for the second year in a row? I think not." She winked.

"*Just* being the operative word here. How did you pull this off in a few days?" He looked around the room at his friends and associates.

"A few days? Baby, I've been planning this since last year's ceremony. There wasn't an ounce of doubt that you'd win again. I mean, you're *the* Quinton Boudreaux."

Quinton's caramel skin tinted crimson. "Well, to be fair, I couldn't have done it without them." He nodded toward a few of his best employees, whom Leah made sure to invite, but not without threatening to do bodily harm if they ruined the surprise. She knew none of Quinton's success would be possible without them.

"And you, Mr. President, are the leader of that group."

Quinton leaned down and pressed his soft lips against hers just as someone approached them.

"Get a room," Harper, Leah's best friend, teased.

"We have five upstairs, thank you," Quinton pointed out.

"Whatever. Congratulations." She held up her wineglass to Quinton. "But, um . . . I know we're celebrating you, but I think your wife and that dress are the real stars." Harper stepped back and admired Leah's red wrap dress that clung to her body. Leah had her mom to thank for her slim waist and round hips.

"Tell me about it." Quinton bit his bottom lip and slid his eyes up and down Leah's body. "Baby, if you only knew what you were doing to me right now."

"And that's my cue." Harper threw up her hand and rushed away.

Quinton and Leah laughed. He pulled her close to his side, and they stood, like the power couple Leah knew they were, and watched as everyone mingled in their formal living room. At first, she wasn't sold on having the party in their home. It still had the new-house smell. She and Quinton spared no expense decorating and furnishing all six thousand square feet. She didn't know how she'd react if she saw even a speck of dirt on the Persian rug for which she had waited a whole year. The smart thing would've been to remove it, but when everyone walked in and raved over it, she was glad she'd left it in place.

Quinton excused himself and went to chat with a few gentlemen on the other side of the room. The music thumped outside, pulling Leah along with most of the inside guests toward it. Their backyard was the reason she finally decided to have the party there.

When Leah's mom suggested that she hire Carmen Dupre to decorate for Quinton's party, Leah wasn't sure that was a good idea. Leah and Carmen both grew up in Bayou, Louisiana. They were elementary-school besties until they both realized they were besties by default. Carmen's older brother, Lance, and Leah's sister, Nova, were the real friends. Leah and Carmen were around each other so much that it just made sense to become friends too. By the time they entered middle school, their friendship was over, and they were both okay with that.

"Are you pleased?" Carmen asked, tugging Leah away from her memories. Carmen towered over Leah, even in her six-inch heels. Although, with Leah coming in at a whopping five feet one, most people towered over her.

"I'm more than pleased. Thank you so much."

At first, Leah had doubts about Carmen; they were very different—different interests and different tastes. However, Leah's hesitation ended when Carmen showed her mock-ups of how she could turn Leah and Quinton's backyard into a tropical oasis. Even she had to admit that the final results far exceeded her expectations. The lights underneath the white tents added a nice touch. She saw elegance when she looked at the round tables with white linen tablecloths.

"Is that Ms. Martha?" Carmen pointed toward the pool, which was covered in glass and was now the dance floor.

Leah smiled when her eyes landed on Martha Lefleur, her mom, who was the true definition of *Black don't crack, crinkle, or crumble*. If Leah hadn't known her mom had just turned sixty, she wouldn't have believed it. Martha's black dress fell above her knees, showing off her thick, shapely legs. The curls in Martha's shoulder-length black hair, thanks to Dark and Lovely, bounced as she made her way to the pool. Leah watched as her mom eased her foot onto the glass.

"It's safe, Mom!" Leah cupped her hand around her mouth and hollered, but there was no way Martha would hear her over Frankie Beverly.

Carmen laughed. "Your mom's a hoot."

"Yes, she is," Leah agreed.

When Leah and Nova were younger, their mom was the one all the other kids wished they had. Leah wasn't sure why, though. Their parents didn't spoil them, and they had rules and expectations like all the other parents they knew. But, for some reason, everyone loved Ms. Martha. As Leah continued watching her mom moving her body to the beat of the music, she figured that that was probably the reason people gravitated to her. Martha was the life of all parties. She and Nova were alike in that area. Leah was more like her dad: They liked to have fun, but they didn't have to be the center of attention. She and her dad were just as happy sitting back and watching Nova and Martha.

"I still laugh when I think of her at last year's Founder's Day festival. She danced on the stage." Carmen laughed at the memory.

"She used to love dancing. It's always good to see her enjoying herself again."

"You mean after your dad passed?" Carmen's voice dropped to a whisper as if mentioning it was a secret. When he lost his battle with cancer two years ago, Leah wasn't sure how she'd survive with the hole his absence left in her heart. A hole she was sure couldn't spread any wider from losing Nova but somehow did.

"Hey, I've been meaning to thank you," Carmen said.

"Thank me? For what?"

"For helping my brother. He told me that he's been meeting with you and . . ."

Leah looked around and prayed Quinton wasn't in earshot. "It's fine. Don't mention it." Leah looked up at Carmen, hoping Carmen could read the seriousness in her expression. "Please."

Carmen's brow lifted to her hairline. "Oh no. I wouldn't dare say anything to anyone else. I understand."

Leah's knees suddenly became too weak to hold her up. She and Lance had an understanding that their sessions were just between them. Had she known he was going to tell his sister, she never would've agreed. The last thing she needed was for Quinton to find out that she'd been counseling the one person he hated more than anyone else. Leah may not have understood the vendetta between the two men, but she did know that their feud went way back to high school and only grew stronger over the years, at least on Quinton's end.

Quinton, Leah's knight in black Armani, came and wrapped his arms around her waist. Her heart thundered at the close call, even though there was no way Quinton could've heard Carmen over the music.

"Excuse me, Carmen. I need to borrow my wife for a second." He took Leah's hand and led her toward the house.

"Be back," Leah turned around and mouthed to Carmen, though she had every intention of avoiding her for the rest of the night.

Quinton walked through the kitchen and down the hallway where his office was located. "You outdid yourself this time." He leaned against his desk and pulled Leah to him.

"Only the best for you." She rested her hands on his broad chest.

Quinton bent toward her and gently pecked her lips. Then another peck that led to a deep, passionate kiss. Before she knew it, they'd swapped places, and he'd lifted her onto his desk. He opened the top of her dress, exposing her red-lace bra, which barely contained her full breasts.

"We can't do this," Leah managed to say between the pleasure of his mouth teasing her. He knew all her spots and never missed an opportunity to give each one special attention.

"I like this much better than anything going on out there." He slid his hand between her thighs.

"Quinton," she said breathlessly as his hand roamed to the most soulful part of her body. His touch made her want to scream. "No, we really can't." Leah somehow managed to break the sexual tension that had taken over both of them. "We don't have time." She jumped down from his desk.

"Are you sure? We can be quick." Quinton held her wrist and gently pulled her back to him.

Leah tilted her head. "Quick? Really?"

He lifted his broad shoulders. "Quick-ish?"

Leah laughed. "But I don't want quick. You know what I like, and we'll need way more than a minute for me to show you just how proud I am of you." She winked before moving around him and crossing the room. Leah glanced through the trophy case at her reflection as she attempted to fix her lipstick.

"Have I told you how beautiful you look tonight?" Quinton stood behind her and stared at her reflection. "I love your hair. You should keep it like that."

Leah's mind once again led her back to her sister. The void of her absence was just as deep as it was fifteen years ago.

"Hey, where'd you go?" Quinton asked, breaking the trance his words placed her in.

"Still here." She smiled. "Come on, our guests are waiting."

"Wait." Quinton stood in front of her and bit his bottom lip. His eyes slid up and down her body. "To be continued."

Leah nodded.

"You promise?" His lips brushed against hers as he spoke.

"Most definitely."

If Leah had to sum up the rest of the evening, the word she would use was *magical*. She and Quinton had been so busy lately, both running successful businesses, that sometimes they forgot to make time for each other and Skye. Not that Skye ever complained. Leah remembered what it was like being a teenager, and the busier your parents were, the better. It meant less time for them to be in their children's business.

As much as Leah enjoyed the celebration, she enjoyed seeing everyone leaving equally as much. She and Quinton stood in their driveway and waved as the last guest drove away. Quinton closed the door and turned off the front porch light.

"I'm going up to shower." He kissed her cheek.

"I'll be up shortly."

Leah walked down the hallway and into the guest bedroom, where her mom was standing in front of the mirror, taking off her jewelry.

Martha's tired smile greeted Leah. "Everything was so wonderful."

"Thank you, Mom." Leah bent down and took off her shoes. "Do you have everything you need?" She glanced around the large downstairs master bedroom that had the same layout as theirs did upstairs. When she and Quinton built their house, a downstairs master bedroom was a must. Leah was a planner, and that included planning to grow old in her dream house with her dream man. Once that happened, and their knees were too weak to take them up the flight of stairs to their current bedroom, they'd always have one that was easily accessible. For now, though, she was happy calling it her mom's room. Not that Martha used it much since she lived in Bayou, only a fifteen-minute drive from Leah and Quinton's house in Baton Rouge.

"I still think I could've gone home," Martha said, as if reading Leah's thoughts. "You know I don't like to be away from my things." She picked up a brush and ran it through her hair like she did every night. One hundred strokes. She still lived by that rule.

"I know, Mom, and I promise I'll take you home bright and early in the morning. But I knew we'd all be drinking and enjoying ourselves tonight, and I didn't want you, or us, on the road."

Martha aimed her brush at Leah. "Okay, but if anyone breaks into my house, I'm blaming you."

Leah couldn't hold in the laugh. "Break in? In Bayou? Mom, we both know that the only laws broken in Bayou are traffic or littering."

"Whatever, just be ready to take me home in the morning."

Leah walked over and kissed her mom. "I will."

"Hey, what happened with Renee? I thought you said she was coming?" Martha asked, sitting on the side of the bed and unzipping her overnight bag.

Leah's stomach dropped at the mention of Quinton's mom. Renee promised she'd be there, but Leah knew better than to get her hopes up. It was a good thing Renee was supposed to be a surprise, and Leah never mentioned it to Quinton. Unlike Leah, Renee's broken promises didn't bother Quinton. He'd shake his head, smile, say, "That's Renee for you," and then move on.

"I haven't heard from her, but I'm sure she'll have some excuse like always," Leah said.

Martha shook her head. "Some people will never change."

"I know, but Quinton had a great time, and he wasn't expecting her anyway, so it's fine." Leah stepped out of the room with her hand on the doorknob. "Good night, Mom," she said, pulling it shut behind her.

One thing Leah never had to worry about was her mom not being there for her. She wished Quinton could say the same, especially since both his grandparents were deceased. His grandfather died two weeks after his grandmother. Everyone in Bayou said it was from a broken heart, and Leah believed it. The thought of being with one person for nearly sixty years, then one day they're gone. She and Quinton had only been married three, and she couldn't imagine life without him.

Leah trudged upstairs, her whole body heavy from tiredness. A part of her wanted to crawl into bed and sleep until next weekend. But a bigger part of her wanted and needed to fulfill the promise she'd made to Quinton. Being with him always had a way of washing all her sadness away. She needed it washed away tonight. Leah wondered how much time had to pass before it healed her wounds, or if the anniversary of her sister's disappearance would always bring the sting of sorrow.

CHAPTER 3

Nova

My hands cramped. I hadn't realized I'd written so much. It was amazing how much you thought about when you felt your life was coming to an end—a painful lump formed in my throat. I closed the notebook and walked to the window. I looked at the sky, which was filled with stars. There was a time when the pain of being without my family was so great I could hardly breathe. When that happened, I had to find a way to cope. Something that would help me feel closer to them in spirit since I couldn't be with them in person.

One night, as I gazed at the stars, it dawned on me that there was so much I could share with my family. The moon, the stars, and the sun were the things that we all shared. No matter the distance between us, we were all looking at the same moon. During the day, it was the sun that brought me comfort.

"I love you all so much," I said to the moon. "If it's possible, can you please shine a little brighter on them? Wherever they may be." I cleared my throat, as the moon became a blurred shimmering light.

I moved to the bed and stared up at the ceiling. My body was tired, but my soul was even more tired. The song "Hush, Little Baby" popped in my head. It made me think of peace. In my mind, I saw Mama sitting in a rocking chair, singing and soothing a baby that I knew had to be me. Then, I saw myself where Mama was, holding my own baby. I whispered the words to the song, but instead of sounding like a smooth melody, the words were cracked and broken. The more I sang, the quieter my voice sounded and the lighter my body became. An indescribable feeling of peace washed over me as my mind told me it was okay to let go. I'd fought a good fight, and I'd been fighting for years, but it was time to rest.

Then the peaceful feeling I had was washed away by the heaviness of dread as I remembered that I only had one life. One chance to do the things I wanted to do and love the people I wanted to love. That chance was now gone. Knowing I'd never have to wake up another day in that room battling with despair when I thought about the finality of my existence.

I closed my eyes and gave in to whatever came next.

An undetermined amount of time passed before I was jolted awake by a woman's screech.

"Oh my God!"

I shot up, and my whole body trembled. My eyes took a minute to adjust to the bedroom light. I had no clue how long I'd been out, but the sun was up, so I'd slept for a while. The woman stood in the middle of the floor, wearing a red top and black pants. Her hands covered her mouth, and her wide eyes took up half of her round chubby face.

"Is this a dream?" I asked, not expecting an answer. It had to be because, other than Adam, no one else had been in this room. My mind struggled to catch up with my racing heart. I opened my mouth to ask who she was, but she spoke first.

"No, it isn't a dream." The woman's head turned toward the door, but her eyes stayed on me. "Darryl, get in here," she called.

I pressed myself against the headboard, my muscles tense. Her unfamiliar presence filled the room and made it feel too small, like the walls were closing in on me. "Who are you?" My voice was so low and so shaky that I barely recognized it.

"I'm Shelia," she said. Seconds later, a tall, round man wearing blue jeans and a white shirt that stretched between each button stood beside the lady. "And this is my husband, Darryl." She glanced over at the man.

"Who's this?" Darryl asked.

"I don't know." She kept looking at me as if the answer was somewhere on my face.

"How'd she get here?" He pulled a pair of glasses from his shirt pocket and pushed them over his eyes.

The lady rested her hands on her hips and looked up at him. "How da hell I'm 'sposed to know, Darryl?"

"I'm Nova," I said, my throat dry and sore.

The one thing I'd learned from Adam was to trust no one. The notebook and pen were still in the bed somewhere. I ran my hand underneath the cover for the pen, held it in my hand, and then plucked off the top. I couldn't take them both, but maybe I could injure one enough to scare the other one away or at least distract them while I . . . What? What could I do? As long as that chain was around my leg, I was helpless.

"Nova," Darryl repeated.

I gripped the pen tighter as the sound of my name coming from his mouth sent a shiver down my spine. I hadn't heard anyone say my name in so long. Adam never called me Nova. I was always Angel or Baby. I wondered if he even remembered my name. Probably not, since who I was wasn't important to him. All he needed was for me to be who he decided I'd be.

"You friends with Uncle Adam?" he asked, easing a step closer.

The lady rolled her eyes. "No, she ain't no friend of Uncle Adam's. I told y'all something was wrong with that man, but did anyone listen? Sure didn't. Talking 'bout, he just wanna be alone 'cause he grieving. Don't nobody grieve that long." She wagged her finger at me. "This is why he wouldn't let nobody in this house."

Darryl didn't look convinced, so I reached over and moved the cover off my legs.

The lady gasped as soon as she saw the chain. She stretched her hand out to the man. "Give me your phone."

My heart raced. My eyes darted between the two of them. Hope flickered in my chest; a tiny flame broke through the darkness that had existed inside me for so long. Could it be real? Were they here to help me? Then, just like that, the flame was extinguished with another thought. I didn't know these people. Had Adam sent them?

"Adam." Anticipation rose through me as I waited for him to barge in.

As soon as they exchanged glances, something else invaded my body. Fear. What were they going to do to me?

"Where's Adam?" I asked again, pushing the words through the tightness in my throat. Somehow, my mind had transformed my predator into my protector. I needed a face I recognized. I knew what to expect from Adam. I didn't know what to expect from them.

"He died last week," the lady answered. "The funeral was yesterday. We just came by to check on the house."

I stared at her and waited for her to say more. Waited for her to tell me she wasn't serious. That she just wanted to see my reaction. She was toying with me like Adam did sometimes. Like when he'd give me his keys and make me believe he was going to let me leave, only to stand behind me laughing after I'd tried every key and none of them worked. My letdown was his entertainment, and I couldn't fall for it again.

"Did you hear me?" Shelia asked.

I nodded before I lifted my head to her. She looked like someone I could trust, but then again, so did Adam. "How do I know you're telling the truth?" I finally asked.

Shelia looked at Darryl before looking at me. "Because we don't play about death." Her words reminded me of ones my grandma would've said.

"How long have you been here?" Darryl glanced at the chains around my ankle.

My brain was trying to remember how many times the leaves had changed colors. My last count was nine, but some time had passed since then. The agony of adding another number was too much, so I stopped counting. "Since 2003." That was the best answer I could give.

I didn't realize the weight my words had carried until they caused Shelia to stumble backward. I wasn't sure if her wide eyes were from the fear of almost falling or hearing that I'd been there so long. Darryl put his hand on her back to keep her steady.

"I'm alright," she told Darryl before moving closer to the bed again. "It's 2018. You mean to tell me you've been here. . ." She lifted her head toward the ceiling and then returned her gaze to me. "Fifteen years?"

The words were like a jolt of lightning slamming into me, knocking all the air from my lungs. "Fifteen years?" I repeated.

"Ms.? Are you alright?" Shelia's voice was muffled.

I tried to speak, but my whole body tightened, including my throat. A dull ache sat in my stomach and grew bigger and stronger each time her words replayed in my ears. To me, fifteen years away from my family may as well have been a lifetime.

"Where's your phone, Darryl?" Her request was more demanding than before.

Darryl reached into his back pocket and gave her something that looked nothing like any phone I'd ever seen.

"Call Sheriff Walker," the lady said into the black, flat, rectangular thing.

"Calling Sheriff Walker."

I jumped when the phone talked back.

"Sheriff Walker. It's Shelia Guidry. I need you to get to Uncle Adam's farm right now. Bring all the men you got and the ambulance. You ain't gon' believe what we done found."

Relief filled my body and poured out through my tears. Joy erupted inside me, and I couldn't stop trembling.

Sam was the locksmith they'd called hours ago. After he'd worked with the lock for what felt like hours, he was finally able to find the right key. Sheriff Walker stepped in and unwrapped the thick chains from around my ankle. The shackles were gone, but their weight remained. I reached down and rubbed my skin where there were now dents that served as a reminder of a life I never asked for.

I didn't feel free while I was still in that room. The air was thick and suffocating. I inhaled and exhaled hard, but no matter how hard I breathed, it wasn't enough to fill my lungs.

"Let's get her out of here," Sheriff Walker said, looking at one of the officers standing next to the door.

He and another officer helped me out of the bedroom and to the stairs.

"It'll be easier for me to carry you down. Is that okay?" the officer with the jet-black hair and thick black mustache said.

I nodded, then closed my eyes as he lifted me into his arms. My body trembled in fear at his touch. He was too close. Way too close. My heart raced, and I reminded myself that I needed him to get out of here. My ankle was too sore, and I felt too weak to make it down those stairs alone. I cringed when I thought of what I must've looked like to them, what I must've smelled like since I hadn't washed anything in days. When death is your final destination, taking care of yourself is the last thing on your mind.

We were halfway down when the front door ushered in sunlight, which felt like a guide to my freedom. The officer walked slowly and carefully when all I wanted was for him to run, sprint if he had to, to get me through that door and out of this house.

As soon as my eyes hit the sunlight, I shielded them with my hand. It took a few minutes for them to adjust. The last time I was outside was a few days before Adam left. Once a week, he'd take me out in the backyard so I could walk around and get some air. I never imagined a life where going outside in a secluded backyard would be the highlight of my week. Adam never let me out of his sight. Maybe he thought I'd find a way to climb the wooden fence that looked as high as the trees.

Once I was off the porch and in the yard, I turned around and looked at the house that had held me against my will all those years. I lifted my gaze to that window. How many times had I pressed my hands against it, yearning for this moment? Now that it had come, there weren't enough words to describe the mixture of emotions that swirled inside me.

The officer slowly placed me on my feet but wrapped his arm around mine to help keep me steady. I looked around and took in everything. The sun's brightness welcomed me back to a world stolen from me. I unwrapped my arm from the police officer's, then bent and picked up a rock. A rock. I hadn't held a rock in fifteen years. It was smooth and beautiful. I squeezed it in the palm of my hand, then rubbed my fingers over it. I limped over to the side, ignored the pain in my ankle, bent down, and rubbed my hand over the prickly grass. I thought of the dead grass and dirt in Adam's backyard before closing my eyes and releasing more tears as I continued rubbing, feeling the moisture from the early-morning dew. Each touch. Each sight. Each sound and every smell, even from the cows in the pasture behind the house, was a reminder that I was free.

Out of everything around me, the sky had drawn me in the most. It was so blue with the fluffiest, whitest clouds I'd ever seen. As I enjoyed its beauty, a couple of birds joined the celebration by circling ahead. It was as if they sensed that something special had happened. I watched as they flew off. They could go wherever they wanted to go. It was strange and magical to be able to say that I could now do the same.

For everyone else, today was just a normal day. The fresh air, the warmth of the sun, the smooth and rough textures of the rocks, the soft yet prickly grass—all of it was mundane, nothing special.

Before I was lifted into the ambulance, I turned around and looked one final time. There was no way I'd ever set foot in that place again. When I turned back around, it symbolized my thoughts from that day forward. All I wanted was to focus on my new life. My second chance with the people I loved.

Machines beeped, footsteps pounded against the floor, doors banged shut and creaked open, and the voices . . . so many voices from so many directions. Had things always been this loud? Had there always been so much noise? I sat alone in the hospital room, gripping the rough fabric from the blanket. My feet hung over the side of the bed because there was no way I was lying down. There was no way I would "get some rest," as the doctor suggested. My eyelids were heavy, but I had to stay awake. Thoughts of closing my eyes and waking up in that house again tortured me, and the only way to make sure that didn't happen was by watching everyone who came near me.

My heart raced with each beep, each step, each creak as they grew louder and louder in my ears.

I didn't need to be checked out by a doctor. I didn't want to stay in a hospital. I wanted to go home. That was it. Nothing else. I didn't want to answer any more questions about Adam or how he'd snatched me from the hotel in Biloxi and brought me an hour away to his house in Picayune. None of it mattered. He lived like a coward and died like one too.

Silencing my mouth was easier than quieting my mind. The day I met Adam was a day I refused to think about until now. I thought he was a godsend. That was what I told him when he sat next to me at the banquet table. My husband had just started his job as an insurance agent, and the agency he worked for hosted a weekend training every year that ended with a banquet.

I hated the thought of leaving our daughter, Skye, who was only two years old at the time, but it was something I had to do. My husband and I were going through a rough patch—a very rough patch—but Mama assured me that all couples went through it at one point. I could never imagine Mama and Daddy going through any rough patches, though. As much as I dreaded leaving Skye, I dreaded the thought of a broken marriage even more. So, I kissed my sweet little baby, promised to be back before she knew it, and drove away.

Adam wasn't in the insurance business but attended the conference with his sister. As soon as he sat down, he asked if I was having as much fun as he was. I thought he was serious until I looked at him and saw him rolling his eyes and shaking his head. He provided a laugh that eased the pain of missing my baby. Sunday, which was the next day, couldn't come fast enough for me. Adam and I weren't there to network and learn, so while my husband and Adam's sister were away from the table, chatting with colleagues, we spent most of the evening at the table talking to each other.

The mood changed from joyful to sorrowful when Adam shared that his wife had passed last year. After offering my condolences, I immediately wondered if he was ready to date or if it was too soon. I thought he'd make a good companion for my mother-in-law. He was her type, chestnut brown, with salt-and-pepper hair, clean-shaven, and in pretty good shape, from what I could tell through his suit.

Later that night, after a huge fight with Quinton, I needed time alone. I didn't give it a second thought when Adam slid onto the empty stool next to me at the bar in the hotel. The conference was held there, and it was where all the attendees stayed, so his being there wasn't alarming.

All that night, I'd entertained a devil disguised as an angel.

As I sat on the hospital bed, I couldn't stop thinking of the unfairness of it all. This wasn't how it was supposed to be. Adam wasn't supposed to die like that. He was supposed to suffer the way he'd made me suffer. He was supposed to spend the rest of his life locked away like I'd been. I was supposed to stand in the courtroom and tell him how disgusting he was. I needed him to know that I only said I loved him all those times because he made me. I could never . . . would never . . . love a pathetic piece of man like him. I needed him to suffer, but he was gone, and I'd never have the chance to say those words to him or to see the look on his face when I expressed the joy I felt at the thought of him rotting in hell.

For years, I dreamed of the day when I could use the voice he'd tried to silence as a weapon against him. But he'd taken that from me, too, because he was dead. He was really dead.

Detective Cox came in and sat in a chair next to my bed. Until a few minutes ago, she hadn't left my side since she arrived at the hospital. She was a tall, thin woman with a beautiful face, but I couldn't say the same about her hair. It was a big puff ball that sat on top of her head. I touched my hair, which was also in desperate need of care.

At least I had an excuse.

"Nova." Detective Cox's voice demanded my attention. "I called your parents' house using the number you gave me." She smiled. "That's amazing that you remembered it after all these years. It's even more amazing that they still have it. Most people don't have house phones anymore."

"I repeated that phone number every day. I needed to be able to call my family when I escaped."

Detective Cox nodded as if she understood, but there was no way that she or anyone else could understand what it was like knowing that your only companion was a notebook and four walls. No one knew what it was like living in a world where time didn't exist and one day bled into the next. Detective Cox had no idea what it was like to live the same day over and over for years. Breakfast with Adam. Lunch with Adam. Dinner with Adam. Bed with Adam. I flinched at the memory of his rough, calloused hands roaming over my body.

"Are you okay?" Detective Cox asked.

I nodded, but I was far from okay. "Did you talk to them? Did you tell my mom and dad that I'm okay?" I asked, holding my breath as I waited for her to speak.

Detective Cox nodded. "I'm sorry, but I didn't get an answer."

A heaviness came over me. That wasn't what I wanted to hear.

"Do you need anything? Some water?" She reached for the pink plastic jug of water on the nightstand.

"I just wanna go home," I whispered through my tears.

"I spoke with someone at the Bayou sheriff's department, and they're going to deliver the good news to your family. In fact, they're probably talking as we speak."

I rubbed my hands back and forth against the cover, then turned away from Detective Cox. I stared out the window and smiled at the thought that soon, I'd get to see my family again.

"I found your sister's Facebook page. Her personal page is private, but I did find her business page." Detective Cox spoke as her head lowered to the same black, flat, rectangle device that Shelia said was a phone, except the one Detective Cox held was bigger.

My mind was foggy as I struggled to understand words that were so familiar to everyone else. *Face book?* I kept trying to make them make sense. I knew what a face was, and I knew what a book was, but I didn't know what a face book was. A book of different faces?

"Oh my goodness." Detective Cox shook her head. "I'm so sorry. You have no idea what I'm talking about, do you?"

I looked away as humiliation vibrated through me. I didn't care about no stupid book with faces anyway. But I did care about Leah, and if her face was in that book, I wanted to see it. "Can I see Leah?" I asked.

"Of course." Detective Cox turned the black thing around and extended her arm toward me. I scrambled to the other side of the bed, my fingers clawing at the sheets. I pressed my head against the headboard and curled my body into a tight ball. I tasted the fear that rose inside me.

"It's okay, Nova." Another voice had entered the room, but I couldn't look.

"Nova, it's Dr. Lee." His voice broke through the wall of fear that surrounded me. "That's it, Nova. Deep breaths."

I did as Dr. Lee instructed. Slowly, my fingers uncurled. The more breaths I took, the lighter my body became.

"Very good," Dr. Lee continued in the same soothing voice. "You're safe here, Nova. No one's going to hurt you. Everyone is here to help you. You understand?"

I turned my head in his direction and nodded.

"Good." He looked at Detective Cox and held out his hand. She gave the black thing to him. "This is an iPad. It's a device that's like a cell phone or a laptop. It can't hurt you. Can I give it to you so you can see your sister?" he asked, holding the iPad toward me.

I looked at it, then at Dr. Lee, before I nodded again.

As soon as I saw her, I knew it was Leah. That was my sister. My Leah. She looked like Mama. I couldn't take my eyes off her fancy red dress and pearls. Her wavy hair was slicked back, showing off her high cheekbones and beautiful smile. *She's so pretty.*

Through my tears, I read that Leah was a therapist. That didn't surprise me. Leah was one of those people who always knew what she wanted to do in life. I was probably her first patient. I may have been the oldest, but Leah was the mature one. She had her hands full, trying to keep me out of trouble. As I stared at the picture, a memory flashed through my mind. Leah and I had convinced Mama to let us camp in the backyard. Leah hated being outside and the thought of sleeping out there even more, but she did it for me. I couldn't remember anything she didn't do for me, even if it meant putting her wants and needs aside.

A knot formed in my throat as I closed my eyes and saw Leah and me on our backs, gazing at the stars. We used to love to talk about our futures. Leah wanted to be a doctor, and I wanted to marry Michael Jordan. I could still hear my sister's small eight-year-old voice telling me how amazing my life would be. In Leah's eyes, there wasn't anything I couldn't do, including marrying Michael Jordan.

When I opened my eyes, Leah was gone. The screen was black. I lifted my head to Detective Cox as I shook the iPad and touched it, but nothing brought Leah back.

"I can fix it." Detective Cox reached for the iPad.

"I don't want it anymore." I lay down and faced the wall. The ache for Leah had grown so much since I'd been out that I could hardly breathe. Leah was as important to me as air, and I needed her more than ever before. If Leah said everything would be okay, then I'd believe it.

CHAPTER 4

Leah

Leah's back was to Quinton, and she was still cradled in his embrace when her eyes opened too early for a Saturday morning. She pushed her body closer to him, which caused him to stir. He groaned and planted soft kisses on her neck and shoulder.

"Good morning, Mrs. Boudreaux," his husky voice whispered in her ear.

Leah's body tensed. After three years, you'd think she'd be used to hearing him call her by his last name. As his wife, she was Mrs. Boudreaux, but on paper, she was Leah Lefleur. When she told Quinton she wanted to keep her maiden name, he was totally against it. Quinton wasn't old fashioned, per se, but there were some traditions that he felt strongly about, and the wife taking the husband's last name was one of them. It wasn't until Leah explained her reasoning that he conceded.

She could still see the name written in a notebook in big pink and purple bubble letters. They were in high school, but even back then, all Nova wanted was to one day become Mrs. Boudreaux. After Nova disappeared, the last thing Leah expected was to fall in love with Quinton. Leah couldn't help what her heart wanted, and as hard as she tried to fight it, it was no use. Her heart was more powerful than her mind. She allowed herself to love

Quinton, but she couldn't allow herself to use the name. Nova loved that name too much. That was what Leah told herself, even though she knew it was the man behind the name who Nova loved.

"Hey." Quinton propped himself up on his elbows. "What's going on with you?"

Leah turned on her back and looked at him. "I'm sorry. My mind's just . . . I can't stop thinking about Nova," she admitted.

Quinton collapsed on his back and stared at the ceiling. His blank stare told her that mentioning Nova's name had extinguished whatever sexual desire he had. She expected him to be upset, but he wasn't.

"I've been thinking about her a lot too. Last week made fifteen years," he said, never breaking his gaze from above.

"I know." Leah laid her head on Quinton's chest as sorrow settled over them. The quiet in the room amplified the heaviness in her heart. "It's like a wound that never fully heals," she whispered, her voice thick with emotion.

Talking about Nova to Quinton never offered the comfort Leah wished it would. The truth was that her grief was always escorted by guilt. She'd hoped after all this time that those feelings would've subsided, but they were still there, which was something she could never admit to Quinton. Her words could come across as regret, but that wasn't the case. She would marry Quinton a thousand times if she could, but she wished the man of her dreams hadn't been the man of her sister's dreams first.

"I'd better get dressed before Mom makes her way up here to pull me out of bed," Leah said, lifting herself off Quinton.

"I can drive her home if you want to rest a while longer," Quinton offered.

"No, it's fine. I think I'll surprise her and take her to the café for breakfast. It's been a while since we've done that."

The idea just came to Leah, and she loved it already. Her mom complained that they didn't spend enough time together, and Leah agreed. Besides, if Leah was feeling heaviness over the anniversary of

Nova's disappearance, then she couldn't begin to imagine what her mom must've been feeling.

Leah showered and dressed, then pulled her hair back in a ponytail before going downstairs, where her mom and Skye were in the kitchen cooking.

Leah looked at her phone and then at Skye. "Are you feeling okay?" she asked.

"Yeah." Skye furrowed her brows. "Why?"

"Because it's Saturday, and it's not past noon, and you're awake. And dressed," Leah pointed out while taking in Skye's ripped jeans and sweatshirt. Her hair, like Leah's, was pulled back, except Skye had braids, which was how she usually kept her hair. Being an athlete came with constant workouts, and Skye's long, thick mane was too hard to wash daily. So, protective styles like braids were perfect for her.

"This is why I keep telling you that you should come stay more often," Leah said, leaning over and kissing Martha's cheek. "You know how much we love waking up to your famous pancakes, and you're the only person on earth who can get Skye out of bed this early."

"Not true," Skye said, cracking an egg over a glass bowl.

Leah refilled the Keurig with water, then opened the cabinet to grab her favorite autumn mug that was shaped like a pumpkin with a green leaf for the handle.

Martha stared at Leah's mug and shook her head. "I'll never understand your obsession with those things."

"They're cute, and I like cute things," Leah said, pushing her mug underneath the Keurig and pressing the silver button, causing the machine to roar to life.

"Did I hear someone talking about me?" Quinton joked.

"You sure did." Leah smiled.

Skye and Martha glanced at each other and rolled their eyes.

"Gross," Skye mumbled.

"Whatever. One day, you'll marry a fine, handsome man like mine, and you'll understand." Leah winked.

"Now that's the truth." Martha pointed at Leah. "I sure married me one, and I couldn't get enough of that man." Martha did a little dance, followed by a moan that Leah prayed she'd never have to hear from her mom again.

Leah looked at Skye. "I get it now. And I'm sorry," she joked.

They all sat at the table, and Leah's mouth watered in anticipation. Her mom's pancakes were light, fluffy, and buttery, the way Leah liked them. Martha said grace, and then the only sound in the room was their forks clinking against their plates.

Once they were done, Leah finished her coffee while Skye cleared the table. Martha wasted no time going into her room and gathering her things. Leah was shocked she'd stayed long enough to cook and eat. That was unusual, and Leah enjoyed every moment of her mom's visit. She wished she could do or say something to get her mom to stay with them more often. She worried about Martha being in that big house, all alone. Martha insisted that she wasn't lonely as long as she had her phone and television. Leah didn't get it because electronics could only hold her attention for so long before she needed human interaction, but she and her mom were different, so she'd stopped pushing the issue long ago.

Quinton was already outside when Leah and Martha came out. He took Martha's bag from Leah and placed it in the back seat of Leah's car.

"Hold on," Martha said, opening her purse. "Let me make sure I have these keys."

Leah chuckled. "You and these keys."

Her mom lost her keys at least once a week. Leah bought every device she could think of to help her keep up with them or find them, but nothing worked.

"Just keep living. You better pray keys are all you lose when you're my age." Martha kept digging.

Leah watched her mom, and her heart expanded more than she thought it could. They'd come so far over the past five years. Their relationship hit a huge bump when Leah and Quinton announced that they were dating. Because of Nova, she didn't expect her mom to jump up and down with joy, but she also didn't expect the backlash she'd received either.

"Thank you, Mom." Leah reached over and touched her mom's shoulder.

Martha stopped searching long enough to glance over at Leah. "For what?"

"For being here for Quinton's celebration. For spending the night. For accepting . . ." Leah cleared her throat.

Martha patted Leah's leg. "You don't have to thank me. You're my daughter, and I love you."

Leah's vision blurred for the third time, and she was over it. She had to pull herself together, but October was always her most challenging month. She'd go from grieving Nova to grieving the children she'd never have. It was a lot, but Leah would be okay because she understood what she focused on grew. So, she'd make a conscious effort to focus on her gains instead of her losses. It would've been nice if her gains hadn't come wrapped in a loss, though. The hysterectomy saved her life but took away her future children. Her relationship with Quinton came because of losing Nova. At some point, Leah would love to experience a win without the loss.

"Got 'em," Martha said, pulling her bundle of keys from the bottom of her purse.

Leah put her car in reverse just as a police car pulled up behind her. Since she knew almost everyone she cared about was safe, she didn't immediately think the worst.

Leah and Martha opened their doors and stepped out.

"Carlos . . . I mean, Sheriff Jones, what are you doing here?" Martha asked the newly elected sheriff of Bayou, who was also the nephew of her best friend, Ms. Cora. Carlos was more like Leah's cousin than a family friend.

"Good morning, Ms. Martha." He looked over. "Morning, Leah. Quinton." He waved toward the house where Quinton was coming toward them. He turned back to Martha. "I stopped by your house. When I saw you weren't home, I called my aunt, and she told me you'd be here."

"Is everything okay?" Martha's voice was steady, but concern filled her eyes.

Watching as Carlos stood in front of her mom dressed in his sheriff's uniform pulled Leah back to the last time they were standing like that. The only difference was it was in the middle of the night, and they were in Bayou at Martha's house. Leah was home helping with Skye. The nervousness Leah thought she'd avoided came. She grabbed her mom's hand as they waited for Carlos to answer Martha's question. The answer came immediately, but it felt like forever.

"Yes, ma'am. Things are better than fine." Carlos's mouth lifted into a cautious smile. "We received a call from a Mississippi police department a little while ago. After I heard what they were calling about, I knew I had to deliver the news personally. It's about Nova."

I gasped when I heard her name. His smile said it wasn't bad, but it was about Nova, so how could it be good?

". . . alive."

I was so into my thoughts that I only caught that one word. "What?" I asked, needing to make sure he'd said what I thought he'd said.

He nodded. "You heard me right, Leah. Your sister's alive. They found her in a house in Mississippi."

"Mississippi?" It was Quinton's voice that entered her space that time. "What do you mean they found her in Mississippi?"

"That's what Sheriff Walker said when he called. She was in Picayune. Y'all ever heard of it? Or know someone who lives there?"

Leah, Martha, and Quinton all shook their heads.

"What was . . . ? Why . . . ?" Martha tried to form a complete sentence, but it seemed too difficult.

Martha's words sounded like Leah's thoughts. Jumbled and confused.

"Nova's alive?" The words tasted sweet on Leah's tongue. Before now, saying or hearing Nova's name left a coat of dread over her heart, but now, having it accompanied by the word *alive* flipped a switch inside her that ignited the good parts of her soul that died so many years ago.

"If you want, we can go inside, and I can fill you in on everything I know." Carlos looked toward the house.

"My daughter's inside. We should hear the details first," Quinton said.

Skye? How would she take the news that, after all these years, her mom was alive?

Carlos continued. "Sheriff Walker said they received a call this morning about a woman locked in a bedroom."

Leah's heart pounded. She turned to Quinton, whose hand had covered his mouth. Martha sniffed, and Leah moved closer to her mom and wrapped her arms around her. They'd only heard one sentence, and it was already too much. Could they handle hearing everything?

"Sheriff Walker said she was pretty dehydrated, and the cha—" He paused, then continued. "Her ankle was pretty sore, but he couldn't see anything wrong with her other than that. Of course, once she's checked out at the hospital, they'll be able to tell you more if there's more to tell."

Leah heard everything Carlos said, but her mind kept going to the word he wouldn't say. "Cha—" Was he about to say *chains*? He said her ankle was pretty sore. Did she have chains on her ankle? Like some kind of animal? Leah stumbled back. The image of her sister locked in a room with chains holding her in place made every part of Leah weak. She held her fist so tight that her nails dug into her skin.

"Who did this?" Quinton's voice was so deep that his words sounded like a low growl.

Carlos reached into his shirt pocket and pulled out a slip of paper. "Adam Guidry? Name ring a bell to any of you?"

Once again, they all shook their heads.

"Adam Guidry?" Quinton repeated.

"You know him?" Leah asked.

"No, but . . ." Quinton's brows furrowed, and then he stared at the ground. "I don't know why the name sounds like I may have heard it before, but I'm sure I don't know an Adam Guidry."

"When can we see her?" Martha asked, her voice just as shaky as her demeanor.

"I can call and see what hospital she's in, and you can go as soon as you're ready. Or you can wait, and someone will bring her home when she's discharged. It's up to you."

Martha shook her head so hard that Leah was afraid she was going to make herself dizzy. "No, I'm not waiting. I want to see my baby, and I want to see her now." She looked up at Quinton. "I want to see my baby." Her voice trembled and her body swayed, as if the news was suddenly too overwhelming to hold any longer.

Carlos and Quinton each took one of Martha's arms and walked her to Leah's car. They eased her into the passenger seat and stood back so she could get some air. Leah and Quinton stayed near Martha while Carlos stepped away to get the name of the hospital where they were treating Nova.

When Carlos came back, he held his phone toward Quinton. "This is Detective Cox. She asked to speak with you."

Leah watched as Quinton listened intently, every now and then offering an "okay" or an "I see."

He gave the phone back and looked between Leah and Martha. "She said Nova's being checked out by the doctor now, but she's been asking for us."

Leah's trembling hands went to her mouth.

"She wants us to call her when we're close. She said the hospital was swarming with reporters. She'll tell us where to park so we won't be bothered with them."

A Sky Full of Love

"I'll go so you folks can get going. Give me a call if you need anything, okay?"

"We will. Thanks, Carlos," Leah said. "I guess we need to go inside and tell Skye," she told Quinton.

"All of this was going on, and she didn't come out once," Quinton said.

"You know she has those headphones over her ears. She can't hear a thing going on around her, and for the first time, I'm grateful for that. I'd rather she hear the news from us."

"Can we tell her on the road?" Martha asked. "I want to get going. The sooner we leave, the sooner I can see Nova." Her eyes popped open as if she'd shocked herself with her words.

"Okay. Come inside and get some water. We'll grab a few things, then we'll go. It'll only take a few minutes," Leah said.

Martha shook her head. "I don't want any water. I'll sit here and wait."

"Mom, you can't stay out here. Come on inside," Leah insisted.

"I'm staying here." Martha crossed her arms, looking more like a defiant child than a sixty-year-old woman.

Leah held up her hands. "Fine. We'll be as fast as we can."

As soon as Leah and Quinton walked through the front door, a thought hit her. "Oh God." Leah's eyes locked with Quinton's. "What are we going to tell Nova about us? She's going to be devastated."

"You don't know that. It's been fifteen years. You don't think she expected me to stay single for fifteen years, do you?"

"No, but she also didn't expect you to marry her sister either. I don't think we should say anything right now," Leah suggested.

"So, what are we supposed to say when or if she asks?" Quinton shifted uncomfortably.

"If she asks, we won't lie about being married. We just won't tell her it's to each other. She's been through so much, and I think it's best if we all just enjoy the reunion without the pressure of this big announcement."

Leah followed Quinton upstairs. He knocked on Skye's bedroom door, but she didn't answer. He knocked again. Still no answer.

Quinton turned the knob, and Skye was lying across her bed with her headphones over her ears, scrolling through her phone. Quinton touched her leg, and Skye screamed before snatching the headphones off.

"Geez, Dad. Are you trying to kill me?" She sat up and scooted to the edge of the bed.

If it were a normal day, Quinton would've given Skye a speech about having headphones on and not being aware of her surroundings. He'd then ask, what if he was an intruder coming in? But since the day was far from normal, he didn't say any of those things.

"Leah and I need to talk with you." His voice was somber.

Skye's long lashes fluttered as she looked from Leah to Quinton. "What's wrong?" Her voice lacked all the attitude it held a second ago.

"It's about your mom . . . um, Nova," Quinton said.

"My mom? What about her?" Skye glanced at Leah, then back at Quinton.

Leah didn't understand why Quinton needed to clarify who he referenced as Skye's mom. It had been clear from the beginning of their marriage that Leah was Skye's aunt and, technically, stepmom, even though Leah hated that term. The uniqueness of their situation made every decision a big deal. They had to think about things that most people didn't, like would Skye introduce Leah to new friends as her aunt or her stepmom.

Then there were even simpler things that they had to explain when asked, like why Skye said *Teeah* instead of *Leah*. Leah usually resorted to a half truth. She'd been in Skye's life since she was a baby, and when she started talking and tried to say *Leah*, it came out as *Teeah*. The part Leah conveniently left out was that Nova had tried to get Skye to say *Tee-Leah*, which came out as *Teeah*.

But for the past fifteen years, Leah had been more than an aunt. She was the only mom Skye knew. Until now, anyway. Leah's chest constricted at the thought of sharing Skye. *What's wrong with you?*

Nova's Skye's mom. You should be overjoyed that they're about to be reunited.

"She's alive?" Skye asked.

Her words alerted Leah to the fact that she'd missed Quinton breaking the news to her.

"Yeah, and she's in a hospital in Mississippi. We're about to go there now, so I need you to throw some things in a bag real quick so we can get going. Your grandma is outside waiting."

"Wait. B-b-but . . ." Skye stammered.

"We'll fill you in on all the details in the car, okay?" Leah told her. "Just do as your dad said." Leah was about to leave when she turned back around. "Oh, and before I forget, we're not telling her that your dad and I are married. Not right away. We have to wait and see when we feel she'll be ready for that news."

Skye nodded, then scooted off the bed and went to her closet. Leah and Quinton went to their room and quietly did the same. They moved around, both caught in their own bubble of disbelief. Leah was pushing the last of her things in her overnight bag when she looked up and saw Quinton staring down at his bag.

"What's wrong?" she asked.

Quinton lifted his head, and his eyes were filled with tears. For a second, Leah just watched. Nova was her sister, but she was also his wife. As much as Leah hated to admit it, there was always a tinge of insecurity that resided in her when she thought of Nova and Quinton. Theirs was a love story that felt like it should've been from a romance novel instead of a small town like Bayou. When people thought of Nova and Quinton, they used words like *soulmates, greatest loves of all time,* a *once in a lifetime kind of love.* No one ever described what they had like that. Theirs was a love that grew from grief. But now that Nova was back and there was no loss to grieve, what did that mean for them?

Dammit, Leah, stop it!

She went to Quinton and leaned her head against him. He wrapped his arms around her and held her so tight she could hardly breathe. "Can you believe this is actually happening?"

"I can't." For a brief second, Leah closed her eyes and allowed herself to imagine the reunion with her sister. That image wiped away everything else she'd thought about. The only thing she cared about was holding her sister and never letting her go.

CHAPTER 5

Nova

Each time the door opened, I expected my family to walk through. My body deflated every time I saw a nurse or Detective Cox. However, I perked up when the detective said she'd heard from the sheriff that my family was on their way.

There was no way I could sleep now.

"What are you doing, young lady?" Ashley, my nurse, asked when she walked in. She put her hands on very round hips and shook her head. "What did they tell you about this?" She pointed to the television.

My hands shook so badly that it was hard to pick up the remote. I managed to press the green button that turned it off. "I'm sorry," I said quietly.

"Oh, sweetie, you don't have to be sorry. It's okay," Ashley assured me. "The doctor just don't want you to overwhelm yourself. That's all."

Dr. Lee didn't realize that nothing on the TV was more overwhelming than what was going on inside my head. I was free, but I didn't feel free. I felt like I belonged to someone else. Like nothing about me was mine. I waited for someone to tell me what to do and when to do it. I wished I felt free, but I didn't know what that felt like anymore.

I did know what fear felt like, though. It was a familiar feeling that I'd hoped would go away once I left that house, but it didn't. It had just got stronger and heavier since I'd been here. Everything was too big. Too open. Too strange, and I hated it.

Ashley stood next to my bed. My body tensed, and my heart raced. She was closer now.

"You mind if I check your blood pressure?" She held on to the machine that sat next to the bed.

I reminded myself that Ashley wasn't dangerous. She just wanted to do her job, and I should let her do that. I nodded. She wrapped something around my arm.

"You okay?" Ashley leaned her head to the side and stared at me.

I wanted to say yes, but I couldn't speak. I was too busy trying to remember to breathe.

"Nova." Her voice was low and soft.

I nodded again. "I'm okay," I whispered.

She paused for a few seconds before pressing the button, and the machine started humming. The thing around my arm got tighter and tighter, and even though I knew it was Ashley standing next to me, my mind told me it was Adam, and the tightness was his hand wrapped around my arm. I closed my eyes and tried to will the image away, but instead, it grew more vivid. I tried to squeeze myself as far as I could into the corner of the bed. I hid my face and begged him to stop. Begged for him to leave me alone.

"Nova." He called my name, but it didn't sound like him at all. I couldn't look. It was a trick. As soon as I lifted my head, he was going to attack. I knew him well enough to recognize when he'd lure me into what I considered a safe space just for him to snatch me right out of it. I covered my ears and continued begging for him to leave, but I sensed him standing there watching me and waiting.

"Nova." Another voice broke through my wall of terror. I knew that voice. I loved that voice. I lifted my head slightly.

My eyes landed on the most beautiful person I'd ever seen, and a tsunami of emotions surged through me.

I launched from the bed, and a sharp pain shot through my ankle. It slowed me down but didn't stop me from wrapping myself around Mama with such force that we almost toppled over. The deep, guttural wail that escaped from my body caused me to tremble. Fifteen years' worth of longing, needing, and eventually hopelessness was expelled through every tear.

"Thank you, God," Mama repeated as she held me tighter.

Mama stood back and looked at me. Her eyes made me nervous, but it was Mama, and I wanted to look at her too. She'd changed a lot. The darkness underneath her eyes wasn't there the last time I saw her. Neither were the lines that exposed themselves every time she narrowed her eyes. Even with all the changes, she was still the beautiful woman Daddy called his Brown Sugar. I inhaled as hard and as long as I could. Mama smelled like safety, and I wanted to fill my entire body with her scent. We shook and cried until every ounce of water we had, or so I thought, had left our bodies. It turned out that I had plenty of tears left over.

I lifted my foot and put most of my pressure on the ankle that wasn't sore. I'd waited too long for this moment, and I didn't want to sit while it happened. Mama moved aside, and Leah sat in her spot. I couldn't stop staring at her. She was just as beautiful in person as she was in the picture I'd seen. Other than a few extra pounds that looked amazing on her and eyes that were still big and beautiful but aged with wisdom and experiences that I missed out on—a realization that sent an ache throughout my entire body, causing a lump to settle in the pit of my throat. When Leah stepped closer, I noticed that her hair, which was pulled back into a ponytail, held a few gray strands, a silent testament to how much time we'd missed.

Leah picked up my hand and gently squeezed it, causing more uncontrollable tears to flow. That squeeze was our code of reassurance, a promise that everything would be okay. Whenever one of us got scared in the middle of the night, the other would crawl into bed next to them, pick up their hand, and squeeze it.

"You remembered," I choked out.

"How could I ever forget?" Her voice was laced with sorrow as she leaned down and wrapped herself around me, just as Mama had done. "I missed you so much."

"I missed you too."

Throughout the room, all I heard was sniffling. Some came from us, and some, even though I didn't see it, seemed to come from the few police officers who stood by the door and witnessed our reunion.

I looked around, and my eyes fell on the most beautiful young lady who was more developed and taller than the two-year-old memory I held close to my heart. She'd changed the most out of everyone, but she was definitely my baby. Everyone moved aside and created a path for Skye to walk through, giving me a better look at the two-year-old, who now stood taller than Leah and Mama. The resemblance to my younger self was uncanny. Tall, slim, and muscular. She had to be an athlete.

My hands trembled as I reached out to her. I was afraid to move too quick. Afraid that any sudden movements would make her image disappear. When my fingers brushed against her soft skin, the joy that I'd buried years ago was revived.

I could tell she was nervous. She held her phone tightly in her hand and close to her body. She looked like she wasn't sure what she should do. That made two of us. The baby I protected in my body and nourished with my milk was a stranger. Her discomfort twisted my heart into a tight knot. I wanted to pull her into my arms and hold her close, but I resisted the urge, and instead, I held out my hand, a silent invitation. Joy exploded inside me when she placed hers in mine. I lifted it to my cheek, closed my eyes, and soaked in the moment. When I opened them, tears blurred my vision. "You used to have the tiniest hands," I told her. "I used to kiss them all the time when you were a baby." I swallowed the huge lump in my throat. "You would laugh when I pretended to bite your fingers off."

Skye managed a small smile. Her discomfort seemed to ease a little. "I'm really glad you're okay."

The sound of her voice caused me to gasp. I'd never heard her voice before. Not the voice she grew into. It was soft and calming. I could listen to her talk all day. I wanted to listen to her talk all day. In fact, it was all I wanted to do.

"I used to dream about you," Skye said.

"You did?" I wanted to know more. Wanted her to keep talking and never stop. I lowered myself onto the bed when my one leg could no longer hold me up.

"It was mainly about basketball," she continued.

"Skye's a star basketball player. She's just like her mom." Mama beamed, confirming what I already assumed.

Skye's cheeks went from brown to crimson as she smiled at her grandma. I had a feeling Mama thought everything Skye did was exceptional. Just as I did, even without knowing for sure.

I tore my attention away from Skye and looked around the room. It wasn't hard to notice that two people were missing. "Where's Quinton and Dad?" I asked.

Eyes darted around the room, but none of them connected with mine. Something was wrong. My heart dropped, and so did my body. Once again, I found myself sitting on the edge of the bed, but that time, it was from fear of what I was about to hear. "Can someone please tell me what's going on?" My voice rose. "Tell me," I said again.

Leah stepped in front of me and then sat beside me. When she took my hand in hers, I stopped breathing. Whatever she was about to say couldn't be good.

"Nova." Leah's voice was sad. Everything felt sad.

"Are they gone?" I asked before she had a chance to tell me.

"Quinton's here." She had what looked like a forced smile. "He's outside talking with Detective Cox."

"What about Dad? Is he out there too?"

Leah shook her head. "No, Nova, he's not."

"Then where is he? At home?" I turned to Mama.

"Nova . . ." Mama's tone set off an alarm inside me.

"No. No. No." I jerked one hand away from her and placed both of them firmly over my ears. If I didn't hear it, then it wouldn't be true. I had two prayers when I was in that room. One was to get out, and the other was to reunite with my family. All my family.

I sat on the side of the bed, singing louder and louder. I closed my eyes and refused to allow anything bad to come in. I did whatever I had to do to block out all the noise. All the bad stuff. I wanted it all to go away.

CHAPTER 6

Leah

Leah stood close to Nova. She looked back at her mom and Skye, who wore matching shocked expressions, although Martha's was filled with more concern than shock. Leah silently motioned for them to step out. She could tell her mom didn't want to leave, but Leah lifted her brows and mouthed, "Let me calm her down."

Martha reluctantly followed Skye out of the room.

Nova was still humming, and her eyes were still closed, but her hands were no longer over her ears. She had them clenched together in her lap, and she'd squeezed her eyes together. Leah moved the chair close to Nova's bed, then reached over and picked up Nova's hand. At first, Nova flinched at Leah's touch, but then she cracked her eyes open, and quickly shut them again.

"I'm not listening to you. I don't want to hear you," Nova repeated as if it was a song and those were the only words she knew.

"Okay," Leah whispered. She gently massaged Nova's hand while softly repeating, "You're okay. You're okay." Leah knew Nova wouldn't hear her words at first, but Leah kept massaging her hands, and eventually, Nova's song grew softer and softer until the only sound in the room was Leah's soft voice, reminding Nova that she was okay.

The door opened, and Dr. Lee, the doctor Leah met when they first arrived, entered. He'd filled all of them in on Nova's condition before they were allowed to go in and see her. Physically, Nova was going to be okay, but mentally, as expected, she had a long road ahead of her.

Leah nodded at the question Dr. Lee never asked. He continued monitoring for a few more minutes before he eased out of the room, closing the door behind him. What took him so long? What would've happened if they hadn't been there? Then again, if they hadn't been there, Nova wouldn't have been fighting against hearing that a huge part of all their hearts was gone.

Nova sat silently as streams of sorrow flowed from her eyes. There was no need to speak the words out loud.

"When?" Nova sniffed.

Leah kept rubbing Nova's hand. "Two years ago. Cancer."

Nova gave a slow nod, then stared across the room. While Nova processed what she'd heard, Leah watched her and thought of how growing up, people used to get them mixed up all the time. They used to look so much alike. At one point, all they heard was, "That's those pretty Lefleur girls." Leah and Nova were convinced no one in Bayou knew their real names. "Those pretty Lefleur girls" had become their identity back then, and they loved it.

Now, Leah struggled to find any similarities between her and her sister. Nova's thick gray hair and the dark circles underneath her eyes made her look way older than the two years that stood between her and Leah. Her once rich mahogany skin was pale and ashy. Leah had a hard time making the woman in front of her be the tall, muscular athlete her sister had once been. Nova was a shell of herself physically, mentally, and emotionally, and more than anything, Leah wanted her sister back. She wanted the sister with the loud mouth who had to be the life of every room, even when the room didn't call for it or desire it.

"Girls should be seen and not heard" was the speech that Martha had given to Nova on more than one occasion. When Nova went missing, Leah remembered hearing her mom in her bedroom, on her knees, crying out to God, asking if she could just hear her baby's voice again. She promised she wouldn't try to shut her up. Leah had prayed the same prayer. Nova used to work her nerves because she always moved like the Energizer Bunny, which was the exact opposite of Leah. After Nova was kidnapped, Leah didn't think she'd ever move again.

"Leah?" Nova's hoarse voice brought Leah's attention to her. "Can you sit next to me?" Nova asked quietly.

Dr. Lee had explained that Nova became anxious when someone got too close. Even though they'd hugged and cried a few minutes ago, Leah still wanted to make sure she was following Nova's lead. If she had it her way, Leah would've hopped on that bed as soon as Nova did, and she would've held her sister as tight as she could until the pain she was feeling at that moment subsided. But she'd studied trauma enough to know that the side effects came in waves. Thankfully, this wave was pushing Nova closer to Leah.

"Of course." Leah pushed herself onto the bed. She and Nova sat, with their feet dangling over the side, just as they used to do when they were kids. And just like back then, Nova's legs hung way lower than Leah's.

"I've missed this," Leah said.

She and Nova hugged, and as soon as their bodies touched, a warmth Leah hadn't expected coursed through her. Tension she hadn't realized she was holding eased from her muscles. Leah went limp. Still in Nova's arms, her whole body shook as she released years of pain.

After she was sure there was nothing left to get out, Leah sniffed and wiped her eyes. "I'm sorry. I don't know where that came from," she joked.

Nova smiled. "You still don't like to cry?"

Leah cleared her throat. "It's not that I don't like to cry."

She hated it. For years Leah tried to remember where this feeling came from. Tears were natural. And shouldn't a therapist, of all people, be okay with people expressing their emotions in a natural way, like crying? Maybe it was the feeling of helplessness it gave her whenever someone cried or even when she cried.

"You used to hate crying. You said tears gave you . . ." Nova lifted her head toward the ceiling. "What was the word? It was a funny word you used to say."

"Heebie-jeebies," Leah chuckled.

"Yeah. That's the word." Nova lowered her gaze and twisted her hands around each other. "You would've had a lot of heebie-jeebies if you'd been in that room with me." She glanced at Leah and quickly affixed her gaze to her hands. "Crying was all I could do. Not that it helped. My tears didn't matter."

A cold shiver traveled down Leah's spine. Her heart ached with rage and sorrow as she thought of Nova, who was so vulnerable and alone. Hearing how her tears were ignored reignited the protective fire inside Leah that had always burned for Nova.

Leah touched Nova's leg. "They matter to me. And crying doesn't give me the heebie-jeebies anymore, so if you need to cry, then cry. If you need to scream, then scream. Whatever you need to do, please do it, and I'll be right here with you. Hell, I'll even cry and scream right along with you."

Nova picked up Leah's hand and squeezed it. "I don't feel the need. Being here with you is the only time I don't want to run away and hide. You've always made me feel like everything would be okay."

Leah's throat tightened, but she refused to cry again. She waited until she was sure her words would come out without cracking before she spoke. "And you've always made me feel the same way. You were . . . are . . . my best friend. I hope you know that that hasn't changed."

Nova's eyes watered. "And you're mine." She adjusted herself on the bed. "Okay, I want to know all about you. Tell me everything. I know you're married." Nova glanced at the ring on Leah's finger. "Tell me about your husband. What about kids? I have so many questions."

Questions that caused the nonstop battle inside Leah to intensify. She and Nova used to tell each other everything. Secrets didn't exist between them—until now. But Nova had been through so much already, so if Leah had to choose between honesty and protection, she'd choose protection, which meant making sure Nova didn't find out about her marriage.

"We do have a lot to catch up on, and trust me, we'll have plenty of time. Believe it or not, my life's not all that interesting." Leah hoped the guilt she held on the inside didn't show on the outside. "Besides, it won't be long before Mom comes barging in. You know she's anxious to get back to you."

"I know, but I just want to be with you now. Please." Nova moved closer and held Leah's hand tighter, but Leah couldn't deny her sister's request. As painful as it was, Leah had to share her life, at least part of it, with Nova.

"Okay." Leah squeezed Nova's hand, hoping to give herself the reassurance she tried to give her sister. "I've been married for three years." Leah told Nova the story that she, Quinton, and Martha had discussed on the way there. She was married. She and her husband were going through some things and were separated. That was the only way Leah could explain why Nova wouldn't meet him. If Leah had her way, Nova would never find out that Quinton was her husband. More than anything, Leah wanted things between her and Nova to be how they used to be. A connection so deep that they could practically read each other's thoughts and feel each other's emotions. She feared that once Nova learned about her marriage to Quinton, what they once had would never be again.

"Is it the guy you were dating in college?" Nova asked.

"Ricardo?" Leah pondered the right answer to that question. Then she decided that there was no right answer because any answer she gave would be a lie other than telling Nova that his name was Quinton. Yes, her Quinton. And there was no way she was about to say that, so she continued with the lie. "No, Ricardo and I broke up. He's someone I started dating after college."

"So, what's his name?" Nova asked.

"Chris," Leah said, the first name that came to mind.

That name tasted like betrayal when Leah thought of Quinton and their beautiful life, which she had to treat like a dirty little secret. Leah didn't know how long she could endure the emotional tug-of-war of protecting her sister and disowning the love of her life.

"Why aren't you and Chris together? Did he hurt you?" Nova asked.

"No, no, nothing like that." Leah hoped to offer her conscience a tiny sliver of relief by telling Nova at least part of the truth. "He's a great guy. We found each other during a time when we both needed love more than anything else. He gave me a reason to smile again. To breathe again when, before him, those were the last things I wanted to do. My life ended when I lost you and began again when I fell in love with . . . with Chris."

"Wow," Nova said breathlessly. "That's so beautiful." She placed her hand over her chest. "For the life of me, I can't understand how that kind of love couldn't fix whatever happened between the two of you." Nova stared across the room as if her thoughts were a million miles away. "That's the kind of love Quinton and I had. Things weren't great between us back then, but I always knew that our love would outlast our problems." Then, as if snapped out of a trance, Nova looked at Leah. "It sounds like that's what you and Chris have too."

The knot in Leah's stomach traveled to her heart and then her lungs. It was so tight that Leah felt she was about to black out. Her saving grace came when Nova jumped to another more pleasant topic.

"Okay, now tell me about Skye. What does she like? What does she dislike? What is she like?"

"Skye is amazing. She's a perfect combination of you and Quinton in every way."

Those words were knives to Leah's heart. They were true, but it hurt that no one would ever say that about a child of hers. People used to compliment Leah on how sweet, smart, and respectful Skye was, but now that Nova was back, it was possible that those words of praise would be directed at her instead of Leah. Caring for Skye was the closest Leah would ever come to being a mom. She started to feel the same way she did when she'd woken up after a miscarriage and learned that the doctor had to do an emergency hysterectomy to save her life. In an instant, the future Leah had imagined was taken from her. Just as it would be now if Skye decided she didn't need Leah anymore. She had Nova, her real mom. Why would she need a substitute?

"She's so beautiful," Nova practically sang. "I wish I could've been there for her special times. I missed so much, and no matter how bad it hurts, there's nothing I can do to get it back." Tears streamed down Nova's cheeks. "All I wanted was to be a good mom and to have the kind of relationship with her that we had with Mama."

Leah pushed past her feelings and focused on Nova. "It's not too late. Skye's not a baby anymore, but she still has a lot of milestones left to reach. You'll be there for all of them, just like Mama was for us when we were Skye's age."

A knock at the door interrupted their talk, and Leah was sure it was their mom, but she was wrong.

"Quinton." Nova said his name as if it was the sweetest word she'd ever spoken.

Nova and Leah both stood. Leah to leave and Nova to embrace Quinton, just as she had with everyone else.

Quinton didn't speak. He walked to Nova, and they hugged and cried as Leah slipped past them unnoticed, lugging her heavy heart with her. The sound of their muffled sobs followed her to the door. In their embrace, Leah saw a bond fractured by time and an unfortunate circumstance. With a final glance toward the room, Leah walked down the hallway with the thoughts of the journey ahead of them swirling around in her head.

CHAPTER 7
Nova

When I saw Quinton, I saw the face of the little boy I once loved, even with the gray stubbles on his chin. I took in every part of him and desperately wanted to know what those parts experienced over the years. What wisdom caused the curly gray hairs to outnumber the black ones? What had those light-brown eyes seen? What burdens did those broad shoulders bear? What was life like without me?

Then I thought of the last time I'd seen him and how I wanted to be as far away from him as possible. Every day after that, I longed to find my way back to him.

Quinton was my high school sweetheart, but I'd liked him ever since he walked into our third-grade classroom and Mrs. Smith introduced him as the new student from Texas. She said that he was living with his grandparents, Coach and Mrs. Boudreaux. Everyone knew Quinton's grandparents, especially Coach Boudreaux, who coached football and basketball at Bayou Middle School. His grandmother, Mrs. Boudreaux, taught English at the same school.

Most of the students in our class didn't talk to Quinton. His face held a permanent mean mug that showed he didn't want to be bothered. Unlike all the other students, I saw Quinton as a challenge. I was determined to make him smile. I did eventually, but it took almost the whole school year before it happened. Once I broke through his tough-boy exterior, I thought he'd want to be friends, but unlike Lance, my best friend back then, Quinton wasn't interested in being friends with a girl.

My body froze at the thought of Lance, the person at the center of the argument Quinton and I had that night. The argument that sent me running away from Quinton and led me right to Adam.

"I'm so sorry, Nova." His eyes begged for forgiveness.

I blinked a few times, wondering if I'd spoken my thoughts out loud or if, like so many times in the past, Quinton somehow knew what I was thinking.

"Sorry?" I asked, lowering myself onto the bed.

Quinton pulled the chair closer to me before sitting. "Yes, for everything. For not listening to you that night. For accusing you when I knew I had no right to. For not being the husband that I should've been to you. For all of it."

Quinton's apology reopened old wounds while also giving me the relief I longed to feel. So many times, I wondered if Quinton hated me. If he thought I'd left him and Skye on purpose. I wondered if he blamed me for ruining the life we were supposed to have together for as long as we lived, like we vowed to do.

"It wasn't your fault," I told him.

"Yes, it was. I shouldn't have let you leave. I shouldn't have said the things I said. I'll never forgive myself for not protecting you."

That night, after the banquet, Quinton and I were in a much better place than when we arrived that weekend. I felt like we were finally getting back on track, which was why I told him that I'd spoken with Lance. I didn't want any secrets between us, plus I was afraid that he'd find out from someone else. The people in Bayou were known to talk too much about everyone else's business.

Quinton blamed Lance for causing his knee injury that ended his chances of getting a scholarship to college and his ultimate dream of playing in the NFL, which Lance went on to do. Things got so bad that while we were in college, right before I found out I was pregnant with

Skye, Quinton told me how much it bothered him that Lance and I were still friends. The last thing I wanted to do was end my friendship with Lance, but I also couldn't risk losing Quinton. I had to make a choice, and once I found out I was pregnant, the choice was made for me. I chose Quinton.

That wasn't the only reason I chose him, though. The other reason was his relationship with his mom, Renee. Quinton shared with me that he moved to Bayou because Renee's boyfriend didn't want any kids. So, Renee sent Quinton away. The one person he needed to choose him didn't. I couldn't do the same.

"I hope one day you can forgive me," Quinton continued.

"I'm the one who ran away. You used to say I never wanted to listen, and you were right. Adam wouldn't have had a chance to drug my drink or get me away from the hotel had I stayed and dealt with our problems instead of leaving."

Adam never admitted that he slipped something in my drink, but it wasn't hard for me to figure out. When I woke up at his house, I felt loopy and disoriented, like I'd taken medicine or something.

Quinton's eyes narrowed. "Adam. Was he the one who sat at the table with us? The one who kept saying you looked like his wife?"

"Yeah. That's him."

Quinton shook his head. "I knew something was off with that guy." His lips tightened, and his hands balled into fists. "Dammit! I told the police about him. I told them they needed to check him out because he was too attentive. Something was off."

My heart raced as Quinton's face changed from Quinton to Adam. I pushed myself away from him. Fear gripped me, and I struggled to breathe. I tried to speak. Tried to run, but I couldn't do anything but retreat to the corner of the bed that had become my safe space.

"Nova, oh God, I'm so sorry. I was angry at him. I'd never . . ." His voice broke. "I'd never hurt you, Nova," he cried, his voice begging for me to understand.

I lifted my head, and tears burned my eyes, but I couldn't go to him. I couldn't comfort him because I had to take care of myself. I had to make sure I was okay. All I could do was watch and wait for him to be okay too.

"I know," I finally said. "I know you wouldn't hurt me. I know." I repeated it until I believed it.

After I'd calmed down, I asked the questions I'd been dying to ask. "Quinton. Did you have a good life? I mean, are you happy?" My words cracked as they flowed through my lips. I wanted him to have a good life, but I was supposed to have a good life too. I was supposed to be a part of his life with Skye.

He hesitated before he answered. "Yes," he said softly, or maybe it was regret I heard in his words. "I have a good life, but a piece of it was always missing," he admitted. "I never stopped thinking about you. And every time I look at Skye, I see you. She's everything you would've wanted her to be. She's smart. Athletic . . ."

"And beautiful," I added.

He nodded. "And beautiful. Like I said, when I see her, I see you."

I turned away from him. "You see the me that I used to be when you look at Skye. You don't see the me I am now. This person is ugly, frail, and hollow. Skye's nothing like me."

"That's not true."

"How can you say that? Look at me, Quinton."

He did, but not for long, and I didn't blame him. "You can barely look at me."

He fixed his eyes on me and locked them there. "What I see is beautiful and strong. I see a survivor, and there's nothing ugly about that."

"I wish I saw who you saw."

"I wish you did too."

"What's her name?" I asked.

Quinton's eyes narrowed. "Who?"

I pointed to the silver band on his ring finger. "Your wife. What's her name?"

"Oh." Quinton stared at the ring like he didn't realize it was there. "Nova, I know you have questions, but can we focus on you right now? I just need to know that you're going to be okay."

"As long as I'm with the people I love, then I'm going to be okay. But part of being okay is knowing that you are too. I know it may not be easy to share your new life with me, but I've missed so much, and I want to know everything. Even if it hurts a little. I can handle it," I assured him.

"I never doubted that for a second. And you're right, it's not easy. For years all I wanted was to have you back. The hardest thing I ever had to do was accept that you were really gone. All of this is a lot to take in, and one day soon, I'll tell you everything you want to know about my new life, as you called it, but for a second, I kinda just want to remember my old life."

I smiled. "I kinda want to remember my old life too."

"Then let's do that."

For the rest of our time together, Quinton and I reminisced about the good days: the first day we brought Skye home from the hospital and Quinton drove two miles per hour on the interstate. The day we moved into our first apartment and neither one of us knew a thing about hanging curtains or picking out furniture. It was hard to believe that life used to be so simple for us, but we thought it was so hard.

"How's Renee?" I asked.

The light in Quinton dimmed. "Renee is still Renee."

There was more I could've asked, but I chose not to. It wasn't hard to see that he'd rather not talk about his mom, which meant she still didn't put him first like a mom was supposed to do.

The hospital door opened, bringing our trip to the past to an end.

"I'm sorry, Mr. Boudreaux, but my patient needs her rest so she can hurry up and get out of here and back home where she belongs." Ashley smiled at me.

"That's all we've ever wanted." Quinton smiled, but it didn't hide the sadness that rested in his eyes and on his shoulders.

Quinton leaned down and hugged me again before he left. Hours afterward, his cologne lingered on my hospital gown. I leaned into it and inhaled. I'd hoped his smell would take me back to the past. Hoped it would cause memories I'd forgotten to fill my mind and push out all the bad ones. It didn't. All I smelled was a life that no longer included me. When we first got married, we had so many dreams we wanted to fulfill together. We used to lie in bed at night and talk about our future with our houseful of children and all the trips we'd take together. We were determined to travel the world and experience new adventures, but after fifteen years, I was sure he'd lived the life we planned with someone else.

CHAPTER 8

Leah

Yesterday was one of the most emotional days Leah had experienced in a while. She'd replayed the moment over in her head when she first saw Nova. Then she thought of the look Nova had when Quinton walked into the room. It was as if someone had flipped a switch inside her and caused her whole face to light up. It was a look Leah would never forget. The look of a woman who was finally reunited with the man she loved.

In addition to the guilt that had settled inside her and made itself at home, Leah also grappled with two new feelings that she hated even more than guilt—fear and inadequacy. From the very beginning, Leah and Quinton's relationship had been overshadowed by the amazing one he had with Nova. Some of Leah's family members, including her mom, warned her that Quinton could've been using her as a replacement for the woman he really wanted but couldn't have. Leah dismissed their words of warning. She ignored the nagging feeling that questioned if they were right and convinced herself they were all ridiculous. But after yesterday, Leah wasn't so sure anymore. When Quinton walked into that room, his gaze never left Nova. He made Leah feel invisible, and he'd never made her feel that way before.

A Sky Full of Love

It was almost ten o'clock before they left the hospital last night. Everyone was exhausted and just wanted to find the nearest hotel and sleep. Everyone except Martha, who refused to leave Nova's side. Leah was too tired to convince her mom to come with them so she could get a good night's sleep. Not that it would've done any good. If Martha felt anything like Leah, then nothing, including a comfortable bed, would offer a good night's sleep.

Leah reached over and picked up her phone from the nightstand. It was three in the morning. She turned over, expecting to see Quinton sleeping beside her, but his side was empty. She didn't have to think twice about his whereabouts. Whenever Quinton had a lot on his mind he always went to the gym. He said working out helped him to think better, and Leah could tell he had a lot to think about after his conversation with Nova. He looked like he had the weight of fifteen years on his shoulders.

Skye was in the adjacent room, hopefully sleeping a lot better than Leah and Quinton were. When Leah pushed her door open, she was surprised to see Skye in bed with the light of her cell phone shining in her face.

"Hey, what are you doing up?" Leah asked.

"The door woke me up. I got up to see if something had happened and if y'all were going back to the hospital, but you were still in bed, so I figured Dad must've been going downstairs to work out. I couldn't go back to sleep after that."

"I must've been more out of it than I thought. I didn't even hear him leave," Leah said, walking farther into the room and taking a seat on the bed next to Skye. "Well, since you're up. How are you feeling about all of this?"

"Okay, I guess." Skye laid her phone down. "I don't know how I'm supposed to feel. I've never had a mom come back to life before."

Leah chuckled. "Technically, you still haven't, since someone has to be dead to come back to life."

"You know what I mean. To us, she was dead, and now she's back."

Leah nodded. "This is true."

"I do want to get to know her, though. She's always been like this fairy tale that I've heard stories about but never seen in person. I feel like I know her, but not really. Does that make sense?"

"Of course. You know her because of what you've heard, but you want to get to know her for yourself."

"Yeah."

"But, honey, I also want you to remember that the Nova you heard about isn't the same Nova that you met yesterday. The Nova you used to hear about would've run to that door and picked me and Mama up and spun us around, and the nurses would've had to come in and tell her to keep it down. It didn't matter where she was, her inside voice didn't work."

"You say the same thing about me."

Leah nodded. "That's right, I do."

"I don't expect her to be the same as she used to be. I just want to know who she is now." Skye yawned.

Leah was grateful that the room was dim, and Skye couldn't see the unease that Leah was sure showed all over her face. Skye's playful, just-want-to-have-fun personality was a lot like Nova's used to be. Leah wondered how long it would take before parts of the old Nova resurfaced and she and Skye formed a relationship that didn't have room for Leah.

Leah leaned over and kissed Skye's forehead. "Get some rest. I'm going to walk down to check on your dad."

"Okay." Skye adjusted her pillow. "Teeah?"

"Yeah?" Leah's hand rested on the doorknob as she turned back to Skye.

"You're okay with me getting to know her, right?"

Leah's hand tightened around the doorknob, the cool metal grounding her as she worked to keep her composure.

"Of course, sweetie," Leah managed to say, her voice steady despite the storm churning inside her.

"Good," Skye said before turning her phone off and snuggling underneath the covers.

Once she was back in her room, Leah quickly washed up and dressed before going downstairs. She walked through the dimly lit lobby, where a heavyset middle-aged woman with a long black weave sat behind the desk. Leah offered her a smile that wasn't returned. It was almost four in the morning, after all.

In the gym, which was smaller than Leah and Quinton's bedroom, she expected to find Quinton working out with the fierceness of a madman, but that wasn't what she saw. Quinton sat on the weight bench with his head lowered, looking like a man who'd been defeated.

The sight of him caught Leah off guard. Quinton was someone who tackled challenges head-on. In fact, he looked more relaxed after the flood of 2016 damaged over one hundred thousand homes and businesses in Baton Rouge and other areas in Louisiana. The flood was so catastrophic that the governor called it a historic, unprecedented event. Quinton's insurance agency was inundated with claims, putting intense pressure on the limited manpower he had at the time. Leah and Skye barely saw him for weeks. And still, he didn't look as overwhelmed as he did now.

Walking closer, Leah felt a tightness in her chest, as a thousand questions raced through her mind; the main one and the one she couldn't stop asking herself was if Nova's return brought back old feelings and he didn't know how to break the news to Leah.

"Hey," Quinton said when he lifted his head, and their eyes met.

Leah pointed to the sign. "The gym's closed."

"I know. I asked Rochelle if it was okay, and she said she didn't care," he said as if Leah knew Rochelle.

"Rochelle?"

"The receptionist."

"Makes sense. She looked like she couldn't care less about anything at this hour."

Quinton straightened his back. "Speaking of time, why aren't you sleeping?"

"I could ask you the same question." Leah sat on the bench next to Quinton.

For a moment, they sat in silence while Leah reminded herself that Nova wasn't the only one who'd suffered. Quinton had lived through his own kind of trauma, struggling with the loss and uncertainty of Nova's fate, not to mention the guilt of not being there to save her. It was more likely that Quinton was submerged in memories and not feelings. And those memories didn't hold any weight to the reality of the life they were committed to living together.

"It was Lance," Quinton said, breaking the silence. He turned his body, so he and Leah were both facing the same way, but his eyes didn't meet hers.

Oh God. Leah's body tensed at the mention of Lance's name. "What was Lance?"

"The argument Nova and I had that night. It was about Lance."

Leah couldn't breathe. "What?" That one word took everything she had in her to push out.

"I didn't say anything because I knew y'all would blame me. Hell, I blamed me, but you and your parents were the only family I had left in Bayou, and I knew how important it was for Nova for Skye to grow up around her family. I couldn't uproot her and move to Texas to be close to Renee. It wasn't like we'd see her much anyway." Quinton paused as if he realized that talking about his mom was veering off track. "I'm sorry, Leah. I know I should've told you, but I didn't know how."

They always knew that Nova and Quinton had an argument, and that was the reason she'd left the hotel room that night, but Quinton told them that it was about money. It made sense to Leah because Nova had already expressed how they were barely making ends meet and they were both stressed out about it.

"I don't understand. Why were you fighting about Lance? He and Nova weren't even friends anymore."

"That's what I thought, too, but apparently, she'd been talking with him behind my back."

Did Leah know about that and forgot? No, she definitely would've remembered. That was a huge deal between Leah and Quinton. In fact, Quinton was so against Nova's friendship with Lance that he had been willing to walk away from their relationship. He didn't trust Lance, and hated that Nova was so close to him.

"How did you find out that they'd been talking? Did Nova tell you, or did you hear it from someone else?" Leah asked, because it wouldn't have surprised her if it was secondhand information. That was one of the reasons Leah didn't want to live in Bayou. She loved the small-town feel but hated the small-town gossip.

"No, she told me. That weekend was about putting our relationship back together, and she said she didn't want there to be any secrets between us."

"So, she and Lance just talked on the phone or something?" Leah asked.

"I don't know. I guess, but that's not the point. She knew how I felt about Lance, and she was talking with him behind my back. Needless to say, I didn't take it well at all. We both said things we shouldn't have, and she left. Everything inside of me screamed that I should go after her, but my stupid pride wouldn't let me. I sat in that room, watching TV while she was being kidnapped." The veins in Quinton's neck popped out. He looked over at Leah again. "You think she'll ever forgive me?"

Leah moved closer to Quinton. "I think she's already forgiven you. The question is if you can forgive yourself."

Quinton shook his head. "I don't know if I can. I thought I had, but now that Nova's back and hearing everything that she's gone through . . . How am I supposed to forgive myself?"

"You have to find a way. Holding on to this isn't doing anyone any good."

"And then . . ." Quinton paused.

"And then what?"

"It's not just the guilt for not being there for her, but . . ." He swallowed. "We have such a good life. We've accomplished so much, and before now, I thought Nova was in heaven, looking down on us and smiling because we were happy, you know. But now . . ."

"You feel guilty that she was locked up and we moved on." Leah knew what he felt because she felt it too.

He nodded.

"But we had no choice but to move on. You know that, right?"

At least that was what she kept reminding herself. Her words didn't seem like they were getting through to Quinton any more than they'd gotten through to her. But then, she thought of the one thing that would help both of them to see things in a different light.

"We also have to remember Skye. She needed all of us at our best. What kind of life would she have had if everyone she depended on had shut down and given up? You moved on because you had no choice. None of us had a choice, and we have to believe that Nova will understand that."

CHAPTER 9

Nova

I couldn't stop staring at Mama. All night, while she slept on the chair that let out into a bed, I watched her sleep. I fell asleep a few times, but it was never for long. It was only when I was awake that I knew all of it was real. Eventually, I gave in and stopped fighting it. The next time I opened my eyes, the sun was shining, and Mama was dressed and sitting in the chair, drinking a cup of coffee.

"Good morning, Sweet Pea," Mama greeted me, using the name she called me when I was younger. As I got older, I hated that name. But now, I could listen to Mama call me Sweet Pea all day. "How'd you sleep?" Mama asked.

"Good." I sat up in the bed.

I couldn't tell Mama that it was hard to sleep because nighttime had always been the worst time in that house. During the day Adam was either out working on the farm or running errands, but at night, he had nothing but time, and he spent all of it on me. I wished I could convince myself that Adam was gone, but my mind didn't believe it.

It was hard to talk about the things I went through in that room and even harder to see the painful look on my family's faces whenever I mentioned the slightest thing. All of it was too much for me.

"You hungry?" Mama stood and walked to the side of the bed. "I can call the nurse and ask them to bring you something to eat. Or I can run downstairs and get you something."

"I'm not hungry," I told Mama.

I doubted I'd be too picky about whatever food they served. The cooks at the hospital couldn't be any worse than the food Adam cooked. Most times, he threw together whatever he could find in his kitchen. I didn't have to be with him to see that. The plates with SPAM, sliced bread, green beans, and peaches gave it away.

"You want me to fix your hair while we wait?" Mama went back to her seat and rummaged through her purse until she found a brush.

I nodded silently and sat on the edge of the bed. Mama unwrapped the silk scarf that she'd given to me to tie around my head. It reminded me of the scarves she always used for Leah and my hair when she'd tied it up every night before bed. I asked Adam for a scarf once. I didn't like the idea of going to bed without something covering my hair. Adam didn't even think before he told me no.

"What you need a scarf for?" he asked.

When I told him I wanted to use it for my hair, he stared at me so long that I thought he was going to say yes.

"Hell no. You think I'm stupid or something?" he'd fussed. "Why do you really want that scarf? What are you trying to do?"

No matter what I said, Adam was convinced that I was up to no good. He didn't punish me that night. The punishment came the next day when he didn't show up with food. By that time, I'd gotten used to those punishments and started hiding packs of oatmeal or cookies, which I only got when he was in a good mood. I hid things I could easily wrap in a towel and tuck in a drawer. Sometimes, the punishments were so spread out that whatever I'd hidden was stale by the time I needed it. That didn't matter to me, though. I just needed to eat.

"You okay, baby? Am I hurting you?" Mama leaned over and looked at me.

"I'm okay. I think my hair is good now." Suddenly, Mama's touch wasn't soothing anymore. It was too familiar, but her hands weren't the ones I felt running through my hair.

"I brushed my wife's hair every night." Adam grinned and insisted on doing the same for me. Or maybe I should say *to* me because I never asked him to do anything *for* me. As the memory grew, so did the feeling of his hands in my hair.

"Okay. I just have to brush this part down."

I looked up just as Mama raised the brush, and without thinking, I swatted it, sending the brush flying against the wall.

Mama's wide eyes stared from me to the wall.

"I'm sorry, Mama." And I was. I hated seeing that look in her eyes and knowing I'd caused it. It was a look I was sure Adam had seen plenty of times, and I didn't want to be him. I didn't want to hurt her like he'd hurt me.

"You don't have to be sorry, baby. It's okay." Mama bent down and picked up the brush just as someone knocked on the door.

I grabbed the scarf from beside me and wrapped it back around my head to cover my thick gray hair that made me look older than Mama.

Leah peeped her head through. "Good morning," she whispered. "Can we come in?"

"Yes," I said, waving them in.

It was the first time we'd all been in the same room. My smile locked in place. I couldn't drop it even if I wanted to. At least, that was what I thought until joy and sorrow mingled inside me, causing my body to deflate by the overwhelming absence of Dad's presence.

Even with the dread of missing Daddy, there was still joy.

As I watched Skye standing between Leah and Quinton, I couldn't help thinking how someone could easily mistake them as a mama, father, and child. The thought caused me to laugh out loud as I remembered how much Leah and Quinton couldn't stand each other. I could tell they got along now, though, but they'd probably get sick at the thought of touching each other, let alone marriage.

"What are you laughing at?" Leah asked, looking like she was about to laugh even though she had no idea why.

"I was looking at the three of you and imagined how upset you'd be if someone had mistaken you two as a couple and Skye as your daughter."

The flash of panic that crossed Leah's and Quinton's faces made me laugh even more. "Those are the looks I expected to see. I knew you'd both find that horrifying." I cleared my throat. "I needed that laugh."

Leah and Quinton laughed too.

"Then I'm glad we were able to give it to you," Leah said, before turning her attention to Mama. "Mom, how about we go to the cafeteria and grab some breakfast and give Skye and Nova a little time alone?"

Mama hesitated for a minute.

"I'd really like that," I said, giving Mama the reassurance she needed to leave.

Skye sat in the chair when everyone else left.

"How'd you sleep?" I asked, needing to say something to get rid of the silence.

"Good." Skye glanced at me and then looked away.

Last night, she only looked at me for a second or two before she'd turn to look at Mama or Leah. I should've been the person she turned to when she needed security, not the person who made her feel uncomfortable. I was her mom, but in reality, I was just a random stranger she'd heard about but never knew. I was no better than Santa Claus or the Easter Bunny. Actually, they had an advantage because at least she looked forward to a visit from them every year.

Never in a million years could I have imagined my relationship with my daughter being like this. When I thought of all the things Adam did to me in that room . . . The times he'd make me go days with very little food because he said I was unappreciative. The time he took away the ring Quinton had slid on my finger and replaced it with the one he'd bought for his wife. All the times he held me and touched me and kissed me. None of that came close to the torture I felt sitting across from my daughter, being so close yet feeling so far away.

"Dad said you may want to know about my life," Skye said softly before lifting her gaze to me. "Do you? Want to know, I mean."

"I want to know everything. Every little detail." I felt like I'd said those exact words to all of them.

"That'll be a pretty boring story if I start at the beginning, especially since I really don't remember much from when I was younger." She twisted her finger around her braid.

Her words sliced a hole in my heart. I was a part of those younger years. Naturally, I didn't think she'd remember anything, being that she was only two, but a small slice of my soul had hoped that somehow, she'd remember our bath times when we'd fill the tub with bubbles, scoop them in our hands, and blow them at each other. Or even bedtime when she'd lie next to me, and I'd read or sing to her until she fell asleep on my chest. I wanted so badly for her to remember the walks in the park or the first time her dad and I took her to the pool in our apartment complex.

"My life now is way more interesting, but only because of basketball. It's the only thing I do outside of school and church." Skye glanced at me. "Dad's pretty strict."

My mouth flew open. "Quinton's strict?"

Skye nodded. "Why is that so shocking?"

"I just never imagined he'd be a strict parent. I always thought he'd be the fun one, and I'd be forced to be the strict one, which I didn't want to be either," I admitted.

Skye leaned forward. "Are you saying my dad used to be fun?"

"What? I'm saying your dad was the fun." I laughed. "Oh, the stories I could tell you about him back then."

And just like that, Skye and I had found something that we were both interested in talking about. There was nothing I loved more than sharing stories from our past with her.

"I cannot believe this," Skye said after I told her about the senior prank Quinton spearheaded. "Farm animals in the school? He would have a fit if I did that."

"Well, you're his baby. He used to say that no matter how old you get, you'd still be his baby girl," I said, thinking that would make her feel better, but it didn't.

"That's the problem. He always wanted me to be a little baby and couldn't accept that I was growing up."

"It's kind of hard for me to accept too," I admitted.

"At least you have a reason for feeling that way. Dad's been with me every day. He should remember what it was like being a teenager. He did say I could go to prom this year, though. Teeah and I had to double-team him to finally get a yes." Skye stopped abruptly like she'd said something wrong.

"Did your dad and Teeah tell you how I used to always have to referee the two of them?"

Skye's eyes wouldn't meet mine. "No, they didn't tell me."

"It's good to see that things have changed between them, though. That makes me happy."

"It does?" She seemed shocked. Skye bit her bottom lip like I used to do whenever I was nervous. It was so hard to watch the uneasiness that I caused her to have. She should've felt more comfortable with me than anyone else. I should've been the person she ran to to feel better, but instead, I was the one who made her uncomfortable.

"But prom, huh?" I said, wanting to erase whatever caused her mood to change. "That'll be fun. Are you taking someone special?"

Skye laughed. "Are you kidding? I was barely able to go. Going with a date would've been pushing it."

Quinton had changed a lot when I heard about him from Skye's point of view. Then the thought hit me. Maybe he was so strict because of me, which meant that I was the reason Skye had so many complaints about her life. I didn't like that. Yes, I wanted her to be safe, but I also wanted her to live her life. I didn't want Quinton to scar her the way

Adam scarred me. I hated that the world felt like a scary place to me when it never did when I was Skye's age. She shouldn't have to miss out because one man decided to steal a life that wasn't his to take. I didn't think I could hate Adam any more than I already did, but it was possible, because I could feel the hate growing inside me. Ruining my life was one thing, but ruining Skye's was different, and I wasn't going to stand by and allow him to have an impact on her or Quinton any longer.

"Now that I'm back, maybe I can talk with your dad, too, and see if I can get through to him."

Skye's eyes grew. "Really? Oh my gawd, that'll be so great. I bet he'll listen to you."

"Well, I don't know about that, but I'll do whatever I can to help you."

That was enough to lift Skye's mood once again, and we spent the rest of the time talking about school, basketball, and her best friend Ava, who she'd been friends with since middle school.

"There's nothing like having a best friend. I hope the two of you can stay friends forever," I said as my mind flashed back to all the fun times Lance and I had.

What had become a barely there ache over time was starting to hurt a lot more now that I was out. I was returning to a world where I had no husband, no father, and no best friend. But I reminded myself that I wasn't alone. I had Mama, Skye, and Leah, and they were more than enough for me.

I hated it when my time with Skye ended. Dr. Lee set up an appointment for me to meet with Dr. Harris, a psychologist, who was there to do something he called a debriefing.

Dr. Harris looked like one of those women who never left home without their face fully made. She looked like the exact opposite of me. I never liked makeup, maybe because I was always sweating from playing sports. Leah and Mama were just like Dr. Harris.

"It's so nice to meet you." Dr. Harris stood in front of me but at a distance. I assumed everyone was told I didn't like it when people were too close. Not people I don't know. "Mind if I sit?" Dr. Harris pointed to the chair next to the bed. She sat when I nodded. "Did Dr. Lee explain why we do the debriefing?" Her voice was proper and soft.

I nodded. "To check my mental state or something like that."

"That's right. You've spent years in a situation that most people couldn't even imagine being in. Going through something like that for so long has to have taken its toll on you. This is your time to share and say whatever you'd like to get out. No one is here to judge you or to tell you what you can and cannot say."

"I don't know what y'all want me to say. I was kidnapped, and I've lived in a room for fifteen years. Was it hard? Yes, but after a while, it just becomes a part of your life."

My thoughts swirled like a storm, battering against the walls that I'd built around myself. Walls that this lady was trying to break through, but there was no way I was going to allow anyone to get that close to me. My thoughts and feelings were only for me. Besides, what was I supposed to say that this woman didn't already know? That I was hurt? Angry? Upset? Betrayed? That every time I thought about all the birthdays and milestones I'd missed with my daughter, I wanted to scream? That the thought of never seeing my father again hurt so much that I could barely breathe? Was that what she wanted to hear? Or maybe she wanted to hear about the numbness that had settled in my bones and had become a part of my identity. Or the emptiness that left me like a shell of the person I used to be. Or maybe she needed to hear how even though I was free, I still felt like a ghost, like someone lurking unseen in the shadows while everyone else lived and laughed and went on with their lives. Was that what she wanted?

Dr. Harris nodded as if she was waiting for me to say more.

"I don't want to keep talking about being in that room, or that house, or that man. I don't see how that's going to help me move forward."

"I understand. Okay, we don't have to talk about that. Let's talk about your life now. Do you have any questions for me? Is there any way I can help to make this transition easier for you?"

I thought about her question for a minute. "I do have one question. When will this feel real? When will I stop waiting for him to come back or to wake me up? Will I ever feel safe again?"

"Nova, I'm not going to sugarcoat it. What you've experienced has left emotional scars that are going to take time to heal. Feeling this is all unreal, even when reality is staring us in the face, is normal. In fact, I'd be concerned if you didn't feel that way. Your mind is going to need time to process all of this."

"So even when I'm home, I'll still feel like this?"

"You'll probably have lingering fears and anxieties. You have to remember that for years, your mind has been in a state of hypervigilance. I'm going to refer you to a good friend of mine in Baton Rouge. I promise if you work with her, she can help you address those intrusive thoughts, and she'll give you techniques to help you reframe your perception of safety. Like I said, it's going to take time, but she'll be there to help you navigate through this journey."

I had to admit that I didn't like the idea of having to work with anyone after I left there. When I made it home, I wished I could pretend that the last fifteen years never happened. Even though Skye was a visible reminder that so much time had passed. My daughter was perfect in every way, but my heart mourned for the little baby I used to rock to sleep at night. The chubby-cheeked baby who would cry if I was out of her sight for two seconds.

"In the meantime," Dr. Harris continued, "I want to give you a technique to use whenever you start to question if this is real. You're going to engage your senses. Physical sensations don't exist in dreams, so you're going to use touch to anchor yourself. Do you want to try it?"

"Okay."

Dr. Harris smiled. "Great." She looked as if my willingness to cooperate shocked her. She seemed nice, but I didn't want to push my luck with her. At any moment, things could change. People could change. One minute they could be nice, and then seconds later, they'd have you pinned down to the bed, daring you to misbehave again. My heart raced as I saw the terror in my eyes staring back at me through my memories.

"Nova, it's okay. Breathe. Just breathe. You're safe. You're okay." Her soothing voice eventually broke through the panic that held me hostage. I did as she instructed, then wiped the sweat from my forehead. Dr. Harris gave me some time to compose myself, but she never left her chair. She sat quietly until I told her I was ready to continue.

In that same quiet, soothing voice, she continued with the exercise. "I want you to pick up the remote control. Now close your eyes and rub your hand across it. Try not to think about anything except how the remote feels."

I did as she asked, fighting against the urge to mentally go back into that room. It was hard to keep my mind on the remote. The more I fought to only focus on it, the harder it became. I opened my eyes. "I can't do it. I can't close my eyes without being back in that room."

Dr. Harris nodded. "It's okay. How about I show you some breathing exercises you can do whenever your thoughts start to feel too real? Is that okay?"

I nodded. If breathing exercises would help to keep my mind in the present, then I'd do them all day long. All I wanted was to focus on being with my family again and eventually getting back home.

CHAPTER 10
Leah

Leah and Quinton sat hand in hand across from Martha and Skye. One of the nurses told them about the garden in the back of the hospital, and they thought it would be a good time to speak openly and honestly with each other while Nova was in her therapy session.

The garden should've offered a sense of peace, but peace was nowhere around, especially after what happened in Nova's room when she couldn't stop laughing at the thought of Leah, Quinton, and Skye being a family. Leah understood why Nova thought they'd find it insulting for people to think that, but that was because Nova only knew the relationship that Leah and Quinton used to have. The one where they couldn't stand to be in the same room with each other. After losing Nova, all the pettiness they held for each other instantly went away. Leah made it her mission to take care of and look out for Quinton and Skye, and Quinton did the same for Leah. Those weren't the people Nova knew yet.

"It's nice out here," Martha said, looking around the garden.

Since it was the second week in October, most of the flowers were gone, but Leah's imagination allowed her to picture the riot of colors that existed there in the spring and summer months. The hospital administration was right; the garden was surrounded by huge hedges that hid everything on the other side. Around the hedges was an iron gate that provided a sense of safety and security.

"Today sure don't feel like a Sunday, does it?" Martha asked, reaching over and closing Skye's jacket.

"I'm fine, Gran." Skye opened the jacket again.

On the inside, Leah laughed because she knew exactly how Skye felt. Martha hovered over her granddaughter just as much as she used to do with Leah and Nova. Back then they didn't know the term *helicopter mom*, so Leah and Nova used to say she was too overprotective.

Turned out that Leah was just like her mom. When it came to Skye, there wasn't such a thing as being too overprotective. Actually, she'd take that back, there was a thing, and it was Quinton, not Leah, who took overprotection to a whole new level. Unfortunately for Skye, Nova's disappearance caused Quinton to become borderline obsessive when it came to protecting Skye. He tracked everything. Her phone. Her car. Leah wouldn't be surprised if he'd looked into putting a chip in Skye so he could track her too. Even though Leah didn't agree, she understood. Skye was his whole world, and keeping her safe was his top priority. She'd probably have done the same had she'd been in Quinton's place.

"No, it doesn't feel like a Sunday at all," Quinton said, answering Martha's question. "To be honest, it doesn't feel like any particular day."

Leah squeezed his hand. The same way she and Nova did when they knew the other person needed a little support, encouragement, love, or maybe all three at once.

"What do you think that therapist is asking her?" Martha asked Leah.

"Well, I've never had a case like this one, of course, but I'd assume she's just talking with her to gauge her mental state before they release her to go home."

Quinton shifted beside her. Leah looked over at him, and his head was lifted toward the sky. Martha's hand was cupped over her mouth, and Skye stared at Leah intently, as if hanging on to her every word.

Leah apologized, but she wasn't sure why. It wasn't like they hadn't heard the details of the abuse Nova endured. Leah and Quinton had seen the pictures of the bruises on Nova's back and arms. They looked old, but still evident. And even though no verbal abuse had been confirmed, Leah was sure Adam had done that too. Leah didn't know any cases where a person was physically abusive but not verbally. She did, however, know of cases where someone was verbally abusive but not physically.

"I know this is hard to hear, but we have to accept that Nova did experience these things. We can't pretend it didn't happen or shut down when we hear it. If Nova wants to talk about it, we need to be a safe space for her," Leah told them. "That means not reacting when she talks, like y'all just did." She looked from her mom to Quinton.

"We understand that, Leah, but it's not easy knowing it happened to someone you love," Quinton said.

Leah stiffened as the word *love* flowed so easily from Quinton in reference to Nova. Leah wished her brain didn't expand everything he said when he talked about her sister. It was hard for her not to question the meaning behind his words. That was what she was trained to do: hear what wasn't said as well as what was and decipher the true meaning behind the words.

"What happens when she goes home tomorrow? That's what the doctor said, right? She may be able to go home tomorrow?" Skye asked, flipping her phone from one hand to the other.

"Tomorrow or Tuesday," Leah corrected, "but most likely tomorrow if nothing changes."

Skye's eyes widened. "I can't miss two days of school."

"Then let's hope it's tomorrow, because we can't leave here without Nova," Quinton said.

"Sure can't," Martha agreed.

Skye sat back and folded her arms. For Skye's sake, Leah hoped the discharge would come tomorrow. In Skye's world, very little came before basketball, and not being able to play in the game this Friday would devastate her. It was the first home game of the season, but it wasn't just any game. Skye and her teammates had been waiting to meet up with their rival team from Baton Rouge, who they lost to last season by one point.

"Hey, let's go grab a snack." Quinton stood and reached his hand out to Skye.

He knew Skye well, and there was never a time when a snack didn't lift her mood. They didn't even know if Nova's discharge would be pushed back yet, and Skye was already sulking about the possibility.

Leah and Martha watched as Quinton put his arm around Skye, and they walked back toward the hospital. Like Skye, Leah could use some comfort from her parent as well. Leah left her bench and went and sat next to Martha.

"How are you doing, baby girl?" Martha put her arm around Leah.

Leah exhaled, unsure if she should be totally honest with her mom or if it was a time to keep her feelings to herself. Martha was always vocal about her disapproval of their relationship in the beginning, and Leah wasn't sure if that had changed now that Nova was alive. She didn't know if she could handle going through the fights and silent treatments again.

"You can always talk to me, Leah. You know that?" Martha said when Leah remained silent.

"I don't know if I should. I don't want to put you in an uncomfortable position," Leah admitted.

"As your mother, it's my job to worry about you. Not your job to worry about me. And right now, I'm worried about you."

"You don't have to worry about me, Mom. I'm fine."

"Are you sure? Because you sat there and talked about your sister being abused like you were talking about a stranger. We were all in shock listening to you say it, but you looked like you were talking about the weather or something."

"It's like Quinton said, I'm used to it," Leah explained.

Martha's head dipped to the side. "You work with rich couples, Leah. That's not the same."

"What makes you think they're rich?"

"Because po' people don't have a therapist. They talk to their pastors and their friends. Free therapy." She opened her purse and pulled out her compact mirror and her tube of blush lipstick.

"That's actually not true." Leah shook her head at her mom's words.

Talking about her clients made Leah think about the one client she needed to deal with as soon as she made it back home. After her conversation with Quinton, there was no way she could continue working with Lance. Quinton saw it as betrayal when Nova went behind his back and spoke with Lance. She didn't want to imagine what he'd think about her helping Lance recover from what could only be described as the darkest time in his life.

"But anyway," Martha said, her words tapping Leah back to focus, "I would still expect you to be a little more emotional when you're talking about your sister, but, as your daddy used to say, I'm not going to borrow trouble. You said you're fine, and I'll have to take your word for it."

Why couldn't she open her mouth and tell her mom how she was really feeling? Why did she always have to be the strong one?

She knew the answer to that, of course. It was the title their dad assigned to her way before she understood the pressure that came along with it.

"Nova's my sensitive child," he'd say, "and Leah's my strong one. She don't let nobody get under her skin."

The funny thing was, what her dad called strong, her mom called bullheaded and stubborn. Leah called it survival. It was easier to ignore her feelings and focus on everyone else's. That way she could fool herself into thinking that she was okay. Of course, Leah knew that her way of dealing with things wasn't healthy. In fact, it was the very thing she warned her patients not to do. Emotions were like boomerangs; they always found their way back.

CHAPTER 11

Nova

Dr. Harris gave me a lot to think about yesterday, and thankfully I didn't have to think about it in that hospital.

"How much longer?" I leaned forward and asked Quinton.

"Less than thirty minutes." He looked at me through the rearview mirror.

I couldn't believe it. In less than thirty minutes I'd be home.

Home?

The word played on repeat, assaulting the sliver of peace that came when I first said it. Where is home? It used to be with Quinton and Skye, but that wasn't my home anymore. Someone else had taken my place. I closed my eyes to stop the room from spinning. It blocked out the space but not the questions that pounded into me.

Where will I live?
What will I do? I don't have a job.
Do I even know what to do to get a job?
And if so, what kind of job?
Who would hire me?
How will I take care of myself . . . of Skye?

I'm her mother. Shouldn't I help take care of her? Will she want me to take care of her?

I reached for Leah when I felt myself getting worked up by my thoughts. I didn't need to explain anything. It was like Leah just knew. She massaged my hand like she did the first day. I stared out the window and only focused on what was right in front of me. Everything else would have to wait.

A brick sign sat in the median. WELCOME TO BAYOU were the words that greeted me. It had probably been there for years, but it felt like it was just for me. As soon as we entered Bayou, we were greeted by people on both sides of the street, waving WELCOME HOME signs, cheering, clapping, and crying. There had to be hundreds of them. The line went down Main Street, where everyone in Bayou shopped and ate, and continued all the way through town. Everywhere I looked there were people and more people. My heart raced, and sweat rolled down my back. My hands wouldn't stop shaking. People were in front of Bayou Park, where I spent hours on Saturdays playing with Leah and Lance. Then, there was Mr. Leroy's Farmer's Market, where more people stood outside and waved. People stood on their front porches as we drove toward Mama's house. I wanted to see everyone. I wanted to take it all in, but it was too much, and I couldn't look anymore. I tucked my head between my legs and hummed a tune, attempting to drown out the cheers, which to my ears was just noise. Too much noise.

I kept my head down until I knew we'd turned onto the lane that led to the house. Because of the trees and the curve, no one could see the house from the street. Privacy. That was what my mind craved. Silence. It needed silence. Coming home didn't feel like I'd imagined. I wanted to enjoy it. I wanted it to feel special, but instead, it was scary.

Quinton got out first, then walked around and opened my door. I couldn't move. I wanted to leave the truck, but I was frozen. I couldn't trust that someone wasn't out there lurking among the trees, just waiting for me. How could I be sure there wasn't another Adam out there waiting to take over where he'd left off? If home wasn't safe, then where could I be safe? Back in the room? As much as I hated it, a part of me yearned for it. For the seclusion. I wanted the feeling the room offered without Adam.

Quinton lowered his body until my eyes were looking into his. "It's okay. I promise I'll never let anything happen to you again." His words sounded good, but even he couldn't make a promise like that. It wasn't like he'd be with me 24-7. He had another wife who he also had to take care of. I wasn't his responsibility anymore.

I looked at Quinton, Skye, Mama, and Leah, all standing and waiting patiently for me. All reassuring me that I should take my time. I inhaled and exhaled before twisting my body toward the door and stepping out of the truck.

I paused as my eyes took in the two-story white house with the front porch that stretched from one end to the other. The house that used to be white was now light blue. I didn't know if I liked it. Actually, I did know. I hated it. At least one thing was still the same. Mama's prized flower bed still sat on each side of the front steps. I couldn't begin to count how many times she'd fussed at Leah and me from running and playing around them.

"All these acres y'all got, and you still choose to run around my flowers. I tell ya what, if you mess them up, I'm gonna mess up your little behinds."

Leah and I would take off running. When we were sure we were out of earshot, we'd burst out laughing. The memory of the good old days gave me such a warm feeling.

Then something happened that I didn't expect. I went from smiling to crying. It was that moment when reality really set in. I was free. I was afraid to get too comfortable before, but that was not home. It was safe to let your guard down at home. I didn't have to fight anymore.

"Welcome home, Sis." Leah wrapped her arm around my waist.

That was when it happened. A flood of memories flashed through my mind—all the family gatherings, holidays, birthday parties, anniversary celebrations, and church meetings, all like a movie playing in my head, and then as if someone had switched off the television, the memories stopped. No more birthdays. No more holiday celebrations. No more anniversary parties or church meetings. Everything came to an abrupt end. For me. Life continued for everyone except me. The agonizing ache of all the missed moments caused a flood of tears. I cried out fifteen years' worth of pain, hurt, suffering, and a longing so deep it was physically painful.

Mama held me until I'd drained myself of all the tears. I wish I could say that all the pain had left with it, but that was too good to be true. While Mama went to unlock the door, Quinton helped me up the steps. My ankle was healing, but not healed yet.

Once Mama opened the door, I stepped over the threshold and back into the past. "It doesn't look the same." I ran my hand along the plain yellow wall in the foyer. The gold-and-cream-striped wallpaper was gone. I hated that wallpaper, but I really wanted to see it. I needed to see it. I looked over at Mama, who stood next to me, smiling. She didn't know there was a war of emotions taking place inside me. "Did Daddy know about this?"

This house once belonged to his grandparents, then his parents, then us. Even though most things in the old house were outdated, Daddy refused to change it. He said it was all he had left of his parents and grandparents. I often felt bad for Daddy. He was an only child, so he was all that was left once his parents died. Maybe that was why I'd clung to him so much. I thought if I was around, he wouldn't feel alone.

"Of course he did. I'd tried for so long to get him to do something about this old house, but it wasn't until he retired and got antsy that he finally decided it was time. He worked day and night on this place."

"How about I call the café and place an order for takeout," Leah suggested.

"That'll be wonderful," Mama said, tucking her hair behind her ear.

Instead of following Leah, Skye, and Quinton into the living room, I continued down the narrow hallway, where Mama always kept a wall of pictures. My steps slowed as I approached. Each image was a window inside a world that didn't include me.

I stopped in front of a picture of Mama and Skye. They were standing in front of our family's church, Bayou Baptist. Skye's head was at Mama's waist. Now Mama's head was at Skye's waist, since Skye was at least five feet, ten inches—the same height I was at seventeen. Both Skye's height and missing two front teeth were the clues that it was an old picture.

My mind struggled to think of Skye at that age. What was she like then? Was she loud like me or quiet like Leah? Was she sneaky like I was, or was she a rule follower like Leah? I didn't want to accept that my daughter, who was nearly an adult now, had experiences and memories that I knew nothing about.

"I missed so much," I whispered. My words didn't feel big enough to capture the emptiness inside me. I was a mother who didn't know what it was like to drop her child off at school. To kiss her boo-boos or scare away the scary closet monsters.

"How old was she here?" I reached to touch the picture, then pulled back and aimed my head toward it instead. That way, I wouldn't mess it up or break it.

Mama's narrowed eyes stared at me. "It's okay to touch it, sweetie."

I smiled but kept my hands to myself as my mind flashed to the room. The cold, dark room where hopelessness was my constant companion. I blinked the image away and focused on the smiling faces in the photos instead of the unwelcome memories that came at the most random moments.

Mama removed the picture from the nail and stared at it. "My mind's not as sharp as it used to be, but I guess she was about seven or eight here. This was one of her dance recitals." Mama chuckled. "We fought so hard to get all this thick hair into a bun."

What I wouldn't have given to have the opportunity to fight with hair instead of fighting for my life. I walked over to the next picture while Mama put Skye's back on the wall. Every picture was a painful reminder that they'd built a life, created memories, probably created different traditions, and had inside jokes that I knew nothing about. I was a stranger in my own home.

While Mama's animated voice told me about each picture, I was battling my mind to stay focused. I was split between paying attention and hoping her stories could fill in some of the gaps I'd missed, but it was hard to stay in the present when I couldn't stop revisiting all the nights I'd lain in bed and wondered what my family was doing. Wondered if they were still thinking about me. If they still missed me. It looked like they were too busy living life to give me much thought.

This was my family. This was my home. Somehow, I had to find a way to belong. To fit in again, but how was I supposed to do that? How was I supposed to belong to a world . . . a family . . . that was so much different than I was?

"Are you okay, sweetie? Do you need to sit? You don't look well." Mama touched my shoulder.

"I'm okay." I forced a smile that felt more like a grimace. "I'm just trying to take it all in. Fifteen years is a lot to catch up on."

"And you don't have to do it all today. You'll have plenty of time, and we'll tell you everything you need to know. You're home now, baby." Mama smiled through her tears.

Home. I bounced the word around in my head and tried to make it feel real, but it didn't. Home used to feel comforting, not complicated and confusing. Mama was right; I was back, but the real question was, did I belong?

I stepped into the living room and immediately noticed that the walls were the same light yellow as the hallway. The furniture was different too. The brown-and-cream-cloth sofa seat was replaced with a tan leather set. I stepped farther into the room and walked to the corner where Mama's clear knickknack case was still filled with all kinds of crystal things. The light from the window across from the case always made the crystals sparkle, like they were doing now. I crossed the room and stood next to Mama's and Daddy's recliners, which still sat on the wall right next to each other—memories of them sitting there watching *Wheel of Fortune* or the news filled my mind. Most times, it was Mama who watched while Daddy slept. A framed picture of Daddy sat on the round table between their chairs. I was drawn to it. I stared down at it, but it was Mama who picked it up and placed it in my hand. I didn't resist. I just kept staring into the eyes of the first man who'd ever loved me—the man who warned me never to take any wooden nickels. I had no idea what that meant back then, but it made sense now.

I released a wail so loud it pierced my ears. The reality that Daddy was gone had just hit me out of nowhere, and the grief was too overwhelming to bear. All those years I'd prayed to see my family again. I'd prayed to have the chance to hug them, kiss them, and tell them how much I loved them, but I'd never have the chance to do any of that to my daddy, and I couldn't breathe.

"I'm so sorry, Daddy." I held his picture close to my chest and hoped he could hear my words. "You warned me to be careful. You told me to never let anyone cheat me out of what was mine, and I didn't listen. I should've listened. Now you're gone, and I'll never get a chance to tell you how sorry I am. I let him cheat me out of something that was worth more than all the nickels in the world. More time with you."

Mama rubbed my back and led me to the sofa, where she sat next to me. I looked around and wanted the void to go away, but it wouldn't. The presence that filled this house every time I stepped through those doors was gone. The smile that used to greet me with open arms and a big kiss, even if he'd just seen me the day before. The deep voice that asked, "How's my baby girl doing?" The spicy cologne that lingered on my clothes long after we'd parted. The first man I ever loved. The only man I knew who loved me no matter what I did or said.

CHAPTER 12

Leah

Leah removed her purse from behind the wooden stool and slid it on her shoulder. "The food should be ready. I'll go pick it up," she offered, hoping no one would volunteer to ride with her. She needed a few minutes of no talking.

Quinton sat on the island next to Nova. Skye walked into the kitchen holding a black book to her chest. "You were right, Gran. The yearbook was in the box." Skye held the book up and shook it from side to side.

"Is that my old yearbook?" Nova asked.

"Yep. Skye was worrying my nerves about it. All your things are still boxed up and in the closet from when you moved out."

"Oh my goodness. I'm almost afraid to look at these pictures." Nova laughed.

"Can we all look at it together?" Skye asked.

"Sure." Nova eased down from the stool and slowly made her way to Skye.

"Come on, Dad, you too." Skye waved for him to join them in the front room.

"Alright. Alright." Quinton tried to sound aggravated, but he wasn't doing a good job pulling it off. There was nothing else he'd rather do than continue his walk down memory lane with Nova.

Seeing Skye and Nova bonding so fast should've been a good thing. No, it was a good thing, but it was also a hard thing to watch. Leah was right. As soon as Skye spent time with Nova, she'd instantly want more. Most people did. Including Leah.

"Mom, can I take your car to get the food?" Leah asked, while trying to tamp down the annoyance she wasn't sure she should've been feeling.

Even though she wanted some time alone, it would've been nice if Quinton had at least asked if she needed him to come. She knew why he didn't ask, though. It was a challenge trying to remember what might seem appropriate and inappropriate to Nova. Not that Leah and Quinton riding to the café to pick up food was inappropriate by any means, but it was still a task that one person could handle. One thing Leah knew for sure was that they had to tell Nova soon, no matter how hard it was going to be. She couldn't keep up the act much longer, and it wasn't fair that she and Quinton had to in the first place.

Leah drove downtown but passed the café. She stopped her mom's car at the edge of the cemetery, then sat for a moment, staring ahead at the wrought-iron gate that was wide open for visitors. That was the last place she wanted to visit her dad, but unfortunately that was her life for now. When she left her mom's house, she thought she needed time alone, but what she really needed was time with her dad, away from the whirlwind her life had become in a few short days. The cemetery, though not ideal, was at least peaceful, a big difference from how her life felt.

Leah walked down the dirt path to the grave site. She was in the middle of reading a text message from Harper, who she needed to call, when she ran straight into . . . "Lance. Oh my God, I'm so sorry."

Lance held up his hands. "It's okay." He flashed Leah the smile that landed him on the 50 Sexiest Men in Louisiana list.

"Guess that's what happens when you're reading and walking." Leah held up her phone and then slid it into her jeans pocket. "Wow, you look very nice." She gave Lance a corny thumbs-up on his appearance for some reason.

Lance smiled, then looked down at his attire as if he'd forgotten what he was wearing. "Yeah, well, I don't have a reason to dress up much these days, but I'm meeting with some of my old teammates about a community project. I thought I should at least put a little effort into my attire."

"Good choice," she said, admiring his dark-blue jeans and tan blazer that paired very well with his rich brown-leather cowboy boots. "Listen, I'm glad I ran into you. I mean, not physically, but I'm glad you're here because I need to talk with you."

Lance's brows furrowed. "Is it about Nova?"

"Nova? No. Well, yeah, but not directly about Nova." Leah stopped rambling and composed her thoughts. "I know I agreed to help you, and you've made significant progress over the past six months, but . . ."

"You're dropping me?" Lance continued the words that Leah seemed to have trouble saying. "May I ask why?"

"As you know, I had my concerns from the very beginning, but I did take an oath to help those in need, and you were in need, but you and I both know how disastrous this could end for me if Quinton ever found out."

"You know I'd never say anything to him about our sessions, right?"

"Yeah, but you did say something to Carmen, who said something to me at Quinton's party. That showed me that we can't continue our sessions. I only want what's best for you, but Quinton's my husband."

Lance sighed. "Dammit, Carmen! I didn't tell her, by the way. She was on my phone and saw it on my calendar. I couldn't lie when she asked about it since it was there plain as day. But I get it. You have to do what you have to do for your marriage."

"I knew you'd understand. Thanks for not making this harder than it already was. And listen, I have a list of therapists whom I trust wholeheartedly. I want you to consider seeing one of them."

Leah hated the thought of him not continuing his sessions. He did make progress, but every now and then he needed someone to talk with. Leah just couldn't be that someone anymore.

In high school, Lance was Louisiana's golden boy. Everyone from Bayou and beyond loved his country charm and Christian values, which he never missed an opportunity to talk about. Lance stayed in the newspaper and on the news because of his football skills. When he was drafted by the Saints right out of college, that sent everyone's love level for Lance soaring to new heights. It wasn't until a few years ago that his name and reputation were smeared by someone he trusted.

Lance moved from New Orleans and back to Bayou where he'd been ever since, refusing to leave the comfort that Bayou offered. When he came to Leah for help, after he felt he'd hit rock bottom, Leah couldn't turn him away. She'd withheld that information from Quinton and hated to think how he'd react if he ever found out that his wife was helping the man he'd blamed for ruining his football career before it ever began. Unlike the rest of Louisiana, when Quinton thought of Lance, all he could see was the man who was living the life he should've been living.

"I don't know, Leah. You know how I feel about having people I don't know in my business. I've been burned by a therapist before, remember?"

"I do, and I can promise you that the people I'm recommending would never sell your information for any amount of money. They're decent and upstanding people."

"And thank you," Lance said. "For getting me over one of the roughest patches I've ever been through. I'm eternally grateful."

"You're welcome." Leah exhaled. "Well, I'd better get in there and visit with Dad before I need to get back."

"Hey, how's Nova?" Lance asked, his eyes filled with concern.

"She's as good as can be expected. Give her some time to adjust and I'm sure she'd love to see you."

Lance stared at his shoes that Leah was sure were shiny before he stopped there. "I'm not so sure about that."

"What happened was a long time ago. And Nova and Quinton aren't married anymore." Leah held up her left hand. "As you already know."

Lance eyes expanded. Apparently, that thought just hit him. "Oh wow, I didn't even think of how that must've gone over."

"It didn't, actually. We're waiting to tell her once she's had some time. I don't think I'll breathe until we do, though."

"I bet it works out better than you're thinking."

Leah crossed her fingers. "Here's to hoping."

"What about us? I mean, our sessions. Are you going to tell Quinton?" Lance asked.

The question alone caused her whole body to shake. "Of course not . . . you know . . . HIPAA."

Lance ran his hand over his beard, then glanced at his watch. "I need to go. I don't want to keep them waiting. Today's my favorite girl's birthday, so I wanted to stop by and put some flowers on her grave."

Leah's heart fluttered. She loved the relationship Lance had with his grandmother. For as long as she could remember, Lance had always referred to her as his favorite girl. If his tall frame and broad shoulders weren't enough to make the women swoon, then the love he showed for his grandmother definitely would. It was his grandma's dementia that sent him spiraling. The one person, other than his mom, who he could always depend on to have his back had no longer known who he was.

Leah and Lance said their goodbyes as Leah made her way to her father's final resting place. She had to admit, talking with Lance wasn't as hard as she thought it would be. He was so adamant that he didn't trust anyone except Leah to help him through his dark days, which turned into months, and the next thing Leah knew, six months had passed, and they were still meeting regularly.

Leah's visit with her dad couldn't last long because her family would wonder what happened to her if she stayed away much longer. Driving to the café, Leah braced herself for the switch from solitude to socializing. Growing up in Bayou meant having to chat with everyone you passed. When she pulled into the parking lot of the café, she was surprised to see so many cars. Most days the café only had a few vehicles at a time.

When Leah walked in, she immediately regretted that she'd come. Most of the people who participated in Nova's welcome-home parade had gathered at the café. Had Leah known that, she would've stayed at her mom's house and cooked instead. She was barely through the doors when the questions came.

"How's Nova doing?"

"Do you have pictures? Can we see her?"

"Is she up for company?"

"I can drop off some food. What would be a good time?"

Leah plastered a smile on her face and maneuvered through the group of people who had surrounded her before she could reach the front counter. Among them were Mrs. Thompson, the choir director, who always had a kind word and a warm hug ready whenever Leah saw her; Mr. Peters, who owned the flower shop next door; and Elaine, one of Leah's former classmates who always told Leah they had to make it a point to get together and catch up, even though both of them knew it wouldn't happen. It wasn't like Elaine and Leah were close back then, so there was really nothing to catch up on.

"Hey! Hey! Give the lady some space." Ms. Dot, who'd worked at Bayou Café for as long as Leah could remember, came over and moved the group away from Leah.

"Thank you," Leah said, finally able to catch her breath.

The questions were coming so fast that Leah didn't have a chance to answer any of them. Which was probably best since the answers to most were no. She understood how anxious everyone was to see Nova, but they had to understand that she needed time and space.

After Leah picked up her bags, she turned to the people who were now sitting at their tables, most still watching her. She waved and smiled at Mr. Harold, the retired school librarian, and Missy, a local journalist who always had her eyes and ears open for something juicy to report. "Everyone," Leah said, speaking loud enough so everyone in the small space could hear. "My family and I, especially Nova, appreciate your concern and well wishes, and I know how anxious all of you are to come and see her, but please understand that Nova's been through a lot, and right now all she needs is time and space to recover. As soon as she's ready, I promise my mom will throw a huge party in her honor. Trust me, she's been waiting to do that for fifteen years." Leah smiled, then waved before leaving.

CHAPTER 13

Nova

I opened my eyes to the moonlight glaring through the window, casting an eerie glow over the room. My breath caught in my throat as everything in me said that I'd been transported back to the small cramped space I'd been forced to live in for too many years. My fingers clutched the soft blanket. Soft? What had he done with the other? The thin, rough blanket that never kept me warm but was the only comfort I had. The memories slammed into me, filling me with dread. A moment of clarity came over me as I recognized the faint sound of leaves rustling on the trees outside. Then, it happened again. The fear crept back in as the rustling sound morphed into scurrying. Rats scurrying inside the thin walls. Running from one side to the other, teasing me night after night with their ability to move from one place to another.

Was it true? Was I back in the prison he'd held me in all those years? Was it all a dream? My freedom? Reuniting with my family?

As my heart raced, each thump caused my panic to rise. Agony strangled me and made it hard to breathe. I pressed my hands to my temples and tried to ground myself, but the thoughts were too powerful. Nothing I did made me believe I was home. I was back in that room, and my whole world deflated with that one thought.

The pain inside me was so unbearable that I knew the only way to end it would be to end my life. A thought that once terrified me now filled me with a wave of relief.

"Nova." Mama's voice rushed to my ears and caused the room that had closed in on me to expand. Mama flipped on the light, and my eyes scanned the room, taking in every familiar object. My dresser. My TV stand. My trophies and plaques. A room that reminded me of the me I used to know. A room that Mama refused to change, even after I got married and moved, because she said she always wanted it to feel like mine, just as she'd done with Leah's. I never loved Mama more than I did in that moment.

My heart continued its wild dance, a thunderous beat that eventually slowed as Mama walked farther into the room.

"I just peeped my head in to check on you before I turned in. Are you okay?" Her eyes narrowed. "Oh, Nova, you're soaking wet." She sat on the edge of the bed and used the back of her hand to feel my forehead like she used to do when I was younger. "You're not hot. Come on and get out of those clothes before you catch a cold." Mama reached for my hand, and I took it and let her lead me to the dresser, where she opened a drawer and pulled out another gown.

"You want me to help you?" She stared at my nightshirt, which was drenched in sweat.

I got the gown from Mama. "I got it." I walked back to the bed and stood holding the gown.

Mama waited for a moment, her hand hesitating on the door handle. "Okay. If you're sure," she continued, standing as if she needed me to change my mind and let her help, but I couldn't.

"I'm sure," I said, before Mama turned and walked away.

The thought of anyone seeing me without clothes, even Mama, was unsettling. I never wanted anyone else to look at me again. My hands trembled at the memory of standing in the middle of the room for hours as Adam stared and instructed me on how to move and what he wanted me to do to myself. The first time Adam tried to sleep with me was one of the worst moments of my life. The only thing that saved me that night, and every night since, was that Adam's *thing* didn't work. It didn't stop him from trying, though. Then, he finally gave up and moved on to other ways to torture me. Living inside a body where you were both the molester and victim was the most distorted feeling ever.

"Can I come back in?" Mama asked from the hallway.

I slid the gown over my body and threw the wet one in the corner of the room. "Come in." I stood in the middle of the floor because I didn't know what else to do. I didn't want to go back to bed because more nightmares awaited me there.

As if reading my mind, Mama took my hand into hers. "Why don't you come lie with me?" Mama suggested, just as she'd done so many times when I was younger and woke from a nightmare in a screaming fit. Of course, back then, the monsters were all make-believe. My monster was no longer alive, but the effect he'd left on my life was, and I was afraid that that unsettling feeling would always be a part of me.

I followed Mama back to her room. I hesitated before I crawled into her bed. My gaze fell on the empty side that was still made up and untouched—a heavy reminder of Daddy's absence. Running to the safety of my parents' bed didn't feel like it used to when I was cocooned between Mama and Daddy, snuggling safely between an extra layer of protection. Mama walked around the bed where I was still standing, staring down at the empty space, and wrapped her arms around me. She held me close to her. Mama pulled the covers back, and I slid underneath them. I moved close to Mama and allowed her powdery scent to soothe me back to sleep.

The following day, I woke up alone. The brightly lit room was a relief. I'd slept the rest of the night without another nightmare. I'd faced Mama's side of the bed and stared at the big red numbers on the clock. I'd gone years without knowing the day, year, or time. Every now and then, Adam would say he needed to be somewhere at a certain time. Whenever I heard his old pickup truck groaning down the driveway, I knew it must've been close to that time. Eventually, I didn't even want to know. It wasn't like I had anywhere to go or anyone to see.

My focus slid away from the numbers and to the framed picture of Mama and Daddy. I leaned over, picked it up, then ran my finger over Daddy's face. I attempted to clear the lump that had formed in my throat, but it was too big, just like my longing for Daddy.

As I stared at the picture, I could hear Daddy's laugh as it echoed in my ear. His deep hearty laugh that always lifted my spirits. I looked into his eyes that were always full of warmth and love. Even through the picture I felt him reassuring me that everything was going to be okay. It would be a lot better if Daddy was here, though. He made life better.

Would I always miss him this much? Shouldn't I be used to not seeing him? But this was different. I didn't expect him to be in that room. I expected him to be here. He was supposed to be here. It didn't feel fair that he wasn't.

The last time I saw him was when Quinton and I dropped Skye off before we left for what should've been a weekend. I could still see Daddy standing in the doorway, holding Skye with one arm and hugging me with the other.

"She's gonna be just fine. Now wipe those tears and go enjoy yourself." He winked, and that was enough to calm my nerves and my spirit. I was leaving Skye in the best hands.

After a while, I put the picture back on the stand and made the bed. Mama used to hate to see a bed unmade. I was the same way. Even in that room, I made the bed every morning. Not only because I wanted to do it but mainly because it gave me something to do. At least for a short time, I had a purpose.

Other than that, Adam did everything. He cooked food and brought it up for us to sit and eat. We only ate breakfast and dinner together. Lunch was a sandwich or cereal and milk, sometimes tuna and crackers. Adam was the worst cook. Most of the time, I didn't recognize what I was eating. It didn't help that I'd always been a picky eater. I was particular about my food, and I hated it when my food touched. Adam mixed everything together and served it as one dish. Meat, vegetables, condiments, whatever he could throw together and call edible. Over time, I learned to tolerate it. It was either eat or die, and I chose to live. Most days, I questioned if I'd made the right choice. What was I living for? To spend another day in a room where, other than Adam, my only visitors were the critters that found their way through the cracks in the walls and floorboard.

"Hey, Sweet Pea," Mama said when I joined her in the kitchen. She stood by the stove, one hand stirring food and the other resting on her round hip. Her hair was still tied in her pink headscarf, and her big blue rollers were underneath.

"Can I have a clock and a calendar?" I asked Mama.

"Sure. You can take the clock from my room."

"Can I have this calendar?" I pointed to the wall where she'd pinned a calendar from some insurance company.

"Of course." Her eyes narrowed as if she had a question but was unsure if she should ask.

"I want to put them in my room," I told her.

She nodded. "I fixed us some bacon, eggs, and pancakes." Mama waved her hand around the stove.

"This is a lot of food." My stomach growled and churned at the same time. I wasn't used to so much food. I'd always had a big appetite. Mama used to say I ate like a grown man. I was also active, so as soon as I ate it, it wasn't long before I burned it off. Adam only cooked enough for a small plate of food, which was okay because it took everything in me to choke down the little he gave me.

I stared at the plate in front of me, and I wanted to dive in and never stop until every crumb was gone, but I couldn't. The doctor said it would be a while before my body adjusted to things again. I'd hoped "a while" would have meant by the time I made it home, but it didn't.

Mama sat in front of me and then reached across the table for my hand.

I stared, confused as to what was going on. "What?" I asked, lifting my eyes from her hand to her eyes.

"We have to say grace."

"Oh, we're still doing that?" I held out my hand but refused to close my eyes. I watched her while what started as grace turned into a regular prayer. I was sure our food would be cold by the time she said amen. Thankfully, I was wrong.

Mama picked up her coffee mug and sipped.

I looked at the counter where the coffee pot used to sit. It wasn't there. "Where'd you get coffee?" I asked.

"I made it. You want me to make you some?" She was about to stand before I stopped her, but I stood first.

"No, I can do it." I scanned the counter once again. I must've been overlooking it.

"Something wrong?" Mama asked.

I looked for a few more seconds before finally asking. "Where's the coffee pot?"

"Oh." She stood next to me. "It's right here." She tapped the top of a tall black thing in the corner of the counter exactly where the coffee pot used to sit.

I stared at it. It looked nothing like a coffee pot. "What is this?" I bent down and leaned closer to get a better look.

"It's a Keurig."

"But I don't want Keurig. I wanted coffee like you have."

Then, it dawned on me that I didn't know if I wanted Keurig. Maybe that was the new name for coffee.

"Keurig is the name of the machine," Mama explained softly. "It makes coffee."

I pressed the buttons on the Keurig, trying to figure it out for myself, but it was no use. I had no idea how to work that thing.

"Here, let me show you. So, you lift this top like this and put the pod in." She held up a white plastic cup that reminded me of the ones we used to use for communion at church, except those were clear. I watched as she dropped the cup into the machine and closed the lid. It looked simple enough, but I still didn't understand what was wrong with the old coffee pot. Why did everything have to change?

"How am I supposed to make it in a world where I need lessons to make a cup of coffee?" My eyes burned with tears. "I feel so out of place, and I just want to feel like I belong, but I don't. I don't fit in anywhere."

"Oh, baby, that's not true. You belong right here. This is your home."

"But it doesn't feel like home. Daddy's not here. Skye's not here. Quinton's not here. When I think of home, I think of the people who lived with me and made the house a home. This doesn't feel like home, and I can't go back to the apartment I used to call home since Quinton doesn't live there anymore. Even if he did, it's not like I could just move in with him and his wife."

"Uh . . . yeah." Mama reached into the sink and pulled out a dish towel. She wiped the countertops that didn't look dirty at all to me. "Nova, you have to give yourself time. It may not feel like home right now, but it will soon. You wait and see. Before you know it, this house will feel like home again. The one thing I never want you to forget is that you're a survivor, okay? You survived everything you went through in that room, and you'll survive this too. One day at a time, Sweet Pea. One day at a time." Mama removed my coffee from the Keurig thing and handed it to me.

I took my coffee back to the table and sat it in front of me. "I just wish I knew how long it'll take to feel normal. I thought if I ever left that house, everything would go back to how it was. Silly, huh?"

"Not at all. Just remember that God never promised things would be easy, baby. He only promised to be there to see us through."

I jumped from my chair, causing it to crash to the floor. "Your God left me in that room for fifteen years!" My voice trembled in anger.

Mama flinched, then shook her head. "Nova, that's not true. God kept you safe through those fifteen years."

"That's easy for you to say. You weren't trapped in a room, waking up every day, reliving the same nightmare over and over again. You have no idea what it's like to plead and cry and cry and plead to the God you grew up hearing about. Hearing how good he is and how he answers prayers, if you just have faith. Well, guess what, Mama? I believed in him. For years, I believed, and he still refused to help me. He wasn't there for me when I needed him the most, and I'll never believe, trust, or love a God who doesn't love me."

I ran from the kitchen and straight to my bedroom. I locked the door and froze. The clicking sound from the lock sent a chill throughout my body that caused me to freeze in place. My hands shook as I reached for the door and turned the lock. I stared at the door and tried to tell myself it was okay if the door was closed, but I couldn't convince myself that was true. I opened the door as wide as it would go and sat on the bed and stared out in the hallway.

CHAPTER 14

Leah

Leah sat across from her client and tried to stay focused, but it wasn't easy. Her mind kept wandering from Nova to her mom.

The conversation she'd had with her mom as she drove to work this morning reminded Leah that she needed to find Nova a therapist sooner rather than later. Her mom said that Nova woke up screaming last night. She thought that everything that happened over the last couple of days was all a dream. Leah couldn't even begin to imagine the torture she must've felt in those first few minutes. To think you were free and back home, only to believe it was all a dream.

Leah's phone vibrated and chimed when the timer went off. She touched the screen, then flashed Ms. Franklin with her biggest and brightest smile. The one that said *it was a pleasure spending this time with you once again*. The one that lied to her patients and everyone else.

"Looks like that's our time." She stood and adjusted her black pencil skirt.

Ms. Franklin lifted her head, but the rest of her body remained seated. She brushed the hair of her gray wig from her face. Each week she wore a different wig. That particular one seemed to be her favorite. She called it Patti after her favorite singer Patti LaBelle. She said every time she put it on, she felt sassy like Ms. Patti.

"Oh . . . umm . . . okay." She placed her oversize purse on her shoulder. She refused to set it on the floor beside her chair like Leah's younger clients did. Leah knew the moment she met Ms. Franklin that she was a woman who believed in superstitions. It was nothing she'd done that gave it away. It was simply the fact that she was an older Black woman from the South. That meant that Ms. Franklin, like her mother, most likely believed that if she placed her purse on the floor, she'd lose all her money. All of it was ridiculous to Leah. She'd placed her purse on the floor plenty of times and still had money. She'd also bought Quinton shoes for Christmas even though Martha said a woman should never buy a man some shoes because then he'd walk . . . away. She shook away the ridiculous feeling those words caused.

"Ms. Lefleur, I hope whatever is holding your mind hostage sets it free soon. I could tell you weren't listening at all." Ms. Franklin used her finger and pushed her glasses closer to her eyes.

"That's an interesting choice of words," Leah said. "I'm assuming you've watched the news then."

Ms. Franklin narrowed her eyes. "The news? No, I stopped watching it a long time ago. Nothing on there but killing. I don't want to see all that." Ms. Franklin wrinkled her nose like she got a whiff of something awful.

Maybe it was just a coincidence that she chose the word *hostage*, Leah thought. Which was strange since Leah didn't believe in coincidences any more than she believed in superstitions.

"I promise to do better next time," she assured Ms. Franklin, deciding it was best to apologize and move on.

There were many clients who Leah needed more sessions with, but Ms. Franklin wasn't one of them. In fact, there were quite a few times when Leah hinted that she didn't need her services anymore. All she needed was a group of friends to spend time with. Her only problem was she was lonely, but according to Ms. Franklin, she didn't like people and would rather talk with Leah. The one thing Leah admired was Ms. Franklin being open enough to seek therapy. Most women her age didn't believe in it. Her mother was one of them.

After Leah's dad died, her mom locked herself inside and refused to see anyone or go anywhere, including church. That was when Leah realized how bad things were. Martha would go to church on her deathbed if she could, so for her to miss, she had to be in a bad place. No matter what Leah said, her mom refused to get the help she needed. Over time, Leah gave up.

Leah sat at her desk, her thoughts on Quinton, Nova, and Skye, wondering what each of them were doing and if Quinton and Skye were really handling everything as well as they seemed to be. There were emails waiting on Leah's response and charts that needed to be completed, but thinking about work was a task Leah couldn't force herself to do. So, she gave up.

Once Leah made it to her car, she called Bayou High. "Hi, this is Leah Lefleur. I'm on my way to check Skye out of school. Can you please let her know? Great. Thanks."

It wasn't until Leah made it to the school and Skye rushed from the front office that Leah realized she should've sent Skye a text to let her know nothing was wrong.

"What happened?" Skye asked.

"Calm down, nothing happened. I'm sorry, I should've texted you. I thought we could spend some time together."

Skye narrowed her eyes. "Really? You're checking me out of school, and it's not an emergency? Well, that's new."

"Are you saying you'd rather stay?" Leah teased.

Skye walked past Leah and practically sprinted to Leah's car. "I have to be back before practice, though. You know Coach don't play."

"I'll have you back before last period. How about that?"

"Miss math class? Oh yes." Skye did a little dance in her seat.

Since their skip day was more like a skip-class day, Leah decided to go around the corner to the ice cream shop instead of driving back to

Baton Rouge for lunch. She watched as Skye twirled her spoon through her melting ice cream.

"Something wrong with your ice cream?" Leah asked.

"No, it's good." Skye filled her mouth with what was now sweet milk.

"Skye, with everything that's going on, I just wanted to make sure you're okay. I mean, I know you're enjoying getting to know your mom and hearing all the stories about your dad and Nova in their high school days, but other than that, are you okay?"

Skye paused, her spoon resting against the side of her bowl. "It's still kind of strange," she admitted. "I mean, a good strange, but still strange. Plus, it doesn't help that now that she's back, I have to explain how she's my real mom. I guess I never gave it much thought, but apparently, everyone assumed you were my real mom. Which makes sense. In a way, you are."

Those were the words Leah needed to hear. She reached across the table and covered Skye's hand with her own. "You know I'll always be here for you, right? No matter what."

"Of course, I know that." Skye smiled, squeezing Leah's hand the way Leah always did to hers. Something she and Nova created, and Leah continued with Skye.

As they finished their ice cream, Leah felt much better than she had a few hours ago. Knowing that Skye still looked at her as her mom was the confirmation Leah needed to know that they were going to be okay.

CHAPTER 15

Nova

I'd been home for four days and every day I woke up and reminded myself that this was real. Hearing Leah's voice coming from downstairs was another pleasant reminder that I wasn't dreaming. I hadn't even seen her face that day and already I felt better. Knowing she was there was all it took to calm me in a way that no one or nothing else could. Leah always had that effect on me. If Leah said everything was okay, then I instantly knew that everything was okay.

"Hey." Leah stuck her head inside the room. "Can I come in?"

"Of course."

Leah held up two white bags. "I got something for you." She waved the bags like they were pom-poms, then pulled out smaller bags of hair. "Remember I used to braid your hair all the time during basketball season. And every single summer." Leah shook her head.

When Mama realized that Leah knew how to braid hair, she put Leah in charge of my hair while Mama still braided Leah's hair. At first, Leah hated that job, but over time, it became our special time. Mama always left us alone, and we figured it was because she didn't want Leah to ask her to help. Whatever the reason, we took advantage of our uninterrupted sister time.

"I do remember that." I couldn't stop smiling. "Are you going to braid my hair?" I asked, pointing to my head that was still covered in the scarf Mama gave me at the hospital.

"If you'd like me to. I figured it would give us something to do today." Leah sat next to me on the bed.

"I would love that." There was nothing more I wanted to do than spend time with Leah while she did something to this head of mine. Maybe then I'd start to feel like a real person again. I was so excited about Leah doing my hair that I wasn't even that mad with Mama anymore. "But wait, it's Thursday, aren't you supposed to be at work?"

"Yeah, but I cleared my schedule today and tomorrow so I can spend more time with you."

I clapped because the excitement of seeing Leah today and tomorrow made my whole day.

Leah washed and blow-dried my hair. When we walked into the kitchen, Mama was sitting at the table with her laptop.

"I'm ordering groceries. Is there anything special you want?" Mama asked me.

"You're ordering groceries online?" Leah and I both asked. Our words were the same, but the questions were very different. Leah had more emphasis on *you*, and I had more emphasis on *online*.

Mama addressed Leah's question first. It was probably easier to explain than mine.

"I'm saving a lot of money ordering my groceries online. I just hate I have to drive to Baton Rouge to get them. Jim needs to get with the time and start letting us order online from his store."

"Mr. Jim's mom-and-pop store will never go online. Mr. Jim is stuck in his ways, and I can't say it's a bad thing. Besides, who's going to bag the groceries and bring them to the cars? Mr. Jim can't keep workers longer than a day."

"I can't believe Mr. Jim is still alive."

Mama and Leah laughed, but I was serious. Mr. Jim was old when I was in high school.

"Jim just celebrated his eighty-ninth birthday. I don't know why he won't go home and let those children run that store." Mama shook her head and went back to her laptop.

"Can someone tell me how you get groceries online?" I leaned down and looked at the computer screen.

"I'll explain it to you while I do your hair. You wanna go on the back porch?" Leah nodded in the direction of the porch.

Leah's hands worked through my hair, bringing back a familiar feeling of comfort that I desperately needed. While she braided, she filled me in on online grocery orders. I couldn't believe Mama trusted anyone to pick out her groceries. She never trusted Daddy, Leah, or me to do it. She used to say we didn't know how to pick fresh vegetables.

"Oh, trust me, she's not ordering any fruits or vegetables. Probably no meat either. She'll find a way to get to Mr. Jim's for that," Leah said when I told her how surprised I was.

"Every few minutes I learn about something new. I don't know if I'll be able to keep up with all these changes. It's too much."

"I know it's a lot, but you'll learn everything you need to know over time." Leah leaned over and kissed my cheek. "How about this? I'll fill you in on some of the bigger news stories that've happened since you've been gone. But not the bad news. You'll have plenty of time to hear about that." Leah stood beside me and pulled her phone from her jeans pocket. She swiped her finger over her phone and stared at the screen. "Okay, let me see." Leah tapped on her screen again. "My mind isn't as good as it used to be. Let's go to Google."

Leah said she was only sharing good news, but the Janet Jackson and Justin Timberlake Super Bowl scandal sounded like pretty bad news to me. I loved Janet Jackson.

"A Black president? You should've started with that news. How did we get a Black president?" I had so many questions. "Was he Black like us or Black like . . . What's her name? We graduated together. Remember, she used to always have to prove to people that she was really Black?"

"Sharon. I don't remember her last name."

"That's right. Sharon."

Sharon's mom was white, and her dad was Black, but she didn't get an ounce of his color. She looked like both of her parents could've been white.

"Was he Black like her?" I asked again.

"No, he was Black like us." Leah turned her phone around and showed me a picture of our former president.

My mouth flew open. I couldn't believe it. I would've loved to have been a part of that. I could only imagine how proud Mama and Daddy felt. "Wait, was Daddy alive when we had a Black president?"

"Yes, he was, and you would've sworn that Obama was his son the way he was acting. All he kept saying was he never thought he'd see the day when Americans would vote in a Black president."

My eyes watered. I wasn't sure if I was sad or proud like Daddy was. I think I was a little of both. "I wish I could've been there."

"I wish you could've been there, too, but trust me, the world is constantly changing. I'm sure we'll have more history-making events to experience. Besides, you coming back to us is better news than a Black president."

Leah finished my braids, and we went to the hall bathroom so I could see her work. I couldn't stop looking at them. "I don't know how to thank you," I spoke to Leah, but my eyes were still on me.

"You being here is all the thanks I need." Leah stood behind me and leaned her head on my back. "I'm so glad you're here."

We both decided to leave the bathroom before we started bawling. I'd cried so much lately that it was starting to give me the heebie-jeebies too. We stepped into the hallway and heard Mama talking to someone on the front porch. Leah went to the door while I stood by the stairs.

She looked back at me. "It's Lance."

I rushed to the door, but didn't go through it. "Lance." Saying his name brought back all the good memories. But they didn't last long because I immediately thought of the bad. How I'd hurt him and the argument Quinton and I had that night about him.

"Nova." Lance walked closer to the door. He looked down at the handle. "May I come in?"

I nodded.

"Oh my God, Nova, it's so good to see you."

"It is?" I said between heavy breaths. "I thought you'd hate me."

"Hate you? I could never hate you."

I wanted to hug Lance. I wanted to tell him how sorry I was, but I didn't do any of that. Instead, I ran away. Not out of fear, but out of guilt. He may not have hated me, but for years I hated him. Hated that he'd called me. Hated that I called him back. And hated that he was the reason Quinton and I fought.

CHAPTER 16

Leah

Sitting in the school gymnasium on a Friday night was just the dose of normalcy that Leah needed. The game had just started, and Leah's palms were already sweating. Quinton cupped his hand over her knee to stop the nervous bounce. With everything that had been happening in their lives, Leah was happy about this distraction, even if it was wrecking her nerves. Watching Skye play basketball was just as intense as it used to be when she watched Nova.

"Are you sure you're going to be okay? We're still in the first quarter." Quinton leaned over and pointed to the time clock on the wall across from where they sat.

Before Leah could answer, a player from the other team fouled Skye. Bayou High was behind by two points, and Skye needed to make both free throws to tie the game. Leah bit her bottom lip as she watched Skye bounce the ball a couple of times then aim toward the goal and . . . swish. All net.

Leah and Quinton sprang to their feet. "Alright, Skye!" they shouted.

When they sat, Quinton talked with the guy beside him about the game, while Leah tried to focus on the basketball court, but an uncomfortable feeling drew her attention away from the game and to her right, where a group of women were obviously engaged in a heavy conversation that had nothing to do with the basketball game. As soon as they saw Leah watching them, they quickly averted their gazes.

"What are you doing?" Quinton shot from his seat again. He cupped his hand over his mouth and shouted, "Are you going to call anything right today, Ref!"

Leah tugged on his T-shirt, the one they both wore proudly announcing that their daughter was number seven. Skye wore the same number that Nova used to wear. Leah's parents loved that Nova chose that number. They said in the Bible, it signified the number of completion. Leah had no idea what that had to do with basketball, and she never asked. Questions like that always came with a long, drawn-out explanation.

Quinton was so fired up he didn't even feel Leah. It wasn't until Skye's coach called a time-out that he finally sat down again.

"I think we're the entertainment tonight," Leah whispered as she leaned over to Quinton.

He furrowed his brow and tilted his head.

"Don't look, but there's a group of women who were staring at us. As soon as they saw me looking, they turned away."

"So what? Let 'em look." Quinton hunched his shoulders.

Leah knew he was right, and she wished it didn't bother her, but it did. This was the only time Leah wished they'd made Skye go to school in Baton Rouge instead of Bayou. There were plenty of schools in Baton Rouge with great basketball programs, but Skye wanted to play for Bayou High. The high school that her mom, dad, and aunt graduated from. Not to mention that it was also the school where her best friend Ava attended.

Once halftime came, Leah was tired of sitting. She needed to move around, and the lady next to her had nachos that made Leah's mouth water. "I'm going to the concession stand," she told Quinton.

Leah stopped and talked to a few of her parents' friends who were sitting at the bottom of their section. The people in Bayou, young and old, loved their sports. Of course, there wasn't much to do in Bayou in terms of entertainment, so attending church and the games was their idea of fun.

"Hey, Leah."

Leah smiled, prepared to greet the person behind her, but her smile immediately faded when she saw it was two of the ladies who'd been staring at them. If Quinton and Nova had a fan club in high school, then Danielle and Monica would've been the president and vice president. They acted like Nova and Quinton set the standard for the perfect high school relationship.

"Hey." The word flew from Leah's mouth so fast that she almost missed it herself. She turned back to the front of the line and away from them.

"Um . . . Leah." Both ladies stood beside Leah. "We just wanted to say how happy we were to hear the news about Nova," Danielle said.

Leah didn't have the energy to fake a smile when she looked at them again. "Thank you."

"I know your mom must be so happy," Monica added.

"We were all very happy." Leah was grateful when the line moved up and hoped they'd leave it at that, but of course that was too much to hope for.

"How are Quinton and Skye? I'm sure they were happy too, huh?" It was Danielle's turn to ask the question.

"We were *all* very happy," Leah said before they went down the whole family tree.

"But . . . um . . . We don't mean to pry," Danielle continued.

Then don't.

"Does Nova know? You know . . . about you and Quinton? We're only asking so we won't slip up and say anything that could give it away, you know?"

Leah forced herself to keep her face from showing the frustration she felt.

"Nova's using this time to heal, so you won't have to worry about seeing her out anytime soon, nor is she accepting visitors, but thanks for your concern," Leah answered as politely as she could without telling them where to stick their fake concern.

"Oh, okay." Danielle smiled, but Leah couldn't miss the disappointment in her eyes.

Instead of taking a step forward with the rest of the line, Leah stood and waited to see if they were going to be bold enough to ask the real question.

"So, we were talking the other day, and our hearts just went out to all y'all. I know this can't be easy for Nova, being away for so long. And even you and Quinton. It has to be hard for the two of you too."

Leah opened her mouth to respond when Quinton walked up and excused himself, moving past the two intruders to get to Leah.

"Hey, I was wondering what was taking so long. Now I see." He nodded toward the people ahead of Leah.

"Hey, Quinton," Monica spoke.

Danielle waved.

"Oh, hey, ladies."

"You're just in time," Leah informed him. "Danielle and Monica were asking if Nova being back was hard on us. I'm assuming you mean our marriage, or in general?" Leah played dumb.

"No, we were just . . . I mean . . . hard on you, Quinton, the whole family," Monica rambled.

"Especially Nova," Danielle added.

"Yeah." Quinton dragged the word out before turning his attention to Leah. "The next quarter's about to start. I'll come get you some nachos once this line goes down." He took her by the hand and left Danielle and Monica standing behind.

Quinton led Leah to the other end of the hallway and away from the crowd going and coming out of the gymnasium.

"You alright? You look like you're ready to spit fire." He gently massaged her shoulders.

"I told you they were staring at us. They couldn't wait to find out if Nova knew about us." Leah was breathing so hard that her chest started to hurt.

"You have to calm down, babe. You know how these people are. They don't have a problem being in everyone's business."

"Well, that's fine. I don't care if they're in everyone's business, I just don't want them in mine."

"Why are you so upset?" Quinton asked.

"Why aren't you more upset?" Leah questioned.

"Because I expected this, and you should've expected it too."

"I guess. I don't know, I just hate the thought of people watching us and asking questions that are none of their business."

Quinton pulled Leah into him. She let him hold her for a quick second before she moved away. "Let's get back in and cheer for our girl. I don't need those two busybodies to know they got to me the way they did."

Leah and Quinton walked back into the gymnasium, and Leah saw and felt the eyes of too many people watching them. What she wanted to do at that moment was go home and stay far away from Bayou for as long as she could. These were the looks they endured at the beginning of their relationship, and now, here they were, getting them yet again. Leah hated it. She hated everything about this whole situation, especially the fact that she was still withholding this information from Nova.

CHAPTER 17
Nova

I could hear Mama talking when I made it to the bottom step. I stood for a minute and listened. I wasn't trying to be nosy. Or maybe I was. I couldn't shake the feeling that there was something they weren't telling me. I already knew Daddy was gone. Nothing could be worse than that.

And, as if on cue, my mind told me all the other things that were just as bad or worse.

Skye's sick.
Mama's sick.
Leah?
Quinton?
And if they aren't telling me, it must be bad. Like, really bad.

I silence my mind so I can hear what Mama was saying. Maybe she'll tell me without knowing it.

"How was she?" Mama asked.

Another voice. A deep male one came from the kitchen. I assumed Mama was on the phone. The thought that someone could've been here didn't cross my mind.

I shook my head, reminding myself I was supposed to be listening.

The male's voice wasn't as clear as Mama's. The only word I heard was *Leah.*

"Leah?" I said her name louder than I intended, then covered my mouth, but it was too late. In the quietness of the house, my voice carried right to Mama.

"Nova?" She called for me. "There you are," she said when I stood. "Lance came to rake up all these leaves for me."

"Morning, Nova." Lance greeted me.

"Morning." I glanced at him and then at Mama. "What's wrong with Leah?"

"What?"

"Leah? You asked how was she? Is she sick?"

"No, honey, calm down. Your sister's fine." Mama's gaze slid over to Lance.

"What aren't you telling me?" I asked, feeling the heat rising inside me.

"I'm telling you the truth. Leah's fine. There were just some busybodies at Skye's game asking questions about you. That's all."

"What kind of questions?"

"Just questions."

"Like what?" I pressed.

Before she could respond, Lance, who I forgot was there, walked behind Mama and put his coffee cup in the sink. "I'd better get started." He touched Mama's shoulder.

"Okay, baby." Mama patted his hand.

Mama took her time turning back to me, but my eyes never left her. "Why are you hiding things from me?"

"I'm not hiding anything from you," she insisted.

"But you are. All of you are. You think I don't hear you whispering, then getting quiet when you hear me coming? I do and I'm sick of it."

"Nova, please calm down."

"And stop telling me to calm down. I am calm."

"Okay. Alright," Mama said, sounding like she was soothing a baby instead of talking with a grown woman.

I clenched my teeth together and allowed them to lock in the words that I knew would hurt Mama's feelings. I stared at my feet because looking at them was easier than looking at Mama while I was trying to compose myself. It wasn't easy when I thought about my family and how they were treating me. I didn't think they saw me as an adult anymore. When we were kids, Mama and Daddy used to say that children shouldn't be in grown folks' business. Was that what they were doing now?

"Nova." Mama paused until I lifted my eyes to face her again. "You're right," she admitted. "We have been discussing things behind your back, but only because it's silly things that we don't want you to worry about."

"And what should I worry about instead? What I've lived through the past fifteen years? Maybe I'd prefer worrying about silly things instead of that. I've spent years in a place where I didn't belong. I don't want to come home just to feel the same way."

Mama shook her head slowly. "You're right, Nova. I'm sorry."

I couldn't talk about it anymore, so I went to the cabinet and pulled out a mug to make myself a cup of coffee.

"I'm going to do some shopping this morning. You want to ride? You don't have to get out," Mama asked.

For a second, I thought about taking her up on her offer. I'd been home for six days now and I hadn't left this house yet. I was so ready to get out and explore the world. So ready to do so many things, but all I did was sit in this house and stare out the window. I hated the fear that came over me when I thought of leaving through that front door. Why couldn't my mind accept that Adam was dead? Why did it want me to leave one prison just to put myself in another one?

I opened my mouth to tell Mama yes, I'd go. "No. Maybe next time." We both knew that next time the answer would be the same.

"Okay, well, I can ask Cora to pick up some things for me. I don't have to go."

"You can go to the store, Mama. I'm okay."

She looked around, as if she was trying to make sure there wasn't anything there that could hurt me before she decided whether she should leave me alone or not.

"I don't know." Mama wrung her hands around each other. "What if someone stops by?"

"I won't answer," I said, repeating the rules she had for us when we stayed home alone as children. "Mama, you do understand that I'm forty years old, right? I'm old enough to stay home alone."

"I know that, Nova. I just like to be here. You know. Just in case."

"In case what? If someone comes, I won't answer. If someone calls, I won't answer. Is it okay if I use the stove while you're gone, or should I wait until an adult is present?"

Mama's eyes widened, and her hand slapped against her chest. She opened her mouth, then closed it. "I'll let you know before I leave."

I abandoned my coffee and went upstairs to my bedroom. Whenever I felt too overwhelmed, being alone calmed me. That was my intention when I walked into my room, to sit on the bed and stay there until my nerves were no longer jumping all over the place. But that wasn't what I did. I passed the bed and went straight to the window that overlooked the backyard. I looked down where Lance was raking leaves into a neat pile.

My body relaxed when I thought of how he used to come over and help Daddy do yard work. Lance loved being outside even more than I did. I think that was what drew us together. That and the fact that Mama, his grandma, and Ms. Cora had a three-member gossip group, and no one's business was safe once it hit any one of their ears.

My body was heavy as the memory of the good times faded and the unhappy played. For years I blamed Lance for what happened to me. My anger was too big for one person, so I had to spread it around to me, Quinton, and Lance, but if I was honest, out of the three of us, I gave Lance the biggest dose.

My life was fine before he called. Yes, Quinton and I had our problems, and we were fighting more than usual, but it was still okay. We could've worked things out, but then Lance had to go and call me. He wanted to see me. Why did he do that? Why didn't he just leave me alone? Why did I go? Honestly, that was a question I'd already answered time and time again.

I went because I missed him more than I'd realized. That wasn't the point, though. The point was he should've left me alone and I wouldn't have gone, which meant I wouldn't have had anything to confess to Quinton that night. He wouldn't have blown up, and I wouldn't have stormed out, and we'd still be married with a houseful of children like we planned. Everything happened because of one stupid phone call.

"Nova."

I whipped around, clutching my chest and breathing like I'd just run for ten miles.

"I'm sorry." Mama rushed to me. "Are you sure you don't need me to stay?" She moved her head from one side to the other, studying my face.

"You look nice," I told Mama, ignoring the question that I'd already answered downstairs.

Mama was wearing dark-blue jeans, a burnt-orange sweater, and brown boots. Her hair hung to her shoulders, and it was still hard for me to believe how little she'd aged. Yes, she looked older than I remembered, but not fifteen years older.

"Thank you." She leaned in and hugged me, and I already knew her sweet perfume was going to be all over me when she left. "I won't be long. Call me if you need anything." She held up her cell phone. "The number is on the refrigerator. Oh, and I put Cora's on there too. And it's not because I think you're a baby."

I didn't protest. Instead, I linked my arm around Mama's. Her eyes dropped to my arm, then made their way back up. She gave my arm the same pat she'd given Lance in the kitchen, but mine was paired with concern in her eyes. Mama worried about me. She didn't know how I'd react from one minute to the next. Actually, from one second to the next. If I knew, I'd warn her what was coming, but I never knew either. I wasn't used to feeling so many things. For so many years my only emotions were anger, loneliness, and hate. Joy and happiness felt foreign in my body. Like they didn't belong there. Was it bad that I felt more like myself in anger than I did in joy?

"Okay, I'll be back shortly. You have my phone number." Mama held up her cell phone again as we walked back downstairs. "Call me if you think of anything you need. I'm going right up the street to Mr. Jim's Grocery so I'm only a hop, skip, and a jump away." Mama continued talking even after she was out of the house and standing on the porch.

"I'll be fine, Mama."

I was ready for her to leave. Mama had barely left my side since I'd left the hospital six days ago. I loved her, but I wasn't used to all the attention and smothering. Being alone in the house wasn't as scary as Mama probably thought it would be for me. If I was locked in, I knew I'd be fine. It wasn't inside that frightened me. It was out there, where she was going, that scared me the most.

I set the alarm by the front door and sat on the sofa. I clicked on the television and went to Netflix. When I wasn't upstairs in my room, I'd sit in the living room with Mama and watch TV. I almost jumped through my skin when she was flipping through Netflix, and I saw *Girlfriends*. It was one of Leah and my favorite shows. *Girlfriends* and *Gilmore Girls*. Whenever they came on, if we weren't together, we'd call each other and sit on the phone and watch. The memory wrapped around me like a warm blanket on a cold day.

Mama showed me how to turn on Netflix, which wasn't very hard since the button was on the remote control. It still amazed me that I could watch these shows, and there were no commercials. It used to feel like I'd be holding my breath waiting for a commercial so Leah and I could talk about what just happened. I guess we could always pause it, but that didn't feel the same.

I was halfway through the show when my stomach started grumbling. I needed to eat. A giddiness that I couldn't even describe came over me when I walked into the kitchen and pulled a pan from the hanger above the island. I pulled out the carton of eggs and bacon from the refrigerator and sat them by the stove. One day, hopefully soon, I could cook breakfast for Skye the way Mama cooked for me.

I poured a little oil into the pan, turned the knob on the stove, and waited for the pan to heat. It was silly, but being alone and cooking for myself made me feel like a real adult. Mama wasn't there to cook for me and fix my plate. Adam wasn't there to make me eat, whether I was hungry or not. His hunger was my hunger. I believed that was what he thought. My mind played devil's advocate and pulled me deeper into the memory of that time. I was snatched out at the smell of smoke and a loud shrill that made me cover my ears before I thought to pull the pan from the eye of the stove. I turned the stove off, moved the pan over, and then covered my ears again while I tried to find the alarm. Sound seemed to come from everywhere. Fear gripped me. I snatched open the back door just as Lance ran toward the house.

"Are you okay?" he asked, still running.

I nodded. "I forgot. The pan was . . . I was just . . ." My words were like puzzle pieces that someone needed to slide into place to make sense of them.

Lance moved past me and waved his hand in front of his face from the smoke. "Stand outside," he instructed.

I didn't move.

"Nova, stand outside." He pointed, his voice louder and sterner than before.

I flinched, then relaxed when our eyes met. They weren't the eyes of a madman but the eyes of a man who cared about me. Always cared about me.

"Go," he said again.

I went out in the backyard and waited for what felt like forever before Lance came out. I lowered my head in shame. I couldn't even cook a simple egg without almost burning down the house. How was I supposed to live on my own one day? I didn't want anyone treating me like a baby, yet that was exactly what I was. Not in age, of course, but in mind. A real adult would know better than to daydream, or rather day "nightmare" while cooking. I slumped to the cold ground, where I sat until Lance came out.

"You okay?" He bent, his arms resting on his legs.

"I'm fine." I focused on everything except him.

Lance stood and reached his hand out to me. I looked at it for a second before accepting his help. He pulled me up, apparently unaware of how light I was because I collided with him.

"Sorry." I moved away, putting distance between us.

He shook his head. "That was my fault." He turned back to the house. "You may wanna stay out here for a while. At least until the smoke clears a little more."

I hugged myself, suddenly aware of the chill in the air.

Lance took off his sweatshirt and gave it to me. I hesitated once again.

"Take it," he insisted.

I wanted to protest, but the chill bumps on my arms told me not to. I pulled his hoodie over my head and inhaled the scent of Lance. "Thank you."

"No problem."

I had so many things I wanted to say to him, but my nerves wouldn't let me. Instead, I turned away from him, intending to sit on the outdoor furniture surrounding the firepit, but then I stopped.

"Something wrong?" Lance asked, his footsteps crunching against the leaves.

I was so caught up in the disaster I almost caused that it didn't even dawn on me what I'd done. I faced Lance, who stood closer to me but not too close. I scanned the backyard, then bent down and picked up one of the yellowish-orange leaves. "This is the first time I've been outside since I've been home." I didn't know if I was talking to Lance, myself, or the air, but I needed to put words to my realization.

"You've been inside for six days?" he asked as if that was impossible.

"Yeah," I said, dropping the leaf.

I looked up and saw a smile that split his face in two.

"I'm sorry. I'm still trying to remind myself that you're here." His smile dropped a little, but not much. "I missed you."

I didn't acknowledge his words because I thought it was the first time I'd really paid attention to Lance. He was bigger and older, but he was Lance. His deep-set rich-brown eyes connected with mine. His once boyishly smooth jawline was now covered in a neatly trimmed salt-and-pepper beard, making him look much more mature than I remembered.

My eyes were locked on him, and I couldn't look away even if I wanted to. I felt a strange mix of familiarity and detachment. It was Lance, my Lance, and yet he was a stranger. But unlike other strangers, he didn't scare me.

CHAPTER 18

Leah

This wasn't how Leah was supposed to feel about her sister's homecoming. She should be planning a welcome-home party, even if they didn't have it until next year when Nova felt more comfortable being around crowds. At the very least, she should be with her sister every day, talking about old times, or Leah could spend each day sharing a new detail about her life over the past fifteen years, but instead she was dealing with ignorant people at basketball games. When she was with her sister, most of her thoughts were on remembering not to say anything that would send off alarm bells to Nova about Leah and Quinton's marriage.

Why did Dr. Yvonne have to be out of the country this week? The sooner Nova started her sessions, the sooner Leah and Quinton could tell her about them. Leah feared what would happen without a professional there to guide Nova through any negative feelings the news may bring.

Leah's heart plummeted. Like most little girls, she used to dream of her wedding day and the life she would have with her husband and all their children. She missed the innocence and delusion that came with being a child. That little girl, the one with the big dreams, couldn't have known that trying to have a child would almost kill her. She inhaled as she thought about one of the worst days of her life. She could still see the look of horror on Quinton's face when he walked into the bathroom and saw all the blood. He rushed her to the hospital, where she was immediately wheeled into surgery. The next thing Leah remembered was waking up to the worst news she could hear.

It was two years ago, and she could still hear the doctor's voice when he explained that they had no choice but to perform a hysterectomy. Leah never hated a word as much as she hated that one.

She picked up her cup of coffee from the kitchen island where she'd been sitting before the sun came up. The coffee was cold . . . again.

Leah gave up on the coffee. Apparently, her adrenaline was high enough without the help of caffeine. She was washing out her cup when Quinton came downstairs and joined her in the kitchen.

"What time did you get up?" Quinton kissed her cheek.

"Four thirty." Leah didn't have to give it a second thought. For some reason, whenever she had a lot on her mind, her eyes would pop open at four thirty on the dot. She could never go back to sleep, and this morning, she didn't even try.

"I hope you're not still thinking about those women." Quinton went to the refrigerator and pulled out a carton of orange juice.

"It's not just them." Leah turned off the water and placed the mug face down in the wooden dish rack to drain. "It's having to go through this all over again. A part of me wishes we could pack up and move away."

"Yeah, but we know we can't do that," Quinton said as if Leah was actually considering it.

He knew how she felt about their house. When most people said their "dream house," they didn't mean it literally. However, Leah literally dreamed of this house years before she and Quinton started dating. She sketched out what she remembered about it and kept it safe, believing that one day she would have that house. She was right and Quinton knew that, which was why his insistence that they couldn't move was throwing her off.

Leah, not one for letting things go, explained, "Well, we could if we wanted to, but we wouldn't because we don't want to."

He placed the carton back in the refrigerator and looked over at Leah. "No, that's what I'm saying. Even if we wanted to, we couldn't. It wouldn't even be an option. Moving now that Nova's back?"

Leah massaged the back of her neck. "Why are we talking about this? We know we're not moving, so let's just drop it, okay." Leah rubbed harder, but it didn't seem to do any good. The tension she felt had made itself at home.

"You want to go by your mom's after we take Skye out for breakfast?" Quinton asked.

"Breakfast?"

"Yeah, they won last night, remember?"

"Ah, right?" Leah snapped her fingers.

It had become their tradition to go out for a celebratory breakfast after each win. Leah and Quinton wanted to do it after each game because Skye always gave each game her all, and to them, that was worth celebrating, but Skye shut it down. She said she only wanted to celebrate the wins. That way, she'd be motivated to push even harder. Leah admired so much about Skye, but it was definitely her drive that she admired the most.

Leah's phone vibrated on the counter. Quinton was closer, so he picked it up and passed it to her.

"Oh, it's Mom." Leah put the phone on speaker. She figured her mom was calling to give them an update on Nova's night. She'd done that every morning since Nova came home.

"What happened last night?" her mom asked, skipping the greeting portion of the call.

"Nothing happened. What are you talking about?" Leah looked over at Quinton.

Quinton lifted his shoulders as if Leah had asked him the question.

"I heard that you'd gotten into it with Danielle and Monica." Martha lowered her voice as if their names were top secret.

"I didn't get into it with anyone, Mom. Who told you that?"

Aggravation stirred inside Leah. Why did these people insist on getting underneath her skin? All she wanted to do was watch Skye's game and go home. Nothing more. Nothing less, but no, not in Bayou. In Bayou everything had to be addressed and talked about and told and retold even if the retelling was a lie.

"Hey, girl!" Martha's voice boomed through the phone.

"Mom, where are you?"

"About to go into Jim's to get a few groceries."

Before Leah could ask another question, Quinton had lowered himself to her phone. "Where's Nova?" His voice gave away his concern.

"She's at home. She didn't want to come."

"You left her home by herself?" Quinton sounded like he'd never heard anything so ridiculous in his life.

"She's not alone, Lance is out back raking the yard. I told him to listen out for her. And she has my phone number if she needs me. I'm at Jim's, for goodness' sake, not out of the country."

Quinton didn't respond because he was no longer there. Leah watched as he fled the kitchen and ran upstairs.

"Mom, let me call you back." Leah ended the call and was about to go upstairs, but by the time she made it to the first step, Quinton was rushing down.

He pushed his wallet in the pocket of his warm-up pants and pulled his cap, the one that matched his outfit, over his head. "I'll be back," he said, not bothering to say where he was going or asking Leah, who was fully dressed, if she wanted to come too.

"Where are you going?" she asked, even though she already knew the answer.

"I'm going to check on Nova." Quinton patted his pockets. "Did I have my keys?"

"I don't know, but Quinton, before you go over there . . ."

"Leah, do not stand here and defend that man like he's a saint."

Leah had no intention of doing that. The fact was that Lance wasn't a saint, and neither were they. She knew that statement wouldn't go over well if she said it out loud, so she didn't. She also didn't remind Quinton that the allegations Lance's ex made against him were retracted the very next day. That wouldn't go over well either. Truthfully, nothing she said in defense of Lance was going to get through to Quinton, and given the fact that up until a few days ago Lance was her client, she thought it best not to say too much, or Quinton would become suspicious. She'd never defended Lance before. However, she never had a reason to. Quinton wasn't concerned about Leah or Skye being alone with him because he knew that would never happen. At least, he may have thought he knew.

"Found them." Quinton held up the keys he'd pulled from the kitchen drawer.

"Quinton." She followed him out of the kitchen, down the hallway, and to the front door.

"Leah, I don't have time for this right now. I need to get to your mom's and check on Nova."

"Or you can just call." Leah held up her phone.

"I'd rather see for myself." He put his hand on the doorknob, then turned back and kissed Leah.

"What about breakfast?" Leah asked.

"Text me where you're going, and I'll meet you."

Everything inside her said no, he wouldn't.

"Where's Dad going?" Skye stood on the stairs and yawned.

No matter how old Skye was, Leah couldn't help but look at her and see the little girl who'd curl up in her arms and fall asleep when they were supposed to be having movie night. After Nova disappeared, taking care of Skye became Leah's number one priority. She found it hard to believe she could love any child as much as she loved Skye. Finding out she would never have children of her own was hard, and the only thing that made the blow just a tad bit easier to bear was knowing she had Skye. The little girl who reminded her so much of Nova. Having Skye was like having the best part of her sister.

"Hellooo, Teeah?" Skye sang. "Where's Dad going?"

"To Gran's. He's going to meet us for breakfast."

"Why didn't he wait so we could all go?"

"He won't be there long. Besides, you still need to get dressed before our breakfast turns into lunch," Leah said, scanning Skye from her pink hair bonnet to her big fuzzy slippers.

"It's called brunch, Teeah."

"No. At the pace you move, we'll miss brunch too." Leah stood next to Skye and bumped into her, hoping her playfulness was enough for Skye not to recognize the irritation she was fighting so hard to hold inside.

One thing Leah hated was when a comment came to her too late to voice. Had she thought about it sooner, she would've reminded Quinton that Lance's past wasn't the news that would crush Nova. It was the secret they were holding that Leah knew, without a doubt, would turn her sister's already tilted world upside down.

CHAPTER 19

Nova

I sat in the chair in front of the firepit and watched Lance raking the leaves. I probably could've gone back inside, but I was enjoying being out there and breathing in the fall air, snuggled in Lance's oversize sweatshirt. Before Adam, fall was my favorite season. Especially fall in Bayou. The people of Bayou were serious about their decorations. All the stores on Main Street would have a display with bales of hay at the front of the door. On top of the hay, they'd have a scarecrow and pumpkins surrounding it. You couldn't drive down any road and not see a house decorated as if everyone had an agenda to outdo the other.

"Nova!" My head swung around toward Quinton's frantic voice, calling my name.

"What's wrong?" I asked when he came outside looking more afraid than I thought I'd ever seen him look before.

"What's wrong?" he repeated. "I'm ringing the doorbell and knocking on the door until I have no choice but to use the emergency key Ms. Martha hid. Then I open the door and smell smoke. I'm looking all over and calling for you, and you're nowhere around. That's what's wrong."

"I'm sorry. I didn't mean to scare you." I backed away from him.

"Hey, Quinton, you need to calm down." Lance stood next to me.

"I am calm. Trust me, this is calm." He closed his eyes. When he opened them the fear and anger I'd seen before was gone. "I'm sorry, Nova. I couldn't find you, and I immediately thought . . ." He pulled his lips in and shook his head as if trying to shake away the scary thoughts that came to his mind.

"Quinton, I'm okay." I walked away from Lance as a familiar pang of anxiety rose inside me as I thought about all the fights Quinton and I had over Lance, and then the last fight that changed my life forever. I stood in front of Quinton and took his hand in mine. "Hey, I'm right here. I'm fine," I kept reassuring him.

Quinton gently pulled me into him and hugged me. His touch didn't feel uncomfortable, so I lingered in it a little longer before we broke away.

"Why does the house smell like smoke?" Quinton asked, pointing toward the house.

"I was cooking eggs and got distracted. The smoke from the pan set off the fire alarm. But it was fine because Lance came in, shut it off, and opened the windows."

A crease formed between Quinton's brows as he glanced from Lance back to me. His jaw was set, and there was a guarded look in his eyes that I remembered all too well. "Can I speak with you for a minute?"

"Yeah, what's wrong? Is it Skye?"

"No, Skye's fine. Everyone's fine. I just need to talk to you in private."

"I'm pretty sure this is about me," Lance said, shaking his head and smirking.

And just like that, it was twenty years ago, and I was caught between my best friend and the man I loved. I didn't like the feeling back then, and I hated it even more now.

"Okay, listen. I know what this is about. For a long time, I blamed Lance, too, for that night. I think a part of me still blamed him, but I don't want to hold on to that anymore, and you shouldn't either," I urged Quinton.

"Blamed me for what night?" Lance asked.

"This isn't about that," Quinton said.

"What night?" Lance asked again.

"The night I went missing." I lifted my head to Quinton, then closed the space between Lance and me. "I'd told Quinton that we'd spoken a couple of times, and, as you can imagine, he didn't take it well. We got into a huge fight, and I stormed out. That's when I went downstairs to the bar and, well, you know the rest."

"You were upset with me?" Lance asked, his words filled with hurt and dread. "Nova, I'm sorry, had I known that call would've caused all of that, believe me, I never would've—"

"But you did know she was married, right? And you did know how her husband felt about you, right?" Quinton questioned.

Lance's jaw muscles twitched. "Yeah, I knew that. Did you know that a husband's job is to always protect his wife?"

I knew those words must've landed like a gut punch to Quinton. He balled his hands into tight fists and the tension circled around us, trapping us all in this atmosphere of anger, and I hated it so much.

I stood between Quinton and Lance. "Okay . . . enough!" I shouted. "I only brought that up because I have a second chance at life, and I don't want to spend it with all those negative pinned-up feelings like I had in that room with Adam. I want to be happy." I looked at Quinton. "Like you're happy with your new life." I turned to Lance, but the words were for Quinton. "And you can't tell me who I can and cannot be friends with anymore." I looked at Quinton again to make sure he understood what I was saying. "I'm not your wife anymore. I can choose my friends."

The hurt that flashed across his face was unexpected. For some reason, I thought he'd be relieved to know that he didn't have to carry that burden anymore. That hate that he held for Lance for so long was about me, and now he could let it go.

"You don't know him like you think you do," Quinton said.

"Of course I don't," I chuckled. "It's been fifteen years. I don't know any of you anymore, if you really think about it. But that's what I want to spend this time doing—getting to know the people I love again. And in order to do that, there can't be any secrets." I looked over at Lance. That's why I wanted you to know how I'd been feeling."

Quinton touched my arm. "I get that, but I'm trying to tell you that . . ."

"What?" Lance cut in. "What are you trying to tell her? Because, like Nova said, she doesn't know any of us anymore." He turned to me. "A lot has happened to me over the past fifteen years, and I hope I can share some of it with you one day. But I can promise you that *I'm* not keeping any secrets from you."

Maybe it was my imagination, but I could've sworn I felt heat radiating off Quinton's body. No one got underneath his skin like Lance.

"There you are," Mama said, standing at the door and looking out at us. "What happened in here?"

Lance walked away and went back to finish up the rest of the yard work. Quinton and I followed Mama back inside. I helped her put up the groceries and explained how I almost burned her house down. Quinton sat quietly. He was still breathing hard, like at any minute he could jump from that stool, run back outside, and tackle Lance.

"I should get going." He hugged me, then Mama, before he left.

"What's that about?" Mama asked.

"I'll be back." I followed Quinton to the front door. "Are you okay?"

He smiled, but I knew Quinton's smile, and that wasn't it. "Yeah, of course."

"Lance really got to you."

"He didn't get to me. He just . . . I don't like him, and I don't understand why no one can see him for who he is."

"Who do you think he is?" I waited for him to fill me in, but he couldn't. "What happened between the two of you? And don't say it was nothing."

He stared at me, and I could tell that there was more that he wasn't saying. When the forced smile returned, I knew he wasn't going to tell me.

"Fine, but just know that you'll feel a lot better once you let it go."

He touched my shoulder. "Talk with you later."

I watched him drive off, and a part of me wanted to call him back and sit with him until I knew he was okay. Then, I reminded myself that he had a wife to go home to. Someone else would comfort him and make sure he was okay. Why did it feel like I just received the news that he was no longer married to me? I thought I was okay with that news. I told myself I was fine, but now I didn't know if I was.

CHAPTER 20

Leah

Leah was fuming, and it had taken a lot for her not to show it. Skye sat across from her on her phone. Leah looked at her phone again. Still no call from Quinton. She'd texted him when they were leaving, then called when they made it to the restaurant, and she hadn't heard from him yet. Even though she knew not to expect him, a part of her wished she was wrong.

"Are you ladies ready to order, or do you still wanna wait?" the waitress asked.

Leah looked at Skye. She was willing to follow her lead. If it were up to Leah, they would've ordered twenty minutes ago, but Skye wanted to wait for her dad.

"We can order." Skye hunched her shoulders.

Leah agreed, even though her appetite abandoned her a long time ago.

"He's probably driving," Skye said after they placed their order and the waitress walked away.

All Leah heard was, "It's okay, Teeah. I'm sure my dad isn't ignoring you to spend time with your sister."

"I'm sure he is." Leah glanced at her phone again.

She didn't want to entertain the thoughts that came to her, but she couldn't help it. Quinton had never given her a reason not to trust him, so the feeling she had was a foreign one when it came to their relationship. Leah had been hurt in relationships before and she knew how devastating it could feel, but what she and Quinton shared wasn't just another relationship. When she agreed to marry him, it was with the intent that they'd be forever, till death did they part. Until now, she never questioned if that would happen.

Why am I questioning it now? He's checking on Nova. That's it.

It wasn't long before their breakfast arrived. Skye devoured hers while Leah managed to swallow a few bites before she was done.

"You're quiet," Skye said, leaning closer to the table. "Something on your mind?" She lifted her arched brows.

"Of course. Something's always on my mind. Right now, I'm thinking about the groceries I need to pick up, the dry cleaning I need to drop off, and the notes I need to make from my sessions this week."

"And that Dad's not here even though we've called him several times?" Skye asked, cutting right through Leah's BS.

"What?" Leah's small laugh sounded nervous even to her ears. "What makes you think that's on my mind?"

"Because you've been looking at your phone every few seconds." Skye put her fork down and waved the waitress over. "Can we have the check and two to-go plates, please?"

"You can finish eating," Leah insisted.

"No, we're going to Gran's to make sure everything's okay," Skye said in a tone that let Leah know there was no need to argue. Her mind was made up, and they were leaving.

All Leah had to figure out was when and how the seventeen-year-old who sat across from her became so wise beyond her years. There were days like that one when Leah had to remind herself that Skye wasn't an adult yet, even though she often behaved like one.

Quinton called as soon as Leah and Skye pulled out of the restaurant's parking lot. "Babe, I'm sorry. I left my phone in the truck and lost track of time. Are y'all still there?"

"We just left."

"Are you all . . ."

Leah's phone beeped. She looked at the screen that showed her mom's number. "It's Mom, I'll see you at home." Leah hung up.

"Hey, Mom."

"It's Nova."

Leah still hadn't gotten used to hearing her sister's voice on the other end of her phone. "Hey, Nova. Are you okay?" Leah wasn't sure why she asked. Nova sounded fine. She definitely didn't sound like someone who needed saving a minute ago.

"I'm fine. Hey, I was wondering if you would like to come over tonight, and we can maybe have a sleepover or something."

Leah's mood lifted. "I'd love that."

"Really? Oh good. Do you think that maybe Skye would like to come too? I thought it could be just us girls for the night?"

"I'm sure she would." Leah almost turned to Skye, then caught herself midmotion. She didn't know if being with Skye would raise any suspicions, even though it shouldn't. Leah liked to think whether she was married to Quinton or not, she'd still have a close relationship with Skye, but to avoid any questions, she had to stay quiet for now. "Do you want me to call and ask her?"

Nova was quiet. "Yeah, that'll be good." Her voice was lower and lacked the enthusiasm that it held a minute ago. "I don't have her phone number, so."

"Oh, she probably didn't think about it. You know how teenagers can be?" Leah said the words before thinking. Because of course Nova didn't know how teenagers could be. Not today's teenagers, who, if you asked Leah, were quite different from how she and Nova were as teenagers.

"Yeah," Nova said nervously. "So, I'll see you tonight then."

Leah could've slapped herself for that slipup. She'd been so careful to make sure she didn't say anything that would make Nova feel any less included than she already felt.

"You need to give Nova your phone number. She'd love to be able to call you sometimes," Leah told Skye.

"Okay."

"And she wants us to come over tonight for a sleepover." Leah spit the words out quickly, hoping Skye would say okay without paying much attention to what she'd said.

"What? But I'm supposed to stay with Ava tonight. You and Dad already said it was okay."

"I know, but that was before Nova wanted us to come there. Come on, Skye, this would mean so much to her. You'll have other nights to spend with Ava."

"And we'll have other nights to spend at Gran's too."

Leah had perfected the "mama look" she learned from the best. All she had to do was bend her head a little and lift her brows, and that look meant, "Just do what I say."

"Fine." Skye folded her arms and turned toward the window.

As Leah pulled into her driveway, she couldn't help thinking how her life was now divided into two parts. Before Nova and After Nova. Before Nova, Leah's biggest issue was making sure her calendar wasn't overbooked and deciding what they should eat for dinner. After Nova, her life was all those things and much more, like wondering if her husband was still in love with her sister and figuring out when would be a good time to unburden herself from this secret that was growing harder to carry by the day.

Was it bad that Leah felt her life was better before Nova? Yes, it was. She knew it was. It wasn't a thought that made her feel good at all. Not that she wished Nova wasn't back. She'd never in a trillion years wish that, but she did wish that things were different. If there weren't a dark, stormy cloud hanging over her head every day, then all of this would be much better.

"Hey, how was breakfast?" Quinton asked when they walked inside.

"It was good. Where were you?" Skye asked, getting straight to the point.

Quinton looked at Leah. "I was at Gran's. Didn't Leah tell you where I was?"

"Yes, but we thought you'd join us for breakfast like we do every single morning after a winning game."

Quinton nodded. "And that was the plan, but I left my phone and . . . You know what, it's not important. I'll make it up to you, I promise." He kissed Skye's forehead.

"When you say make it up to me are we talking monetary orrr . . ."

"I mean however I feel is a good way to make it up to you," Quinton clarified.

"Gotcha." Skye pointed, then ran upstairs to her room.

She knew not to push the issue because he had been known to change his mind. Like earlier, for instance.

"How was Nova?" Leah asked, folding her arms and waiting for him to tell her what she already knew.

"Not good."

"Really, because she sounded good when she called me a little while ago."

"Did she tell you about the conversation we had?" he asked.

"No. What conversation?"

Quinton nodded toward the family room. "Let's talk in here."

Leah followed Quinton and sat next to him on the sofa. She listened as he told her about the smoke and how Nova acted like Lance was this great savior when there wasn't even a fire, just smoke. His words, not Leah's.

"I didn't get a chance to tell her about him. I don't want her around him."

"Quinton, Nova's not a child. I understand that you want to protect her, but you don't need to protect her from Lance. You know, like I do, that Lance would never do anything to hurt her."

"I don't know anything, and neither do you. People only show you the person they want you to see, Leah. You, more than anyone, should know that."

"Me more than anyone?"

"Yes, a therapist. You think your clients tell you everything about themselves or just what they want you to know?"

"Of course they tell me what they want me to know. Isn't that what everyone does? Isn't it what we're doing right now with Nova?"

"Yeah, he brought that up too."

Leah's body was like a bottomless pit and her heart never stopped dropping. "What?" She was barely able to speak. "What do you mean he told her?"

"He didn't say it outright, but he hinted to the fact that I had a secret that I wasn't sharing too."

Leah couldn't sit any longer. "And that's exactly why I didn't want you going over there in the first place. What would've happened if the two of you had gotten into it and he let it slip that we're married? Who do you think she would've felt more hurt and betrayal from, him or you?"

"What was I supposed to do?"

"Nothing. You were supposed to go eat breakfast with your wife and daughter like we do every morning after a winning game. That's what you were supposed to do."

"And leave her alone with a guy who we both know was accused of rape."

"Oh my God, Quinton!"

"Hey! What's going on?" Skye's eyes were wide as they darted from Leah to Quinton. "I've never heard y'all fight before. I don't like it."

"We're not fighting," Leah said.

"You were shouting. It sounds like fighting to me."

"It's fine, Skye. Just go to your room and give us a minute."

Skye didn't move.

"Now." Quinton's words were more forceful than Leah had ever heard him speak to Skye.

Skye rushed away from the doorway and up the stairs. Leah's heart was being pulled with each step Skye took.

Leah flopped back on the sofa. She held her head in her hand. "What are we doing? This isn't us," she said, feeling drained.

"I know." Quinton exhaled. "I don't expect you to understand how important this is to me, Leah."

"But I do understand. You have to know that you're not the only person who wants to keep Nova safe. We all want the same thing, Quinton. If my mom thought for one second that Nova would be in danger, then she never would've left. Plus, she told Lance to listen out for her."

Quinton shook his head. "And for some reason you still don't understand that he's the danger I'm trying to keep her away from. If you're asking me to let it go, then I'm sorry, I can't do that. I'll never sit back and wait for something to happen to her again."

"You weren't sitting and waiting for something to happen to her back then. Don't you get that? If you thought for one second that she was in danger, you would've flown out of that room, snatched her away from Adam, and probably tried to beat him within an inch of his life. You didn't fail her then, Quinton, and being overprotective now isn't going to erase the past."

"I hear what you're saying. I just wish you could hear what I'm saying."

Quinton walked out of the room, leaving Leah sitting and replaying their entire conversation from beginning to end. How could she get him to understand that Nova was no longer his responsibility without sounding like a jealous wife?

A better question was what could she tell herself to convince her that she wasn't a jealous wife?

CHAPTER 21

Nova

Mama went all out for that night's dinner. When I told her that Leah and Skye were coming to sleep over, you'd think it was Christmas the way she was cooking, baking, and singing all afternoon.

"I can't believe I'm going to have all my girls with me tonight," Mama said when I joined her in the kitchen.

Mama changed from her jeans and sweater into her cooking dress. That was something that hadn't changed over time. Mama never wore her good clothes to cook. Her dresses were ones that she said she didn't mind messing up, plus, they were cheap. Leah and I hated those big grandma-looking dresses, but Mama had loved them, and apparently, she still did.

"Can I help do anything?" I needed something to occupy my time until Leah and Skye came. That way I wouldn't keep thinking about the look on Quinton's face when he drove away. It was gnawing at me, and I needed to get Leah alone so I could tell her what happened and ask what I should do. If anyone could guide me in the right direction, it would be Leah.

"You can go get the tea from outside and sweeten it up. You know how we like it." Mama winked.

Mama loved sun-made tea. She'd put the tea bags in a pitcher of water and set the pitcher outside in the sun until she felt it was ready. I walked outside, picked up the tea, and smiled when I realized that, once again, I'd walked through those doors without a second thought. Maybe tomorrow, I'd try going out the front door. It wasn't much, but it made me feel like I was making progress. Leah said once I met with Dr. Yvonne on Monday and started my sessions regularly, she felt that I'd make even more progress. I really hoped so because as safe as I felt inside the house, I also knew that I didn't fight to get out of that room just to stay inside for the remainder of my life. I was ready to live so badly I could taste it.

By the time Mama and I finished in the kitchen and dressed, Leah and Skye were pulling up. Leah must've picked Skye up from her house because they were riding together. I loved that my sister and my daughter were so close, but I'd be lying if I didn't say I wished it was me who had that kind of relationship with Skye.

"It smells great in here," Leah said, holding her overnight bag on her shoulder and a plastic container in her hand. "I made ooey gooey cake. Even though I know Mom probably made enough sweets to open a bakery." Leah laughed before kissing Mom.

"Oh hush." Mama took the container from Leah and walked over to Skye. "Hey, Gran's baby."

"Hey, Gran." Skye leaned down and kissed Mama. She then walked over to me. "How are you?" she asked.

"I'm good. How are you?"

"Same." She stepped closer, and I wasted no time going in for a hug. Even though it wasn't a warm hug that you'd expect to feel between a mom and her daughter, it was still a hug, nonetheless.

"Okay, girls, let's eat." Mama beckoned for us to come to the kitchen, where we all sat around the island. Skye sat across from me, and Leah sat beside me. I didn't think I could feel any better even if I tried.

"What are you girls going to do tonight?" Mama asked.

Leah and Skye both looked at me for the answer. I guess I was the one who put this whole thing together, and I probably should've had plans, but I just wanted them here. We could've sat on the sofa and watched TV for all I cared, as long as they were there with me.

"Umm . . . Nothing much, just sit and chillax."

"Chill who?" Skye asked, her brows dipped together.

"Chillax. You know, chill and relax . . . chillax."

"I've never heard that before, but you know what, I think I'll bring it back. I like it." Skye laughed. "Chillax," she repeated the word.

"What about crunk? Do kids still get crunk?" I asked Skye.

She laughed even harder. "No, and I don't think they want to. What does that even mean?"

I looked over at Mama, then Leah. "How could y'all not teach her these words?" I joked.

Leah held up both hands. "Don't look at me. I didn't use them even when they were popular."

"Me either. I could barely understand a word you young kids used to say." Mama laughed. "Still don't know what they're saying half the time."

"Well, that makes two of us," I said. "Only for me it's young and old. At least for you, it's just words that you don't understand. I don't understand most of the changes around here. Like pods for instance. Why are there so many of them?"

"Pods?" Mama repeated. "What pods?"

"Coffee pods." I raised a finger. "Dishwasher pods." I raised another finger. "Detergent pods." I raised a third finger. "I'm sure there are more that I haven't heard of yet."

They all wore matching expressions, like I'd just given them a lot to think about. Maybe I did. I guess when you were used to it, you didn't think about it much, but it was all I thought about. Not pods necessarily, but all the new things that weren't around back then.

After dinner, we were all stuffed. The only place we could go was to the sofa, where we watched a few episodes of *Gilmore Girls* until Skye had enough and suggested another idea.

"Listening to you talk about words you used to say back then made me want to know more. How about we have a dance party? We'll each play songs from our generation. That way we can also work off some of this pie and ooey gooey cake we ate."

"Hey, you're the only one who needs to work it off. The rest of us don't have to run up and down the court," Leah told her.

"That's why the rest of you should definitely get up and work it off now," Skye said, looking for something on her phone. "I'll go first," she said, playing a song that I didn't know, but I liked the beat. "Who's this?" I asked, moving my shoulders more than anything else.

"Bruno Mars." Skye stopped singing long enough to insert his name before she started up again.

Skye made all of us, including Mama, get up and dance. I could only do so much because my ankle was not totally healed, but that didn't matter.

It was Leah's turn to choose the next song.

"What's your song, Teeah?" Skye asked, ready to DJ for Leah.

"Oh no. My song requires a video so we can get the moves right."

Leah picked up the TV remote control and went to the YouTube station. Mama and I didn't watch that channel—only Netflix—but YouTube seemed to have a lot of movies and other things too. Why did anyone need so many movies? I'd never understand.

When Leah chose her song, I recognized the name.

"I remember Beyoncé. She was with the group . . . what's the group?" I knew it had to do with children.

"Destiny's Child," Skye and Leah answered.

"I like Beyoncé." Mama was snapping her fingers and moving her hips. Seeing her dance reminded me of when she and Daddy would put on one of their records and dance in the middle of the floor while Leah and I begged them to stop. As a child, seeing your parents dancing and kissing was gross, but not so much now. Our parents were in love, and they didn't have a problem expressing it. I'd give anything to see them together now.

Daddy would be right here with us. It wouldn't have bothered him at all to be with all the girls. It was what he was used to, anyway.

"Alright, get ready," Leah instructed.

The video started, and we all did our best to follow along with the dance moves to "Upgrade U," but we were too busy laughing at each other to get them right. There was no way I could move like Beyoncé even if I didn't have a hurt ankle.

After Leah's song, we decided to take a break. As much as I was enjoying our dance party, I needed to sit and catch my breath. That was the most exercise I'd done in years, and my body was feeling all of it.

"What's the guy's name who was in the video with Beyoncé?" I struggled to speak and breathe at the same time.

"Jay-Z," Skye reminded me, sounding like she'd been relaxing the whole time instead of dancing. "He and Beyoncé are married."

"That's so funny because when your dad and I were dating, I loved Beyoncé, and he loved Jay-Z," I told Skye.

Skye's mouth opened so wide I could see her tonsils. "Are you serious?" she asked. "I need to hear everything about Dad listening to Jay-Z."

"I can't believe he didn't tell you that. Not only did he listen to Jay-Z, but he tried to be a rapper himself. You remember that, Leah?"

"Um . . . No, not really."

"Of course you don't." I looked at Skye. "Your Teeah didn't like it when I'd tell her things about your dad. They had a love-hate relationship back then."

Leah coughed like she was choking on something.

"Are you okay?" I was about to go to her, but she stood. "I just need some water. I'm fine." She hurried to the kitchen.

"Hold on. Dad. My dad. Quinton Boudreaux was a rapper? The man who only listens to talk radio or jazz? That Quinton?"

"Talk radio and jazz? No way." That time I was the one shocked by the news.

The Quinton I knew would never listen to jazz. If he did it would be to make fun of it. He definitely wouldn't listen to it for enjoyment. Although he wasn't the twenty-five-year-old I'd been taken away from anymore. Maybe getting older changed his taste in music. I wondered what else changed about him. Did he still like going to the movies? Was Popeyes still his favorite fast-food restaurant? There was so much about him that I suddenly wanted to know so badly.

"I cannot believe my dad tried to be a rapper," Skye said. "I can't even picture it."

"Yep. His rap name was Q-Dog."

Skye laughed so hard she had tears rolling down her cheeks. "I wish I would've known him back then. He sounds like he was a lot of fun."

"He was. We used to have the best times when we were together. I guess that's why we were always with each other." I pretended to whisper, "Which your Gran and Teeah didn't like very much."

"I get wanting to be together, but all the time. That's the part I didn't understand. Everyone needs a break from each other every now and then," Mama said.

Mama definitely didn't understand. When things were great between me and Quinton, the last thing we wanted or needed was a break. That felt more like a punishment than anything. Back then, being with Quinton was everything I could have wanted—it was comfort, excitement, and security all wrapped into one. I wished I still felt that way, but Quinton was a stranger now. And bigger than that, he was someone else's husband.

"None of that sounds anything like the dad I know," Skye said.

"Well, I think I brought a lot of his silly side out of him. He wasn't always like that. He used to be like the person you're describing now . . . minus the jazz music and talk radio. That was never him." I laughed. "But the more we were around each other, the more he loosened up."

"That must be it then."

"I'm surprised your stepmom hasn't pulled it out of him already. Unless she's not the silly type either."

Skye didn't respond. She just kinda hunched her shoulders, but I could tell she wasn't comfortable talking about her stepmom, so I moved on. "Like Teeah, for instance. She's more serious than I used to be. I bet my brother-in-law, who I still haven't met," I hollered into the kitchen, "is probably just like her. Serious and all business."

Skye laughed nervously, then all our attention was drawn to the kitchen when something shattered.

"Sorry. It's fine," Leah called to us.

"I'll be back." Mama jumped up and rushed into the kitchen.

"Is she okay?" I asked Skye. "Did she seem like something was bothering her when you all were on your way here?"

Skye shook her head. "I'm sure it's nothing. She's probably busy with work or something like that." She laughed again.

Skye had a tell, and it didn't take long for me to pick up on it. She laughed when she was nervous, and people only got nervous when they were hiding something. As much as I wished I could shake the feeling, I just knew that there was something my family was keeping from me, and whatever it was had to do with Leah. I felt it in my spirit.

"You know what?" I told Skye. "I bet I still have some of your dad's old tapes that he used to make for me. They're probably in one of those boxes in the closet."

She wasted no time leaping from the sofa and running up the stairs. I enjoyed spending time with her, but I needed to check on Leah and figure out what was going on.

CHAPTER 22

Leah

Leah was sweeping up the glass when her mom came rushing into the kitchen. "I'm sorry. I'll buy you another one," she said, looking down at the pieces of the mason jar she'd used for water.

Martha flicked her wrist at Leah. "Don't worry about that. I'm more worried about you."

"I'm fine," Leah said, bending down to sweep the pieces onto the dustpan.

"Yes, I can tell." Martha put her hand on her hip and stood next to Leah.

When Leah rose, Martha put her free hand on Leah's arm. "You're shaking. You've got to get it together. Your sister already thinks we're hiding something from her," Martha whispered close to Leah's ear.

Leah leaned back. "What? Why does she think that?"

"Because she said she sees us talking and then stopping when she comes around. She's not blind, you know. She can feel that we're not telling her something, and I think it's time that all of us unburden ourselves from this secret," Martha said, practically using the exact same words Leah had been using every time she thought about the secret they were keeping from Nova. It had indeed become a burden. A bigger one than Leah imagined and one she was tired of holding.

"I know. I'm going to talk with Quinton tomorrow. We wanted to wait until she started her sessions with Dr. Yvonne, but it looks like we'll need to go ahead and do it before she hears it from someone else. It's already been a risk with Lance coming around. Not that I think he'd say anything on purpose, but things can slip out."

"Is the party in here now?" Nova asked, coming into the kitchen.

"No, I was just cleaning up my mess." Leah looked around. "Where's Skye?"

"She ran upstairs to look in my box for some of the old tapes Quinton made for me." Nova glanced over at Mama. "Do you know if they're still in there?"

Mama hunched her shoulders. "Chile, I don't know what's in that box. I hadn't looked at it in years. But Nova, I do want you to be careful what you're sharing with Skye. She's a teenager, and I don't want her to get caught up in what her parents did and think it's okay for her to do it too." Mom lifted her brows. "You understand what I'm saying, right?"

Leah agreed with her mom but didn't feel it was her place to say anything. In any other situation, she'd have no problem telling someone what they should or shouldn't share with Skye, but Nova wasn't just any someone, and Leah had to remind herself of that. As much as she wished Skye was her biological child, that wasn't her reality.

"Of course, Ma. All I'm trying to do is bond with my daughter, and this is the most she's talked to me since we've reunited. And if you're worried about the marijuana, then you can relax. I didn't tell her that part, and I don't plan to. Even though she's around the same age as I was when I first tried it. I wouldn't be surprised if she's already tried it too."

Mom's eyes were about to pop out of their sockets. "Don't say that. Skye's a good girl."

"And I wasn't?"

"That's not what I'm saying. I'm just . . . Just be careful, okay?"

"I know I may not know much about being a parent, but I do think I can figure out what's appropriate and not appropriate to share. Why can't you just be happy that we're getting closer?"

"I am happy about that. You have no idea how happy that makes me. I just don't want you to overshare, that's all."

"I hear you," Nova said, sounding more frustrated than before.

Leah's head ping-ponged between her mom and her sister. She was glad they didn't try to pull her into their conversation and get her to side with one of them. She used to hate that. Even if she agreed with Nova, she couldn't go against her mom. So, Leah endured Nova's silent treatment when she decided that Leah was the enemy for not agreeing with her. The silence never lasted long, though. It hurt Nova more than Leah. There were times when Leah purposefully upset Nova so she could be quiet for a little while.

"How about we watch a movie? It's late, and we're all tired," Leah intervened.

"You girls go ahead. I think I'll call it a night." Mom kissed Leah, then Nova.

"Good night," Nova and Leah both said.

"So." Nova leaned over the island. "I've been wanting to speak with you alone."

"Oh yeah? About what?"

"Quinton."

Leah clutched her hands together, hoping Nova wouldn't notice how badly they were shaking. Her mom was right. She had to get herself together and fast. "What about him?" she managed to say without the words coming out a jumbled mess.

"He was over earlier today, and I know you're going to say leave it alone because he's married, and I get that, but I feel like there could be something still there between us." Nova held up both hands. "Don't get me wrong, I'm not interested in anything romantic. Nowhere near ready for that, but I think Quinton and I should spend more time together. You know . . . just to see."

"See what? Like you said, he's married."

"I know, but . . ."

Leah's chest tightened. "Nova. You don't want to put yourself through that. Let's focus on what's important right now like filing the necessary paperwork that shows you're alive and getting your driver's license and seeing what career path you want to take. There are so many other things you should think about right now." The words flew from Leah's mouth so fast that half of them were unexpected. She just needed to say whatever was necessary to put Nova's mind off the idea of a Nova–Quinton rekindling.

"Don't you think I'm focusing on that too? Quinton was my husband, Leah. He wasn't just some guy I was seeing. We didn't end our relationship. It was snatched away from us, and you weren't here earlier. You didn't see what I saw or felt what I felt. Quinton still loves me, and I believe a part of me still loves him, too, but we won't know if we don't at least spend time together."

The room was thick with tension, each word hanging heavier than the last. Leah felt her heart race, her palms sweaty as she listened to Nova pour out her feelings about Quinton—her Quinton.

"And what about his wife?" Leah asked.

"The wife that he's too ashamed to bring around? That wife?"

"I don't think he's ashamed."

It's not personal. She doesn't know it's you. Leah recited those words like it was an annoying song that she just couldn't get out of her head.

"Then explain why he hasn't brought her around. Every time I ask about her it's another excuse. Sounds like he's ashamed to me."

Leah's mind raced, thoughts colliding painfully into each other. How could she get through to Nova without telling everything? What could she say that would get her to see that a life between her and Quinton could never happen?

"Okay, Nova," Leah's voice cracked, frustration and anxiety knotted in her chest as the conversation spiraled. She needed to steer this away, to protect Nova's heart from the hurt she was sure to follow.

"Why are you getting upset? Is she your friend or something?"

"No. I mean . . . it has nothing to do with friendship or anything else. I just think it's wrong to go after a married man. That's all."

"Why do you even care so much? And please don't tell me you're still holding some kind of grudge against him like he's holding against Lance. At some point, both of you are going to have to let the past go and move on."

"It's not like that either."

"Then what is it like? Stop telling me what it's not like and tell me what it's like. Tell me what you're trying to say."

Leah took a deep breath, her entire body tensed, her voice barely a whisper as she confessed the truth that would change everything. "I'm married to Quinton. I'm his wife."

CHAPTER 23
Nova

Tonight was definitely a night filled with laughs. After hearing Leah say that she and Quinton were married, I understood how Skye felt when I told her that her dad used to be a rapper. Just like Skye, I couldn't stop laughing. Then, when I thought about the two of them together, I laughed even harder.

"I found the tapes," Skye said, running into the kitchen holding a cassette tape in her hand. Her smile dropped. "Did I interrupt something?" She stared at Leah.

"No. Teeah just said something that made me laugh."

Skye narrowed her eyes. "Why isn't Teeah laughing?"

I looked at Leah, who was apparently trying hard to make me believe she was telling the truth.

"Skye, could you give us a minute, please?" Leah asked.

"Okay, I'll go see if Gran has a tape player somewhere around here."

"Leah, seriously, you'll never convince me that you're married to Quinton, so please stop. Besides, even if you didn't hate him, you'd never do that to me." I went to the refrigerator and pulled out the pitcher of sweet tea. "You want some?" I asked.

"No, but Nova, we really need to talk."

"Talk. I'm listening." I opened the dishwasher and grabbed a glass.

"I'll wait." She pulled out a stool and sat.

After I fixed my tea, Leah motioned for me to sit across from her. I was hesitant because I didn't want to continue that conversation. There was no way Leah was married to Quinton. My mind refused to believe that could ever be true. Yet, a part of me knew that it was, and that was the part I worked hard to ignore.

"This isn't easy for me, and I need you to really hear me, okay?" Leah spoke slowly, like I had bad understanding.

"Okay."

"Quinton and I are married." She held up her hand, showing the wedding ring I'd seen at the hospital.

"You already told me your husband's name is Chris. Why are you lying like this?" I went from amused to not so amused anymore.

"It isn't," she said softly. "I told you that because it wasn't the right time to tell you the truth."

The more she spoke, the more I couldn't pretend. If her words didn't convince me, then the tears that fell from her eyes did. My body was numb. I couldn't think. I stared at her and tried to form words, but words were too hard to pronounce. Sweat dripped down my back, and my head pounded.

"Nova, please say something."

"This isn't a joke?"

Every cell in my body begged and pleaded for her to say it was. I needed to hear the words. I needed her to say that she was kidding. But she didn't say anything. She shook her head and cried harder. I'd never seen Leah so upset, and if this were any other situation, I'd run around the island, pull her in my arms, and hold her until she felt better, but this wasn't another situation. She was crying tears that I should've been crying. Feeling hurt that I was supposed to be feeling.

"Why?" was the only word I could get out before my throat tightened.

Her bottom lip was shaking. She opened her mouth, then closed it again. "We didn't mean for it to happen."

"You accidentally fell in love with my husband?" I asked, speaking just as slowly as she did earlier. I needed to see if those words sounded just as ridiculous to her ears as they did to mine.

"I know it sounds strange."

"No, it sounds stupid!" I shouted. "How do you not mean to fall in love with someone?"

"If you'll let me explain." More tears fell.

"I'm listening." I crossed my arms and bounced my leg against the floor so fast and hard that I knew there would be a dent when I moved.

"Please." She looked up. "I don't want Skye to hear any of this."

The room felt unbearably small as the revelation taunted me. The woman I'd been imagining, the unknown figure who had been filling my place, caring for my daughter—it was Leah. It was always Leah. My sister. The betrayal sliced through the confusion and left me breathless.

Every image of Leah and Skye together flashed through my mind—them laughing, talking, and sharing jokes that only they understood. Leah sharing precious moments with my daughter that should've been mine. Anger, disbelief, and an overwhelming sense of loss mingled inside me and rose to my throat, threatening to suffocate me. How could she? How could he? How could they keep this from me?

Then, another memory came to me and sent a dagger straight through my heart: "That day in the hospital. I said you all looked like a family, and no one said anything." A chuckle escaped me. "I thought your silence and your facial expressions were out of disgust at the thought of being married to each other, but, boy, was I wrong. You were scared. That's the familiar look I saw in both of your eyes. You were afraid that I would figure it out."

"Nova . . ."

"Why didn't you say anything then?" The question tore from my throat, raw and riddled with hurt.

"It wasn't the right time." Leah's voice cracked.

"And this was the right time. The one night I wanted to have where we didn't do anything but have fun. All I wanted was one night of fun, but I guess that was too much because you had to mess that up too."

Mama and Skye came rushing into the kitchen. Both their eyes were wide and darted between Leah and me.

"What's going on?" Mama asked, tightening the belt on her robe. "We can hear y'all all the way upstairs."

Leah's face looked pale, and her eyes rimmed with redness from tears I could tell she was fighting to hold back. She cleared her throat before saying, "I told her."

"Told her what?" Mama asked, stepping closer to us. The shakiness in her voice told me that she knew exactly what Leah was talking about.

I stared at Mama as another more unsettling question hit me. Had my entire family, the people I trusted most, seen me as so fragile, so broken, that they felt they couldn't tell me the truth?

"Everything," Leah answered softly, sounding like she did when she was a child and had to answer for something she knew she wasn't supposed to be doing.

"Leah." Mama's body slumped in disappointment, but I didn't understand why. It wasn't like it was news to her.

"So, it is true?" I asked for confirmation even though I already knew.

"I'm sorry, Nova. I didn't plan on telling you tonight, but when you were talking about your feelings for Quinton, I couldn't listen and not say anything." Leah's explanation was the confirmation I'd been waiting for.

Her words were heavy and piercing as they entered me, puncturing every part of my body. I looked around and inhaled the irony of that whole situation. I was in the kitchen, which still held the sweet smell of cinnamon and sugar from Mama's sweet-potato pies, yet everything around me felt sour and out of place.

Leah's shaky hand covered her mouth. Her eyes locked on me, and then she lowered her hands. Her mouth moved, but I didn't hear what she said. The announcement she made ricocheted off the walls and slammed into my ears over and over.

A surge of anger rushed through me as the heat inside me burned my nose. My head snapped toward Leah. "My entire family has been lying to me since the moment we were reunited."

"Nova, calm down, baby. You're getting yourself all worked up." Mama touched my arm, and I jerked away.

"Don't touch me!" I hollered so loudly that my ears rang.

Mama's eyes filled with tears. "I know you're upset . . ." Her voice dropped, but not so low that I didn't hear the tremble in her words. "We can talk about this."

Leah moved from her spot at the table to stand next to Mama. "It's not Mama's fault. Don't be upset with her."

As my gaze shifted and fell on Skye, stillness took me over for a moment amid my storm of emotions. Seeing her there, leaning against the doorway, one hand over her chest and the other hand lifted to her mouth, biting her nails, brought a pang of sympathy. Skye was caught in the middle of this whole mess. As angry as I was with everyone else, my heart ached for Skye. She was the only innocent person here. She didn't ask for this. She was forced into it, which sent me to another level of anger for Leah and Quinton.

"I'm sorry. I'm not upset with you, okay?"

Skye didn't respond. She just glanced at me, then back at Mama and Leah. Before, Skye seemed so mature to me, but as I watched her standing there, I saw the eyes of a little girl who was afraid. *Is she afraid of me?* The thought sank in heavy and hard.

"It's okay, Skye," Leah said.

"Don't talk to my daughter," I spat.

"Nova, don't do this," Leah begged. "Not in front of Skye."

Mama walked past me and over to Skye. "Go upstairs. I'll be there in a few minutes."

Skye's eyes were still on us as if she was in a trance and couldn't move.

"Go on," Mama urged.

Skye did as she was told, leaving me once again with the two people I wanted to be as far away from as I could get. How? That was what I kept asking myself. How? Leah and Quinton? That didn't make sense. They didn't make sense.

I couldn't stand still any longer. My feet needed to move. My body needed to move. I walked around the island, talking to no one in particular, but stating the truth filled me with a hurt I'd never felt before. I hated Adam for stealing my life, but I didn't love Adam. I didn't trust Adam. Adam didn't betray me.

My hand ran across the smooth granite as I made my second trip around the island. "So, what you're saying is that while I was in that room, fighting to stay alive, fighting to come home to my family, you and Quinton were busy falling in love and living happily ever after." I stopped when a thought occurred to me. "I guess me coming home wasn't the news you'd hoped to hear, was it?"

"That's not true." Leah came back to the island. She and Mama on one side and me on the other. Them against me. Or me against them. Either way, we were no longer on the same team.

I walked around the island and stood in front of Leah. "I never thought you'd hurt me like this."

"I wasn't try—"

"I hate you." I turned to Mama. "And I don't care what your Bible says about hate. If it sends me to hell, so what? It can't be any worse than this life has been." I walked out and left them standing there. I had nothing left to say. Nothing left to give. No more tears left to cry. I was empty of everything.

CHAPTER 24
Leah

Leah couldn't move. She wanted to. She *really* wanted to, but how could she when she was sure her heart had disconnected from the rest of her body? Was it possible to be living and dead at the same time? Because dead was how she felt on the inside.

"Leah. Sit down." Martha took her hand and pulled her into the living room.

As if on autopilot, Leah followed behind her mom. *I hate you . . . I hate you . . . I hate you.* That was what Nova said, wasn't it? Leah was sure she'd heard her sister say those words to her. No one had ever told her that they hated her, and Nova would've been the last person she'd expect to hear that from.

"I knew she'd be upset." Leah rubbed her chest. There was a tingling that wouldn't go away. Was she having a heart attack? How could she when Nova had snatched her heart out and thrown it away?

"Are you okay?" Martha sat beside Leah.

"Yes," Leah said, her breathing hard and labored. "I'm . . . fine."

"You don't sound fine. Let me get you a glass of water." Martha stood. Leah grabbed her mom's hand. "No. Don't go. Sit with me."

Martha did as Leah asked. Leah needed her mom to tell her that everything was going to be okay, but she'd never ask her mom to lie to her. Everything wasn't going to be okay because Nova hated her.

"I don't know what to do. How do I make this right?" Leah asked, or rather begged. When she was a child, she couldn't wait to grow up so her parents couldn't tell her what to do. Now it was all she wanted.

"There's nothing you can do but give her some time," Martha advised. "She needs to cool off, and maybe then she'll be ready to hear what you have to say."

"Or it could give her time to decide that she really does hate me," Leah said, afraid that too much time and space could backfire on her.

"She doesn't hate you. Her heart is wounded. A wounded heart makes an angry tongue. Remember, I used to tell you girls that all the time whenever you'd get into it with one of your friends."

Leah did remember. Of course, back then the angry tongues didn't mean as much to her as Nova's did. Her sister was her whole world. She couldn't lose her. Not again.

Footsteps on the stairs caused Leah and Martha to turn in that direction. Leah's heart thumped with anticipation, hoping it was Nova coming back to talk.

"Can I come down now?" Skye asked.

Martha waved Skye over. "I think Teeah can use some support."

When Skye sat, Martha stood. "I need to go and check on your sister." She looked back at Leah. "You're going to be okay. Our family will heal from this. God didn't get us this far to let everything fall apart. You have to believe that."

Leah nodded, but she didn't believe it. Her faith was never as strong as her mom's. Disappointment after disappointment made it hard to believe that everything would work out when sometimes it didn't. What if this was one of the times when it wouldn't? When Leah and Quinton married, Leah went against her mom's wishes. Every action came with a consequence. Sometimes it was good, and sometimes it wasn't. Experiencing the unbelievable miracle of having Nova back just to lose her again felt like a harsher punishment than Leah felt she deserved. How much was she expected to pay for her disobedience? Wasn't the hysterectomy enough?

"Teeah?" Skye laid her head on Leah's shoulder. "Gran's right, you know? You're going to be okay. We all are."

Leah leaned her head on top of Skye's and embraced the overwhelming feeling of love. Nova was in her room, hurt and broken, while her daughter was downstairs comforting Leah. That should've made Leah feel good. Skye chose her. But that would only matter if it were a competition. Leah and Nova never competed. That wasn't their relationship. They were always too busy celebrating with each other to compete.

"Are we still spending the night?" Skye asked, lifting her head long enough to ask the question, then laying it down again.

"Do you want to?" Leah knew it was best for her to leave, but if Skye wanted to stay, there was no way Nova would reject her.

"I'd rather go home."

Leah patted Skye's leg. "Then let's go."

Their bags were in the corner of the living room. Leah held hers on her shoulder and dug in her purse for the keys. Once she pulled them out, she looked at Skye, who was standing by the door waiting. "You mind going up and telling Gran we're leaving? I don't want to upset Nova any more tonight."

Skye dropped her bag and ran upstairs. She wasn't there long before she came back down. Her body drooped as she slowly made her way back downstairs.

"What's wrong?" Leah asked, her stomach clenched.

"Gran's really upset." Skye looked upstairs, then back at Leah. She lowered her voice. "She's in her room crying."

Leah put her things down.

"No, she said to tell you to drive safely and let her know when we make it home. I don't think she wants you to come up there," Skye said.

As badly as Leah wanted to comfort her mom, she also wanted to honor her wishes. She'd caused enough trouble for one night, so the least she could do was leave before she made things worse.

Leah was very familiar with the dark, narrow road that led out of Bayou. She should've been, since she'd been driving it since before she was legally able to drive. Unlike her mom, her dad was a risk-taker, which he'd proven when he'd allowed both Leah and Nova to drive him around Bayou since they were in elementary school and barely able to see over the steering wheel.

Tonight, though, the road was too dark and too narrow since her tears had stolen part of her sight.

"Teeah, are you sure you don't want me to drive?" Skye offered.

Leah lifted the top of her T-shirt to her eyes and wiped away the tears, which did no good since a steady flow was falling right after those were gone. "I'm fine," she said, her voice failing to convince either of them that she truly was.

Skye didn't offer any more words of comfort. She touched Leah's shoulder, which, for Leah, said enough.

Her mom and Skye wanted her to believe that Nova's words were out of anger, but Leah knew Nova. She may have changed over the years, but when it came to her words, her sister was still the same as Leah remembered. She didn't say anything that she didn't mean unless it was to save her life, like when she was in the room with Adam. When she told Leah she hated her, she meant it. Maybe not forever, but for tonight.

"I've never seen you this upset before." Skye's normal, upbeat tone was replaced by a quaver that Leah hadn't expected.

"Skye." Leah struggled to say her name without breaking down even more. The pain she heard in Skye's voice was overwhelming. Everything was a mess, and it was all Leah's fault—Nova's pain, Skye's hurt, and Martha's distress as a mother.

Leah was tangled in her thoughts for the rest of the ride home. Should she have waited to tell Nova? But how could she when she saw where Nova's thoughts were going? She didn't care that he had a wife. She wanted to explore the possibility that something was still there. Leah would've felt even worse knowing she'd allowed Nova to think that could happen when Leah knew the truth. She did know the truth, right? Then she remembered Nova's words.

"We didn't end our relationship. It was snatched away from us, and you weren't here earlier. You didn't see what I saw or felt what I felt. Quinton still loves me, and I believe a part of me still loves him too."

What did he say? What did he do to cause her to feel that way? Those were questions she needed Quinton to answer.

Nova's words haunted her until she pulled into her driveway. Leah parked and stared at her house. The blinds were closed, and all Leah could think about was Quinton in bed, sleeping peacefully, unaware that his world, like hers, was about to change forever.

"Skye." Leah shook Skye awake. "We're home, sweetie."

Skye reached down and picked up her backpack, which she used as her overnight bag, and opened the door. Leah didn't have the energy to bring anything inside except herself. Leah and Skye moved slowly through the house and up the stairs. No words were spoken as they gave each other a quick kiss and a tight hug, much tighter than their normal good-night hugs. But this was no normal night.

Leah opened her bedroom door and was greeted by a pitch-black room. She couldn't sleep without some type of noise, either the TV or radio. Something had to be playing in the background, or her mind would fill in the silence, and Leah would find herself up all night staring at the ceiling. Quinton, on the other hand, preferred a dark, quiet room. It didn't take long before he adjusted to Leah's need for sound.

Quinton stirred when Leah turned on the lamp that sat on the nightstand. He narrowed his eyes to give them a minute to adjust to the light. Once they did, he sat up straight. "Leah. What . . ." He looked toward the window. "What time is it?"

"Midnight." She sat on the bed next to him.

"What happened? Why aren't you at your mom's?"

"Quinton." His name was all she was able to get out before she broke down again.

"Leah, what's wrong? What happened? Where's Skye?" He scrambled from underneath the covers.

"She's fine." Leah reached for his hand as he tried to get out of the bed. "Skye's in her bedroom."

"What happened to the sleepover?"

"I told Nova." Leah bit her bottom lip.

"Told Nova what?"

"About us. I told her the truth."

"Why? We said after we talked with Dr. Yvonne. We said we would go to her together. What happened?"

"I know, and I wanted to wait, I really did, but . . ."

"But what?" Impatience coated his words.

"What happened when you went over there earlier?" Leah asked.

Quinton's brows dipped. He shook his head. "Nothing. I told you I tried to talk to her about Lance."

"Anything else?"

"Like what?"

"I don't know, but whatever you said or did gave her the impression that there was possibly something still there between the two of you. She started telling me how she thought the two of you should spend more time together to see if what she's feeling is true."

Quinton stood. He clasped his hands on top of his head. "That doesn't make sense. She knows I'm married even if she didn't know it was to you."

"And she didn't care about the wife that you were obviously embarrassed by, since you never brought her around." Leah held up both hands.

"That's what she said. When I saw that nothing I said was going to get through to her, I had no choice but to tell her the truth."

Quinton sat back on the bed. His head dropped into his hands. He stayed that way for several agonizing minutes.

Leah's stomach coiled into knots. Was he upset with her?

With his body still leaning forward, Quinton turned his head in her direction—just enough for her to hear his words but not enough for her to look into his eyes—or for him to look into hers.

"How's Nova?" he asked. "Never mind; I know how she is. Upset, obviously." He sat upright.

"Yes. She's upset. She's angry. And she's hurt." Leah paused before adding, "But so am I. Me. Your wife. I'm hurt. I'm hurt, Quinton," Leah cried. She repeated the words, and each time she sobbed harder.

Quinton erased the space between them and pulled her into his arms. He held her tight. "Okay, babe. Okay. I know you're hurting."

Leah pushed herself out of his embrace. "Then why don't you act like it? I get why you asked about Nova, but for once, can you check on me first? I just want to be someone's number one. Is that too much?" Leah spoke words that she'd never said out loud. Never even realized it bothered her until that moment. It was how her life had always been, and she accepted that for what it was, but tonight that wasn't good enough.

"What do you mean? You are my number one." He said words she wished she believed, but they both knew that she wasn't.

"Mom was Daddy's number one. Nova was Mom's number one. Mom would say that's not true, but everyone knew it. Nova's the oldest, she and Mom had a bond that I never had, and I was okay with that because I knew that one day I'd have a family of my own, and I'd be someone's number one, but Skye's your number one. As she should be," Leah added quickly before Quinton could dispute it. "She's your baby girl, and for years she was all you had, but the reality is that I've never been anyone's number one."

"Leah." That was all he said. He didn't deny it, and he didn't protest it because how could he?

"Actually, I'm wrong. There was a time before you and Nova started dating when I was her number one. I always knew if no one else in the world loved me, my sister did." Leah paused because the lump in her throat blocked her words. "But now she hates me."

"She doesn't hate you, Leah."

"She literally said *I hate you*."

"You know what they say about hurt people. She wanted to hurt you as much as she was hurting," Quinton explained.

Leah shook her head. "You didn't see her eyes when she spoke those words. She may as well have been looking at Adam. That's the level of sincerity she held in her eyes. She really does hate me."

CHAPTER 25

Nova

I woke up the next morning in the same position I was in when I lay down last night. The only time I moved was when Mama came up to check on me. I turned my head to the wall, and eventually she got the message that I wasn't going to talk.

Before last night, morning was the only peaceful time of my day because that meant all the bad dreams were left in my sleep. Not anymore, though. The bad dream followed me as I slept, and it was still there when I woke up. My sister was really married to my husband. Ex-husband? I didn't know what to call him since we never got a divorce. How did that work, anyway? I would ask Mama, but I was just as upset with her. Well, maybe not just as upset, but I was upset. She lied to me, too, and I bet she went to their wedding. Did she wear the same dress that she wore to mine? Did she help Leah with her hair and makeup like she helped me? Did she and Daddy dance all night at their wedding too?

There were too many questions and no one to answer them. No one I wanted to talk with, anyway. My body felt like it weighed a ton as I pushed myself off the bed and slowly made my way down the hallway and to the bathroom. Like I did every morning, I looked at myself in the mirror, but the image didn't feel the same as before. I touched the braids that Leah did and once again . . . rage.

I rummaged through the drawers but didn't find what I needed. I went into Mama's room. She was sitting on the side of the bed, still dressed in her pajamas, which wasn't like Mama. She acted like sleep was a terrible thing that she did only because it was required, not because she wanted to. As soon as the sun came up, Mama was out of the bed and dressed for the day. She'd always been that way.

"Good morning." Mama's groggy voice greeted me when I walked past her and into her bathroom. "What are you doing?" She came to the doorway.

I was too busy pulling out drawers and moving things around to answer her. Then, in the last drawer, I found them. I held up the scissors and stomped past Mama and back into the hall bathroom.

"What do you need with those?" Mama asked, sounding more alert than she did a moment ago.

I didn't answer. I still had no words for her right then. Instead, I proceeded with my task of removing all traces of Leah from my life, starting with those braids. I cut the first one.

"Nova!" Mama's eyes were about to pop out of their sockets. "Why are you doing that?"

I kept cutting. It didn't matter if I was cutting my own hair, which I was sure I was, but I didn't care. Mama could only stand to watch me for so long before she bolted from the doorway and closed herself in her bedroom. I kept cutting until every single braid was on the bathroom floor.

When I saw myself in the mirror this time, I didn't recognize the person who stared back at me. Almost like I didn't recognize her when she was locked in that bedroom. I ran my hand over my hair, which was about a couple of inches long. Other than a monthly trim at the salon, I'd never had my hair cut before . . . ever. Maybe, if I had any feelings at all, I'd be upset by this new look.

Mama's room door opened, and she came back and stood in the doorway again. Through the mirror, we stared at each other. Mama's hand covered her mouth. Tears ran down her face. My eyes slid back to my reflection. Once again, I felt nothing.

"I'll get you some shampoo and conditioner," Mama said.

"Don't bother." I dropped to my knees, scooped up all the hair, and pushed it into the small trash can. "I'll take it out later," I told Mama when I walked past her and back into the bedroom. I opened the top drawer, removed the silk scarf, and tied it around my head.

I threw on a warm-up and tennis shoes and skipped breakfast and coffee. There was only one place I wanted to be. Outside in the backyard. Alone. That was the plan for today, but I should've known things wouldn't go my way. Did they ever?

It felt like I'd just sat when Mama opened the back door and stole the dream I had of being by myself.

"Nova. Dr. Yvonne's here to see you." Mama stood aside, and a woman who looked to be around the same age as Mama walked down the steps and across the yard to me. Dr. Yvonne's gray locs caused me to touch the silk scarf that covered my new hairstyle.

"Hi, Nova. It's really nice to finally meet you." Dr. Yvonne's voice was warm and rich like molasses. She extended her hand to me.

I shook her hand, which was unbelievably soft.

"Mind if I join you?" Dr. Yvonne asked, slipping her purse from her shoulder as if I'd already agreed with her sitting and invading my space.

My immediate thought was to push her away. To create the distance that I craved today, especially since Leah was the person who arranged my sessions with Dr. Yvonne. Even knowing all that, I still found myself nodding in agreement. A part of me wanted to hold on to the hate that I felt so deep inside me, and another part wanted . . . no, needed . . . someone to tell me everything was going to be okay. That I wouldn't feel this way forever.

Dr. Yvonne took the chair across from me. The firepit sat between us.

"This is really nice," she said, looking around the backyard, which wasn't as big as the front, but almost. "I'd love to have land like this where I can garden."

Mama would love Dr. Yvonne from that statement alone. They could spend time together in the yard, gardening and drinking tea.

If Dr. Yvonne loved to gossip, then she and Mama would be friends for life.

"Let me guess," I said, drawing Dr. Yvonne's attention away from the landscape. "Mama called you and asked you to come over because she thinks I'm having a nervous breakdown. Is that right?" I crossed my arms and tilted my head while I waited for confirmation.

Dr. Yvonne's small black glasses sat at the edge of her nose. She looked over them and at me. "Believe it or not, I was the one who called. I wanted to see if it was okay for me to come and meet you today."

"Not," I said.

"Pardon?" Dr. Yvonne narrowed her eyes and leaned forward.

"You said, 'believe it or not.' I choose not."

Dr. Yvonne smiled. "Oh, but it's true."

"So, you always see clients on a Sunday?" I asked, thinking I'd caught her in a lie.

"Not always, but I felt bad that I wasn't here to meet you sooner. However, to be honest, your mom did fill me in on the news you received last night."

"Figures."

"But"—she held up her finger—"that doesn't change the fact that I initiated this visit. You've been back home, what, almost a week now, right?"

"Seven days since I've been home and nine days since I was freed from that house," I answered without hesitation.

"Seven days," Dr. Yvonne repeated. "How have you been feeling?"

I laughed. "Are you sure you want that answer?"

"Of course." She crossed her legs and smoothed out her long wool skirt, which covered most of her leather boots. "This is our time to sit and chat. I want to get to know a little more about you."

"There's not much to know. I spent fifteen years locked in a room. Now I'm out, and I don't know if that's a good thing anymore."

"I know it can't be easy coming back after all those years apart from your family and the world, but you have to know that being out here and having your freedom is a gift that you may not feel right now, but you will one day."

"When? Maybe I'd believe it if you could tell me when that'll happen. I'm a stranger in my own life. I don't fit in anywhere anymore. You can't even begin to imagine what that feels like."

"No, I can't, but I do know that there's something incredible waiting for you on the other side of your journey. My job is to be here with you and help you get there."

I stared at a leaf that drifted from the tree and onto the ground and thought about Dr. Yvonne's words. It was hard to imagine what the other side of this journey could look like. Based on how my life had gone so far, I'd say that the other side was just as bad or worse.

"Do you believe that some people were born to be miserable?" I asked Dr. Yvonne as I thought about my existence.

She didn't answer right away, which I liked. It meant she was giving my question some serious thought. I felt like everyone said what sounded right without really thinking about the answer. Then again, maybe not. I thought of how quiet Leah, Mama, and Quinton would get whenever I asked about Quinton's wife. They took forever to answer, and it wasn't because they were giving my question some serious thought. It was to think of a lie.

"No, I don't believe people are born to be miserable." Dr. Yvonne unfolded her legs and pushed herself to the edge of her chair before she continued. "Life can certainly deal some incredibly difficult and painful experiences, which can cause you to feel like you're trapped in a cycle of suffering. But I believe that everyone has the capacity for growth, healing, and finding those special moments of joy and peace. And I believe that all of that can happen even in some of our darkest times."

"All of that sounds amazing, but it's really hard to find joy and peace from my darkest times. What's joyful or peaceful about having your life stolen away from you? About coming into a world where you can't even make a simple cup of coffee without help? Or where you find out that the people you trusted the most betrayed you the most?" I shook my head. "I'm sorry, Dr. Yvonne, but I'll never believe that there's anything more for me than what I'm feeling right now."

"And Skye?" She lifted her thin arched brows. "I saw that you have a seventeen-year-old daughter. What do you think about when you think of her?"

I gave her question some thought, just as she did with mine. "Skye gives me a bittersweet feeling," I admitted. "Yes, I love my daughter, but she doesn't feel like mine. She's more Quinton and Leah's daughter than mine." Those words jackhammered through my heart.

I wrapped my arms around myself, attempting to provide comfort that didn't reach the places that needed it the most.

"You're cold." Dr. Yvonne stood. "I won't keep you out here any longer. Like I said, I wanted to stop by and get to know you, but tomorrow we'll start our first session, and don't worry." She reached back and picked up her purse. "I have enough faith and hope for the both of us. You're going to be fine, Nova. I'm going to do everything in my power to make sure that you are."

I nodded instead of speaking because my throat was swollen with uncertainty. I could tell she really believed her words, and I almost felt bad about the disappointment I knew she'd feel when she saw for herself that no matter how hard she tried, my life wasn't meant to be one of joy and happiness.

Mama came into the kitchen while I was making a sandwich to take back upstairs to my bedroom. That short session with Dr. Yvonne was exhausting.

"Dr. Yvonne seems like a nice lady." Mama stood across from me.

I spread mayonnaise on my bread as if it were the most important task in the world. "Yep."

Mama cleared her throat. "Nova, the only reason I didn't tell you about Quinton and Leah sooner was because the thought of anything else hurting you broke me into pieces. I'm your mother, and my job is to try as hard as I can to protect you however I can. I know it may have made things worse, but you have to understand that I was only doing what I felt in my heart was the right thing to do at the time. I did the same thing you would've done if it was Skye—if you had a choice to share something that could hurt her or give her a few more days of happiness. Can you say that you would've chosen the hurt over the happiness for Skye?"

Her words were an anchor that caused my heart to sink.

"I have to be honest. I didn't agree with their relationship, and I didn't agree even more with the marriage. I know you feel hurt and betrayed and everything else, and you have a right to that, but let me tell you this. Even though I didn't like it, I knew they didn't fall in love to hurt you, me, or anyone else." Mama exhaled. "And that's all I need to say about that, so whenever you feel it in your heart to forgive me for trying to protect you, well, you know where to find me." Mama walked out of the kitchen, leaving me to ponder the words she expelled.

Tears burned my eyes, and I quickly wiped them away. I was so tired of crying. For once, I wanted to be happy. I wanted to be normal, whatever that was. I was about to put the bread, meat, and the rest of the fixings away until I had an idea.

I walked into the living room where Mama was in her recliner reading her daily devotional. She removed her readers and looked up when I sat next to her in Daddy's chair. The first time I'd sat there a few days ago, I'd curled up and cried so long that I'd fallen asleep. Somehow sitting where he used to sit gave me a sense of comfort that I needed.

"I thought you might be hungry." I gave Mama the sandwich I'd made for her.

A wide smile spread across her face. It wasn't until she bit into the sandwich and made a face that I remembered.

"I'm sorry, I forgot you don't like mustard," I said, reaching for the sandwich.

Mama moved the sandwich out of my reach. "I love it today," she said, taking another bite, followed by a pained expression that she tried unsuccessfully to hide behind a smile.

I wanted to laugh, because that was definitely something I could see myself doing for Skye. I didn't care if she'd served me dirt pie. I'd painfully eat that pie like it was the best food I'd ever tasted.

"I don't know what I'm supposed to feel or how I'm supposed to react. But I do understand why you didn't want to tell me. I would've done anything to protect Skye from bad news, too, if I could."

Mama's eyes watered. "So, you understand, then? You know I wouldn't do anything to hurt you on purpose."

"I understand why you didn't say anything, but it still hurts—just not as much as the hurt that Leah and Quinton caused. I don't know if I'll ever be able to forgive them. I don't know if I want to."

My reality was that I lived in a world that I didn't understand and was too afraid to explore. Even if I wanted to, I couldn't stop talking to Mama forever. I needed her, but more than that, I didn't want to be angry with her. She was my mama, and it was bad enough that I didn't have a daddy, and it wasn't like Mama was so young. I couldn't spend the rest of whatever time we had together upset with her.

"Forgiveness won't be easy, but the Bible tells us . . ."

"Mama, please don't start with that Bible stuff, or I'm going back upstairs to lock up in my room. I said I understood how you felt as a mother, but I need you to understand that I'll never get how you feel as a Christian. How you can believe in a God that allows us to suffer. Or who can take a father away from his family, like he did with Dad, or a mother away from her child like he did with me." My heart raced, and I closed my eyes to calm myself down.

"Okay, I don't wanna upset you." Mama held her hands toward me as if to block the impact of my words.

"Then stop talking about God. Don't ever speak to me about God or the Bible or church again, and you won't upset me."

The corners of Mama's mouth turned down, and she pressed her lips together as if she had to physically block the words that she wanted to express so badly. She released her lips, and a soft sigh escaped. Even though it was barely audible, it was enough for me to feel the weight of her disappointment. Growing up, Mama and Daddy always used to say that as long as they gave us a good Christian foundation and made sure we knew Jesus, then they had no doubt that we'd be okay. It wasn't easy for Mama to accept that I didn't believe in her Jesus anymore, but that was something she'd have to learn to get over. Nothing she could say or do would change my mind on that subject.

The crunch of someone's tires against the gravel was a welcome distraction. Until I realized that meant someone was here. I looked over at Mama, who was looking toward the front door. I abandoned Daddy's chair and walked to the stairs, prepared to escape into my bedroom if I needed to. I wasn't ready to see Leah or Quinton. They'd both been calling, because I'd overheard Mama answering questions that only they would've been asking.

Mama got up and looked out the front window. She looked back at me and smiled. "It's Lance. He's dropping off a box of decorations I left at the church."

It was hard to believe it was yesterday when I almost burned Mama's house down and Lance came to my rescue. It seemed like forever ago with everything else that came after that. Before yesterday and being out in the backyard watching him working like he used to with Daddy, thinking of Lance would cause dread to come over me, but I was serious when I said I wanted to let all of that go. When Mama said his name, a flood of memories hit me out of nowhere. Lance and I rode our bikes to Ms. Rose's house, the candy lady, for candy that we'd hurry and eat before either of us made it home. Lance and I camped outside in the backyard and talked about all the things we'd do when we were grown and had families of our own. In middle school, we tried to learn the latest dance moves or coach each other on how to talk to someone we liked. Both of us feeling those first-day jitters when we hit high school and reminding each other that we'd always have each other's back, no matter what.

My heart shattered at the memory of us sitting underneath our tree, the big one in the backyard where we'd spent many summers enjoying snowballs or frozen cups. A tree that once held our best memories now held my biggest regret. The look on Lance's face when I told him we couldn't be friends anymore. I threw away the only true friendship I've ever had, and for what? To marry a man who could turn around and marry my sister? I was such an idiot.

"Hey, Nova." Lance held a big box in front of him.

"Hey." I stood. "Need some help?"

He chuckled. "Nah, I think I can handle it, but do you mind removing this for me?" He leaned forward, as if he was taking a bow.

I reached over and pulled off his hat. "Still don't wear caps inside, I see."

"Your dad only had to get on to me one time for me to remember. I'll never make that mistake again." He laughed.

Mama playfully hit Lance's arm. "That's because you were at the dinner table. You know that."

"He said inside . . . period. I'm never taking any chances." He shook his head.

"Well, Frank's gone now, bless his soul. I think you're safe," Mama said, giving Lance a sad smile.

"I don't trust it." Lance shifted the box. "If anyone can come back and get on to me, it's Mr. Frank."

We all laughed.

"Come put that box in here for me," Mama said.

They weren't gone long before Lance came back alone. I didn't need to ask where Mama was. I already knew she was going through that box and pulling out her decorative pumpkins and other fall decor to put around the house. Mama loved that kind of stuff. Between the house and the church, she was always decorating for something.

"Can I talk with you for a second?" Lance asked.

"Sure." I pointed toward the back of the house. "You wanna go out back?"

He held out his hand as if to say, "After you."

"I was out here earlier talking to my therapist . . . Well, doctor, actually. She's a psychiatrist. Can you believe it? I have a psychiatrist. What does that say about me?" I chuckled nervously. I wasn't sure why I shared all of that with him, but it didn't feel wrong.

"It says that you're smart enough to let someone help you. The world would be a better place if more people did that."

Needing to change the subject, I asked, "So, what did you want to talk about?"

"Yesterday." He rubbed his hands together. "You said something that I couldn't stop thinking about."

"I did? What?" The only thing I clearly remembered about yesterday was what was said to me. "Quinton and I are married," Leah's voice played in my mind.

"You said that you blamed me for what happened to you. Nova, I had no idea that . . ."

I held up my hand. "No, Lance, listen." I exhaled, then twisted the hanging edge of my headscarf around my finger. "I did blame you, but a huge part of me knew that it wasn't your fault. It was easier to blame you than myself."

"Why would you blame yourself? Nova, no one is to blame for what happened to you except the guy who kidnapped you. He's the only bad guy in that situation."

"I know, but . . ."

"No buts. You had every right to leave out of your hotel room, go to the bar for drinks, and make it back to your room unbothered. The fact that you didn't isn't because of anything you did wrong."

"Everyone keeps saying that. Maybe one day I'll get it." I tried to unwind my finger from the edge of the scarf, but somehow, I pulled the scarf off my head.

Lance's eyes shot up to my hair. I waited for the laugh I knew was going to explode through him, but it never came.

"You cut your hair?" Not even a hint of a smile played on his face.

"Something like that." I frantically tried to untie the scarf, which was now in a knot. My hands were shaking. I couldn't lift my eyes to look at Lance even if I wanted to.

The next thing I knew, Lance had taken the seat right beside me. He reached over and removed the scarf from my hands, which were still shaking. After he untied the knot, I waited for him to give it back, but he didn't. He stood. "May I?" he asked, holding the scarf, already folded and ready to go over my head.

I twisted my body to the side so my back was to him. That was when it happened. My heart pounded, but the rest of my body froze. As soon as he put the scarf on my head, I jerked around, then jumped from my seat.

"What's wrong? Are you okay?" He held up his hands.

I tried to speak while trying to remind myself to breathe. *It's Lance,* I told myself. *It's just Lance.* I tied the scarf over my head. "I'm okay," I told him, still struggling for air.

"You don't sound okay." He took a step back. "Do you need to go inside? I can get you some water." He took another step back toward the house.

"No. No, I'll be fine. I just need a minute," I said, focusing my attention on the white fence that lined the yard. Once I was able to speak, I turned to him. "It's okay. You can sit." He seemed hesitant at first, which made me feel even worse. He didn't do anything wrong, but he was acting like he had, and that was because of me. "I think being out here and talking with you almost made me feel like I was normal again. Then, when my back was to you, I kept thinking . . ."

"Thinking what?" he asked.

I couldn't say the words out loud. I couldn't tell him that I expected him to hurt me because I wasn't waiting on *him*. I was waiting on

Adam, but Adam wasn't there, and if I told Lance that, he'd think something was wrong with me, and he wouldn't be wrong.

"I just wanted to do it myself," I said, knowing he'd never believe that, but he didn't push the issue.

"Nova."

All he said was my name, and that was all it took for the dam that had built inside me to erupt. I'd held it together all day, but ever since I was a little girl, Lance had always been the person I could cry to and not feel ridiculous. Of course, there was Leah, too, but once I knew how much Leah hated Quinton—which was laughable now—and after she made it clear she didn't care for him, I stopped telling her about little fights we'd have. I knew she didn't want to hear it. Lance probably didn't, either, but he never let on that it bothered him, so I kept sharing.

Lance leaned closer and pulled me into him. "Everything's going to be okay, Nova," he whispered.

I pulled myself together and wiped my eyes. "Leah told me that she and Quinton are married." I could barely say the words without bursting into tears again.

"Oh." That was all Lance could say.

That was when I remembered something he'd said yesterday. "Is that what you meant when you said I'm not the one keeping secrets from you? Were you talking about Leah and Quinton?"

Lance lowered his head, then looked at me. "Yeah, but that was childish, and I shouldn't have said it. Quinton just gets to me sometimes."

I thought about that night in the hotel room. I needed to leave because of that very reason. I loved Quinton . . . had loved Quinton . . . or maybe it was still love. I had no idea anymore, and it didn't matter now. When his wife was a faceless person, I was open to the idea that maybe there was a chance, but not only did his wife have a face, at one time our faces looked very similar.

"But anyway," Lance continued, "I wanted to ask how you're doing after finding out, but I guess I already know." He glanced down at the spot on his cotton shirt where my tears were still evident.

"Sorry." I reached over and wiped the spot, as if that would help.

"I'm kidding. It's all good." He smiled, showing off his deep dimples that I used to stick the eraser end of pencils in.

"So," I said, straightening my back and wiping away any leftover moisture that was still around my eyes. "Enough about all that. I want to know about you. How's your life been?" I gasped when I remembered his sister. "Carmen. How is she?"

"Carmen's good. Still aggravating as hell, but other than that, she's doing great. She lives in Texas now, but you wouldn't know it as often as she's here."

"I'd love to see her one day."

"She's coming back this weekend to do a gender reveal for her best friend."

"What in the world is a gender reveal?"

Lance laughed. "That's what I asked when I first heard of it. It's like a baby shower, but the parents reveal the sex of the baby. Carmen said that some people cut a cake, and if the inside is pink, it's a girl, and if it's blue, it's a boy, but they have different ways of announcing it." Lance reached into his jeans pocket and pulled out his cell phone. "Look, I'll show you." He found a video on his phone and gave it to me to watch. The video showed different couples finding out the sex of their baby, so, apparently, the gender wasn't just revealed to their family and friends. Everyone was surprised when they saw pink or blue balloons flying from a box or the cannon with pink or blue smoke. It was obvious that these gender reveals were a big deal.

Once I'd seen enough, I gave Lance his phone back. "I still don't get it. When I was pregnant with Skye, all I did was tell Mama I was having a girl, and fifteen minutes later, everyone in Bayou knew." I held on to that memory and the warm feeling that flowed through me when I thought about being pregnant with Skye. I could honestly say that other than my wedding day, finding out I was having a baby girl was one of the best days of my life.

"Yeah, I remember my grandma called and told me." Lance rubbed his hands against his jeans, then cleared his throat.

I didn't know what to say. Lance and I weren't friends then, so I didn't call him and tell him that I was having a baby. I knew his mom had told him, though. She and Mama were good friends, and I had no doubt that his mom kept him as informed on my life as Mama had kept me informed on his. Mama and Daddy loved Quinton like a son, but it wasn't the same as the love they had for Lance. He was truly like one of theirs, and neither of them was pleased when they heard that we weren't friends anymore. To this day, I still didn't know how they'd found out. It wasn't like Lance and I announced it.

"I'm sorry," I said softly. "I'm surprised you're even talking to me after the way I hurt you back then."

"Hey, you were in love. I didn't expect you to choose me over Quinton."

"I shouldn't have had to," I said, voicing what I'd always felt.

"Listen," Lance said, "we have all the time in the world to discuss past choices and mistakes or what have you. I'm just happy to have you back now."

"Me too." I leaned over and rested my head on Lance's shoulder like I used to when life felt heavy. Of course, back then, nothing was as heavy as the load I'd been carrying around the past fifteen years. "I missed you so much."

"I missed you, too, Nova Boo."

A laugh from the deepest part of my stomach flew through my mouth.

"Nova Boo. Wow, I'd forgotten all about that." He started calling me that when he was at our house one day, and Mama was fussing about someone who'd worked her nerves. She said the person was such a bugaboo. Lance had never heard that word before, and when Mama told him she called all annoying people that, the name Nova Boo was born. The only difference between Mama's people and me was that I annoyed Lance on purpose. It was fun. The first time I heard Destiny's

Child's song "Bug a Boo" was after our friendship had ended. That was one of the worst times ever. I couldn't escape that song for nothing. It was played on the radio, on television, at parties . . . everywhere. The more I heard it, the bigger the pain of missing him grew.

Lance's visit was what I needed that day. Even though I knew the day would come when we'd have to talk about the hurt I caused him and myself, I was relieved that he didn't want to deal with it today. Today, we stuck to safe subjects for the rest of our visit, which meant not talking about Leah or Quinton, and I was fine with that.

CHAPTER 26
Leah

Something yanked Leah out of her sleep. She sat straight up and looked around the room. The other side of the bed, where Quinton should've been, was empty. Her mind was so jumbled that for a second she thought he must've left for work, which meant she was late, but then everything came back to her, and she realized it was Sunday.

Leah was still groggy since it had been almost two o'clock in the morning when she decided to take one of her pills. She didn't take them often, only when she really needed them, like after she lost her dad. The grief was overwhelming, and Leah finally admitted it to her therapist, who urged her to see her doctor and ask for a mild anti-anxiety medication. She told Quinton they were for her migraines. She could barely admit to herself that there were days when she needed a pill to help her deal with everyday life. Taking the pill almost had the opposite effect. It made her feel like maybe she wasn't the strong person her dad always said she was.

The one thing Leah wished the pill did was erase all her memories from last night—the ones that haunted her while she tried to sleep. The look of pain and then anger that she saw on Nova's face was something she'd never forget. She'd also never forget that she was the cause of it all.

"No, I can't do this," Leah said, throwing the comforter off her. "I'm going to get up. I'm going to get dressed." She looked over at Quinton's empty side of the bed. "I'm going to find out where my husband is." As soon as the words left her mouth, the answer entered her head. It was Sunday, and Quinton was going to church with his friend Mario, who was running for city council. Why didn't he wake her up, though? Unless he didn't want her to go. Was that it?

"Stop it!" Leah fussed to herself.

She pushed herself off the bed and went into the bathroom to wash up. The reflection that greeted her in the mirror wasn't one Leah was used to seeing. She couldn't remember the last time she had a good night's sleep, and the bags underneath her eyes showed it.

Leah was moving in slow motion. She didn't have the energy to do anything but lie down and wait for the day to pass, and tomorrow she'd have work to keep her mind busy. What she really wanted to do was go to her mom's and try to talk with Nova, but that would be a waste of time. As angry as Nova was last night, there was no way she'd want to see Leah, let alone talk with her.

By the time Leah had dressed and pulled her hair up into a bun, she started to feel a little better. Something about fixing herself up always helped her mood. It wasn't a huge uplift, but she'd take whatever she could get.

The bedroom door opened, and Quinton walked through, with his coat to his black suit draped over his arm. "Hey, you're up," he said, throwing the coat on the bed and walking to the bathroom door where Leah was standing. He leaned down and kissed her lips. "How are you feeling?"

"I'm okay. How was church?" she asked, wanting to talk about anything other than last night.

"It was good. I started to wake you, but you'd just gone to sleep a few hours ago." Quinton loosened his tie and then disappeared into their walk-in closet.

This Sunday, like all the other days since they found out Nova was alive, didn't feel like it used to. How could eight days change their lives so much? After church, Quinton, Leah, and Skye usually went to brunch, then came home and relaxed until Leah or Quinton, and sometimes both, cooked dinner. Sundays were their days to simply exist with each other, and Leah loved it.

"What are you doing today?" Quinton asked.

That question always meant there was something he wanted them to do together or something he wanted or needed to do, and he had to make sure that Leah didn't have plans for them already.

"I'm not—" A knock on their door cut off her words.

"Come in, Skye," Leah said.

"Hey, are we still going to the bookstore?" Skye asked Leah.

"The bookstore?" Leah repeated, trying to remember why they were going there today.

"Remember my project? I have to do a report to go along with the display. I told you about it a few weeks ago. We were supposed to go last Sunday, but we were in Mississippi, so are we going today?"

Leah nodded, the details clicking into place. "Right, the new bookstore with the coffee shop." She and Skye visited a few weeks ago, and both of them loved how vibrant and creative the space felt. A few people were sitting at tables working on their laptops, and they agreed that would be their new weekend workspace whenever they wanted a change from working at home or the neighborhood library.

Leah looked at Quinton. "I guess I'm going to the bookstore."

"Great," Skye said. "I'll go get dressed."

"You asked what I was doing. Did you make plans for us or something?" Leah asked, pulling the covers back to straighten the sheets on their bed.

Quinton shook his head. "Nah, that's perfect, actually. I thought I'd go and hang out with Mario for a little while today. A lot's been going on with him. I think the campaign is starting to get to him and Jen."

"Well, she wasn't too happy about him running in the first place," Leah said, recalling the conversation she and Quinton had about Mario and his fiancée, Jennifer.

The one thing about the whole conversation that bothered Leah the most was Quinton's siding with Mario. Even though Jen, as they all called her, made it clear that she wasn't interested in being a politician's wife again, Mario still moved forward with his plans. Jen had gone through so much scandal with her first husband, a former mayor of Magnolia, another small town not far from Baton Rouge. She'd had enough of that life, so meeting Mario, an attorney who had no political aspirations, was ideal for her.

"Things change. People change. Jen should understand that," Quinton said when Leah expressed how wrong Mario's move forward was, knowing how Jen felt about it.

That was the first time since they'd been together that Leah feared that the Quinton she knew and had fallen in love with had gone back to the Quinton she couldn't stand. When Nova and Quinton were dating, Quinton had an idea of the woman's role and the man's role in the relationship. Nova used to tell Leah how Quinton didn't cook or wash dishes because that was the woman's job. Leah hated it. Nova worked and took care of Skye, so Quinton should've been willing to help her out. Of course, whenever Leah said something, Nova defended him, so eventually, Leah let it go.

That wasn't the Quinton Leah fell in love with, though. The man who won her heart was the one who was at her apartment every day cooking and cleaning when she fell and broke her arm. He was the guy who combed Skye's hair almost better than Nova did. He played tea parties and polished Leah's nails when she said she couldn't stand to look at them anymore. That was her Quinton.

"I know I keep asking this, but you're sure nothing's wrong?" Quinton asked, standing in front of Leah and buttoning his light-blue shirt, which he wore with dark-blue jeans.

"Well, I'd be better if my sister didn't hate me, but I guess we can't always have what we want, right?"

"I'm telling you that she'll come around. Give her some time, and you'll see."

Quinton tried to put on a brave face, but she knew it was bothering him too. How could it not? He was already dealing with the guilt of what happened to Nova, and now, there was the guilt of hurting her. He'd never admit it to Leah, though.

It wasn't until Nova went missing that Leah learned how much she and Quinton were alike. They both had the need to protect. To make sure everyone else was okay. It was almost two years after losing Nova when Leah and Quinton saw each other break down for the first time. Leah had gone to help him clean out Nova's things, which she'd finally convinced him to get rid of. It wasn't healthy for him to sit in the house, looking at her clothes every day, knowing the likelihood of her coming back was, in their minds back then, impossible. That day was almost as hard as the day they'd learned she was gone. It was the final act, and Leah didn't expect it to hit her as hard as it did. Skye was with her parents so they could work uninterrupted. It was a good thing that she was because Leah couldn't imagine a four-year-old walking into that closet and seeing her dad and her aunt wailing like babies.

"Come here." Quinton pulled Leah into him. "I hate to see you like this." He tightened his hold on her.

Leah laid her head against his chest as Nova's words about feeling that there was still something between her and Quinton echoed in her mind. What should've been a simple, comforting moment between Leah and her husband was overshadowed with doubt. What happened to make Nova feel that way? "It won't feel like this forever. That's what I keep reminding myself," she said, reminding herself more than Quinton. Leah lifted herself off him. "I'd better get dressed. Skye will be ready to go soon."

After Leah finished dressing, she stopped by the door to Skye's room. "I'll be downstairs when you're ready."

"Okay," Skye said over the music she had playing.

While Leah waited, she sat in the family room and called her mom. It wasn't like she and her mom saw each other every day or talked every day, but today, Leah really missed her. She needed her, but so did Nova.

"How's Nova?" Leah asked when her mom answered the phone. Martha's deep sigh was the answer.

"I'm sorry, Mom," Leah said, wishing she could carry all the pain she'd caused them.

"You don't have anything to be sorry about," her mom said, her voice shaking with each word. "Like I told you last night, we'll get through this as a family."

"Where's Nova now?" Leah asked.

"She's outside, sitting by the firepit. But she had somewhat of a breakdown or something this morning. She cut her hair."

"What?" Leah almost dropped her phone. "Cut it how?"

"Cut what?" Quinton asked, causing Leah to really drop the phone that time.

She held her chest as she glared at him. "What are you doing?" she fussed, reaching down to pick up the phone.

"I'm sorry, I thought you heard me coming downstairs." He pointed toward the stairs.

"Mom, I dropped the phone. What were you saying?" Leah put the phone on speaker so Quinton could hear as her mom explained how Nova found some scissors and cut almost all her hair off.

Leah didn't have to ask why. She already knew. Nova was trying to cut out the braids that Leah had done for her. The fact that her sister would go to those extremes to get rid of them showed Leah how bad things were. Not that she needed proof, but it was confirmation.

"Hold on, Leah. I think this is Dr. Yvonne calling the house phone. I'll call you later," Martha said before Leah could respond.

Leah held the phone in her hand and stared straight ahead. How was it that she'd spent countless hours fixing families every day and managed to destroy her own in one night?

"I should've waited," Leah said. "I shouldn't have said anything last night."

"It wouldn't have mattered." Quinton sat next to her. "What difference would it have made? She was going to be upset no matter when we told her. We lied to her, and it sounds like that's what she's upset about the most."

"That's what she focused on last night, but I don't think that's what's most upsetting to her." Leah twisted her wedding ring around her finger. "Quinton, are you sure that you didn't say or do anything that would've given her the wrong impression?"

Quinton leaned away from her. "What? No, I didn't do . . . Are you asking if I led her on?"

"I'm trying to figure out what happened to make her suddenly think that maybe there's a chance for the two of you," Leah explained. "I know you wouldn't do anything like that on purpose."

"On purpose or otherwise." Quinton stood. "Look, all I did was go over there and try to talk to her about Lance. That's it. Nothing more or less. And no matter how many times you ask, the answer will still be the same." His words were as sharp as his stare. "I'm done with this conversation."

Quinton left the room and then the house without saying another word. Leah couldn't remember a time he'd left without kissing her. Even if they were in the middle of a disagreement, he'd still kiss her before he left. Her body ached with an unfamiliar emptiness, and a knot of fear and sadness tightened her chest. Was this the beginning of their unraveling? Leah shook away the thought. She refused to accept that. No matter what her mind wanted her to believe, what she and Quinton built over the years was strong and could withstand anything, even the return of the one person he never wanted to lose.

"Ready," Skye said, standing in the doorway dressed in her ripped jeans, crop top, and a hoodie that Leah had the urge to zip to hide Skye's midriff.

"I'll drive," Skye said, holding up her car keys.

Leah ran upstairs to grab her laptop. She fooled herself into believing that she could get some work done while Skye worked on her paper. When Leah suggested that they try the bookstore, which was also a coffee shop, she thought it would be a nice change while she and Skye worked. Of course, that was when her life wasn't in shambles, and it sounded like a perfect idea. Not so much anymore when the last thing Leah wanted was to be around people. She wasn't in the mood to fake a smile or make small talk, as she often found herself doing whenever she was out. She wanted to go back upstairs, peel out of her clothes, and crawl back underneath the covers.

Skye pulled into a parking space at Literary Lattes and turned off the ignition. She reached behind Leah and pulled her bag up front.

The door chimed when Skye and Leah stepped inside the building. There weren't a lot of people, which was good.

"Let's get something to drink first," Leah suggested, pointing straight ahead at the coffee counter. Leah and Skye had settled into their seats when, to Leah's horror, they had company.

"Hi, Ms. Lefleur." The lady smiled.

"Mrs. Matthews, how are you?" Leah added an extra lift to her voice to hide the annoyance she felt.

On any other day, Leah wouldn't mind running into her patients—or, in Mrs. Matthews's case, former patients—but today wasn't any other day.

"This has to be your beautiful daughter." Mrs. Matthews smiled at Skye. "She looks like you."

It wasn't unusual for people to assume that Skye was Leah's daughter. There was no reason for them to think otherwise. Skye favored Leah, but only because Leah favored Nova.

"This is Skye," Leah said.

Leah had never considered denying or confirming it in the past, and she hated that she thought about it now. In Leah's heart, Skye was her daughter in every way that counted. Leah was the one who'd coached Skye through all her firsts. Her first menstrual cycle, her first crush, her first heartbreak, which was caused by her first crush. It was Leah who taught Skye that ice cream and a rom-com were the perfect cures to ease a broken heart. There was no rhyme or reason behind the cure. Leah just knew it worked.

Leah liked to think that Skye was the wonderful young lady she turned out to be partly because of her influence. What would happen if Skye didn't need Leah anymore? If she experienced another heartbreak or friendship troubles, would she come to Leah, or would she choose Nova? Leah's spirits, which she was sure were as low as they could get, somehow dropped even lower. She couldn't lose Skye. And yes, it was selfish because she'd had fifteen years with her, but she wanted all the years. She couldn't help how she felt.

"I'll be back." Skye stood. "It was nice to meet you, Mrs. Matthews."

"Um. How are Mr. Matthews and the kids?" Leah asked when it was clear that Mrs. Matthews was making no effort to move along.

Mrs. Matthews's face lit up. "They're wonderful. Thank you for asking. You know, it's funny that I ran into you today because Phil and I were talking about you the other day."

"Oh really?" Leah sat up a little straighter, waiting to hear the good things they had to say about her. She certainly could use some words of praise.

"Yep." Mrs. Matthews pointed to the seat next to Leah. "May I?"

"Sure, I'm sorry. I should've offered you a seat." Leah reached across the table and moved the papers Skye had taken from her bag out of Mrs. Matthews's way.

"So, as I was saying, Phil and I were talking, and we were both saying how we were so thankful that we decided to go to therapy. You have no idea how much you helped us."

Leah smiled for what felt like the first time in years. "And you have no idea how happy I am to hear that."

"Yeah, because of you, we were able to stop arguing and start listening. At the end of the day, we both realized that we weren't happy as husband and wife. We were trying to hold on to something that was never meant to be."

Leah's shoulders dropped. "What?"

Mrs. Matthews waved her hand as if trying to stop Leah from reacting, but it was too late. The news had already sucked the little glimmer of happiness she felt a second ago.

"No, don't be upset," Mrs. Matthews continued. "Getting a divorce was the best decision we could've made. Phil and I are better people, better parents, and believe it or not, even better friends because of it."

"I'm sorry," Leah said, feeling the need to apologize even as Mrs. Matthews sat across from her with the biggest smile on her face. Clearly, she was happy, but Leah couldn't help but feel as if she'd failed them somehow. Failed the children whose two-parent home was now split.

"Please don't apologize. I'm telling you that you helped us."

"I hear that, but it doesn't sound like I did. I became a marriage counselor to save marriages, not help tear them apart."

"But marriage is just a title. Aren't the people in the marriage the most important thing? You helped those two people, so you didn't fail. When you asked us to remember how we began and what made us want to get married, it was a huge eye opener. We got married because I was pregnant. We spent years trying to make it work. And I spent years in second place. I tried to deny it. Tried to convince myself that it was my imagination, but it wasn't. Phil's heart was somewhere else. He never looked at me the way he looked at the woman he really loved. I knew if we hadn't gotten pregnant, he would've asked her to marry him. But Phil has always been a man who wanted to do the right thing, so he married me, but he never stopped loving her. We let each other go to live the lives we were meant to live."

She shared many more words, but Leah's mind couldn't stop replaying. *Divorce. First wife. Never stopped loving.* Leah and Quinton's situation wasn't like theirs, but it wasn't that much different either. Quinton and Nova may have been having problems back then, but they didn't fall out of love.

Mrs. Matthews stood. "I've taken up enough of your time. Thanks again for everything. You may not see it as a good thing, but I promise you it is." She reached across and touched Leah's hand.

Leah forced a smile and watched as she walked away.

Failure never felt good in Leah's body, and it seemed that was all she had been experiencing lately. First, she'd failed as a sister, and now, she failed as a therapist. What was next? She shuddered to even think about it.

CHAPTER 27

Nova

I couldn't pretend that I was happy about my appointment with Dr. Yvonne. During our short session yesterday, which she called a meet and greet, she didn't ask about anything that Adam had done to me, and I was thankful because I hated talking about that. Living it was bad enough, but talking about it wasn't much better.

"I don't know what I'm supposed to talk about?" I looked over at Dr. Yvonne, who sat in a chair while I sat on the sofa in the living room.

Mama left to run some errands and to give us some privacy. I told her she didn't have to leave because I didn't plan on talking about anything that she couldn't hear or didn't already know about, but I could tell that Dr. Yvonne wanted Mama to go.

"Sometimes it's hard for people to open up around family members," she explained after Mama left.

"Open up about what?" I asked, twisting my finger around the edge of the scarf, but stopping as soon as I remembered the horror from yesterday.

"About anything you'd like," she said.

"Skye's coming over today," I said, sharing information about the only person I cared to talk about. "I haven't seen her in a couple days, so I'm glad she's stopping by after school."

I talked more about Skye and how much fun we had that night until Leah ruined it, but I left that last part out because it was all about Skye.

"Well, it seems that our session is almost up," Dr. Yvonne announced after looking at her watch. "I have an assignment for you." She removed her glasses. "I want you to set a goal. What's one thing you want to accomplish this week?"

I gave it some thought, but I didn't have to think long because it was the one thing I'd wanted to accomplish since I'd left that room. "I want to leave the house," I told her.

"Okay. Then I want you to work on doing that. Even if you only get as far as the end of the lane before you have to turn around. It's still farther than you've been, right?"

I nodded as the thought of driving away from the house caused the horses that lived in my chest to start galloping all over the place. "Okay," I managed to say.

I walked Dr. Yvonne to the door after our session was done. I stood in the doorway and watched as she drove away without a care in the world. She wasn't worried about anything happening to her. Or, if she was, it didn't stop her from going. That was what I wanted. That was the kind of freedom I wanted to feel again.

Dr. Yvonne wasn't gone long before Mama came back. "Nova, I have a surprise for you," she said, smiling as she walked through the door.

"I don't like surprises," I reminded her.

"It's not a real surprise. I called your cousin Bianca. You remember Bianca? She's your second or third cousin. I can't remember right now, but Bianca's a beautician. The shop she works at isn't open on Mondays, so I asked if she'd mind coming over and doing your hair for you."

I touched the silk scarf that I was ready to get rid of. Even though I hated that Leah did my hair for me, it was the only time I felt like a real person again. I hated that anyone had to see what I'd done to my hair. It was bad enough that Lance had seen it.

"I told her I'll let her know if you're okay with her coming," Mama said.

"I don't know . . ." Then I thought about Skye. The last thing I wanted was for her to see what I'd done. I wanted to look like someone Skye would be proud to call her mom. Not someone she'd be embarrassed to be seen with. "Yes, I want her to come. How soon can she get here? How long will it take?"

"I don't know how long it'll take, but she only lives about five minutes up the road. She's waiting for me to call."

"Call her now."

Mama was right. It seemed like she'd just hung up the phone when a car pulled up to the house. I looked out the window and saw a short, stocky woman with purple hair pulling a black bag out of the car. Bianca was quite a few years younger than me, so we weren't close. Her dad and my dad were cousins, but like Mama, I didn't remember which number they were. In Bayou, it never mattered, though. A cousin was a cousin, no matter if it was first or fifth.

Bianca, like most of the people on Dad's side of the family, talked a lot. She told me about everyone she thought I should've known, even though I didn't. I listened and pretended to be interested, but my mind was on Skye and hoping Bianca would be done before Skye made it.

"I'm glad I grabbed all my products," she said, squeezing something into her hands. "I forgot that you and Leah both have 3A hair. I can't tell for sure without testing it, but y'all have those loose curls. A lot of my clients have 4C or 4D hair," she continued as if I had any idea what she was talking about.

Since when did hair come in numbers? I started to ask but didn't. I had a feeling it was more information than I needed to know. There were more important things I had to learn about, and hair wasn't one of them.

"How is Leah, anyway?" Bianca asked, massaging the product into my freshly cut and washed hair.

Her fingers felt good until she asked about Leah. That name soured everything.

"I don't know. I haven't talked with Leah," I said, praying she would move on to something else. At that point, I wanted to hear about another cousin I didn't know.

Bianca laughed. "I remember when I was little, I used to want to be y'all's little sister so bad. Y'all were so pretty and so stylish. I used to beg my daddy to bring me around here so I could play with y'all. Not that you wanted to play with me. I mean, you were, what, in middle or high school when I was still in elementary."

"Yeah," I said.

"I used to do Leah's hair all the time, but I think she does it herself now. Or maybe she found someone in Baton Rouge to do it. It always looks nice, though."

"Did you know that Leah and Quinton were married?" I asked.

I couldn't see her face, but I felt the stiffness in the air that my question caused.

"Um . . . yeah."

"And did you remember that I was married to Quinton first?" I continued.

"Yeah . . ." she said, her voice lowering to barely a whisper. "I didn't know if you knew, though, so I didn't . . ."

"I know, and I don't want to talk about Leah, I don't want to hear about Leah, and I don't care about Leah," I said, my fingernails digging into the palms of my hands.

Bianca continued working in silence. "All done," she finally said, placing a hand mirror in front of me.

"Oh wow!" I said, turning my head from one side to the other.

My hair was short and curly, and I loved it. I didn't think I'd like short hair on me, but I never knew for sure. I looked different. In comparison to the braids, it wasn't a good different or bad different. Just different.

Mama came downstairs as Bianca was packing up her things. Her eyes were wide, and her mouth flew open. "Oh my, Nova," she said, smiling so hard she could hardly talk. "You look amazing."

"You can have these," Bianca said, pointing to the products she used in my hair. "Use the daily moisturizer every morning and a little of this gel—not much, just a little dab," she explained.

"Let me go grab my purse," Mama said, turning to go upstairs.

"No, you don't have to pay me," Bianca said.

"Nonsense. You're working on your day off. Of course, I'm paying you."

"You may as well let her pay because she's not going to let you leave until she does," I said, standing and pushing the chair back underneath the table. "Thank you so much. And I'm sorry for snapping at you. I was just . . . It's hard talking about Leah." I swallowed the lump that her name caused.

Bianca reached over and grabbed my hand. "I understand. Believe it or not, I've gone through something similar. It wasn't my sister, though. It was my best friend. I don't talk with her or want to hear about her either." She smiled, but it didn't get rid of the sadness in her eyes.

"You still miss your friend?" I asked.

She nodded. "I do, but it is what it is, you know?"

Would I always miss Leah, or would the pain of not having her in my life eventually go away?

"Here we go." Mama came back and pushed some money into Bianca's hand.

By the time Skye came, I'd changed into jeans and a long-sleeved shirt. I'd even put on a little makeup and lip gloss like I did when I had the braids.

When Skye walked through the door, still dressed in her practice uniform, her reaction to my new hair was the same as Mama's.

"I'm so jealous," she said, tugging at one of her braids. "I want my hair cut so bad, but Daddy would have a fit."

I knew that to be true. Quinton was one of the biggest reasons why I never cut my hair. He loved my long hair. I guessed it was probably why Leah didn't cut hers anymore. She used to always chop hers off and let it grow back. As long as her hair was now, I was sure she hadn't cut it since she and Quinton started . . . I couldn't finish the thought. It was too hard.

"I think you'd look great with short hair," I told Skye.

"I know I would. My friend Amber has this short wig. I tried it on one day, and I loved it on me."

"Then you should do it," I told her. "We can call Bianca. I'm sure she wouldn't mind doing your hair too."

"Cousin Bianca did your hair? I should've known. She's so good. She goes to the hair shows in Atlanta and everything. She does makeup too. She can beat a face better than anyone I know."

"What?" I gasped.

Skye laughed. "Not literally. It means she'll have your makeup looking flawless."

I pretended to understand but couldn't get my mind to connect a beat face with flawless makeup.

"So, what do you think?" I asked. "Do you want me to get Gran to call Cousin Bianca?"

"What?" Skye smiled. "No way. I'd have to check with Dad and Tee . . ." She looked away from me.

As much as it pained me to say it, I had no choice. "It's okay. You can say Teeah's name."

"I know, but—"

"Nova," Mama called from the kitchen, interrupting whatever Skye was about to say. "Can you come and help me with something real quick?"

"I'll be right back."

Mama stood in the kitchen's opening and waited for me. She motioned for me to follow her. She walked across the room and over to the sink.

"Yes?" I asked, looking around to see what she could've needed help with.

"Nova, what are you doing? You can't tell Skye she can cut her hair," Mama whispered.

"And why not? I'm her mother." I crossed my arms over my chest.

"I know that, but Quinton's her father. A decision like that should come from both parents, not just one."

"But it's okay for him to tell her no?" I asked.

"I didn't say that. I said it should come from both parents, which means you two need to talk before you tell her it's okay."

"Why do I need permission from Quinton?"

"I didn't say *permission*," Mama said.

"That's what it sounds like. And what's the big deal anyway? It's her hair, and she should be able to cut it if she wants to. I don't want her to think she needs permission from anyone to do what she wants to do to her body."

Mama nodded. "I understand what you're saying, and I'm not saying that you're wrong. All I'm saying is parenting is a partnership between both parents. One doesn't get to make a decision about the child without talking with the other. That's all. I don't want things to get any worse than they already are."

"I don't think things can get any worse for me than they already are," I told Mama. "And I know you're just trying to help me, but Quinton has had fifteen years of parenting without having to discuss anything with anyone. Now, it's my turn."

"Nova," Mama called for me, but I was already leaving and didn't plan on going back. As far as I was concerned, that conversation was over.

"Is Gran okay? Does she need more help?" Skye put her phone down.

"No, she's fine. Hey, why don't you stay for dinner? I know Gran would love that. And so would I."

"I can't. I'm working on a project for school, and I kind of need Teeah's help with it. But how about another night?"

"Sure." I forced a smile. "I'd like that."

"Speaking of Teeah. Do you think the two of you will ever make up?" Skye asked.

Not a chance.

"I don't know. Maybe. But listen, I know your dad and Leah were there for you, and that won't change, but I want to be there for you too. If you need anything, I want you to know that you can come to me."

Skye's visit was shorter than I wanted it to be, but she needed to get home and start on her project. Something occurred to me while Mama and I were eating dinner.

"How is Skye able to go to school here in Bayou if she lives in Baton Rouge?" I asked.

Mama had taken a bite of her meatloaf. She covered her mouth with her hand while she talked. "She used my address," Mama said. "As far as the school knows, she lives here with me."

"Then why doesn't she?" I asked.

Mama's eyes narrowed. "Why doesn't she what?"

"Live here with you . . . with us? She should live here if she's going to school here."

Mama's stare went from narrow to wide. "What? No, she doesn't want to live here. She wants to live at her house."

"But this could be her house now. She's lived with Quinton for all this time. I want some time with her too. After next year, she'll be leaving for college, and who knows how much time I'll get to spend with her."

Mama shook her head. "Nova, don't do this. Don't go disrupting things in Skye's life. Now, she's happy where she is. If she wanted to live here, she would've asked."

"Or maybe she doesn't know it's what she wants."

"She's seventeen, Nova. She knows what she wants."

I didn't care what Mama said. Everyone assumed they knew what was best for Skye, but I bet no one bothered asking Skye what she wanted. Maybe she would want to live here with us.

"You're right. I'll leave it alone," I told her because I didn't want to hear any more of her unwanted advice.

Mama reached over and touched my hand. "I know it feels like nothing is going your way, but I think I have something that will make you feel a little better." She wiped her mouth and excused herself.

A few seconds later, Mama came back holding an envelope.

"What's this?" I looked at the envelope that she'd pushed toward me.

"Open it."

I ripped it open and pulled out a sheet of paper. "A bank statement?" I looked over at Mama.

"A few years ago, I sold some land that your dad and I bought. I didn't plan on doing anything with it, and someone inquired about it, so I had it appraised, and I sold it. The money in that account is from the sale. I hadn't touched it because I didn't need to." She tilted her head to one side. "I've felt so hopeless these last few days, wishing there was something I could do to make you feel better. The other day you said you're not a baby and wanted us to stop treating you like one. Well"—she pointed to the paper in my hand—"that money will help you get started. Part of feeling like an independent adult is having your own money."

I scanned the paper again, looking closely at the number at the top. "Is this how much money's in there?" I asked.

Mama leaned over to see what number I was asking about. "Yep."

"Oh . . . Mama, I can't take this. This is too much." I folded the paper and stuffed it back into the envelope. As much as I needed it, I couldn't take that much money from Mama.

"Yes, you can, and yes, you will. You'll get it either way," she said.

"What do you mean?"

"Now or once I'm gone. I'd rather you take it now so I can see you rebuilding your life. Besides, things still cost money. You can use it to pay for your sessions with Dr. Yvonne until we get you some insurance. You may want to go back to school one day, and what about a car? You may want to buy one once you get your license."

My head started swimming when I thought about everything I had to do to put the pieces of my life back together. In order to get a license, I needed a social security card, but according to the state of Louisiana, I was still dead. I guess I needed to clear that matter up as well.

"Okay." I stood, leaned down, and hugged Mama. "Thank you, Mama. I don't know what I'd do without you helping me."

"And let's pray you won't have to find out any time soon."

CHAPTER 28

Leah

The only thing Leah wanted to do after her evening group session was go home, but she'd ignored her house and the empty refrigerator long enough. She pulled into the parking lot of Fresh Finds Grocery. The prices were higher since it was a small family-owned grocery store not far from Leah's office downtown. Leah only went out of convenience. She couldn't deal with long lines, and Fresh Finds was her spot where she was in and out.

Shopping without a grocery list was never a good idea, but Leah only had the mindset for one task, either make a list or shop. Leah assessed the items in her shopping cart and dropped her shoulders when she realized there wasn't anything there that would make a complete meal. Once she gathered her thoughts, she continued shopping until she was satisfied with her choices. Leah pushed her cart to the checkout lane. She was mentally running through all the places she would pass on her way home because even though she had a shopping cart filled with food, the desire to cook it was no longer there. Not that ordering out was any easier since everyone in her house liked different things. She and Skye liked pizza, but Quinton didn't. Skye and Quinton liked hot wings, but Leah didn't. Leah and Quinton liked sushi, but Skye didn't.

"I'm open if you're ready, Mama." A young girl waved Leah over.

Leah put all her things onto the conveyor belt and waited while the young lady, who must've been training, since someone else was standing next to her assisting, scanned her items. It took the young lady a little longer than Leah was used to, but she didn't mind. The cashier was probably around Skye's age, and Leah would hope if it were Skye that the customers would be patient with her too.

"I'm sorry," The cashier smiled nervously while her trainer showed her how to find the produce on the register.

"No problem, sweetie." Leah smiled.

She looked around, and something caught her attention. "What the hell?" she whispered.

Nova's picture, not a recent one but an old one from before she was kidnapped, was plastered on the cover. The title in big bold white letters read: Missing Woman Found Alive After Fifteen Years. It was the first time Leah had seen anything in print. Everything else was on the news or internet blogs. For reasons Leah couldn't explain, her hands shook as she reached over and pulled the magazine from the shelf.

"Will that be all, Mama?" the young cashier asked.

"Uh . . . this too," Leah said, giving her the magazine. Then, she reached into her purse for her debit card.

Once Leah loaded her bags in her car, she got the magazine, which sat at the top of one of the bags, and slid into her car. She locked the doors and then opened the magazine. The glossy pages flicked underneath Leah's trembling fingers, which trembled even more as she turned. Just like the cover, the pictures on the inside were old and showed a vibrant, happy Nova during happier times.

Leah read the words of an article that seemed to rehash details from Nova's time in that house, but that couldn't be because Nova wouldn't have done an interview without saying anything. Or maybe she did and didn't tell Leah. Her stomach lurched at the thought. Nova used to tell her everything. Was this how their lives would be from now on? Leah wasn't used to hearing information about her sister from secondhand sources.

The one thing the article did get right was the exhaustive searches and the years of heartache that the family suffered. What it didn't mention was all the weekends Leah and Quinton spent of their own time and money driving from Louisiana to Mississippi, knocking on doors, passing out flyers, talking with anyone who was willing to talk, and praying someone saw something . . . anything. None of that mattered anymore, though. Nova was home and safe now.

Leah was about to close the magazine, having read enough, when one word, well, two, caught her attention: *family friend*. Leah found the beginning of the sentence, which read: "*Nova's resilient, but even though she's home and safe, her ordeal is far from over,*" *a family friend told us*. "*She not only has to heal from what that freak did to her but also from family hurt that occurred while she was away.*"

"What?" Leah screamed and didn't care who heard, but thankfully no one did.

Leah sat outside her mom's house and waited until she'd built up the nerves to go and ring the doorbell. Going there was a spur-of-the-moment decision. Maybe she should've gone home like she'd planned to in the first place. She was thirty-eight years old, and there was never a time when she needed courage to walk through her parents' door. Not even when she and her mom were at odds over her relationship with Quinton. Tonight, though, knowing that Nova was on the other side made Leah second-guess her decision to stop by without checking first.

Leah jumped when her phone rang.

"Where are you?" Quinton asked.

"I'm sorry. I forgot to call, but I'm at Mom's. I won't be long." Leah pulled her keys from the ignition.

"Are you sure this is a good idea?" Quinton asked. "I thought we agreed to give Nova some time."

"We did, but . . ." Leah looked over at the magazine that sat on her passenger seat. "I need to talk with Mom about something. I'll fill you in when I get home."

"Okay, be careful," Quinton said.

Leah slid the phone into her purse and stopped stalling. After two knocks, her mom answered the door wearing her lounging dress and slippers. Leah was wrapped in warmth when her mom hugged her so tight that she could barely breathe. Leah hadn't seen her mom since she and Skye left Saturday night, and Martha was hugging her like it had been years instead of a day.

"Mom, is everything okay?" Leah asked, concerned by her mom's reaction to her visit.

"I'm fine." Martha stood back and scanned Leah up and down. "How are you? Are you okay? You look beautiful. I always loved your hair like that."

Leah's hand went to her hair, which sat on her shoulders. It was day one after a wash, and Leah could only stand her hair down for one, maybe two days before she pulled it into her signature top bun.

"Thank you, Mom, and yes, I'm okay." Leah realized she was still standing in the doorway. "Can I come in?"

"Oh . . . yes . . . of course. Come in." Martha moved aside and closed the door behind Leah. "Did you come to see your sister?"

Leah heard hope in her mom's voice. "If she's willing to talk with me, then yes," she said.

"You have to keep trying," Martha advised.

"There's something you should see." Leah pulled the magazine from her purse.

Martha's eyes narrowed, then widened before she looked at Leah. "It says exclusive details inside. What exclusive details?" She asked, flipping through the magazine.

"According to the article, a family friend said Nova had to heal from Adam and from us. Us being Quinton and I," Leah clarified.

"Oh my God!" Martha closed the magazine. "Who would say something like that? What family friend?" Martha asked.

"I have no idea, but I intend to find out," Leah assured her mom.

Leah sat with Martha a few more minutes before she once again built up the nerves to go upstairs and face Nova. Outside of Nova's bedroom door, Leah reminded herself that she needed her sister. And whether Nova realized it or not, she needed Leah too. That fact was made apparent more than ever once Leah saw that magazine article.

You lost her sister once, Leah, and you're not about to lose her again without a fight.

Leah knocked and waited for Nova to invite her in, but no invite came. Maybe she couldn't hear the knock. "Nova, can I please come in?"

"Go away, Leah."

"Nova, please." Leah turned the knob and cracked the door open. When Leah peeked in, Nova was sitting on the side of the bed with her head turned toward the window. The first thing Leah noticed was Nova's new cut. She looked amazing. Leah studied Nova's side profile and looked for signs of anger, but it wasn't there. All she saw, even from the side, was hurt and disappointment. The two things Leah never wanted to cause her sister.

Leah opened her mouth to speak several times, but each time, nothing came out. On her way over, she'd prepared a whole speech in her head. Now that it was time to use it, she couldn't think of anything that didn't sound wrong.

Nova lifted her chin, but she still didn't look at Leah. "Do you remember that day I came home from school and, like always, I sat on this bed, and you sat next to me, and I told you about my day, but that day was different? That day, I told you that Quinton finally asked me to be his girlfriend." Nova smiled through her tears. "I was so happy. Do you remember that?" Her red, swollen eyes met Leah's.

Leah stood in the middle of the room and nodded. She remembered it well. She'd never seen Nova so happy before. Not even when she did well in a basketball game, which, up until that time, was the only thing other than her family that Nova loved.

"You were the only person who knew how much I liked him. You were also the only person who knew I'd written *Mrs. Quinton Boudreaux* in all my notebooks. It was special, and I didn't want to tell everybody. Only the person I trusted."

Leah's chest tightened at the memory. Not only because of the pain she heard in her sister's words but also from her reaction when Nova told her the news. Leah thought Quinton was a playa, and she didn't trust him. She didn't want him to hurt Nova the way he'd hurt so many other girls before. The irony of her past distrust of Quinton was like a knot tightening in her gut. How could she have known that she would be the one who'd inflict the deepest wound?

"I was so excited," Nova continued. "Then you asked me if he was good enough for me. Remember that?" She looked at Leah again.

Leah's throat tightened, her voice coming out as a hoarse whisper. "Yeah, I remember, Nova. I remember all of that."

Nova chuckled. "You said he didn't seem smart enough for me."

Leah's heart pounded so hard she felt it in her ears. Leah understood the message Nova was relaying. "That was a long time ago, Nova. We were all kids back then." The excuse felt as hollow as it sounded.

Nova laughed hard before her laughter abruptly stopped. "So, at what point did you realize he was good enough? Was it before we got married or after?"

Leah's mouth fell open. Guilt, shame, and fear battled for dominance inside her. Her chest was too tight, each breath a struggle. She wanted to explain, to make Nova understand the years of loneliness, grief, and unexpected love that led them to this moment. More than that, she wanted to beg for forgiveness, to turn back the hands of time and undo the hurt she caused. The only problem was the only way to undo the hurt would be to undo the love she had for Quinton. Both felt like impossible tasks.

"You know it wasn't like that." Even as the words left her mouth, Leah knew they were inadequate. The truth was, there was nothing she could say that could make Nova understand.

"I don't know anything. I'm still trying to make you"—Nova held out one hand, her palm facing up—"and Quinton"—she did the same with the other hand—"make sense in my head, but no matter how hard I try, I can't." She shook her head as she stared back and forth at both hands. "Quinton. The person you called a dumb jock," she said, bouncing one hand up and down. "And you." She did the same with the other hand. "The person he said would never get married because no man would ever put up with your smart mouth and snooty attitude."

Leah's heart raced, and her voice trembled. "Like I said. We were kids. We all said things back then that we wouldn't say today. You want to know the real reason I didn't want you with Quinton?" When Nova didn't answer, Leah continued. "It was because I knew how much you liked him, and I was afraid you'd start spending more time with him than with me. I was afraid of losing you." Leah didn't bother stopping the tears. "Just like I'm afraid of losing you now."

"I don't understand how you could look at the man I loved. The man I had a child with and see anything other than me and him. How, Leah? I need you to help me understand." Nova's voice was low but pleading.

Leah took a step closer to Nova. "For years, I did only see you and him, but as the years passed, he became just Quinton. Not Quinton and Nova. I know this is painful, Nova, but I fell in love with the Quinton he became. Not the Quinton he used to be. Not *your* Quinton." When Nova didn't say anything, Leah took her chance and sat on the bed next to Nova.

"Every weekend for over a year, Quinton and I were in Biloxi and other parts of Mississippi putting up flyers, talking to people, trying to do everything we could to find you. For years, Nova." Leah's voice cracked. "Neither one of us wanted to believe that you were really gone. That the one person we both loved more than our own lives was no longer with us. When everyone else told us we had to stop. We couldn't keep doing that to ourselves. Mama would've been with us, but the grief of coming back every time no closer than we were when we started was weighing on her too heavy."

"None of that has anything to do with how you ended up marrying my husband."

"He wasn't your husband anymore, Nova," Leah's voice was louder than she intended. She took a breath. "When things changed between Quinton and me, you'd been gone for over ten years. Ten years, Nova. All hopes of you ever coming back were gone by then."

Nova's nose flared as if she was struggling to keep her composure. Between clenched teeth, she said, "That still didn't mean it was okay for the two of you to get together."

"I understand that, and you have to understand how hard we both tried to pretend that what we felt wasn't there. We tried to make ourselves believe that it was in our minds. We were both looking for someone in each other that neither of us could have. We believed that who we both really wanted was you."

"And then you both realized that it wasn't me you wanted at all. It was each other."

Nova was quiet for a minute. She lowered her head and stared down at her feet, which she swept back and forth across the shaggy carpet. Leah was stuck in disbelief at Nova's words, which caused a mixture of shock and anguish to press down on her chest.

Nova lifted her head and looked at Leah. "Tell me the truth. Did you fall in love with Quinton because your relationship grew over time, and you couldn't help it? Or did you fall in love with him so you'd finally know what it feels like to be me?"

The question hit Leah like a physical blow. The air had been sucked out of the room. "What? No, why would you ask that?"

Nova stared at Leah. "Because you've always been jealous of what Quinton and I had. You didn't like him because you didn't have anyone who would love you the way he loved me. And guess what, Leah? Quinton will *never* love you the way he loves me. And you will never love him the way I did. I hope you can handle it when he shows you because eventually he will." Nova pulled her legs onto the bed and curled into herself, resting her head on her pillow as she turned away from Leah.

The room fell silent, but their conversation lingered, a stubborn presence that made itself at home in Leah's mind. The weight of Nova's words sank inside Leah and jackhammered through her heart.

Leah picked herself up and silently walked to the door. She put her hand on the knob but couldn't walk out. Leah turned back to Nova. "You're right, Nova. Quinton will never love me the way he loved you. And I will never love him the way you did. Do you know why? Because I'm not you. I've never wanted to be you. Believe it or not, falling in love with Quinton had nothing to do with you. Maybe one day you'll see that."

With nothing left to say, Leah walked out of the room. She'd made it to the bottom step when she flopped down and leaned her head against the wall. Leah swallowed hard, her throat tight with emotion. *Will he ever love me the way he loved her?* Doubt crept into her mind; unwelcome thoughts festered like a wound. She tried to push the thoughts away, to rationalize that Nova's words were a product of hurt and pain, but it didn't matter because the seed of doubt had already been planted, and Leah didn't know how to stop it from blooming.

"Leah." Martha rushed over to her, still sitting on the step, trying to pull herself together.

"I'm fine." Leah pushed herself to her feet and tried to steady herself on her heels, which didn't feel as sturdy as they did a moment ago. "I need to go. I'll call you later." Her attempt to rush out of the house was unsuccessful as she fumbled with the locks.

"I got it." Martha moved around Leah and turned the locks. "Are you sure you're okay?"

Leah kissed her mom and walked away.

CHAPTER 29

Nova

I don't know what it was. Maybe it was the new haircut, or the money Mama gave me at dinner, or Leah's visit. No matter the reason, I was grateful for it because I woke up with a new sense of determination. Dr. Yvonne told me to create a goal, and I was ready to achieve that goal and much more. I was going to do this. I was going to open the front door, walk out, and keep walking until I got to the end of the lane.

Mama left early this morning to go down the street to check on her friend, Ms. Cora. She hadn't been feeling well, and Mama had been worried about her. I wanted to have some good news to tell her when she came back—something to help lift her spirits and take her mind off her sick friend and everything that was going on between Leah and me. Leah's visit last night really bothered Mama. She didn't say anything, but I could tell she was down about it, which made me even angrier with Leah. Mama and I were fine before she showed up, ruining both of our moods.

Anyway, that was neither here nor there. Today was all about being positive and reaching my goal. My hand gripped the doorknob, but I was frozen. I couldn't turn it. I closed my eyes and visualized myself doing it like Dr. Yvonne told me to do this morning during our session. I saw myself walking through the door and down the steps and taking one step after the other until I did it. Only, that was much easier in my head than it was in real life.

I was still standing by the door when someone knocked and nearly gave me a heart attack. I lifted to my tiptoes and looked through the glass at the top of the door.

"Hey," I said when I swung the door open and let Lance inside.

"Whoa!" Lance stepped back. "You look amazing."

I lowered my head and hoped he didn't see the heat that I was sure had colored my face. "Thank you."

"Are you blushing?" he teased.

"No," I said firmly, but the smile on his face said he didn't buy it. I turned and made my way to the sofa, hoping by the time we sat that my face would return to its normal color.

Lance sat next to me. "What are you doing today?" he asked, smiling like he had something up his sleeve.

How in the world was he still single? It didn't make sense to me. Back when we were best friends, I didn't see what all the other girls saw in Lance. I mean, yes, he was always good looking, but to me, he was just Lance. Now, though, after being away from him for so long, I can see why they were all fighting to be on his arm.

"Let's see. You know my calendar stays booked these days," I teased.

"You wanna do something?" he asked.

"I wanna do everything. The problem is my mind won't let me. This wasn't something I thought I'd have to deal with when I left that house. I thought my problem would be trying to do everything at once and wearing myself out. Not stuck in the house, afraid to go outside. The one place I prayed to be for fifteen years."

"I get that."

"You do?" I asked, waiting to hear how he could possibly know what I was talking about.

"Not exactly, but . . ." He moved closer. "When I played football, there were a lot of times when we'd be in the fourth quarter, down by a touchdown, and the whole stadium was watching. Some cheered for us to do well, and others made noise to distract us, so we didn't."

I shook my head. "I'm sorry. What does anything I said have to do with football?"

He laughed. "I'm getting to that."

How did I forget that Lance always took forever to get to the point of a story? He traveled all around the world and back again before he finally said what he wanted to say. Most of the time, he'd forget the point before he reached it.

"What I'm saying is this. The people in the stands who were making all the noise to distract us, that's what's going on in your mind. We had to learn how to block out the noise and focus on the play. And that's what you're going to do. You're going to block out all the things that your mind is trying to tell you to stop you from making your touchdown."

"What?" I laughed even harder. "I'm not playing football, fool."

"You know what I mean."

"I do." I stood. "And before you came, that's what I was about to do. I was determined to open that door and walk outside."

"Then let's do it." He opened the door, reached for my hand, and walked me out to the front porch.

We stood there, holding hands while I stared ahead and tried to block out the people in the stadium . . . or in my case, the thoughts in my head.

"What's the worst that could happen?" Lance glanced down at me.

"What do you mean?"

He tilted his head forward. "If you walked down those steps and into the yard. What's the worst that could happen?"

My mind raced with all the thoughts that replayed in my head when I imagined walking out the door and away from the safety of this house. "Someone could come and take me away again." I voiced my biggest fear, my voice shaking as much as my body.

"And if we walked down there together"—he squeezed my hand—"who's going to take you away from me?" He released my hand and flexed the muscles in his arms, which bulged through his long-sleeved cotton shirt. "I'm six two, two hundred twenty pounds of steel." He hit his chest. "I'll be like Black Panther out there fighting off any and everybody. Young and old. It doesn't matter."

Tears rolled down my face, but they were from laughing so hard at him. I was still wiping my face when he took my hand again, and we, in unison, took the three steps down to the ground.

Lance looked at me, smiling like a proud father who'd watched his child take their first step.

"I did it."

"You did it." He held my hand a little tighter. A reminder that he was still there and as long as I had Lance, my best friend, I was safe. I believed that.

"Who's Black Panther?" I asked as we strolled away from the house and down the dirt road.

"You don't remember Black Panther? Part of the Fantastic Four in the comics."

"No idea what you're talking about?"

"Ah, come on." He threw his hand up and his head back. "You know what? You're in luck because the Black Panther movie came out in February. I'm going to find a way to show you that movie. You have to see it."

Before I knew it, we'd made it to the end of the road, and a funny thing happened. Each step I took was electrifying, like there were jumping cables inside me, jump-starting something that had died long ago. I wanted to keep walking and talking with Lance. So, that was what we did. We strolled down Main Street and kept going until we made it into town. My grip around his hand tightened. I didn't know if I was hurting him, but if I was, he didn't show it.

"Today was a good day to do this," Lance said. "Tuesday morning means people are getting ready for work, so you won't have to worry about anyone bothering you."

That part made me feel good. All I wanted to do was walk and talk with Lance. And see what changes had taken place in Bayou since I'd been gone.

"Oh my goodness," I said, stopping on the sidewalk and putting my hands over my mouth.

All the stores had handwritten posters with my name on them. Some I recognized from people holding them and cheering when we drove into Bayou. I couldn't look too long then, but now all I wanted to do was read each sign expressing how happy they were that I was home and safe. In front of Mr. Jim's store, his scarecrow held a wooden sign with WELCOME HOME, NOVA painted in white.

"Your mom didn't tell you they'd done this?" Lance asked.

"No, she didn't. I guess she was hoping I'd get to see it for myself," I said, taking short steps and reading every sign. It didn't matter that most of them said the same thing. I read it anyway.

Farther down the street, I stopped in front of Southern Sweets. There were a few iron tables and chairs outside of the bakery that weren't there before, but other than that, everything else looked the same as I remembered. I couldn't begin to count the number of times Leah and I begged Mama to buy us some donuts or let us split a cinnamon roll because they were so big. Mama rarely gave in, but Daddy always did.

The more I walked, the more memories came, and the bigger the why-can't-I-be-happy wave washed over me. All my happiest memories were escorted by a feeling of despair. Every corner of this town held a story that included Leah and Daddy and, in most cases, both of them together.

"Not much has changed, as you can see," Lance said.

"And yet, everything has changed," I said as we stood at the edge of Main Street and in front of the park. The park, I remembered, had a swing set, a slide, and a sandbox. Now, there was all of that, plus more things for kids to play on, along with a pond in the center of the park, a walking trail around the pond, and covered areas with picnic tables underneath.

We were about to walk away from the park when a bronze plaque caught my attention. "What's that?" I pointed.

"It's nothing. Just a plaque. You ready to go back?" he asked, sounding more rushed than before.

"In a second." I left his side and moved toward the plaque.

"I'm telling you, it's nothing," he said, walking behind me.

I stood over the plaque and started reading. "Oh my goodness," I said, swinging around to him. "What are you talking about it's nothing?"

"Because it's nothing."

"This park stands revitalized through the generosity and vision of Lance Dupre," I started reading.

"Please don't." Lance held his head.

"A son of Bayou whose dedication to our community and commitment to nurturing the joy and health of our children are embodied in this renewed space. May this park serve as a lasting tribute to his legacy of giving back and fostering spirits as strong and resilient as his own. Dedicated in 2015 by the people of Bayou." I put my hand over my chest. "Awww . . . Lance." I walked over and hugged him. "That was so sweet."

"Don't do that." He blushed.

"And that's not nothing. It's something. A big something, and I don't know why you wouldn't be proud of that."

"Because it was before . . . It was a different time then. Like Quinton said, a lot has changed."

"Like what?" I asked.

"Like too much to get into now, but one day I will, but please don't press me about it, okay?"

"Okay," I said, more worried than nosy.

Whatever it was, based on his response, couldn't have been good. The mood shifted, and I regretted going over to the plaque. It was obvious it bothered him for some reason.

"I'm sorry," I said, hoping it would make him feel better, but I knew it wouldn't. Words didn't heal hurt—not for me anyway.

"No, don't be sorry. You're good. I promise. Today's a big day for you, and I want to focus on that and nothing else."

"I can do that," I said, reaching for his hand again and soaking in the feeling of being with my friend.

When Lance and I were kids, we used to walk or ride our bikes all over Bayou. Our parents and grandparents never worried about anything bad happening to us. When we left home, they knew we'd come back. I used to believe that too. Maybe one day I would again.

CHAPTER 30

Leah

It had been years since Leah woke up early enough to go jogging with Quinton. When she made it home last night, she wasn't in the mood to talk about her visit with Nova. She still couldn't believe that her sister had the nerve to say that Leah always wanted to be her.

When? Leah never wanted to be Nova—not ever. She hated sports, which Nova loved, and being outside, which Nova loved. Then there was Quinton, and Nova had made it very clear how Leah felt about him back then, so she certainly wasn't jealous of their relationship. So, why would she say that?

To hurt Leah. She knew that, of course, but it didn't make her feel any better. She had always been Nova's biggest cheerleader, and she played that role proudly. To think that Nova would accuse her of being jealous was beyond hurtful.

When Leah made it home, she had to tuck her feelings inside and deal with them later. They'd eaten a late dinner, then she and Skye finished Skye's project that was due today. Leah had planned to tell Quinton about the magazine article, but by the time she made it to bed, Quinton was asleep, and she was too tired to talk.

"What made you want to walk this morning?" Quinton asked now. "Not that I'm complaining. I'm happy to have the company. I'm not used to it anymore." He reached down and touched his toes.

Leah followed his movements. "I figured it'd help clear my mind. I haven't exactly been myself at work, which isn't good when you're a therapist, you know?"

"No, I guess it's not." He leaned to one side and touched his foot.

After they finished stretching, both started their smartwatches to record their exercise. "Can we walk for a little while first? I want to talk to you about something," Leah asked, taking long strides to keep up with Quinton's normal ones.

She remembered then why she'd stopped walking or jogging with him. She had to give twice as much to keep up with his normal pace. It was more exhausting than relaxing.

"Yeah . . . sure," Quinton said. "What do you want to talk about?"

Leah told Quinton about the magazine article and how it quoted a statement that supposedly came from a family friend.

Quinton stopped walking. "What?" He pushed the word out with more force than Leah expected.

"What's wrong?" she asked, taken aback by his reaction. "Do you know something?"

"Yes. It's exactly what I'd been saying all along. Who do you think the family friend could be?" he questioned.

Leah didn't know why it didn't cross her mind that Quinton would immediately think the source was Lance. Maybe because she knew that was highly unlikely.

"It wasn't Lance," Leah said, looking down at her watch, which asked if she wanted to pause her workout.

She started walking again.

Quinton slowed down to her pace. "How do you know?" he asked.

"Because . . ." Leah had become very creative with her answers about Lance. "Carmen told me how much he hates the media after they dragged his name through the mud during that whole ordeal. He'd never talk with them about anything." Leah pumped her arms because Quinton was starting to move faster.

"Money can make anyone talk, Leah. No matter how much you supposedly dislike them."

"But he has money," Leah added.

Quinton looked over at her. "Did Carmen tell you that too?"

"No, she didn't have to. He played in the NFL."

"Leah, there are a lot of broke men who played professional ball."

And at that, Leah dropped the conversation. She was already dealing with the aftermath of one confession. She wasn't ready to add another one. The more she thought about telling Quinton that she'd been Lance's therapist, the more she was against the idea. Leah understood that many times, mates felt the need to confess to what they, or their partner, might view as a betrayal in order to clear their conscience. Oftentimes, all it did was offer unnecessary hurt to the other spouse. There were times when what they didn't know really wouldn't hurt them. And her confession about Lance was one of those times.

"Even if it's not him, which I'm willing to bet it is, you still need to tell your mom, if you didn't already. She needs to know so she can watch what she says."

"I told Mom last night, but I'm pretty sure she doesn't suspect Lance. She trusts him just like she trusts us. Anyway," Leah said, moving the conversation away from Lance, "my visit with Nova wasn't very successful."

"I figured as much. I kept waiting for you to say something about it last night, but when you didn't bring it up, I figured you didn't want to talk about it," he said.

"No, I wanted to talk about it, but not in front of Skye. All this messy grownup stuff should stay between us as much as it can. She's already been exposed to enough."

When it came to Skye, Leah had the mama-bear role down to a science. She'd failed in her position Saturday night, though. Had she been thinking about Skye, she never would've told Nova about their marriage. She would've found a way to change the subject, as she'd done before, and moved on. After that, though, Leah vowed to herself that she'd always think about the repercussions her words would have on everyone, not just one person. The only thing she wanted Skye to think about was teenage drama. Who was dating whose boyfriend this week? Who'd posted what on social media? Silly stuff like that.

"I agree. I don't want Skye in the middle of all this either. So, what happened when you talked with Nova?" Quinton asked, slowing down his pace again.

Leah started from the beginning and shared everything. She ended with the gut punch that Nova had delivered. "She said that you'd never love me the way you loved her, and I'd never love you the way she did."

"Whoa," Quinton said.

That's it? Whoa? Leah didn't overreact because people processed information differently. Once it hit him, then he'd react with the outrage that Leah expected.

It never came.

"What happened after that?" Quinton asked.

"I was about to leave because I couldn't believe she'd said that to me. That she would intentionally hurt me like that," Leah said, once again waiting on a flabbergasted Quinton to comment. "But I couldn't leave without making things clear for her."

Quinton's pace slowed even more.

"I told her that she was right. We wouldn't love each other like the two of you did because I'm not her. You love me for me."

"You told her that?" he asked.

Leah finally heard the disbelief she had been waiting to hear. Only it was on the wrong side of the conversation. The words lodged in her throat seemed to scorch her whole body.

"Yes, I told her that. Did I lie?" Leah asked.

"No, but I don't know if you should've said it to her."

"Are you kidding me?" Leah's voice rose above the we-are-still-in-our-neighborhood-so-let's-not-cause-a-scene level.

Quinton looked around to make sure none of their neighbors were outside, listening to the conversation that Leah knew he'd rather die than have in front of them. When they chose that neighborhood, they were the only Black couple. The unspoken rule in the Boudreaux family was to always make sure the neighbors knew they belonged. This meant don't be loud, always smile, only wear outside clothes when leaving the house, even if you're only going to the mailbox—no bonnets, and no sleeping clothes.

Leah and Quinton tabled the conversation until they made it back to their house. Leah tried to taper down the frustration and resentment that started simmering inside her. The more she thought about Quinton's lack of concern for her feelings, the bigger her internal storm grew. Leah had realized she'd been clenching her teeth until her temples started to throb.

Instead of going inside, he unlocked his truck and opened the door for Leah to get in. Leah happily obliged. She had a feeling there were words she needed to say that she didn't want Skye to hear, and she'd held it in too long already while she finished her walk.

"I'm not sure what happened back there, but you know this isn't us," Quinton said as soon as he closed his door. "We don't argue in the streets. We're not those people."

Leah exhaled slowly, reminding herself that anger wouldn't solve anything. When she felt calmer, she said, "We weren't arguing. We were discussing," Leah corrected.

"Fine. Then, we don't discuss that loud outside of our house," he corrected.

Leah glanced at her watch. "We both have to get ready for work soon, so are we going to discuss the real issue?" Her voice was steady, but inside, her heart raced. Leah felt the weight of the biggest issue they had to face. Whether Quinton was still a part of her team or if he'd moved his membership over to Nova's.

"What's the real issue?" he asked.

"For me, it's the way you responded when I told you what Nova said to me versus the response to what I said to her. Where was the outrage for me?" She felt herself getting worked up again, so she closed her eyes and took deep breaths.

Quinton leaned his head against the headrest and stared at the roof before lowering his gaze back to Leah. "First, I wasn't outraged. And you know why my response was different. We both said we had to be careful how we handled Nova. She's dealing with a lot of trauma. That's why I responded that way."

"Yes, we did say that, and maybe I shouldn't have said what I said. Maybe I shouldn't have said anything at all. Hell, maybe I shouldn't have even gone over there last night, but all of that is beside the point."

"Then what is the point, Leah, because I'm missing it."

"The point is when I express how someone said something with the clear intent to hurt me, I expect my husband to say something other than whoa," Leah said, her nails digging into the palm of her hands.

Quinton exhaled sharply. His expression softened, and his shoulders dropped. "Okay. You're right. I'm sorry, but all of this is new to me. There's no handbook for husbands on what to do when the wife you thought was dead for fifteen years comes back after you've fallen in love with and married her sister."

"Really? Because there's not one for sisters who thought their sister was dead for fifteen years and came back after you've married her ex-husband either." Leah added extra emphasis on *ex* since Quinton seemed to keep forgetting that Nova wasn't his wife, and if she was, then that made him a bigamist. But he wasn't, because Nova was declared dead, and their marriage ended with that declaration.

"Okay, look. I may not have responded the right way, and again, I'm sorry, but . . ."

"Why is there always a but? Why can't you apologize and be done with it."

"Because it's not as simple as that. What I was trying to say is that you have to give me some grace here."

"That's the thing, though. You shouldn't need grace—not for that. Coming to my defense and making sure I'm okay above everyone else should be automatic for you. It shouldn't have to be something you have to think about or remember to do." Leah opened her door, then looked back at Quinton, feeling more isolated than she'd ever felt before.

"Where are you going?" Quinton reached for her. His brows furrowed, and his eyes showed a hint of panic. "We can't leave things like this."

"I have a client. I have to get ready for work."

Leah was surprised to hear movement in the kitchen. Most mornings Leah or Quinton had to drag Skye out the bed.

"Is Skye cooking?" Quinton asked.

The answer came as soon as they walked in and saw the table set with eggs, bacon, toast, and orange juice.

"Good morning," Skye sang. "Sit. I made breakfast."

Leah and Quinton exchanged glances. Of course, Skye was up to something. She never cooked breakfast or anything else.

"What do you want?" Quinton asked, taking a seat at the table.

"Okay, since I don't have a lot of time, I'll make it quick. Friday night after the game, some of my teammates are getting together to hang out at the lake. I want to go," Skye said, clasping her hands together and rocking back and forth.

"Absolutely not," Quinton said without giving her request any thought. "You think I don't know what goes on at the lake at night?"

"Kids hanging out," Skye said innocently.

"Yeah . . . okay." Quinton laughed.

"Dad, I'm serious. We're going to hang out. That's it."

"And I'm serious too. Maybe they're going to hang out, but you're not."

Skye narrowed her eyes and glared at Quinton. It was a look Leah had never seen from her before, and she was nervous. What was happening?

"You know, my mom was right. She said that I should be allowed to do what I want, and no one should be able to tell me what to do with my body," Skye said.

Leah and Quinton exchanged a look that conveyed much more than confusion—it was a silent conversation where they were both asking what in the hell was Skye talking about? And bigger than that, why in the hell was Nova giving her that kind of advice? Not that it was entirely wrong, but it didn't apply to them. Did Nova clarify that, or was she just throwing out incomplete advice?

"I know that this has nothing to do with my body, but the point is that I'm glad I have a parent who trusts me and understands that I'm not a baby anymore." Skye yanked her book sack off the counter and stormed out of the kitchen.

Quinton sat in stunned silence. Skye's behavior seemed as shocking to him as it had been to Leah.

There was one thing Leah wished she'd said before Skye left, though. She wished she'd told Skye that Nova wasn't the only person fighting for her to have a little more freedom. Leah had been fighting for years for Quinton to give in a little, but he wouldn't budge. It wasn't that he didn't trust Skye. It was all the other people he didn't trust. He felt that he'd failed Nova, and unfortunately, Skye was paying the price for that.

One thing Leah learned that morning was that exercising didn't always make you feel better—not when you were doing it with a partner who somehow forgot that you were on the same team.

Leah looked up from her computer when someone knocked on her office door.

"Come in." She put on her brightest smile and stood, expecting her temporary assistant, Tanja, who was filling in for Leah's real assistant who was still out on maternity leave, to walk in with her first appointment. They were a new couple, and Leah had been excited when they contacted her last month.

"Ms. Lefleur, the Smiths called, and they're running a little behind," Tanja announced.

Leah sat, confused as to why she didn't call with that information instead. "Thank you, Tanja."

"But"—Tanja's face lit up as she made her way closer to Leah—"Lance is here to see you. He said it'll only take a few minutes."

"Lance Dupre?" Leah questioned.

"Yes, the football player." Tanja's eyes were almost wider than her smile.

"Okay. Please send Mr. Dupre in," Leah said, correcting Tanja's informal use of Lance's name.

Tanja glanced toward the door, then back at Leah. "Would it be okay if I asked Mr. Dupre for an autograph for my son?" she whispered.

"How about I get one for you?" Leah suggested.

She knew Lance wouldn't mind, especially when it came to children, but Leah was curious about his unannounced visit and didn't want to waste any more time before she found out.

Tanja nodded before sashaying to the door and ushering Lance inside.

"Well, this is a surprise," Leah said to Lance. To Tanja she said, "Thank you, that'll be all."

Tanja closed the door behind her.

"I'm sorry to drop in like this," Lance said. "I finished my appointment with my new therapist, and you were right. I can tell that Dr. Brown is going to be a great fit for me. He was easy to talk to. Like you were," Lance said.

"Good. I'm glad to hear that." Leah leaned against her desk.

"But that's not why I'm here."

Leah was hoping his visit would be quick. With so much attention on Nova these days, she didn't know who was watching them. Then her mind went to the magazine. She thought about what Quinton had said. They didn't know who was sharing information about them. It could've been someone they didn't even know, as far as Leah knew. It wasn't like they'd shared anything personal. Leah assumed the family hurt the "family friend" was referring to was Leah and Quinton's marriage. It wouldn't have taken an inside source to assume that Nova may have been hurt once she was informed.

"So why are you here?" Leah asked once she realized she hadn't responded.

"I figured since you're no longer my therapist, and I was in the area, then it would be okay for me to stop by and check on you. Nova told me what happened."

Leah leaned back in her seat and crossed her arms. "I'm fine."

One corner of his mouth turned up. "Yeah, you look like you're fine. Come on, Leah, I see the pain written all over your face."

"What you see all over my face is Fenty number three ninety."

Lance narrowed his eyes. "I have no idea what that means, but I saw how hurt you looked when I mentioned Nova's name. The two of you were closer than any siblings I'd ever met. I know you can't be okay."

Leah desperately wanted to talk with someone about everything that was going on in her life, but that someone couldn't be Lance. Not only because she already had enough guilt from sneaking around and working with him all those months but also because Lance was Nova's friend. His reaction to Leah's story would be even worse than Quinton's. Leah needed someone who would side with her, whether she was wrong or not. Who she needed was Harper. Her best friend would give Leah all the outrage Leah needed, but Harper was busy with her vlog and her family. Leah didn't want to dump all her issues on her, even though Harper would insist.

"I don't know what you think you saw in my eyes," Leah said, "but I promise you that I'm fine. It's not like I wasn't expecting this to happen.

I knew Nova was going to be upset. I also know that after she's had some time, she'll come around." Leah stood. "And when she does, we'll talk, and all of this will be a thing of the past."

Lance stood too. "I believe that as well."

That made one of them because Leah didn't believe a word she'd said. All she needed was for him to leave so she could go on with her day. She liked Lance, but she didn't like the feeling she got whenever she was around him. She wasn't doing anything wrong, though. She was simply doing her job and shouldn't have felt bad about that, but she did.

"Oh, before you go." The magazine article popped into Leah's mind. "Did you, by any chance, say anything to anyone about Nova?"

Lance furrowed his brows. "You'll have to be more specific. The whole town of Bayou is talking about Nova. You know that."

"I know. I mean." Leah paused. "One second." She walked around to her desk and pulled the magazine from her bottom drawer. She gave it to Lance, then explained the quote from the family friend.

Lance was quiet as he read the part that Leah had pointed out. He lifted his eyes to her. "You think I'm the family friend?"

"I didn't know, but I had to ask."

Lance gave her the magazine back. "Well, I can assure you that I never said this to anyone. And you know there's no way I'd ever talk to a reporter about anything. After the way they dragged my name through the mud." He shook his head.

"I know. I'm sorry if I offended you, but . . ."

"No, I understand. I don't know who said it, but it sounds like a family friend that you all may want to distance yourselves from," he warned.

"I agree."

"Take care." Lance touched her arm. "And thanks for everything."

"Don't mention it." Leah smiled, but she meant it literally.

"I see what you did there." Lance wagged his finger at her.

They were both laughing when Leah opened the door to let him out.

"Oh, I completely forgot." Leah looked at Lance. "Would you mind signing your autograph for Ms. Peterson's son?" Leah asked, pointing to Tanja, who was standing behind her desk, still beaming.

Tanja gave Lance a sheet of paper to sign while looking over at Leah. "Ms. Lefleur, these are for you." Tanja lifted a beautiful glass vase filled with sunflowers.

Leah loved sunflowers, and there was only one person who knew that. Her heart expanded with the love she felt for Quinton. Yes, her husband had his faults, as did she, but he was an amazing man who loved her so much. She needed that reminder today.

"That man," she smiled, lifting the flowers to her nose to smell.

"Your husband dropped them off. You just missed him. I told him you were meeting with Lan—I mean, Mr. Dupre, and you wouldn't be long, but he didn't want to wait."

Leah froze. Her gaze flicked between the bright sunflowers and Tanja's oblivious smile. A knot tightened in her stomach, and she struggled to keep the flowers steady in her shaky hands. "You told him what?" Leah asked, keeping her voice as calm as possible.

Tanja's smile melted. "Did I say something wrong?"

"Yes. You did," Leah said, working hard to keep her tone even. "You don't ever share information about who I'm meeting with to anyone. There's a such thing as client privacy, you know?"

Tanja smiled nervously. "I know, but I thought since he wasn't a client, then . . ."

Leah held up her hand. "It doesn't matter who it is. Client or otherwise," Leah snapped.

"I'm . . . I'm sorry." Water pooled in Tanja's eyes.

Leah was furious, but Tanja didn't do it on purpose. "It's fine. Just make sure it doesn't happen again."

"Here you go." Lance handed Tanja the paper he'd been holding. "Are you good?" He looked at Leah.

"Yeah, of course. I'll see you soon." She left them both standing there while she retreated to the safety of her office. Leah closed the door behind her and leaned against it for some much-needed support. She took deep breaths and tried to calm the storm that started brewing inside her.

As she placed the flowers on her desk, she told herself not to overreact. Besides, Quinton may not be upset. Her situation with Lance was nothing like Nova's. Leah wasn't hiding her meetings with Lance because of personal reasons . . . only. She had legal reasons too. However, Lance wasn't there as a client, so that reasoning didn't apply to today's meeting. But Quinton knew that Lance was a big supporter of mental health. He always served on some board or donated to some foundation. He even started his own foundation a few years ago. After Leah talked herself off the edge, she picked up her phone to call Quinton. He didn't answer. He had to be driving. Even though he didn't like talking and driving, he still did it.

She was about to call again when her intercom buzzed.

"Mr. and Mrs. Smith have arrived," Tanja announced, sounding a lot more somber than she had earlier.

Leah didn't have time to focus on Tanja's hurt feelings. She only had the energy to fix one problem at a time, and at the moment, her marriage ranked above Tanja's emotions.

"Send them in," Leah said, once again pushing her problems aside to focus on her clients.

Surprisingly, Leah was able to focus long enough to get through their entire session without her mind wandering off. The Smiths were the first couple she'd counseled who didn't have a traditional marriage. Leah's interest as they talked about their other partners was enough to keep her engaged. There was no way she could imagine sharing

Quinton with anyone. When it came to her husband, she was selfish and wanted him all to herself.

Once the Smiths left, Leah dialed Quinton again. No answer. She didn't have any more clients, so she called Harper and did the one thing she said she wouldn't do . . . unload all her problems on her friend.

CHAPTER 31

Nova

I didn't want to jinx myself, but I couldn't help feeling that today was one of the best days ever. We still had a lot of day left, so I tapped my knuckles against the wooden swing that I'd been sitting on for most of the day.

Lance and I had been on the front porch when Mama made it back from Ms. Cora's. He left shortly after Mama returned. He was waiting to get a package from her—something she needed him to take to Baton Rouge. It turned out that was why he'd stopped by in the first place. The funny thing was, I hadn't even thought to ask why he was there so early. I thought it was perfect timing, which, in a way, it was.

"You plan on sitting out here all day?" Mama asked through the screen door.

"Probably." I smiled back at her.

"I'm so proud of you," Mama said for the hundredth time that day.

I was excited about my walk with Lance and how great it felt to be out, but I think Mama's excitement had mine beat. I knew she hated seeing me cooped up in the house all day. She was ready for us to start going out and doing things together. I was ready for that too. I could see myself going to run errands or grocery shopping with, or for, Mama. I could see me and Skye going out to eat or to the movies. The thought had me pumped.

I'd closed my eyes and was lost in my thoughts when the sound of a vehicle made me sit up. My body tensed. A reminder that I still had a long way to go.

Seeing Quinton didn't help put to rest my desire to run inside and lock all the doors. I hadn't talked to him since finding out that he'd married my sister. I wasn't too surprised, though. Quinton never liked dealing with issues. He'd rather avoid it or act like everything was okay. I guessed that was why I was so upset that night in the hotel when he was angrier than I'd ever seen him before. It was the one time I decided to avoid it instead of him. In fact, I remember thinking that it wouldn't be long before he would leave the room, so I wanted to beat him to it. I couldn't even begin to count the number of times I wished he would've stormed out first.

"I know I'm the last person you want to see," Quinton said, propping one foot on the step while the other stayed on the ground.

He was dressed in a beige plaid suit with a burnt-orange tie. Quinton had always been one of the best-dressed men I knew. In high school, when Nike would come out with a new pair of Jordans, Quinton had them before anyone else. It was the same with name-brand clothes. I was so jealous until I understood that sending clothes was his mom's way of making up for not being there for him.

"What do you want?" I asked, glancing at him and then looking over his shoulder and toward the lawn, focusing my attention on anything except him.

"I wanted to see how you were doing." He stuck his hand in his pants pocket.

I turned back to him, but only long enough to say, "Well, you see. Now you can go." I folded my arms.

"I'll leave as soon as you hear me out." He stepped closer to the porch.

"Why can't you and your wife leave me alone?" I asked, glaring at him.

"Because we love you."

"Love?" I laughed at the word. "I think the two of you have a different definition of love than I do."

Quinton took another step, then another until he was standing on the porch. "I wish there was something I could say that would make this better."

"You can't, so don't bother."

Quinton exhaled, then sat in the rocking chair closest to me. It faced the other side of the porch, where I saw Quinton staring with a faraway look in his eyes. I may have been away from him for years, but I still felt like I knew him, and something told me that there was more to his visit than he was saying.

"Is that it, or is there something else you need?" I asked.

"I never meant to hurt you," he said. "I know I've said that before, and you may not believe it, but it's true. One day you said that you knew the minute we met that you wanted to be with me forever. You remember that?" He looked over at me.

"Of course I remember because it was true," I answered.

"And I asked you how did you know? You said it was hard to answer that question, but it was just a feeling. Just something you knew." He paused. "That's the only way I can describe what happened between Leah and me. It wasn't something we forced. It wasn't something either one of us desired or wished to happen. It just did. Honestly, I think we were more surprised than anyone when things changed."

I could tell he was trying to be careful with his words, but they still stung. They still poked at wounds that I wished I could numb. When I didn't say anything, he continued.

"You have no idea how much I wish I could change things."

My attention snapped in his direction. "Are you saying you wish you didn't marry Leah?"

He didn't answer immediately, but then he shook his head. "I'm saying I wish we weren't the cause of your hurt. If I could take it away and carry it myself, believe me, I would in a heartbeat."

"But you can't, and knowing that the two of you are married does hurt, but I guess there's nothing I can do about that except live with it."

Quinton was quiet once again.

"Is that it?" Nova asked again.

"No, actually, there's something else I want to talk with you about."

The screen door opened. "Oh, hey, Quinton. I didn't know you were here."

"Hey, Ms. Martha." Quinton walked over and gave Mama a kiss on her cheek.

"How's it going?" Mama asked, leaning against the door with a mason jar of sweet tea in her hand.

"I can't complain," Quinton said, going back to the rocking chair. "Something smells good in there." He nodded toward the house where Mama had been working her magic in the kitchen as she'd done every day.

"You're welcome to stay for dinner."

He chuckled. "I may take you up on that."

Quinton and Mama continued their small talk until Mama went back inside. I was ready for her to leave so he could tell me the other reason he'd stopped by. The sooner he said what he needed to say, the sooner I could tell him that he shouldn't stay for dinner. I wasn't ready to sit and eat with him.

"So, what were you saying?" I asked.

"Skye," he said.

Her name caused me to perk up. It always did. "What about her?"

"She said something this morning that kind of bothered me, and I thought we should talk about it."

"What did she say?"

I listened as Quinton told me about his conversation with Skye, which started with her wanting to go hang out at the lake, and him saying no, and ending with her telling him that I said no one should tell her what she could and couldn't do with her body.

"Okay . . . and?" I asked, wondering what was so wrong with that.

"I was curious about that statement. I agree that no one should tell her what she can and cannot do with her body, but were you telling her that about other people or about me?"

"It was about anyone who tried to tell her what to do with her body." I leaned closer to him. "Which includes her hair." I pointed to my hair.

"So that's what the conversation was about? Her wanting to cut her hair?" he asked.

"Yes, and I told her she could."

"You what?" His voice rose.

I flinched.

"I'm sorry. Why did you tell her she could cut her hair without talking with me first?"

"You sound like Mama. Did you talk with me when you told her she couldn't?"

"No, because that conversation happened months ago, before you came back." He loosened his tie.

"And what about this morning when she asked to go to the lake? Did you tell her you needed to speak with me first?"

He narrowed his eyes. "No. Why would I say that when the answer was still going to be no."

"Oh, I see." I nodded slowly. "You don't have to check with me, but I have to check with you. Is that how this works?"

"Right now, yes. You just got home, Nova. And I get that you're Skye's mom, and you want a relationship with her, but part of being a parent is being responsible."

"Are you saying I'm not responsible?" I stood, unable to sit any longer.

He stood. "I'm saying you've never raised a teenager before, and it's not all fun and games. Skye needs structure. She needs discipline. She doesn't need a friend."

"I'm not trying to be her friend," I argued. "All I want is to be her mom."

"You are her mom. You don't have to try to be that," he said, his voice a lot calmer than before.

"It's hard to feel like her mom when I only get to see her every now and then."

"That's because it's basketball season. Once it's over, she'll have more free time," he said.

"Or if she lived here with me and Mama, I could see her every day like you do."

He shook his head and smiled, but not a real smile. More like a what-are-you-talking-about kind of smile. "Live here?" he said, his finger pointing down.

"Yes, here," I repeated.

"That's not going to happen. Skye isn't moving out of her home, Nova. Be for real."

"I am being for real. You've had her all these years, Quinton. I want some time with her too. It's not like she'll be moving out of state. You can see her every day."

"And so can you," he said, rubbing his hand back and forth over his hair. I remember he did that when he was agitated. "Can this day get any worse?" he mumbled.

"I'm not trying to ruin your day," I said.

"It was ruined before I got here." He walked to the steps and then looked back. "I need to go, but I'll talk with Skye and tell her to try and stop by more."

I didn't respond because he wasn't getting it. Or maybe he was and was too selfish to try and see where I was coming from. I'd love to know how he'd feel if he'd missed fifteen years of our daughter's life. Would he be happy seeing her every now and then? No, he wouldn't. He'd want her all the time. I didn't care what Quinton said. It wasn't his decision. If Skye wanted to come and live here with me and Mama, then that was what she'd do.

CHAPTER 32

Leah

The more Leah called Quinton, the more worried she became. Quinton had never ignored her calls before. Sure, there were times when he couldn't answer, but he always called back. It was almost four o'clock, and he should've been home. She thought about calling Mario, but that might make things worse. Quinton was private, and if Leah called Mario to look for him, then Mario would know that something was wrong. Which would upset Quinton even more. Unless something was wrong? Something more than him being upset about Lance's visit?

When the front door chimed, Leah resisted the urge to go running down the hallway and wrap her arms around him. She didn't care about him being upset with her. She needed him to be okay.

"Hey." Skye walked in and leaned against the doorway.

"Hey, yourself." Leah hoped her disappointment wasn't evident in her voice. "How was your day?"

"Fine," Skye said, offering her usual answer to that question.

"Hey, can we talk?" Leah asked, peeking at the lasagna she'd put in the oven. She led Skye down the hallway and into the family room.

Skye slumped on the sofa and folded her arms. "What's up?" she asked, her voice just as dry as before.

"I know you're not happy about this weekend."

"No, I'm not. And why don't you ever speak up for me? Tell Dad that he's being unreasonable or something."

"I do speak up for you. I don't do it in front of you. I thought I could get through to him if I talked with him alone."

"A lot of good that did." Skye rolled her eyes. "He's never gonna let me grow up."

"You know how your dad is when it comes to you," Leah said.

"Yeah, possessive."

"Protective," Leah corrected. "Let's go with that one instead."

"Protective from what? My friends? It's ridiculous, and you know it."

It wasn't the first time that Leah had seen Skye upset over Quinton's unreasonable rules, but she'd never been upset to this degree. Normally, she'd pout for a while, then she'd move on. How much of this was Skye, and how much was Nova?

The front door chimed again, and a wave of relief washed over Leah. Skye stood and picked up her backpack. "I have homework."

She was at the doorway when Quinton walked up. "Hey." He leaned down and kissed Skye. "How was your day?"

"It was okay." She played with her nails and didn't look at him.

"I talked with Nova, and I think we need to talk," Quinton said, his eyes still fixed on Skye.

It wasn't lost on Leah that he didn't speak to her, nor did he include her in the talk that he and Skye needed to have. That was evident in the way he successfully made her feel as if she wasn't even in the room.

Quinton waved Skye back into the living room. Skye sat next to Leah, and Quinton sat on the edge of the sofa on the other side of Skye. He'd angled his body so that he was looking directly at Skye, and still not acknowledging Leah. She wondered if Skye noticed. Probably not. Skye was too wrapped up in her own issues with her dad to notice the cold shoulder he gave to Leah.

Leah's heart sank as the disconnect between her and Quinton grew wider by the second.

"I want you to try to spend more time with Nova. She really misses you. I know you have practice and all that, but whenever you can, stop by there for an hour or so."

"Okay," Skye answered, staring straight ahead and not bothering to look at her dad.

"Good. Maybe now she'll give up this ridiculous idea about you moving in." Quinton touched Skye's leg. "But don't worry, I shut that down quickly. She knows that's not about to happen."

"She wants me to move in?" Skye sat up straight, sounding more like herself.

"Yes, but like I said, I already told her no, so if she brings it up, I don't want you to get worried that it could happen."

Leah didn't understand how Quinton was missing the look on Skye's face and the tone in her voice. Their daughter was far from worried. She looked like she was open to the idea. Leah's heart pounded. There was no way Skye would want to leave them . . . right?

"What if I want it to happen?" Skye asked.

Leah's head shot toward Skye, then over to Quinton, whose shocked expression matched how Leah felt.

Quinton's squared shoulders made him look much bigger than he had a second ago. "What do you mean what if you want it to happen?" he asked, his voice low, as if he was straining to get the words out.

"I'm not saying to live forever, but at least during the week. I've been thinking about staying with Gran since last school year, but I didn't say anything because I knew you wouldn't approve," she said to Quinton.

"And I still don't," he asserted firmly. "You're not moving out." The finality in his tone should've ended the discussion, but it only seemed to add fuel to Skye's fire.

"You see." Skye stood. "This is exactly why I want to go. You never listen to me. Every time there's something I want to do, you automatically say no without giving it any thought. At least when I'm with my . . . Nova . . . she listens to me. She doesn't treat me like a child who can't think for herself."

Quinton's posture stiffened. "Well, right now, you're acting like a child," Quinton shot back. "It's the middle of the school year, and you all of a sudden want to move?"

"During the week. That's it. I'll be here on the weekends." She pointed toward the stairs. "In my bedroom doing nothing while all my friends are out having fun, as usual."

The wrinkles in Quinton's forehead disappeared as his body seemed to deflate. "I don't know where all this is coming from." Quinton paused. "Actually, I do know. Nova has put all of this in your head. I understand why she wants to spend more time with you. I get that, and I'm not going to stand in the way of the two of you doing that, but you don't have to move during the week or otherwise for that to happen."

Leah listened to Skye as she expressed her desire for independence and to be heard. A part of Leah empathized and understood Skye's argument, but a bigger part of her was gripped by fear. She couldn't lose their Skye. Their connection was one of the few bright spots Leah had, and she needed to hold on to it as long as she could.

Skye threw her backpack over her shoulder. "Of course. Whatever you say, Dad." She took long strides out of the room. The next sounds were her footsteps pounding against the stairs.

"I need to check on the food; then we should talk," Leah told Quinton.

"I don't want to do this tonight." Quinton left the room, leaving Leah standing alone. The feeling of rejection had settled in like an unwelcome guest. Was this their life now? Running away from their issues instead of dealing with them? Leah knew all too well the negative impact the lack of communication could have on a marriage.

Leah pulled the lasagna, which was too dark for her liking, out of the oven and placed it on the stove to cool. The likelihood that anyone would be eating it was slim, but that wasn't her greatest concern. As she made her way to Quinton's office, everything in her said to turn around and go the other way. As a marriage counselor, Leah always advised her clients not to discuss serious issues when they were upset. Her directives were to give things time to settle and heads time to cool. Ignoring her own advice, Leah knocked on Quinton's office door.

She pushed it open when he didn't respond. "Are we really not going to talk about what happened earlier?"

Quinton narrowed his brows. "What happened?" he asked.

"Seriously? That's how you're going to act?"

"I told you I didn't want to talk about it right now, but fine, you wanna talk . . . talk." He waved his hands away from his body as if giving her the floor.

Leah took a deep breath and then steadied her voice. "I didn't know Lance was going to stop by. He was telling me about Nova."

"What about her?" Quinton asked.

She continued. "Just that she left the house this morning, and they walked into town. He said she was nervous at first, but she was determined to do it."

"And he came all the way to your office to tell you that," Quinton questioned.

"No, he didn't come just for that. He was in the area, so he stopped in."

Quinton shook his head. "I still don't understand why he needed to tell you that. Your mom could've told you about Nova. Why is he that comfortable stopping by unannounced, anyway?"

"You're making a big deal out of nothing," Leah said. "He was there all of five minutes. Not long at all."

"It may not be a big deal for you, but it's a very big deal to me. If I hadn't stopped by, would you have told me?"

Leah didn't answer because they both knew that he really didn't want the answer to that question.

"That's what I thought."

"The only reason I wouldn't have told you is because I knew you'd act like this, and why would I want to get you all worked up over nothing? Lance is Nova's friend. He's like a son to Mama. And bigger than that, he's heavily involved in a lot of the mental-health programs in the area. We're going to run into each other, and it'll be kind of awkward if I ignore him every time I see him," she tried to explain.

"Seeing him out is one thing, Leah, but you didn't see him out somewhere. He was in your office. Your personal space. That's where my issue lies. How would you feel if someone you had a problem with was popping in to see me?"

Leah didn't know how she'd feel. There wasn't anyone she could think of that she had a problem with. "I'd like to think if it was someone who was involved in the insurance industry, that I'd understand. Not only that, but I trust you, so I'd know whatever you were meeting about had to be professional or, at the very least, not inappropriate."

"This isn't about trust. It's about respect. I came up there because I felt so bad about how we ended things this morning, and I wanted to apologize. I was going to tell you that you were right, your feelings are the only ones I should be worried about, and no one else's. Then . . ." He laughed sarcastically. "While I'm standing there, holding the flowers I thought you'd love, I find out that the very person I have an issue with is sitting in your office." Quinton's voice was louder and deeper with each word he spoke.

"This was a mistake. No matter what I say, you're going to be upset, so why am I even bothering to explain?" Leah said, throwing her hands in the air.

"I don't know," Quinton mumbled.

Leah believed in talking things out, no matter how uncomfortable the conversation may have felt, but that night, she couldn't. It felt like she was handed a new burden to carry every day while still holding on to the one from the day before. It was getting too heavy, and Leah needed a release, or she was definitely going to break.

She left Quinton's office and didn't bother going back into the kitchen to her overcooked lasagna. In her bathroom, Leah unscrewed the top of her anti-anxiety medication and popped one in her mouth. She'd gone from needing them every now and then to every day. Leah thought grieving death was the worst thing she'd ever have to go through, but she was wrong. At least she understood death and the process of healing from it. There were no written steps or a process for everything that was going on in their lives. There was heaviness around all of them, and all Leah wanted was to somehow find a way through so she and everyone she loved could be happy again. It didn't seem like too much to ask, but it felt almost impossible to achieve.

CHAPTER 33

Nova

Lance and I had gone for a walk every day this week. Always early in the morning before too many people were out and about. In the evenings, when Skye stopped by, she'd fill me in on her practice. The more time I spent with Skye, the more time I wanted. That was why today I was going out with Mama. There still wouldn't be a lot of people out since it was Friday, and people were still at work. Mama said Bayou was pretty dead during the day since a lot of people worked in Baton Rouge. It wasn't like there were very many jobs in Bayou, so it made sense for people to commute to the city for work.

"You look beautiful," Mama said as she stood at the bathroom door, her hair pulled back in a ponytail, showing off her high cheekbones, which she'd lightly dusted with blush.

I wondered if I was the only person who thought Mama looked young for her age. Or maybe I didn't know what a sixty-year-old woman should look like.

"Not as gorgeous as you look," I told her.

Mama said it was a beautiful day and we should go out for lunch. I wanted to have something more to share with Dr. Yvonne on Monday, so lunch today was a perfect idea. I kept reminding myself of Lance's advice to drown out the noise. All the negative thoughts that tried to make me believe something bad would happen. I also reminded myself that this was Bayou. Nothing bad happened in Bayou. I was safe here, with Mama and Lance and all the other people who thought of me as family. They wouldn't hurt me.

We pulled in front of Bayou Café, and the parking lot was fairly empty, like Mama said it would be. When I stepped inside, it felt like I'd stepped back into the past. I'd spent so much time in that café. Quinton used to bring me once Mama and Daddy finally started letting me go out on dates. It wasn't fancy, but it was all he could afford as a broke high school student.

"Nova! Oh my gosh." The short, thin lady behind the counter put her hands over her mouth. I immediately recognized her as Ms. Dot, short for Dorothy. Her eyes watered as she continued staring at me.

"Hey, Ms. Dot." I walked closer to the counter.

"It is so good to see you." Her voice cracked. "So . . . so . . . good."

"It's really good to see you too," I said, and it was.

Ms. Dot wiped her eyes. "Grab yourselves a table wherever you like, and someone will be over to take your order," Ms. Dot instructed.

"Thank you, Dot. I'm glad you're feeling better," Mama said to Ms. Dot before we found a table near the back of the café.

Mama sat across from me, facing the door. As soon as I sat, my heart raced. "Switch seats with me, please," I asked.

Mama narrowed her gaze but didn't ask any questions. Since it was my first time out, I hadn't realized how paranoid I'd feel with my back to the door. I felt vulnerable and unaware, and I didn't like it at all.

My heart rate slowed the minute I sat. I had a view of everything around me. "This was a good idea," I told Mama after the server brought out a pitcher of lemonade and three cups. "Oh, it's only two of us." I picked up the extra cup to give to the woman.

Mama was about to say something when I looked over her shoulder and saw Leah. "What is she doing here?" I hissed at Mama, heat rising in my body as Leah got closer.

Pretending not to hear me, Mama poured her lemonade and waited until Leah was seated before she spoke.

"Hello." Leah leaned down and kissed Mama before she sat.

"Hey, sweetie," Mama greeted Leah. "I know you're both wondering why you're here, but you shouldn't have to wonder. You know exactly why you're here." Mama looked at me, then over at Leah. "I've sat back long enough and waited for you to fix this thing between the two of you, but you're taking way too long for my liking."

I felt my chest tighten with shock and anger. How dare Mama do this to me? My palms began to sweat as I realized I was trapped in a situation that I wasn't prepared to deal with.

"I'm sorry, Mama, but I don't know how long it's supposed to take before someone can accept that their sister married their husband." My voice was as tight as my throat. The frustration made it hard to speak. I shot a glance at Leah as a fresh batch of resentment settled inside me.

"Ex-husband," Leah mumbled.

I narrowed my eyes so much that they almost closed. "But I only found out six days ago."

"I understand that, but you've already lost enough time together. You can't afford to lose six days. And you two aren't the only ones who are missing out. Leah don't come over like she used to because she doesn't want to upset you, Nova. I'm missing out on time I could be spending with both of my girls."

Leah bit her glossy lips while she made circles on the table with her finger. I watched her and noticed for the first time how small and vulnerable she looked. It reminded me of when we were kids, and she was bothered by something. It didn't happen often, but every now and then, she needed me to tell her that everything was going to be okay. I wished I could tell her that now, but I couldn't because I didn't know if that was true.

"I don't plan on going anywhere anytime soon," Mama continued, "but I have more days behind me than ahead of me, and I don't want to go another day without my *whole* family." She stressed the word *whole*.

I hated it when Mama talked like that. I didn't want to think about how many days she had left. I wanted to pretend that she had more ahead than behind. The reality of Mama's words hit me hard. The sadness in her eyes made her look much older than she had a few minutes ago. It was as if time had sped up since we sat down.

"I don't like it either," Leah said. She looked at me, her eyes glossy from unshed tears. "I don't know how we can move past this or what to do so you can forgive me, but I truly am sorry." She was barely able to get the words out before her sobs took over. Leah covered her face with her hands, and her body shook. Mama moved from her seat and pushed the empty chair next to Leah. She hugged Leah, and then Mama's eyes, filled with pain, connected with mine.

The agony in Leah's voice and the misery I saw in Mama pierced through my anger and caused it to seep from my body. For the first time in forever, the sadness I felt wasn't for me. It was for the two women my heart had ached to be with for fifteen long years. I'd been so consumed with my own hurt that I hadn't recognized anyone else's.

I swallowed, then said, "I know you are." I paused before adding, "I don't know how to be okay with all this. I mean, you and Quinton."

Mama reached across the table, and I placed my hand in hers. "Do you still love Quinton?" Mama asked.

I hesitated, feeling the entire weight of that question. The vision of the life I used to have with Quinton surfaced, but it wasn't as clear as it used to be. The image was now blurred and distorted. "I . . . I don't know. I don't think I love him the way I used to," I admitted. "But it wasn't about Quinton, not really. For so long, all I wanted was to be able to go back to how things were before Adam took it all away. That meant being Quinton's wife and Skye's mom and living together as a family, like before. It's learning to accept that the life I had before is truly gone."

Leah's shoulders dropped. "Because of me."

"No," I said softly. "Because of Adam. At some point, I have to stop blaming everyone else." My eyes burned. "I hate him so much, and I'm scared that I'll have to carry this feeling around for the rest of my life because he's gone, and he'll never have to pay for what he did to me. What he took from me."

Mama nodded. "You're carrying so much, baby. But holding on to that much hate will only hurt you. Not him. I'm not saying letting it go will be easy, but if anyone can get through it, you can."

The truth of her words resonated deeply, but the path to forgiving Adam seemed impossible.

"Nova, I know none of this is easy for you, and I am really sorry that my actions contributed to your pain. Hurting you in any way is the last thing I'd ever want to do."

Mama reached for both of our hands that time. She looked from me to Leah, then back to me again. "You can't control what happened in the past, but you've got a chance to build a brand-new future—a future with us and Skye. Adam may have stolen part of your past, but he and no one else can steal your future."

"She's right, Nova, and we're all here for you." Leah lowered her head, then glanced at me again. "If that's what you want, of course."

I smiled, then nodded. My throat was too tight to speak. I was overwhelmed, but that time it wasn't a bad feeling. I was overwhelmed by their love and support.

As the conversation ended, Leah announced that she needed to get back to her office.

Leah stood and kissed Mama. "I'll call you later." She looked over at me. "Bye, Nova."

"Bye . . . Leah."

She walked away, and something tugged at my heart. I fought it as long as I could, but the next thing I knew, I was pushing the chair back and walking toward the door. I caught up to her before she made it to her car.

"Leah," I called after her.

She turned toward me, her dark sunglasses covering her eyes.

I didn't speak. I just closed the space between us and wrapped my arms around my sister. Leah's body relaxed as she hugged me back.

"I don't know when or how I'll be completely okay with you as Quinton's wife, but right now, I'm more concerned with you as my sister," I said before we released each other.

"I'm so proud of you girls," Mama said when we drove away from the café. "Your dad is smiling down on you right now."

We made it home as Lance was backing away from the house. I was excited to share the news about my outing with Dr. Yvonne, but I was even more excited to share it with Lance. It amazed me that after all these years and after everything we'd gone through, our friendship felt as strong now as it did when we were kids. Now that he was back in my life again, I couldn't imagine him not being there. The Nova I was today could never end a friendship so strong and so important.

"Hey, there," Lance said when Mama and I got out of the car. "I was coming to see if you wanted to get out today, but I see I'm too late."

I looked at Mama, who was waiting by the front door. "You go ahead, I'm about to take a walk with Lance."

"Into town?" Lance asked.

"No, right down the lane. I want to tell you what happened today."

As we walked, I shared everything from Mama's suggestion that we go to lunch to my embrace with Leah. Lance listened intently, nodding and smiling at all the right moments.

"Nova, that's so good," he said when we made it to the end of the lane and the end of my story. "That explains that big smile on your mom's face," Lance said, as we turned and made our way back to the house.

"Yeah, she's the main reason why I'm trying so hard to be okay."

Lance stopped walking. "I understand why you want to fix your relationship with Leah for your mom, but you're also doing it for yourself, right?"

"Yes. Of course I'm doing it for myself too. I missed Leah."

"Good." He started walking again. "Sounds like everything is working out the way it was meant to."

"Almost." The pain in my heart stretched when I thought of Skye and the little time I got to see her. It all felt so unfair, but the more I thought about it, I knew Mama was right. That was her home, and I couldn't disrupt her life like that, no matter how bad I wanted to.

"You're quiet. What's up?"

"Nothing. Just thinking about Skye and how much I miss her when she's not here."

"It's not because she doesn't want to spend time with you, though. Basketball season is demanding with all the practices and games. You remember how it was."

"Doesn't mean I like it." I folded my arms and pouted like a baby.

"Aw." Lance pulled me into him and draped his arm over my shoulder. "I bet I have an idea that'll make you feel better."

"Is it Skye coming to spend more time with me? If not, I doubt it'll make me feel better."

"No, it's not that, but trust me. You're going to love it," Lance said when we made it to the front porch.

I did trust him, so when he told me to tell Mama we'd be right back, I didn't ask any more questions. Lance and I drove through town, past the park, and kept going until he pulled up to a big beige building.

"What's this?" I asked, looking at the building that looked to be new.

"It's a recreation center. I built it a few years ago." He pointed up to the sign on the building.

"The Frank Lefleur Athletic Center," I read aloud. "You named it after my dad?" My throat tightened.

"Of course. In a way, your parents are the ones who made this possible. Your mom sold me this land, and I was able to build the center."

I pointed at him. "You're the one who bought the land?"

"She told you about it?"

"She told me she'd sold some land, but she didn't say who she sold it to. I wonder why she didn't tell me it was you?"

A Sky Full of Love

"I don't know." Lance pulled another set of keys from his jacket pocket and unlocked the door.

The building was huge—much bigger than it looked from the outside. Lance gave me the grand tour, which ended in the gymnasium. In my world, there were two places that made me feel at home, and one of them was the basketball court.

"Stay right there." Lance jogged across the court and into a room. He came out bouncing a basketball back across the court. "In the mood for a little one on one?"

I laughed, my voice echoing through the empty court. "You can't be serious."

"Why not?" He bounced the ball through his legs.

"Because I haven't touched a basketball in years. I probably don't even know what to do with it anymore."

"Oh, come on, you know that's not true." He ran toward the basket and attempted a layup but failed.

"That's so pathetic," a voice said from the doorway.

Lance and I both turned, and my day went from good to great when I saw Skye standing there laughing.

"Skye!" I said louder than I intended. "What are you doing here?"

"Oh, I forgot to mention that Skye helps out here from time to time."

Skye pressed her hands together like she was praying. "But please don't tell my dad or Teeah. They don't know, but I love helping with the youth basketball team. If Dad finds out, he'll make me stop coming."

I looked at Lance. "Let me guess, because of you."

"Bingo." Lance aimed his finger at me and then glanced over at Skye. "Wait, what are you doing here? Don't y'all have a game tonight?"

"Yeah, I just need to get my knee brace. I forgot it the other day." She looked around. "I don't see it out here, though. Can I check the back office?"

"Sure, go ahead."

Skye jogged to the back of the building. Lance tucked the basketball underneath his arm. "Just so you know, I rarely see Skye when she's here. I make it a point to stay away during the youth-league practices. Quinton can't stand me, and I'm trying to be respectful of that when it comes to Skye. She's a child, and I don't want her in the middle of this mess."

"I still don't understand why he hates you so much. It's not like we were together anymore."

Lance furrowed his brows. "You think you're the reason he hates me?"

"Well, isn't it?"

"Not hardly. Quinton's dislike for me goes back to high school. Remember the practice that ended his football career?"

My mouth flew open. I'd completely forgotten about that. "He still blames you for his injury?"

"He's convinced that I did it on purpose. It didn't help that the coach put me in his position for the last few games. You know, the ones with the scouts that recruited me on the spot."

"Found it." Skye came back, holding her knee brace. "Can I talk with you for a minute?" she asked me.

"You two go ahead. I have some things I need to handle in the office before we leave," Lance said before tossing me the basketball.

"Everything okay?" I asked, tucking the ball underneath my arm.

"Dad said you'd talked with him about me moving in with you and Gran," she said.

I held my breath. Was she upset that I'd done that? Did I overstep? "I did, but I was just talking. I knew you wouldn't want to come and live with us."

"But I do. Want to come, I mean," she said, lowering her head.

"You do?" I nearly dropped the ball.

"Dad won't be happy about it. He made that clear, but I can't take it anymore. Do you know how it feels to go to school on Monday and listen to your friends talk about all the fun they had when you know the only thing you did was sit in your room or hang out with your dad and aunt?"

"No, I can't say that I know how that feels, but it doesn't sound too fun."

"It's not. Do you think you could go with me and talk to Dad? Maybe the two of us can get him to agree to let me move in with you and Gran."

I wanted Skye to move in with Mama and me more than I wanted to breathe. "Okay. When do you want to talk with them?"

"Tonight. After the game? Are you coming to the game?"

"Umm . . ." I swallowed. "I'm going to try to come, but . . ."

"It's okay. I understand."

I didn't think she did, but she did a good job of pretending that it was okay. Knowing that Skye wanted me at her game made me want to be there even more. I didn't know how I was going to do it, but somehow, I was going to go and watch her play. The only problem was that blocking out the negative thoughts was a lot easier than blocking out a crowd of people. If the basketball games were anything like they used to be, then the whole town would be in one space. Packed into the gym. The thought of being in there with them made my heart race with anxiety.

"It may be too late to do it tonight, but how about tomorrow?"

Skye looked at her watch. "I have to get back to the school, but do you promise we can talk with him tomorrow?"

"I promise."

I was still wrapped in my happy bubble when Lance came back out. "What's that smile about?"

I filled him in on my conversation with Skye, but instead of being excited for me, his face showed something totally different.

"What?" I asked, already on the defense.

"Are you sure that's a good idea?" he asked, his voice low and cautious.

"Why wouldn't it be?"

"Because we both know how Quinton's going to react to that request. Plus, you just fixed things between you and Leah. And"—he held his hands out toward me—"hear me out. Skye's a teenager. That's a huge responsibility. Are you sure you're up for that?"

I turned his question around in my head. "Am I sure I'm up for being with my daughter? Is that the question?"

"Yes, but only because I know how dedicated you've been this week to meeting your goals. If you're taking care of Skye full time, then it may pull you away from that, don't you think?"

"No, actually, I don't think so. First of all, Skye's not an infant. She doesn't need me to take care of her full time. Most of the time she'll be at school anyway. And whether she's there or not, I'm still committed to meeting my goals. She's the whole reason I want to meet those goals. If anything, she'll motivate me more."

"Okay, I can tell you're getting upset, and I don't want to do that."

"Too late." I threw the ball down. "Take me home."

How did I go from happy to happier, then make a swift left to angry and annoyed? I was sick and tired of people telling me what I should and shouldn't do as Skye's mom. At some point, they needed to understand that I was perfectly capable of taking care of my teenage daughter.

CHAPTER 34

Leah

When her mom called that morning and invited her to lunch, Leah couldn't have been happier to accept. She needed to talk with her about Nova wanting Skye to move in and about Quinton being upset over Lance's visit. Normally, Leah didn't discuss her relationship issues with her mom, but she was the wisest woman Leah knew, especially when it came to relationships. More than anything, Leah needed the reassurance that everything would be okay.

For the first time since they'd been married, Quinton didn't sleep in their bed. When Leah crept downstairs in the middle of the night, she found him asleep in the guest bedroom. She couldn't believe he was acting like that. She'd explained why Lance was at her office, but Quinton refused to understand. It was almost as if he was looking for a reason to be upset with her, but why would he do that? Leah couldn't stop thinking that the change she saw in Quinton had more to do with Nova than Lance. Was he starting to regret marrying her? Maybe he realized he still loved Nova and didn't know how to tell Leah.

Leah thought of waking him and telling him to come to their bed, but she didn't. Clearly, he was where he wanted to be, so she went back to bed alone. By the time she'd dressed and come downstairs this morning, he was gone. She didn't realize until later that he'd sent a text letting her know that he had an early meeting and would be unavailable all day.

What was happening with them?

Whatever it was, it was bigger than Leah could handle alone, which was another reason she needed her mom. However, everything she planned to say disappeared when she saw Nova sitting at the table with her. It was then that Leah understood that her mother already had an agenda and there wouldn't be time or an opportunity for Leah's. Since her relationship with Nova was also an issue she desperately wanted to fix, Leah didn't mind that her mom tricked her into coming. Not that she had to be tricked. Leah would've shown up even if she'd known Nova would be there. *Especially* if she'd known Nova would be there.

That's strange, Leah thought when she pulled into the empty driveway. She looked at her phone, but there wasn't a message from Quinton. His meeting must've gone longer than he thought. Leah sent him a message letting him know that she'd made it home and would be ready by the time he got there.

She and Quinton tried to get to the school at least thirty to forty-five minutes before the game started. The time never felt long because they were always talking and eating snacks that Leah stopped to buy before they got to school. She figured they donated enough money throughout the school year, so she didn't have to feel bad about not visiting the concession stand during every game since the proceeds went back to the school. Plus, they didn't sell the snacks she liked anyway.

Leah was tying her tennis shoes when her phone dinged. She tied them faster, thinking it may have been Quinton telling her he was outside or pulling up. That didn't make sense, though, because he had to change too. Leah tapped the screen, and part of her thought was correct: it was a text message from Quinton. **Meeting ran over. Going straight to the school.**

Leah stared at the message and tried to make sense of it but couldn't. Skye had been playing basketball since elementary school, and Leah and Quinton always made it a point to attend the games together, wearing their matching T-shirts or sweatshirts, depending on the weather. Even when Leah had events or meetings that ran over and insisted that Quinton go without her because she didn't want him to miss a second of the game, he still waited for her.

By the time Leah made it to the school, the parking lot was packed, as expected. She drove around looking for a space, but it was no use. She'd have to park down the road and walk back to the school.

Leah pulled over and called Quinton. Maybe he could come out and walk with her back to the school. There was no way she was going to walk down that dark road alone. Quinton didn't answer, but Leah wasn't totally surprised. The games could get really loud, and he wouldn't hear his phone. Unless he was holding it, he wouldn't know she'd called. After sitting outside in the dark for longer than she should've, Leah gave up. The only time Leah missed a game, or any of Skye's events, was when she'd had the flu years ago, and the thought of missing this one filled her with dread. Leah didn't want to go home, so she called Harper.

"I need an ear," she said when Harper answered.

"And I need a drink. Wanna meet at our spot?" Harper asked.

Leah drove away from the school and out of Bayou. Her thoughts kept drifting back to the game and the guilt she'd felt from missing it. She'd have to find a way to make it up to Skye. Leah knew how much it meant to Skye to look in the stands and see Leah and Quinton cheering her on. Leah's emotions ping-ponged from guilt to anger. She had no doubt that Quinton was purposely trying to hurt her. Before, she questioned if his attitude was about Nova, but now she knew without a doubt that it was all about her meeting with Lance. If Quinton thought she was going to sit quietly and accept what increasingly felt like manipulative behavior, then he was dead wrong.

As Leah merged onto the interstate, she thought of the best way to approach Quinton. Throwing out accusations, which she knew to be facts, would only lead to denial and more conflict. But she also had to stand her ground and make it clear that she would not be ignored or left behind ever again. She was his wife, and she needed him to remember that and treat her as the partner and love of his life, just as he'd always done before.

Moments later, Leah had pulled into a parking spot at the Wine Loft, a wine bar she and Harper used to visit often. They called it their wine-down spot after a long week of work. Harper was the genius who came up with *wine down*, and tonight that name was fitting because Leah definitely needed it.

CHAPTER 35

Nova

It wasn't the best night to be upset with Lance. Mama wanted to go to Skye's game, too, so getting there wasn't a problem. The problem was working up the nerve to go inside. I remembered the games being a big deal, and I expected the whole town to be there. I guess I didn't think to include the whole town plus the visitors from the other team. There wasn't anywhere to park near the school. As Mama and I walked from our car, which she'd parked down the road, my heart banged with the rhythm of my footsteps.

"You okay, baby?" Mama asked, reaching for my hand.

"No, but let's keep going."

We made it all the way to the front door of the school before I got lightheaded. I was sure I was going to faint. I needed to sit. Not far from the door was a raised flower bed that was bricked in and made a perfect seat.

"Take your time," Mama encouraged me while rubbing my back.

The front door swung open, pushing out the loud cheers from inside. Everything inside me ached to be in that building, among the crowd, cheering and jumping up and down for Skye.

"Martha! What are you doing out here? You missing your grandbaby. She's in there cutting up on that court," a lady said, standing next to Mama. She gazed down at me. "Nova? Oh my God, Nova, is that really you?" She stepped closer to me.

"Pearl, can you run back inside and get Nova a bottled water, please."

Ms. Pearl nodded. "I'll be right back." Her concerned stare stayed on me until she opened the door again and rushed inside.

"Bless her heart, she don't have the brains God gave her. She sees you in distress, and she's just looking. Not bothering to see if she can help or nothing."

As soon as Mama finished fussing, the door opened again, and Ms. Pearl unscrewed the top and passed the water to me.

"Thank you, love," Mama said, her voice soft and sweet.

I would've laughed if I wasn't busy trying to calm my nerves. I sipped the water and felt a little better, but it was still not good enough to go inside the building. It was bad enough that Mama and Ms. Pearl were still standing over me, staring.

I was relieved when the door opened again and diverted their attention away from me. When I glanced up, Quinton was walking out of the building with his phone to his ear. He looked over and saw us, then lowered his phone, a flicker of surprise crossing his features.

The moment I saw him, my mind instantly went back to all the times he and I had walked through those very doors, hand in hand as boyfriend and girlfriend. We had our whole lives ahead of us and so many dreams to fulfill. Then, those thoughts were ripped away by our reality. He was fulfilling dreams with Leah now, not with me.

"What's going on?" Quinton asked, his voice a blend of concern and curiosity. His gaze shifted back and forth from Mama to me, his eyebrows knitted together in a puzzled frown as if he was trying to make sense of what was happening.

"She wanted to see Skye play tonight, but it's a little too much. She's okay, though, aren't you, honey?" Mama asked me.

I nodded, but I wasn't okay. I wouldn't be okay until I was able to walk in a building without the fear of something bad happening. I wanted to surprise Skye so bad, but it didn't look like that was going to happen.

"Come on." Mama reached for my hand. "Let me get you home."

I shook my head. "No, Mama, you really wanted to see Skye play, and I don't want you to miss it because of me. You go inside, and I'll sit here. I'll be okay," I said, looking around the parking lot, fear gripping me at the thought of sitting out there alone.

"How about I take you home," Quinton said to me, "and you can go in and watch the second half of the game. Skye will be happy to see you," he told Mama.

"I don't know . . ." Mama looked toward the building.

"Come on, Martha. You have to see your grandbaby playing. I'm telling you she's on fire tonight," Ms. Pearl said, grabbing Mama's hand.

"Okay, but here." Mama reached into her purse and gave Quinton a key. "This is a key I had made for Nova. I meant to give it to you earlier but forgot," she told me.

Quinton and I were on our way to his truck when a car pulled up beside us.

"Hey, you two." The man spoke to Quinton and me.

I didn't recognize him, but Quinton did. "You may as well go home now," Quinton teased.

The man stepped out. He was tall like Quinton, but he didn't have his muscular build.

"Nova, this is my friend Mario," Quinton told me. "Mario, this is my . . . this is Nova."

Mario extended his hand to me. "Nice to meet you, Nova."

I shook his hand. "Nice to meet you too."

"Hold on one second," Quinton said to Mario before walking me over to his truck and opening the door for me to get in. "I'll be right back, okay?"

I nodded. Quinton walked back over to Mario's car, where they talked for a few minutes. Quinton kept looking back at me, I guess to make sure I was okay, which I was. As long as I could see him, I was good.

Quinton's posture was rigid, and his hands wouldn't stop moving. Mario stared at him, almost without blinking, and gave an occasional nod. Years of living with someone like Adam meant I had to learn how to read his body language. It was helpful to know what to expect before it actually came. I knew the kind of night we'd have based on his footsteps and his arm movements. If his footsteps were light and his arm swung a little when he walked, he was in a good mood. If his footsteps were heavier, not stomping, but heavier than the good-mood steps, and his shoulders were rigid with no arm movement, then he wasn't in a good mood, which meant by the end of the night, I wouldn't be either.

I could tell that whatever Quinton and Mario were discussing was very serious. Quinton's posture was intense. He and Mario gave each other a quick hug, followed by a pat on the back before Quinton turned and came back to the truck.

I was weighed down by guilt. Maybe he was telling Mario that I was messing up his night. And what about Leah? Didn't he need to tell her that he was gone?

"I'm sorry," I told Quinton when he slid behind the steering wheel.

"For what?" He glanced over at me.

"You're going to miss the start of the second half because of me. Not to mention, Leah is probably looking for you. Unless Mama told her what happened."

"Don't sweat it. Skye will understand. Besides, she won't even notice I'm gone. You remember how it was when you were in the zone. You don't know anything that's going on around you. And I was actually trying to call Leah when I walked outside. She didn't make it."

"Is she okay?"

"I'm sure she's fine. I'll try again after I get you home safely."

The floodlights around the house brightened the yard when we pulled up. I stood next to Quinton and waited while he unlocked the front door. Once inside, every muscle in my body relaxed. "Thanks again." I stood next to the front door. "But you need to get going before you miss the whole game."

"I'm not leaving until your mom gets home." He reached around me and locked the door.

"Are you sure? I promise I'm okay," I insisted, stepping slightly away to put some distance between us. Quinton's presence was so familiar, yet so changed. It still left me dealing with feelings that needed to be placed in some category, but I didn't know where they'd fit. I was working toward letting go of the anger I held for him and Leah, but being alone with them reminded me of the depth of what we used to have together. I was trapped between the roles of wife and sister-in-law, and neither of those positions felt right to me. So, where did that leave us? What was he to me now? Just a friend? My child's father? It was hard to see him as only those things when he'd always been that and so much more.

Quinton sat on the sofa, turned on the television, and made himself at home. I guess, in a way, Mama's house was just as much home for Quinton as it was for me. While we were dating, Mama and Daddy didn't allow me to visit Quinton at his grandparents' house. That was because his grandparents were rarely home. It wasn't like they asked to raise another child. They were retired and spent a lot of time fishing and traveling. As soon as Quinton was old enough to stay at home alone, not legally, but maturity-wise, his grandparents had no problem leaving for a few days, trusting that he'd get himself ready for school, which he always did. I didn't know any of this until we were much older. Quinton kept a lot about his home life to himself, but after he told me, I understood why he always devoured Mama's food like it was his last meal.

Because I needed a little extra comfort, I curled into Daddy's recliner and wished I could get a whiff of his smell. I needed to know a piece of him was still there, but his smell was gone.

"You wanna talk about it?" Quinton asked.

"Talk about what?"

"What happened tonight."

I shrugged. "There's nothing to talk about. I guess I overestimated myself. I went to lunch with Mama, and that felt good. Then I went to the youth center with Lance, and that felt good. I thought I was ready to keep going, but I wasn't."

I didn't miss how Quinton's body language changed at the mention of Lance's name. I thought of my first session with Dr. Yvonne when I told her about my feelings toward Quinton and Lance and how a part of me blamed them, even though I knew they weren't at fault.

"I'm not a therapist, but something Dr. Yvonne told me made me think about you and your feelings toward Lance."

"I try not to feel anything toward Lance," Quinton said.

"But you do, and I don't think you're upset with Lance."

He narrowed his eyes.

"Hear me out." I unfolded my legs and leaned toward him. "Dr. Yvonne told me once that it's not unusual for people to have what she called misplaced anger."

"Trust me, my anger for Lance is not misplaced. He's the one who ruined my knee." He put up one finger. "He's the one who stole my position on the team." Another finger. "And he's the one who got the scholarship that was supposed to be mine." The third and final finger.

I nodded, remembering all of that clearly, but as torn up as Lance was, I didn't believe that Lance hurt Quinton on purpose. In fact, what Quinton didn't know was that Lance was going to turn down the scholarship, but I convinced him to take it. So many times, I'd come close to telling him, but the fear of losing him or him hating me always stopped me. And now, years later, that still hadn't changed. It wasn't like Quinton would get it if Lance didn't. Quinton's knee was too damaged. He needed therapy for a while before anyone would even think of putting him back on the field. The fact that he hated Lance and not me told me that Lance was true to his word and didn't tell Quinton about our talk. Not that Quinton would've listened to anything Lance had to say.

"I know you think that all your anger is about Lance, and maybe some of it is, but I believe a big part of it is for your mom, not Lance."

"What? You think I'm angry at Renee?" he asked.

"Yes. You call her Renee. You can't even call her Mom or Mama," I pointed out.

"Because she's never been a mom or a mama. That doesn't mean I'm angry with her. Renee and I have a very good relationship."

Maybe he believed his words, but I didn't. Not for a second. I moved from the recliner and sat next to him on the sofa. "There was a time when we used to share everything. We admitted our deepest feelings to each other, knowing that that's where they would always stay. Between us. Remember that?" I asked.

"Of course I do."

"I know you hated that your mom was never there for you. And you hated that she always chose her boyfriends over you."

He squirmed uncomfortably. "What does any of this have to do with Lance?"

"I also know that getting that scholarship and playing college ball was your way of proving to her that you were special too. All you could talk about back then was her seeing you play on TV. You wanted her to see you as successful. Then, when Lance accidentally ran into your knee, you were angry because that chance of her seeing you as this big-time football player was gone. You blamed Lance, but you and I know that Lance would never hurt you on purpose."

Quinton stared straight ahead. His tense and rigid shoulders slumped. He lowered his head. And that was when I knew he heard me, and he knew I was right.

"You have to find a way to let go of whatever you've been holding against Lance all these years and deal with the real issue. You need to fix things with your mom before it's too late."

Sitting with Quinton reminded me of the deep connection we once shared. The familiarity tugged at my heart and stirred a sweet feeling of comfort. It reminded me of all the times we'd sat and had deep, and sometimes not so deep, conversations that lasted well into the night. Our relationship may have changed, but what could never change was the history and love we once shared.

Car lights shined through the window, and I figured Mama was back early. There was a knock on the door. Quinton and I glanced at each other. His brow furrowed slightly before he went to the door. I walked behind him. I didn't know what to expect when I saw Lance. I hoped his presence didn't undo the breakthrough I'd hoped I'd made with Quinton.

Lance looked around Quinton at me. "Hey," he said. "Can I come in?"

Quinton's posture was rigid, which wasn't a good sign. There was a moment of hesitation before he moved aside so Lance could step inside.

As Lance walked over to me. I caught Quinton's gaze. His light-brown eyes were filled with questions, and his downturned lips hinted at the discomfort he still had when Lance was around. Quinton crossed his arms over his chest. His T-shirt pulled tight across his shoulders while his eyes stayed on Lance.

"I guess your mom thought you were here alone." He looked back at Quinton. "She asked if I'd come by and check on you. While she was at the game, she got a call that Ms. Cora was rushed to the hospital. It doesn't look good. Your mom and Ms. Pearl are on their way there. The sheriff's out of town, so they didn't want Ms. Cora to be alone."

"Oh my God. Poor Ms. Cora. Poor Mama." I put my hands over my mouth, hoping with everything in me that Ms. Cora would be okay. She and Mama were closer than friends. They were like sisters, and it would break Mama's heart to lose her longest and dearest friend.

"I can stay here with you until she gets back if you want," Lance said, keeping his gaze on me.

I nodded, then looked over at Quinton. I wasn't sure what his reaction would be to me being alone with Lance, but I hoped he didn't make a big deal of it because after the night I had, and now being worried about Ms. Cora and Mama, I didn't need any more stress. Lance's presence brought a sense of calm that I desperately needed. I hadn't realized, until that moment, as I stood between Quinton and Lance, just how different I felt around Lance in comparison to Quinton. Despite how upset I was with him earlier,

I still wanted him there with me. Lance had a way, without saying a word, of making me feel like everything would be okay.

Quinton stepped closer to me and put a hand on my shoulder. "I'm gonna head out." He leaned down and kissed my forehead. "Thanks for the talk."

I smiled. "Anytime."

"That was easier than I expected," Lance said once Quinton left.

"Yeah," I agreed, while my mind was still on Mama.

"Listen." Lance clasped his hands together. "I'm sorry about earlier. I overstepped."

It wasn't always easy to forgive someone who hurt you, but I never found it hard to forgive Lance. His words and actions always came from a place of love and concern. They were never meant to hurt me.

I walked closer to him and then leaned my head on his chest.

Lance held me tight. "I got you," he whispered.

And I believed him because he always did.

CHAPTER 36

Leah

Leah and Harper were seated in a cozy corner of the wine bar, their table illuminated by a small candle flicking inside a glass holder. Plush velvet chairs in a deep-burgundy hue enveloped them as they chatted.

"I'm so glad you called. I was about to lose it," Harper said, swirling her white wine around in the glass.

"Why? What's going on?" Leah asked, glad to have something else to occupy her mind instead of Quinton.

"Girl, same story, different day. I'm trying to juggle work, children, homework, and housework by myself while Justin comes in and relaxes without even trying to help. It's aggravating and exhausting." Harper hit the palm of her hand against the table. "Do you know when I told him I was coming to meet you, he had the nerve to ask if I'd be back in time to bathe the twins." Harper rolled her eyes. "I should get a hotel room when I leave here and let him have them all night by himself."

"You know he'd have a fit," Leah said before taking a sip of her wine. "But you're right. It is the same story, different day, so I have to ask, have you talked with him like I suggested?"

"Talk with him for what? I keep telling you that talking does no good. It's not like he's blind. He sees what I'm doing every day. He knows I need help. I shouldn't have to beg a grown man to help out."

Leah shook her head. "I didn't say beg. I said talk. And you're assuming he knows, but he may be thinking that you have it handled since you hadn't said anything. All I'm saying is to sit him down and have a calm conversation with your husband," Leah said, putting an extra dose of emphasis on the word *calm*. "Otherwise, nothing will change except you growing more resentful, and we don't need that."

"Fine." Harper exhaled loudly. "I'll talk with him, and when it doesn't work, I want my money back for this session," she joked.

"Deal." Leah shook her head before taking a sip of her wine.

"Anyway, enough about that. What's going on with you?" Harper asked.

"I wasn't ready to go home. The thought of going back to that house alone was unbearable," Leah admitted.

Harper was one of the few people who knew Leah's weaknesses. She hated being alone. She hated feeling like she wasn't good enough, and she hated with a passion not being in control. Basically, everything she hated she now had to face.

Harper narrowed her eyes. "Wait. I thought Skye had a game tonight. Why aren't you at the game?"

Leah filled Harper in on the events of the day, starting with how good it felt to sit and talk with Nova and to finally feel like they were at least in the direction of healing. Leah would never fool herself into thinking it would be easy and that they wouldn't have some regression along with the progression, but she was up for the challenge, as long as the end result was that she and Nova were together again.

"That's so good, Leah. I'm happy for both of you." Harper pouted. "But sad for me because now you won't have time for me since your real sister is back," she teased.

"You need to stop it." Leah pointed her finger at Harper. "You know no one could ever replace the one and only Harper Miller."

"That's good to hear. I still need you, too, you know?"

"And I still need you. Now more than ever, because I've only told you about the good part of my day. Now comes the drama."

"Uh-oh. Hold on, let me refill my glass first." Harper poured more wine into her half-full glass.

Leah filled Harper in on what had been going on between her and Quinton since last night. Saying the words out loud was almost as hard as going through it. One thing Leah hated to admit was that her marriage wasn't as perfect as everyone assumed it was. In the past, she never shared when she and Quinton had their disagreements, unlike Harper, who was always sharing everything she and her husband went through. Leah liked when Harper would say that she wished Justin was more like Quinton. Because of that, she made sure Harper always saw Quinton as the sweet, attentive, romantic husband that she believed him to be. Not that any of that was a lie, but like all men . . . like all people . . . he had flaws too. Leah just didn't talk about those.

"That doesn't sound anything like Quinton," Harper said. "Do you think he's that upset over a meeting? Even if it was with Lance, that's a lot. To not sleep in the bed with you."

"What else could it be? He showed up with flowers, so he was fine before he found out that Lance was in my office."

"That's true. You have to find out what Lance did. You think he killed somebody?" Harper widened her eyes.

Leah laughed. "What's wrong with you?"

The wine and Harper's humor was the distraction that Leah needed. Leah placed her credit card on the table. "Tonight's on me."

"I won't argue." Harper finished the last of her wine.

Outside, Leah and Harper hugged as they always did before they parted ways.

"Go home." Leah pointed her finger at Harper. As soon as Leah was in her car she pulled her phone from her purse. She had a missed voicemail from Quinton, which caused her heart rate to quicken slightly as she tapped to open the message. Her thoughts swirled with what he might have said. Was he calling to apologize? To offer an explanation about why he didn't come and pick her up? Or had something bad happened? She was about to listen when Harper tapped on her window, causing Leah to jump.

"I'm sorry," Harper said when Leah lowered her window. "You forgot your wine." Harper passed Leah a bottle of white wine.

"I didn't buy any wine."

"I know. I did. Love ya," Harper said, then ran to her car and drove out of the parking lot.

Leah took a moment to inhale the immense gratitude she felt for having a friend like Harper who was always there when Leah needed her the most. She reached across and placed the wine on the seat, then listened to the message. It didn't take long for her to realize he must've called her by mistake.

"What's going on?" she heard Quinton ask.

Leah listened, worried that something may have happened to Skye. She pressed the phone to her ear because the voices weren't clear. As she listened, she could make out her mom's voice. Leah had the same question as Quinton: *What's going on?*

She continued listening, trying to piece together what was happening on the other end of the phone. There was a lot of movement from the phone, making it even harder to hear. Then she heard Mario's voice, and Quinton introduced Mario to Nova. *Did Nova go to the game?* Leah asked herself, not that she had the answer. If her sister did go, that was a huge step for her.

Leah was thinking about how far Nova had come in such a short time when the conversation between Quinton and Mario drew her back to the phone.

"Is that a good idea?" Mario asked.

"What? I'm taking her home. It's no big deal," Quinton explained.

"No big deal. You're about to be alone with your ex-wife. The ex-wife that you're pretty sure you're still in love with. I'd say that's a very big deal."

Leah gasped. Her hand flew to her mouth. She wanted to rewind. She needed to make sure she'd heard Mario right, but her hands were shaking, and she couldn't do anything but keep listening.

"Would you calm down? And I never said I was in love with Nova. I said I didn't know. I still don't."

"But you do still love Leah, right?" Mario asked.

"Why are you asking the same questions we've already talked about? Yes, I love Leah."

"And possibly Nova," Mario added.

Quinton sighed. "And possibly Nova."

Leah's hand trembled as she lowered the phone, unable to listen anymore. The echo of Quinton's confession reverberated in her ears. His words landed like a physical blow, draining all the color from her world. Leah felt a cold numbness spreading through her as the realization of her deepest fears materialized before her. Quinton was still in love with Nova. He said he wasn't sure, but in Leah's world that meant that he was.

Leah needed to leave the parking lot, but first, she needed to get herself together. She couldn't breathe. Couldn't think. The image of the love story she held for her and Quinton suddenly felt like an optical illusion, and if Leah blinked, the picture she'd seen would somehow disappear.

Leah exhaled and pulled out of the parking lot. As she drove, she was accompanied by too many questions that she couldn't answer.

Was she just a placeholder with the hopes that one day Nova would return?

Was she a Nova substitute? A replica since he couldn't have the real thing?

Was anything about their love real to him?

Their love story never had the ending either of them wanted, and now, both Nova and Quinton were stuck in a place of uncertainty.

The more the questions came, the harder her tears flowed. Leah pulled into the driveway, then opened the glove compartment and pulled out a napkin to wipe her eyes. Holding the napkin made her think of Skye. She used to always keep paper towels or napkins because it never failed that Skye was going to spill something on herself or make some kind of mess whenever they were out. Leah rested her head on her steering wheel as she thought about Skye. If Quinton and Nova rekindled things, then where would that leave Leah and Skye? Yes, she would always be Skye's aunt, but Leah was much more than that. Losing Quinton would devastate her, but losing Skye would kill her.

After Leah felt composed enough to leave the car, she grabbed her things and then walked to the front door. When she looked back, she realized Skye's car wasn't there. That wasn't a surprise to Leah. After every game, Skye's coach always kept them at least thirty minutes to an hour talking in the locker room. That was the best part about Skye driving herself now. They didn't have to wait.

The house was dark except for the kitchen light that illuminated from down the hallway. Leah walked in and saw Quinton through the glass sliding doors. He was sitting outside on their back deck. She crossed the room and placed her hand on the door, then stopped. She watched as he stared ahead into the backyard. Leah thought about his surprise party and how hopeful she'd felt for their future on that day. Her lips lifted into a smile as she remembered them dancing and laughing like they were the happiest couple in the world. Back then Leah thought that they were.

She looked down at her hand, which was still resting on the door handle, and realized that the conversation she was about to have could be the turning point in their relationship. The question for Leah was in which direction it would turn.

Leah stepped outside and sat on the wooden chair next to Quinton. In his hand was a glass half filled with an amber liquid that Leah was sure was whiskey. Quinton didn't drink often, only when he had a lot on his mind. And Leah didn't have to ask what was occupying the space in his head tonight.

Quinton turned his gaze toward her, his expression hinting at wariness. The outdoor light broadcast his features, revealing the tension in his jaw and the furrow of his brows.

"I tried to call you," Quinton said, shifting slightly in his seat but maintaining eye contact with Leah as she sat. "You didn't make it to the game."

"No, I didn't." Leah crossed her legs and her arms. "I went to have drinks with Harper."

Quinton nodded slowly. His eyes briefly dropped to the ground before meeting hers again. "Skye played a good game. I'm sure she would've loved for you to have seen it."

"I would've loved to have seen it, too, but . . ." Leah paused. "This isn't about Skye or her game. Is it?" Leah said, cutting straight to the heart of the matter. Her eyes searched Quinton's face, looking for any sign of remorse.

Quinton was the master of deflecting. Too bad for him that Leah was the master of redirecting.

"We both know why I wasn't at the game tonight. Maybe we should talk about why you didn't want us to go together like we've done for years."

Quinton took another sip. "I explained that already. My meeting ran over. Coming over here then going to Bayou would've been out of the way," he said, shifting his gaze back toward the backyard.

Once again Leah thought of all the times it had been out of the way before and had never been a problem.

"You have no idea how much I wish that was really the reason," Leah said, her voice slow and steady. "And had I not overheard your conversation with Mario tonight, I would've made myself believe it."

Quinton stared ahead, allowing a painful silence to stretch between them. "I'm not sure what I'm supposed to say." His once powerful voice was low and subdued.

"I don't know if there's anything more to say. You're still in love with Nova," she stated, the words feeling more like a conclusion than a question.

Quinton looked at her. His eyes were heavy with what Leah assumed to be regret, maybe even shame. "I said I didn't know how I was feeling. I know that I love you, though. That hasn't changed."

His words caused a physical ache inside her. It wasn't the declaration she needed to erase her fears or heal the wounds of uncertainty she held about their future. "I don't doubt that, but you not being sure about your feelings for Nova is a big concern for me." Her voice sounded calmer than she felt.

Leah grappled with the implications of his admission. His love for her didn't offset the uncertainty of his feelings toward Nova. She felt herself starting to build a barrier around the trust and security she used to feel. The very things her past relationships had stolen from her and Quinton had restored. It was as if he'd given her a gift that he'd decided he no longer wanted her to have, or maybe he felt she no longer deserved it. Not from him, anyway.

"Even if the feelings are there, it means nothing. It's not like I'm leaving you for Nova. You know I'd never do that."

"I used to know that. But I'm not sure of anything anymore. Do you understand how unfair this is to me? I love you totally and completely. My feelings aren't split between you and anyone else. Don't you think I deserve that too?"

Quinton looked away. "So, what now?"

Leah wasn't ready to give a voice to the thoughts she'd had all the way home.

"I don't want to lose you," Quinton said, his husky voice laden with emotion. His eyes locked on Leah as if he was too afraid to look away.

"I don't want to lose you either," Leah admitted solemnly. "But we can't pretend that your feelings aren't real because they are. Every second I'll wonder if you're thinking about Nova. If you're feeling stuck or have regrets."

Quinton straightened his back, and lifted his head before saying, "I don't have any regrets."

"Now you don't. But what about a month from now? A year from now?"

"I'll still feel the same way," he said.

"Torn between my sister and me?"

"No. With you. In love like we've been these last five years."

Leah wished those words were enough to erase all her doubts. All she wanted was to go upstairs, take a hot bath, and slide into bed next to her husband, as she'd done almost every night that they'd been married. But how could she? For the rest of their marriage, Leah would always wonder if Quinton was with her because he wanted to be or if he was there out of obligation. She couldn't live like that, so she had no choice but to let him go. As they say, if he came back, it was meant to be. If not, then she was in for a major heartbreak. She hoped it was one she could eventually bounce back from.

CHAPTER 37
Nova

Me and God still weren't on good terms, but as much as I tried to convince myself that he didn't exist, I knew that he did. Which, in a way, made it much harder to talk with him like I used to. He ignored me for fifteen years, so my plan was to ignore him now. Which was too bad for him, because if I was talking with him, I'd tell him thank you for making sure I was here for Mama when she needed me the most.

Ms. Cora died early today. Mama was asleep when the call came. She hadn't left her room at all this morning. She said she was tired from the late night, but I recognized the difference between fatigue and grief. Poor Mama had lost so many people she loved over the years. All I wanted was to do something to put a smile on her face.

I wasn't sure what time Skye would be calling. I promised her that I'd go with her to talk to Quinton about her moving in with me and Mama. The thought of having that conversation made my heart race. Quinton and I already had one heavy talk last night. Two in a row may be pushing it, but I'd do whatever I could to help Skye, especially if it meant her coming to live here. I wanted that more than anything.

I woke up early to cook breakfast. I didn't burn anything, and that was a sign of improvement. I used to be a really good cook, but I hadn't used those skills in so long I wasn't sure if I still had them or not. Maybe today I'd cook something special for Mama for dinner. She deserved a break, even though Mama wouldn't see it that way. Cooking was her therapy. Whenever she was upset or had a lot on her mind, she liked to bake. Leah and I used to say Mama made the term *bittersweet* a real thing.

After the coffee finished brewing, I took it up to Mama, along with a plate of eggs, bacon, and toast. I knocked on her bedroom door before pushing it open.

Mama sat up when she saw me with the tray of food. "What have you done?" She smiled.

"I made your breakfast." I lowered the tray so she could see the food and her coffee, with a little cream and a little sugar, just how she liked it.

Mama took the tray and placed it on her legs. "Thank you, baby." She patted the space beside her.

I kicked off my shoes and climbed into bed with Mama. "You okay?" I asked, which was a pretty crazy question being that she'd lost one of her closest friends. Of course she wasn't okay.

"I will be," Mama said. "You know, I was going to spend the night with her last night. She was weak, but she was still able to talk. She told me to go home and get some rest and come back today." Mama chuckled. "That old cow knew she was leaving me." Then her eyes watered.

I leaned my head on Mama's shoulder. "I've heard that people wait until their loved ones are out of the room or away from the hospital before they transition. You think that's true?" I raised up to hear her answer.

Mama nodded. "I know it's true. Your dad did the same thing. The doctor told us it would be the day before. They didn't see him making it one more day, but he did. The day they thought he would pass, I didn't leave his side for a second, other than to run to the bathroom. That next morning, I went downstairs for coffee. One of the nurses told me that I probably hadn't even made it downstairs before he went."

I wanted to crumble, but I had to be strong for Mama. I wasn't there when Daddy passed, but I was here now.

I stayed with Mama until she finished her food. One thing I could say about Mama was that she refused to let life keep her down. By the time I cleaned the kitchen, Mama was dressed for the day.

"Going somewhere?" I asked, thinking the answer was going to be no.

"Yeah, I'm going to meet Carlos." Mama raised her hand. "Excuse me, Sheriff Jones, at Cora's house. He's in charge of all the arrangements, and Cora would haunt me if I let him pick out her burial outfit."

"You need help?" I asked, drying my hands on the dish towel.

"No, I think I need to do this alone." Mama hugged me.

I didn't push because I understood the need to be alone when you were working through your feelings. Mama was halfway out the kitchen before she turned back to me. "Last night I asked Lance if he'd take you to get a phone. Now that you're venturing out more, I think it'll be good for you to have one."

"I was thinking about that too. Guess the likelihood of getting one like I had before is probably slim, huh?"

Mama laughed. "You can get one like that, but be prepared to be talked about. Your sister and daughter talked about me for a long time because I didn't want to get rid of my flip phone. I still think I could've kept it. These things are distraction machines," Mama said, holding her phone up.

"I can tell." I thought of how everyone looked at their phones. I noticed it in the hospital, at the café yesterday, when I had lunch with Mama and Leah. There weren't a lot of people in there, but the ones who were there kept their heads lowered to their phones.

When Mama left, I called Lance to see what time he'd be coming by. He had business to take care of today, so he wouldn't be over until later. After I hung up with him, I called Skye. She didn't answer. I may not have known a lot about raising a teenager, but I did remember what it was like to be one, and I was pretty sure Skye was probably sleeping in. That was what I used to do on a Saturday. Especially a Saturday after a game.

Since I had nothing to do and nowhere to go, I started prepping for dinner. Mama loved red beans and rice with cornbread and yams. I was pretty sure I could still cook red beans. The yams I wasn't so sure about, but I'd do my best.

I was peeling the sweet potatoes when someone knocked on the front door. Lance had said he'd be later, but I thought he meant a lot later than that. I wiped my hands on Mama's apron and went to the door. When I peeped out, I was surprised to see Skye. She didn't call, and I wasn't ready to leave yet.

"Hey, I was waiting for you to call," I said, opening the door to let her in.

"Sorry," she said, looking around. "Is Gran here? I need to talk with her."

I was confused but tried not to let it show. "No, she's at Ms. Cora's. She passed away last night."

Skye looked at me for the first time, and her eyes were red like she'd been crying. "Ms. Cora died?" Her eyes watered again.

"Oh my God, I'm so sorry. I didn't realize you were that close to Ms. Cora." I pulled some Kleenex from the box next to Mama's recliner and gave them to Skye.

"I'm not, but I know how much she meant to Gran. Is she okay?" Skye asked, sniffing and wiping her eyes.

"She's handling it well. You don't have to worry about Gran. She's a strong woman." I tried to reassure her. "Did something happen? You didn't talk with your dad without me, did you?"

It wasn't until the questions were out that I figured her visit had nothing to do with any of that, unless she'd talked with Mama about living with us.

"No." Skye sat on the sofa and slumped back. "I'm not moving out."

My stomach flopped. "Okay." I swallowed, unable to push any words past my disappointment.

"I want to, but I can't leave Dad right now." Her voice broke.

I sat next to her and braced myself for the question I had to ask and the answer I was afraid to hear. "Is something wrong with your dad?"

Skye lifted her eyes to me. Tears ran down her cheeks. "Teeah's gone."

My world stopped, and every part of my body went numb. "Teeah's gone?" I repeated the words that I was sure I'd heard her say. "What... Gone how?" I held my breath and waited for what felt like a lifetime before she answered.

"She moved out."

I closed my eyes and exhaled the biggest sigh of relief. I held my chest, which was burning at that point. With so much happening at once, the only gone I could imagine was death. I didn't know what would've happened if Skye had said that, but once I was coherent and able to think straight, I should've known that wasn't what she meant. There was no way Quinton would've allowed her to come and share that news. Come to think of it, I doubted he knew she was sharing the news that she'd moved out either.

Skye and I sat for a minute in silence, my mind running through all the questions I wanted to ask but couldn't.

Why did she move out?
What happened?
Did they have a fight?
What was it about?

I wanted to know the answer to all those questions, but Skye shouldn't be the one answering them. "Do you know where she went?" I asked, figuring that was okay to ask.

"Dad said she's staying at the condo for a while," she said, as if I knew about the condo.

"The condo?" I asked.

"Dad and Teeah bought a condo in Perkins Rowe. It's a rental property, but no one's staying there right now."

"Oh yeah, Mama told me about Perkins Rowe. I thought it was a shopping center."

Skye nodded. "It is. There are also eating places, a movie theater, and in the back are condos."

I didn't know what to say after that. Should I tell her everything was going to be okay when I didn't know if it was or wasn't? Did I sit there and wait until she told me what she needed from me? I felt so lost. I had no idea how to help her. How to make her feel better. In the midst of trying to figure out how to help Skye, those burning questions were still nagging at me.

I silently celebrated when I heard a car pull up outside. I understood why Skye was looking for Mama. At that point, I wanted her myself. She'd know exactly what to do and say to make Skye and me feel better. I couldn't help but wonder if Leah moving out had anything to do with me. I didn't see how it could, but I felt like my being back was doing more harm than good, so I automatically assumed that if something bad happened, it involved me in some way.

Whoever drove up knocked on the door. I peeped out again, then looked back at Skye. I opened the door, and Leah walked in. Skye jumped from her seat and ran to her, almost knocking her back out the door.

Skye cried in Leah's arms. I stood back and watched as my daughter sought comfort from my sister. The woman who'd played the role of mom to her while I was gone. I swallowed my tears. It wasn't the time to be jealous, but I was. I wanted to comfort her. I should've hugged her. That was what she needed, but I stayed back, too afraid to overstep. I wished this were easier.

"It's okay," Leah whispered, tears running down her own cheeks while she rubbed Skye's back.

Leah's eyes met mine, and the pain I saw in them was excruciating. Leah finally calmed Skye down while I stood feeling like a complete outsider.

"Are you okay?" I asked Leah when she and Skye pulled apart. I was worried about her. I'd never seen Leah look so broken before. I said Mama was strong, but truthfully, there wasn't anyone I knew who was stronger than Leah.

"I'm making it." Leah nodded as she spoke. "I came by to check on Mom. I heard about Ms. Cora."

"She's not here," I told Leah. "But she shouldn't be gone too long. She went to pick out a burial outfit."

"Poor Mom," Leah said, moving farther into the house.

Leah and Skye sat where Skye and I had a few minutes ago. I sat on the side of Dad's recliner. As much as I wanted to comfort Skye, I could tell it was Leah she really needed.

"Why'd you move out?" Skye asked Leah.

Leah looked at me, probably wishing I wasn't there for that conversation. Maybe I should've excused myself to give them some time alone. I thought of all the food I still had out on the table waiting for me to finish prepping, but I couldn't leave. I needed to know what was going on.

"I didn't move out," Leah corrected. "Did your dad say that I'd moved?" Leah asked.

Skye shook her head. "No. He just said you stayed at the condo, and he didn't know how long you'd be staying there."

Leah nodded. "I'm only staying for a couple of days."

"But why?" Skye whined.

"Your dad and I need some time to think."

Skye narrowed her eyes. Neither of us bought that answer. It couldn't have been easy for Leah to talk about that in front of me, or Skye, for that matter. I remembered how I used to feel when Quinton and I had our disagreements. I never wanted Mama or Daddy to know about it, but I always told Leah. Had she been married to anyone besides Quinton, I'd like to believe she would've called and told me too. I didn't know how we were going to move forward as sisters when it was so hard for us to talk openly about things as serious as relationships. Maybe one day she could talk to me about him, and I wouldn't feel anything other than concern for both of them. Not that I wasn't concerned, because I was, but it was concern mixed with uneasiness because it was Quinton.

"You have to stay in the condo to think?" Skye asked. "That doesn't make sense." She sounded frustrated with Leah's answer.

As Skye's questions continued, I couldn't help but notice how Leah seemed to deflate right in front of me. Her shoulders dropped, and she clasped her hands together, but not before I caught the slight tremor. I could tell she was trying hard to hold herself together for Skye.

"I'm sick of all of this," Skye continued. "You and Dad never fight . . . ever. Now, suddenly, you need time to think? Well, I'm not buying that at all. Did he cheat on you?" she asked.

"What? No. Your dad wouldn't do that," Leah said, averting her gaze away from Skye.

What is Leah not saying? That was my burning question.

Skye crossed her arms and tilted her head. "Did you cheat on him?"

"I'd never cheat on your dad." Leah's voice sounded as if it was weighed down by hurt.

But why was she being so vague when it was clear to Skye and me that there was way more that she wasn't telling us? Or maybe it was that she didn't want to tell Skye. Leah had to be protecting Skye from something, so I remained silent and didn't add my own questions to the conversation.

"Then what could be so bad that you need time apart to think? And what exactly are you thinking about? If you still love each other or not?" Skye's hands were waving all over the place by that point.

Leah looked away.

Skye's mouth fell open. "That's it, isn't it? You don't know if you're still in love with each other?" Her words were shaky.

"We still love each other," Leah said.

"But . . ." Skye needed more.

Leah bit her bottom lip before saying, "It's complicated."

"You know what? Forget it. You and Dad act like this is only affecting the two of you. Neither of you are thinking about me and how this makes me feel. As long as I can remember, I've had a happy family, but now I don't know what's happening." Skye grabbed her keys from the coffee table where she placed them when she first sat and ran out the door.

Leah and I both ran behind Skye.

"Skye, wait," Leah urged.

"Let me try." I moved past Leah and followed Skye to her car. "Hey, listen to me." I was anxious to hear what words of wisdom I had to share because I had no idea what I was about to say to her. "I know you're hurting right now, but I promise you that I'm going to find out what's going on, and I'm going to do whatever I can to make things right, okay?"

Skye glared at me. "I know what's going on. Everything was going fine until you came back." She opened her car door, slid in, and slammed it with such force that it seemed to rattle my bones. I watched as Skye drove away, dragging my heart along with her. I was rooted in place as the dust settled around me and sadness stirred inside me.

CHAPTER 38

Leah

Leah couldn't hear what Skye and Nova were saying to each other, but Skye slammed her car door, and Nova walked back to the house looking dazed and confused. "What did she say?" Leah asked.

Nova shook her head and kept walking. Her shoulders were stiff, and her pace quickened. She looked as if she was physically trying to outrun whatever emotions she was feeling.

"Nova, what's wrong? What did Skye say to you?" Leah asked again.

Nova looked at Leah. "The truth." That was all Nova said before turning to go upstairs.

Leah watched helplessly, and her heart sank with each step, taking Nova farther away. Leah didn't need answers to know that whatever Skye said to Nova had cut her deep. Leah thought of staying until her mom made it home, but she couldn't sit around and wait. Her mind was all over the place, mainly on Skye. She wanted to call and talk with Skye, but she was driving, and Leah didn't want her trying to answer the phone while she was that upset.

She sent Quinton a text message: Skye just left Mom's. She's really upset. Let me know if I need to come by.

Maybe she should've gone by anyway, but Leah didn't. She wasn't ready to see Quinton. It was hard enough packing last night while he tried to convince her that he wasn't in love with Nova, that he was just talking, and it meant nothing. They both knew he was lying.

Leah was glad that Skye had spent the night at Amber's. There was no way she could leave if Skye were there. That's why she had to do it last night instead of waiting till morning like Quinton suggested. Actually, he suggested that he be the one to go and Leah stay, but she needed a change of scenery.

Leah stopped at California Pizza Kitchen, one of the many restaurants in the same complex as their condo. She didn't have an appetite, but she might have one later and since there was nothing to eat at the condo, the salad and pizza was her backup.

Next to her house, the condo was Leah's favorite spot. She loved how bright and open it was. The white cabinets and walls were a perfect contrast to the dark wood and furniture. Leah always thought that one day, the house would be too big for her and Quinton, and they'd move to the condo. It was the perfect size and convenient, with entertainment and restaurants within walking distance. When Leah was younger, she wanted to move to New York. She craved city life, and in her mind, she'd be like the characters on *Friends* who lived in the city and had a swanky little coffee shop hangout. Perkins Rowe wasn't New York, but it was as close to it as Leah would get in Baton Rouge.

The one thing Leah didn't like was how quiet it was. She couldn't hear Skye walking too hard upstairs or running down the hallway while she was downstairs trying to relax. Quinton wasn't hollering at the TV while he watched some game. It was just her and her thoughts, and that wasn't good for an overthinker like Leah.

The one thing she did have was the wine Harper brought her. She'd taken it out and placed it in the refrigerator last night, feeling that it would come in handy. Leah poured a glass and went outside to sit on the balcony, then called Harper to fill her in on the drama that unfolded after they parted ways.

"Have you lost your ever-loving mind?" Harper shouted through the phone when Leah told her what she'd done. "You left your house? Why would you do that?"

"I know it sounds bad."

"Um . . . yeah, because it is bad. How can you work things out if you're not home?"

"It's hard to understand if you're not going through it, but believe me, in order for us to work things out, we have to be apart right now. If I'm there, we're going to fall into the routine of normalcy, but we'll still have this issue between us."

"Quinton loves you. Everybody knows that."

All Harper had ever known was Quinton and Leah, so she would probably be the only person Leah knew who'd say that even with Nova being in the picture. Everyone else, those who knew Quinton and Nova, wouldn't bet their money on Quinton choosing Leah over Nova.

"I know he loves me, and he'd never leave me, but that's not enough." Leah explained to Harper the same thing she'd told Quinton.

"I hate this," Harper said.

"You and me both." She watched a couple on the sidewalk across the street walking hand in hand. They looked like they were young and in love. Leah tried to remember the last time she and Quinton walked anywhere while holding hands. In the beginning they did, but they'd only been married for three years. Wasn't this still technically the beginning? In Leah's mind they were still newlyweds. Why didn't it feel new anymore?

"I get nervous when you get quiet. What's going on in that brain of yours?" Harper pulled Leah from her thoughts.

"There's no way I could make you understand everything that's going on in this head of mine."

The doorbell rang. Leah looked, wondering who could be at her door. Her immediate thought was Quinton. She didn't think he'd show up without calling first, though. He said Perkins Rowe was too far out, so he'd call to make sure she was there before he drove all the way over.

"Harper, someone's at the door. Let me call you later," Leah said when the doorbell rang again.

Leah checked the peephole. "Mom?" She swung the door open. "What are you doing here?"

"Same question I had for you." Martha stepped in holding plastic bags in each hand and looked around the space. "Never mind. This is nice." She walked to the kitchen and placed the bags on the counter.

"Mom, what is this about?" Leah stood on the other side of the island and watched as her mom pulled ingredients from the bag.

"When I made it home Nova told me what happened." Mama set a can of seasoning on the table, resting her hand on top. "She also told me what Skye said to her. It took me an hour to calm her down."

"What did Skye say? I asked Nova, and she said Skye said the truth." Leah sat on a stool while her mom moved around the kitchen, opening cabinets and pulling out pots and pans.

"My poor Nova. Skye was upset, understandably, with whatever's going on between you and Quinton. We'll get to that in a second, but Skye told Nova that things were better before she came."

Leah's heart fell to her feet. "No, is that what she said? There's no way I would've left Nova had I known what Skye said to her. I mean, I knew she was upset, but . . . This is all my fault. Maybe I should've waited and talked with Skye before I left home."

"About that." Martha pulled a knife from the wooden holder on top of the counter. "Why are you here? I had to call Quinton to get the address. He sounds awful, by the way." Mama glanced up at me.

"Well, that makes two of us." Leah didn't know if she sounded awful, but she sure felt it. "Where's Nova?" she asked, needing to change the subject.

"She's with Lance. These days, he's the only person who can pull her out of her funk. Thank God for him." Martha washed the vegetables she'd bought. "Since Lance was taking care of one of my daughters, it gave me a chance to come and check on the other one." She started chopping the vegetables. "And make sure she's eating."

Her mom knew her so well.

"I know you." Martha pointed the knife in Leah's direction. "You take care of everyone else and pretend like you have everything under control. It's okay to admit you need help, too, Leah. And it's okay to admit that you're not okay."

Leah's first thought was to do exactly what her mom accused her of, to try to convince her mom that she was fine. Sure, her marriage might be over, and it was a real possibility that Quinton would realize that his feelings for Nova were a lot stronger than he thought, but that was life, right? Instead of spewing lies that her mom would detect immediately, Leah tried something different.

"You're right. This hurts a lot." She bit her bottom lip. "And I don't do well with uncertainty. Nor do I like the feeling of someone else being in control of my destiny, but what choice did I have? My love for him didn't change."

"And you think his love for you did?"

"It's hard to say. Maybe . . . maybe not. I need him to be sure before we can move forward and even think about fixing things between us."

Martha nodded. "My prayer for my girls was that you'd find a man who loved you a tad more than you loved him. I think that you both found that. I hate that it happened to be with the same man, but what can you do? You love who you love, right?" She continued chopping.

Leah sighed but didn't respond. It sounded bad to say she wished she'd fallen in love with someone else, even though she'd thought it more than she'd like to admit. However, that would mean loving someone other than Quinton, and she didn't want that either. She loved him. She hated that her sister did, too, at one time. The more Leah thought about it, the more she wondered if Nova was being honest when she said she didn't love Quinton anymore. It was only a week ago to the day when Nova was sure there was something still there between her and Quinton.

"How about we talk about why you're really here?" Leah said.

Martha stopped chopping long enough to look at Leah before starting back again. "I told you why I'm here. To check on you."

"And it has nothing to do with you not wanting to be alone right now. Which would make sense given what you're going through." Leah softened her tone. "It's okay to admit that you're not okay." She repeated her mom's words.

Martha sniffed, then shook her head as if trying to get rid of whatever emotions Leah's words caused. She cleared her throat before saying, "I'm making corn and shrimp soup. You still like that, don't you?"

"Mom."

"Leah, I'm fine." Martha removed a clear bag with ears of corn inside. "If you want to help, you can come and shuck this corn." Martha held the bag toward Leah.

Leah took the bag and stood next to her mom. "You know you can buy these already shucked and cut from the cob, right?"

Martha rolled her eyes. Leah expected that reaction. When it came to cooking, her mom was as old school as they came. She stayed at the farmer's market for fresh vegetables. She wasn't against the canned or frozen, but those were used sparingly.

For the next hour, Leah and Martha worked side by side, cutting, chopping, stirring, and tasting until the soup and garlic bread were ready. They took their plates outside on the balcony to eat. They'd sat when Martha's phone rang. It was a number she didn't recognize, but she answered, which surprised Leah. Her mom hardly ever answered unknown calls.

"Hey." Martha's voice was excited. "Is this your new number?" She looked over at Leah. "It's Nova. She has a new phone."

Leah never thought she'd be happy to hear that someone got a cell phone. Maybe because everyone she knew had one already. That was another step forward for Nova, and no matter what, Leah only wanted the best for her sister, even if that meant stepping away from the best love she'd ever experienced. The option to go back and live as though

Quinton's confession never existed was always there, but that wouldn't be fair to any of them. They all deserved what was meant for them.

"That's great, Sweet Pea," Mama said, her southern drawl blossoming as it tended to do from time to time. "Okay, y'all be careful, and I'll see you later on."

Leah forced herself to push thoughts of Quinton and Nova as a couple out of her mind. "She's making amazing progress in a short amount of time. Can you believe it's only been two weeks since we got the news that Nova was alive?"

"I think about that all the time. Some days, it feels like she's been there a lot longer, and then something will happen, like last night at the game, to remind me that it hasn't been long at all. She still has a ways to go."

Leah nodded while filling her mouth with a spoonful of soup. She savored the rich flavors. "This is so good, Mom. I didn't realize how much I needed this." Leah wiped her mouth. "And I'm not just talking about the soup."

Martha reached over and squeezed Leah's hand. "Me too."

CHAPTER 39

Nova

During the drive back to Bayou from Baton Rouge, Lance had to take an important call. That meant I had nothing but time to sit and think while I played with the apps on my new phone. I'd named them colorful boxes until Lance told me the real name. Why did a phone need so many apps anyway? And what did *apps* mean? Those were questions I'd have to wait and ask. His call sounded serious. One of his major donors was trying to back out of their original commitment, and Lance wasn't happy about it at all.

"You okay?" I asked when he opened the console between us and tossed the phone inside.

After a slew of curse words, Lance glanced at me. "I'm sorry. I hate when people say they're going to do something, then at the last minute come up with a million reasons why they can't."

"Anything I can do to help?" I really wanted to do something for him for a change. Ever since I'd been back, he'd been going out of his way to make sure I was okay.

"Nah, it's fine. It'll work itself out."

"You say that like you really believe it."

Lance nodded. "That's because I do."

I chuckled. "Spoken like a man who's never been disappointed before."

He narrowed his eyes and aimed them at me for a second longer than I liked, since he should've been watching the road. "Are you serious? Me? Never disappointed? Now that's funny."

"I'm not talking about football disappointment. Not that that's not real, and doesn't hurt, but I mean life disappointments."

Lance's jaws clenched.

I'd overstepped and made him angry. Why was I hurting everyone I loved today? "I'm sorry." I didn't know what I was apologizing about, but I felt that I needed to say it anyway.

"Don't be." The smile he flashed her wasn't real. It didn't take over his whole face. "Are you in a hurry to get home, or do you have time to go to the lake? I have something I want to talk with you about."

My mind froze in the memory of the last time we were at the lake together. My heart raced when the image of his pained face came into view. Every day, I'd wanted to tell him that I changed my mind. I missed him so much, but I couldn't hurt Quinton either.

"Are you sure we should go to the lake?" I asked, turning the phone over and over in my hands.

"We don't have to if you're not comfortable. We can go back to your house or to mine," he suggested.

"No, it's not that I'm uncomfortable. It's . . . Well, the last time we were at the lake, it wasn't a good experience," I reminded him.

"I know, but the lake has become kinda symbolic for me. It's where I go to release all the bad stuff and take in the good."

"Is that what you think I was doing? Releasing the bad stuff? Because that's not . . ."

"No," he laughed. "That's not what I meant. But after you left that day, I stayed there a while longer. I fished and talked with God. I wasn't too happy with him then, but afterward, I got it all out, and I felt better. For the time being, anyway."

I didn't tell Lance what happened with Skye earlier, but if the lake was a place to go and feel better, then it was exactly where I needed to be. "Okay, let's go to the lake."

Lance turned on the road that led to his house. "Let me grab a couple of blankets. It's getting cool."

"Oh my goodness." I leaned forward in my seat and tried to make sense of what I was seeing.

Lance told me that he'd built a house instead of moving into his mom's house. Neither he nor Carmen could stay there after their mom passed away. When he said he'd built a house, I thought he meant a regular house, not the massive building in front of me. It had to be the largest house in Bayou.

"That's your house?" I pointed ahead.

"This is it," he said, turning off the engine and walking around to open my door.

I was in awe as I stepped out and walked up to the widest front porch I'd ever seen. There were rocking chairs and flowerpots. "I never imagined you as a flower person."

"I'm not. I don't know anything about flowers or decorating. Carmen did everything." Lance unlocked the door. "Want a tour?"

"Of course I do." I moved past him like I knew where I was going.

I didn't think my eyes could get any wider, but somehow, they did. I stepped into the living room, which, like the porch, was cozy and huge. His plush sofas were arranged around a large stone fireplace. On the mantel were black-and-white family pictures all in silver frames.

"This place is amazing," I said, looking up at the ceiling that had to be as high as the sky itself. "How do you clean those?" I pointed to the ceiling fans.

Lance looked up there, too, then back at me. "I don't."

"You hire someone to clean them?"

He shook his head. "I guess I should, though, huh?"

"Show me the rest of the house." I followed Lance out of the room and throughout the rest of the house.

I couldn't be sure, but it felt like we'd walked at least two miles by the time we finished the tour. The final thing to see was the backyard, which wasn't a yard at all. Lance opened the french doors that led to a deck overlooking a pasture, which stretched out farther than I could see.

"You have horses?" I sounded like a little girl at an amusement park.

"Of course. Why do you think I always wear cowboy boots?" He pointed to the boots he was currently wearing.

"Because you like them." I hunched my shoulders. "I didn't know you were a real cowboy."

He chuckled. "I don't know about all that, but I do love horses." He looked over at me. "Maybe one day we can go for a ride."

"On a horse?"

"Yes, on a horse."

I stepped back as if we were going right then.

"Oh, come on. What happened to that girl who was always up for a challenge?"

My head dipped. "I wish she were here too," I said, barely above a whisper.

"Hey." Lance placed his finger underneath my chin, then tipped it up so my eyes could meet his. "She's still in there. She needs time before she's ready to come out."

He sounded so sure that I almost believed him. "Promise?" I asked.

He held out his pinkie, and I wrapped mine around it. "You got this . . . We got this."

Lance stared at me, and for some reason, I couldn't look away. A warm feeling flowed through me, which didn't make sense because the temperature had dropped. Lance smiled, and I could've sworn that someone had turned the thermostat up to a hundred.

"I'd better go get those blankets," he said, breaking whatever hold his eyes had on me.

"Okay. I'll wait for you by the front door."

My thoughts as we drove farther down the road to the lake were very different than they were before. I was still trying to make sense of what happened back at Lance's house. I'd never felt that way around him before. He was Lance. I didn't feel warm around Lance. At least I didn't before today.

Lance backed his truck up to the lake and pulled the tailgate down. We sat with our legs dangling as we looked out at the water. The main attraction wasn't the lake, though. It was the orange and purple sky.

"I don't think I ever realized how peaceful it is here," I told Lance.

It amazed me how I could be surrounded by serenity and beauty and still feel so distraught on the inside. I kept reminding myself that Skye's words were out of pain. I understood that deeply from the times I'd lashed out at Mama. By the next day, the only thing I wished was that I could take them back and tell her how sorry I was. Maybe Skye would feel the same way. Even if she didn't apologize, I wanted to know that she didn't hate me.

"Still thinking about Skye?" Lance asked.

I'd filled him in on our way to the phone store. As always, Lance was the calm I needed at the time. I didn't deserve his friendship. He had every right to turn his back on me the way I'd turned mine on him.

"Yeah." I lifted the cell phone. "I keep hoping that Mama may have given her my number, and she'd call and say she didn't mean what she said."

"She will. Maybe not today, but it won't be long before she realizes you're not to blame for whatever's going on between Leah and Quinton. Skye's young. She doesn't understand that almost every relationship goes through tough times."

I thought of all the arguments Quinton and I had when we were married. They always took place after Skye was asleep. Even though she was young, I thought she could still sense that something was wrong between her parents, and I didn't want her to feel that. It wouldn't surprise me if Leah and Quinton did the same thing when they argued . . . if they argued.

"Maybe their relationship was as perfect as Skye thought it was," I said to Lance.

Lance laughed. "Trust me, they had their issues too."

"How do you know? You aren't close to Quinton. Did Leah tell you? Are you close with Leah?"

"Only professionally, but I don't need to be close to either one of them to know they have problems. Quinton's stubborn, and Leah may not be as stubborn as he is, but she has her ways too. She's a control freak. I can imagine that the two of them butt heads a lot at home."

I probably would've asked more questions if it still didn't weird me out to think of them as a couple.

"But Leah's good people, though," Lance continued. "That's actually what I wanted to talk with you about. Not Leah specifically, but I wanted to tell you about something I'd gone through. I'm sure it was what Quinton wanted to talk with you about that day when he interrupted us in your mom's backyard."

"Okay. What is it?" I asked, glad that I had something else to focus on other than Skye and the words that wouldn't stop playing in my head.

Lance stared quietly at the water for a second before he spoke. "After my grandma died, I went through this period where I thought the only way to ease the pain from that loss was to do something big. My grandma felt like my whole world, you know that. I still had my mom, of course, but she was dealing with her own grief."

I nodded.

"I felt like there was something missing in my life. I guess I wanted the family I used to have, but since that wasn't possible the next best thing was to start a family of my own. I wanted the whole shebang, the wife and kids. I thought that would make me feel better. That it would fill that hole. At the time, I was dating this . . . young lady . . . and I stupidly asked her to marry me."

"Why was it stupid?"

"Because I knew I didn't love her. Not like a man should love the woman he was going to marry. I realized, or rather, I acknowledged that a little too late. Every day, I told myself I was going to have a talk with her and explain that I wasn't thinking straight. That it was the grief talking and not me, but every day, it was harder and harder to say those words to her. She'd put so much into planning our dream wedding. That was actually her dream wedding because I couldn't even tell you the colors. That's how far removed I was from everything."

My heart pounded as if I was waiting for him to break the news to me instead of some woman I'd never met.

"It was bad enough that she was all excited, but then she pulled Carmen in, and she was just as excited. She'd taken our mom's death even harder than I did, and to see her happy again . . ." Lance shook his head. "I didn't know how to take that away from her."

"But you didn't have a choice," I said as if I needed to remind him that he did what had to be done.

"I didn't. I wished I'd manned up and done it before money was spent, venues were secured, and invitations were printed."

My eyes stretched. "Oh wow."

"Oh wow is right. So, as you can imagine, when I broke the news to her, she was fierce. I still believe if she'd had a weapon on her that night, she would've used it."

"That must've been so awful for you."

"It was even more awful for her. I recognized that, but I didn't know what to do to make it better other than go along with the wedding, which I wasn't willing to do. When she left my house that night, she promised me that I would regret what I'd done to her. She was convinced that, for some reason, I did it on purpose. Like I had some longtime vendetta against her or something."

"But she eventually got over it?"

"Yeah, eventually, after she told the whole world that I'd raped her."

My mouth opened slightly, and I tried to think of words that my brain wouldn't form. Rape? Lance? His name and that word should never be that close to each other. Lance was my friend. Lance would never do that. He couldn't do that. It wasn't who he was, and nothing inside me questioned that fact. Which meant a lot because I questioned everything, but not that.

"It's okay, Nova." He moved closer to me and wrapped the blanket around both of us.

I didn't realize I was crying until he wiped my face. "How could anyone do that to you?"

"People who are hurting tend to make others hurt with them. That's what she was doing. She felt like I embarrassed her, so she set out to embarrass me."

"But that was more than embarrassing. She could've sent you to prison. She could've ruined your life."

"She did," he said. "Not my whole life, but she ruined that period of it. I was arrested, and my face was plastered all over the news, in the newspapers, and on social media. I don't think I've ever been more embarrassed."

"Oh my God, Lance." I looped my arm around his and closed the space between us.

At that moment, I wanted to be close to him. The need to make all his hurt go away was so strong. Stronger than I ever imagined it could be. Then, in an instant, my emotions went from sad to angry. Livid. I hadn't felt that kind of anger since I'd left that house, and it scared me. Maybe it was the news Lance had just shared on top of how I was already feeling about myself from hurting Skye. Even if I didn't know what I'd done wrong, it didn't matter. The fact that she believed my return ruined everything was enough.

"What happened to her? Did she go to prison for trying to ruin your life?" My scalp heated at the thought of her getting off easy after causing him so much pain. The same way Adam got off easy after stealing years of my life.

"She took a plea deal and was hit with a healthy fine and probation. I could've sued for defamation of character, but I didn't want to do that. I wanted it over and done with," he explained.

"Over and done with? She accused you of one of the worst things a man can be accused of other than murder, and you wanted it over and done with? Why? You should've sued her. She should've gone to jail for the rest of her life."

"Hey." Lance wrapped his arm around me. "It's okay. I'm okay."

"It's not okay." My voice vibrated with rage. "I'm sick and tired of people getting off easy after they've done wrong. It's not fair," I cried. "It's not fair." I laid my head on his shoulder.

Lance held me tighter and continued telling me that everything was going to be okay. His voice and words were annoying at first, but then they became soothing and mixed in with the scenery around us. His words penetrated the hard exterior I attempted to build and found their way to my core. Lance kissed my forehead and ignited pieces of me that hadn't felt alive in forever. That was when I reminded myself that I wasn't supposed to feel that way. Not with Lance. He was my friend. The feelings that tried to creep in couldn't because it didn't make sense. I shouldn't feel that way about Lance or anyone else. No man deserved the woman I was now. The woman that Adam defiled and damaged and left to die alone. Lance didn't deserve that version of me. After everything he'd gone through, he needed a woman who was whole and beautiful. And that wasn't me.

"You okay?" Lance asked.

I lifted myself off him. "Do I look okay to you?"

"No, not really." He used his finger to wipe underneath my eye.

"You're not funny. But I do have a serious question."

"Yeah, what is it?"

"You said you've never been more embarrassed in your whole life, and I was wondering if that included that time you wore those high-water pants when your mom was out of town, and you forgot to do your laundry?" I made my face as serious as possible.

Lance howled in laughter. He threw his head back and kept laughing. Tears streamed down his face, and he wiped them away while he tried to stop himself from laughing. He'd barely regained his composure when he said, "I hate you so much."

We both laughed until the laughter slowly died.

"I missed you, Nova. Life without you isn't the same. You don't bring me joy. You *are* my joy. And still my best friend. Promise you'll never leave me again." He held out his pinkie.

I latched mine with his, and that sealed the deal. Lance had to be a part of my life forever because the pinkies never broke a promise.

My phone rang, and I reached into my pocket and pulled it out. "My first call." I showed Lance the screen. "It's Mama. Oh my goodness, I forgot to call and let her know where I am." I hurried and accepted the call. "I'm so sorry. I'm fine. I'm with Lance. We're at the lake."

"Nova, have you seen Skye?" Mama asked.

"Yeah," I said slowly, wondering if Mama was okay because I told her that Skye had come by earlier today and what she'd said to me.

"Oh, thank God. Where is she? Leah and Quinton are worried sick."

"What?" Panic took over. "What do you mean, where is she? I haven't seen her since earlier when she came by the house."

"I thought you said . . . I was asking if you'd seen her recently," Mama clarified.

"No. Did you call her?" I leaped off the truck and ran my hand over my short curls. "Of course you called her. You wouldn't have called me without calling her first," I rambled to myself.

"What's wrong?" Lance stood in front of me.

I looked at him, almost unable to see him through the pure terror that had taken over my entire body. "Skye's missing." I somehow managed to say the words that I wished like hell I'd never have to say.

CHAPTER 40
Leah

Leah paced the length of the family room, her phone clutched tightly in her hand. The air was thick with tension, and the silence only made her worry louder. She stopped by the window and looked out at the front of the house, praying so hard that Skye's car would pull into the driveway, and all of this was one big misunderstanding. Maybe she'd told them she was going somewhere, but they'd forgotten. How was it that the whole day had passed and no one knew where Skye had gone? Leah knew the answer to that question, and it made her feel more awful than she had before.

Everyone was so wrapped up in their own mess, and assumptions were made that could turn out to . . . No. She would not go there. Skye was going to be okay, and she and Quinton weren't going to play the would've, could've, should've game. It was an easy mistake. Quinton thought Skye was with Leah, and Leah thought she was home with Quinton. She was sure she'd sent the text message letting him know she was on her way home, but she didn't. Her mind moved faster than her hands, and she never pressed send.

"Where could she be?" Leah muttered under her breath, running her hand through her hair that she'd nervously pulled back into a ponytail and released at least five times.

"Is there anyone else we should call?" Martha asked, sitting next to Quinton, trying to be a source of strength for him even though she looked like she needed someone to be that for her.

Quinton looked at his phone again. "It doesn't make sense that her car and phone are still at that store, but she isn't. I talked with everyone, but no one saw her. I called Amber and sent a message in the team's group chat. No one has seen or heard from her all day."

Quinton sat on the edge of the sofa, his head buried in his hands and his shoulders slumped. He'd been calling everyone he could think of, and each call seemed to cause him to sink lower and lower.

"Maybe she's somewhere cooling off. Nova did say she was rather upset earlier today." Martha's voice trembled slightly as she spoke.

Leah could tell that her mom was trying to sound hopeful, but she wasn't executing it well. Leah shook her head, her throat tight. "I don't know, Mom. I doubt it, though. You know Skye would never do anything like this." Leah fought hard to keep her panic at bay, but it was creeping in, making it hard for her to think straight. Every second felt like an eternity.

How could she have let this happen? That was the question Leah couldn't stop asking herself. No matter what issues they were facing, Skye should've been their number-one priority, just as she'd always been up until that day. Guilt surged through her as she thought of her and her mom sitting on the balcony eating soup and talking while Skye was only God knew where and with whom.

Blue lights illuminated the family room. Leah saw the police car sitting in the driveway. Quinton called them after he'd contacted everyone he could think to call.

"I'll let them in," Martha said.

Leah sat next to Quinton. His eyes were bloodshot. He looked like he didn't sleep at all last night. That made two of them. She reached over and picked up his hand. In spite of what was going on between them, they both needed each other if they had any chance of making it through what could only be described as a pure nightmare.

Leah, Quinton, and Martha sat with the officer and answered question after question.

"What was she wearing when you last saw her?" the officer asked.

Leah's mind went blank before images of Skye flashed through, all in different outfits, from her school uniform to her basketball uniform. Neither of which Skye had on that day, Leah knew that much for sure. She and Quinton exchanged guilty glances. How could they not know what their child was wearing today? What could be the most important information needed to find Skye was the one that Leah nor Quinton had an answer to.

"Okay, think about it, and I'll come back to that one." The officer didn't sound as appalled as he should've been.

The doorbell rang again, and Martha got up and left the room.

Nova rushed inside the family room with Martha trailing behind.

Leah sat on the sofa and Nova sat beside her. Despite the chaos of their situation, having Nova there gave Leah a sense of reassurance. When Nova first returned, Leah saw her presence as a painful reminder that Skye wasn't Leah's biological child. Not that Leah needed that reminder, but it was easier to fool herself when Nova wasn't there. Now that Skye was missing, Nova's presence held a whole new meaning. In Leah's eyes, Nova was a warrior. She was a hero, and Skye was Nova's daughter, which meant she was a warrior, too, and, just like Nova, she'd return home safely. Leah had to believe that to be true.

"Did something happen? Did you find her?" Nova asked, her eyes pleading with them for good news.

"No, not yet," Leah said. "We're giving the officer some information about Skye."

"What do you need to know that's more important than being out there looking for her?" Nova asked.

"We need to know who we're looking for," the officer explained. "I have a picture, but I still need to know what she was wearing today so I can send that information to the dispatcher."

"She had light-blue jeans that were torn at the knees, a red, black, and white flannel shirt that's unbuttoned with a white tank top underneath, and red and white Converse." Nova described Skye's clothes as if Skye were standing right in front of her.

The officer was still writing when Nova finished. "Okay, that's perfect. And you are?" He asked Nova.

"I'm Nova. Her mom." Nova's voice was shaky as her eyes darted toward Leah and Quinton.

The officer stood. "This should do for now. In the meantime, stay put in case she comes back," he said before Martha walked him out.

"I'm so sorry." Nova's voice cracked. "This is all my fault. She's missing because of me. She—she said I ruined everything, and she's right. I don't know how to fix it. I just—"

"Nova, stop," Leah interjected, turning to face Nova and placing her hand on Nova's arm. "None of this is your fault. If anyone's to blame, it's me." The heaviness of Leah's words weighed her down.

"You're both wrong," Quinton said weakly, pulling both of their attention toward his slumped figure. "How did I think I could protect Skye when I couldn't even protect you," he said to Nova, his eyes filled with regret. "I knew something like this could happen. That's why I tried . . ." His voice trailed off as he lowered his head again and hid behind his hand.

Leah knew he'd still blamed himself for not being there for Nova, but he'd never been so open about it. Seeing him so vulnerable made Leah's heart ache even more than it was already.

"Quinton, you can't keep doing that to yourself. Like I told you before, I was the one who left that night. And anyone with eyes and common sense can see what a great job you've done with Skye. She's amazing, and that's because of you." Nova looked over at Leah. "And you."

Nova's words were the validation that Leah didn't realize she needed. They renewed Leah's spirit and strengthened her faith. There was no way that Skye wouldn't come back to them safely. Everyone in that room had too much love for her, and they all needed her there to receive it.

"It's okay," Martha said, walking into the room and talking, but it didn't seem that she was speaking to anyone in the room.

They all looked up and saw Lance standing next to Martha. It was the first time Leah had seen him since his unexpected visit to her office. Seeing Lance now, Leah felt a stir of apprehension about how Quinton might react to his presence. She glanced up at Quinton, but he didn't even seem to notice Lance's presence. Quinton stared straight ahead like his thoughts were only on Skye.

"I'm sorry," Lance said, looking in their direction. "I was waiting on Nova. I didn't want to come inside," he said, looking over at Martha.

"Listen, we don't have time for any of that foolishness tonight. My grandbaby is missing, and we need all the ears, eyes, and hands we can find. If the two of you want to hate each other, then fine, but do it after Skye's home and safe. Is that understood?" Her authoritative tone dared anyone to disagree.

No one did.

"Good," she continued. "Now, come on in. Nova needs you."

Lance had only taken another step into the living room before Nova moved away from Leah and Quinton and wrapped her arms around Lance. He held her head against his chest, and Leah couldn't help but notice how they'd seemed to effortlessly ease right back into the friendship they'd had before it ended.

Leah glanced over at Quinton, who seemed to be completely zoned out from everything that was going on around him. She couldn't be sure that he even realized that Lance was in their house. Leah reached behind Quinton and rubbed his back, attempting to offer comfort. She wasn't sure she had it in her to give, but whatever she had, she needed to give to him.

Then, as if something shook him out of his trance, Quinton jumped from his seat. "I don't care what that officer said. I'm not sitting here for another second doing nothing. I'm going to look for Skye."

"I'll come with you." Leah stood too.

"No." Quinton put his hands on her shoulders. "You need to be here in case she comes back before I do."

Leah nodded. She wasn't in the mood to argue. All she wanted was for Skye to come back safely. As much as she didn't want to think about it, she couldn't stop the memories of the night they'd learned that Nova was missing. The images came to her in vivid flashes.

As if he'd seen her thoughts, Quinton pulled Leah into him and held her with the right amount of tightness, comforting her like only he could. "I'll be back," he said softly before walking to the doorway, past Nova and Lance. "I need something." He looked around. "What am I looking for?" he asked no one in particular.

"Do you have your keys?" Leah asked, figuring that couldn't be it because of course he knew he needed his keys.

"My keys. Yeah, I need my keys." He still stood there like his thoughts were all jumbled and he couldn't figure out the next move without being told.

"I'll drive. I have my keys." Lance held up his truck keys.

Quinton looked at Lance for a long, silent moment. His jaws tightened, but he didn't respond to Lance's offer.

"Listen, I know I'm the last person you'd want to go anywhere with, and I get that, but you're in no condition to drive. You can sit in the back seat, and we don't have to talk. I want to help you bring your daughter home."

Quinton nodded. He turned, and his eyes met Leah's before he followed Lance out of the house. The thud of their footsteps filled the quiet house until the click of the door behind them ushered in more silence.

Nova looked as helpless as Leah felt. Leah sat next to Nova, who was curled into Martha's arms.

"Do you need something to drink?" Leah asked.

Focusing on others and ignoring her feelings was how Leah made it through some of her darkest times. At least, she thought they were her darkest times until today. Losing a parent was painful, but something children expected to do one day. Losing a sibling was something you didn't want to have to endure, but it wasn't unreasonable to think that it could happen, especially when you were close in age like Leah and Nova. But losing a child, whether you gave birth to them or not, was a darkness unlike any other and something no parent or stepparent should have to wrap their minds around. So, Leah had to take care of everyone else because she didn't know what would happen if she stopped. She couldn't promise that she'd be okay.

"We're fine, Leah. Just sit." Martha used her free hand and reached for Leah.

The ache in Leah's heart grew when she settled next to her mom and allowed her mom to comfort her as she was comforting Nova. Leah realized that no matter how old she was, she'd never stop needing her mom. When she was a little girl, she used to think there was nothing her mom couldn't do or make better. She wished her mom could work whatever magic Leah used to believe she had because the fear of what was happening with Skye was suffocating. Leah tried to pray, but she couldn't form the words. All she could do was hope that God could read the thoughts that her mind wasn't coherent enough to form.

CHAPTER 41
Nova

Mama, Leah, and I sat in the family room and waited for news. Leah constantly checked her phone and Facebook. She said she was checking Skye's page to see if she'd posted anything, but she hadn't. I couldn't sit any longer, so I got up and walked around the room, taking in every part of the house that Leah, Quinton, and Skye had made into a home.

It was the little details that stood out to me the most. The built-in bookshelves lined the wall and were filled with books, keepsakes, and framed photographs, capturing priceless moments between the three of them. Skye's school portraits, her wide smile beaming from the frames. There were pictures of family vacations, birthdays, and holidays. I picked up the picture that someone took of Leah, Skye, and Quinton on a beach, laughing like they'd heard the funniest joke ever. None of them were looking at the camera, which made the moment feel more authentic, not staged.

The more I stared at the picture, the harder I attempted to swallow the tears that were scorching my throat. I no longer had to imagine what their life must've been like. I was holding the evidence of a life full of love, experiences, and happiness. There was something bittersweet in that realization. It was a sense of gratitude mixed with sorrow as I stared into Skye's face, which glowed almost as bright as the sun behind her.

In that picture and all the others, I saw the life I always wanted for Skye—a life filled with more love than her little heart could contain. Of course, I wished I was standing with them on the beach, next to Skye as she blew out the candles on her birthday cake, and on the other side of her as she received a basketball trophy for player of the year. But in all those pictures I also saw the love Leah had for Skye. There wasn't a picture that she wasn't in, smiling like she couldn't have been prouder if she tried. Other than Mama and Quinton, I didn't know anyone else who loved Skye, even before she was born, more than Leah did.

"You okay, Sweet Pea?" Mama stood next to me.

I put the picture back on the shelf and forced my lips to cooperate enough to convince Mama that I was fine. I looked around Mama and over to Leah, who was leaning forward with her hands steepled in front of her mouth. "Where's the bathroom?" I asked.

Leah stood. "I'll show you."

I followed to the end of the hallway. "Thanks," I said before closing myself inside.

I didn't have to use it. I needed some time alone. Maybe the bathroom wasn't the best place. This one only had a toilet and a sink. It was too small and too confining, but it would have to do. I leaned against the sink and gripped the edge to steady myself as my chest heaved with emotions.

I raised myself up and stared at the person in the mirror with swollen eyes. How had I gone from sitting at the lake with Lance to this nightmare? During my first few weeks in that room, I often wondered how Mama and Daddy must've been feeling, not knowing where I was. If I was alive or dead. Now I knew. I told Mama that she couldn't compare what she'd gone through to what I'd gone through, and I was right, because what she'd gone through was so much worse. Even back then, when I was locked in that room with no hope of escaping, I still didn't feel as helpless as I felt now.

Tonight, I not only felt useless, but I also felt desperate. Desperate enough to reach out to the same God who'd abandoned me. Maybe he loved Skye enough to hear me on her behalf.

I slid down to the floor, pressing my back against the wall, and hugged my knees to my chest. I closed my eyes and let the darkness wrap around me as I searched for the right words. It had been so long that I didn't know if I remembered how to pray, but I tried anyway.

"God," I whispered. "I don't know if you can hear me or if you even want to hear from me anymore, but I know you know Skye. I'm sure you still love her, right? Because who wouldn't love Skye? She's beautiful and funny, and she has a heart of gold. I know that's true because the people who raised her have hearts of gold." I paused, shocked by my own words. "So, even if you don't protect Skye and bring her back safely for me, then at least do it for Quinton and Leah and Mama. Please don't let them hurt any more than they already have. None of them deserve that. Okay. I think that's all I have to say. Amen."

I stayed on the floor for a few more minutes before I forced myself to stand. My legs wobbled. I braced myself against the sink and stared at myself in the mirror one last time. I looked the same as before, but I didn't feel the same. There was a flicker of something that I hadn't walked in there with, but I couldn't name it. All I knew was that I didn't feel quite as heavy as I did a few minutes ago.

When I stepped into the hallway, I followed what sounded like the clatter of dishes back down the hallway and into a large kitchen. Leah sat at the counter, her back to me, while Mama stood in front of her, pouring hot water from a glass tea kettle and into a mug.

"You want some tea?" Mama asked, raising the tea kettle.

"No, thanks." I slid onto the stool next to Leah and inhaled the smell of cinnamon and spices. "I don't know how to do this," I mumbled.

"What's that?" Mama asked, stirring sugar in her tea.

"I really wanted Skye to live with me, and everyone tried to tell me that it was too soon, but I thought they were being negative and not supporting me, but after this. . ." I looked across the table at Mama and then over to Leah. "What if she'd done this while she was living with me? What if Mama was gone, and I was all alone? Would I have known what to do? Probably not . . . Who am I kidding? Definitely not. I would've panicked," I rambled on.

"Nova, don't do that." Leah leaned closer to me. "You think I didn't panic? You think Quinton didn't? But after that, adrenaline kicks in, and you start thinking straight. I'll be the first to admit that the thought of Skye moving out and living with you and Mama did break my heart, but not because I didn't think you could handle it. Skye's not my child, I know that, but I love her so much." Leah closed her eyes and inhaled.

I moved from my seat and hugged Leah. It was my turn to comfort her the way she'd comforted me when I first walked in. As Leah hugged me back, I could feel the steady beat of her heart against mine. As I held my sister and felt her pain mixed with mine, it was more apparent than ever that Leah had become more than a guardian in my absence—she was a pillar for Skye, just as she'd always been for me.

"Nova," Leah said breathlessly. "You're hurting me."

"Oh." I stepped back. "I'm sorry, I didn't realize how tight I was holding you."

The chime from the front door caused all of us to rush from the kitchen and into the hallway. I expected to see Lance and Quinton and prayed they had Skye with them, but it wasn't them.

"Skye!" Leah ran to the front door and grabbed Skye in her arms.

Mama and I were right behind her. We couldn't wait for Leah to release the hold she had on Skye, so me and Mama joined Leah in the hug. We were all so focused on Skye that it took a minute before we realized she wasn't alone.

"Bianca?" Mama left the group hug and went to the door where our cousin Bianca was still standing. "Where did you find her?" Mama asked.

"I didn't find her, exactly." Bianca played with her fingers while she spoke. She cleared her throat. "Skye rode to New Orleans with me."

"What?" we all responded.

"I'm sorry." Bianca glared at Skye. "I didn't know she didn't have permission to come. She told me she asked, and her dad said it was okay." Bianca hunched her shoulders. "I didn't have a reason not to believe her."

"Why would you do that?" Leah asked Skye. "You scared us half to death. Do you know your dad is out there right now riding around looking for you?" Leah's finger jabbed toward the front door. "And not just your dad but also the police. Yes, that's right, instead of spending their time on real issues, they're out there looking for a seventeen-year-old runaway."

Skye's hands were clasped tightly in front of her, and her eyes darted around the space, as if she was unable to look at Leah. "I wasn't trying to scare anyone," Skye murmured. "I was so upset. I was going to come straight home when I left Gran's, but I couldn't come back here." Her eyes shimmered with unshed tears.

"Why not?" Leah asked.

"Because you weren't here." Skye lowered her head.

Leah's face softened.

I didn't want to feel jealous, but it was still there. Skye's love for Leah was so loud and clear.

"Skye," Leah said softly. She hugged Skye again.

"I'm so sorry." Bianca looked between Mama and me.

"It's not your fault," Mama said, her eyes glued to Skye. "Before tonight, I wouldn't have questioned if she was lying, either, but now I see that I should."

Skye looked like she was ready to crumble. Like the last thing she wanted to do was hurt her grandma.

"I'm sorry, Gran." A frown distorted Skye's beautiful features.

"I guess I'd better call and tell your dad that you're home," Leah said, walking back into the kitchen where she'd left her phone.

"Wait, Leah, before you go, there's something I need to tell all of you," Bianca said, sweeping a gaze from Leah to Mom, then finally landing on me.

"What is it?" Leah asked, sounding rushed.

"It's about the magazine article."

I looked at Leah, whose eyes had narrowed into slits. Mama's arms were crossed over her chest.

"What article?" I asked.

Instead of answering my question, Leah asked her own. "You were the family friend?" She glared at Bianca.

Bianca shook her head. "No. I mean, I didn't do the interview, but I think one of my clients may have. Well, former client now."

"What article?" I asked again, that time a bit more forcefully than before.

Mama filled me in on the article. Once again, they'd kept something from me, but that time I didn't care. With everything I was dealing with back then, and had just learned about, I'm glad they didn't give me more news to deal with.

"Why do you think it was your former client?" Leah asked.

"Because we were talking about it." Bianca's head lowered. "She said everything I'd told her almost verbatim." Bianca looked up again. "I'm really sorry."

Mama walked over to Bianca. "It's okay. It wasn't what was said that bothered us the most. It was thinking someone close to us was talking to the press behind our backs. That's the part we were most concerned about. I mean, it's not like the article said anything that was a secret." Mama smiled.

Bianca looked at me and Leah.

"Thank you for telling us," Leah said. "Just be careful who next time. Mama's right. You didn't share any deep, dark secrets or anything, but now you know you can't trust everyone who sits in your chair."

Bianca nodded. "Yes, I've definitely learned that lesson."

"Good. Well, I need to go call Quinton," Leah said, turning away from us.

"I'm going to go." Bianca opened the door.

"Bianca," Skye called after her. "I'm sorry I lied to you. I wasn't thinking. When I saw you at the store, and you said you were going to

New Orleans, all I knew was I had to get away for a while. I shouldn't have pulled you into my mess, though."

Bianca's face softened. "No, you shouldn't have," she said before walking through the door.

Leah was walking back down the hallway as we were returning to the family room. "Quinton was already in the neighborhood," she said.

I sat next to Skye on the sofa. She looked as nervous as I felt. It wasn't long before we heard the front door opening, and Quinton rushed into the family room.

"Skye, oh my God." He held her for a long time.

"I'm sorry, Daddy," Skye sounded more like a five-year-old than a seventeen-year-old.

Quinton held Skye at arm's length and looked at her from her head to her feet. "Are you okay? What happened? Where were you?" He asked question after question, not giving her time to answer any of them.

"Let's go sit," Mama suggested.

"Where's Lance?" I asked, looking toward the door.

"He left. He said he'll call you later," Quinton said, holding Skye's hand and walking her to the family room with Mama and me following behind.

Skye repeated the story to Quinton, and the more she talked, the tighter his lips became. Skye finished speaking, and Quinton sat quietly, as if his mind needed time to register everything she'd said.

"Have you lost your mind?" Quinton practically leaped from the sofa.

I jumped, then held my chest. My heart raced, pounding against my rib cage as if it was trying to break free. Quinton stood over Skye. His finger aimed at her. His voice boomed throughout the room, causing my body to tremble uncontrollably.

"Stop. Please stop," I shouted over Quinton. My plea drew the attention of everyone in the room.

Mama came over to me and placed her hand on my back. "It's okay, baby," she whispered.

Skye's eyes had gone from sorrow to shock. Even Leah looked like she was too afraid to move. I probably should've apologized for startling them, but I wasn't sorry. I just needed him to stop. Watching Quinton—his anger mirrored the aggression I had once endured from Adam. It was too painful. I understood that Quinton's words were out of love and fear, but I didn't want Skye to feel that kind of love. There had to be another way.

"Go to your room," Quinton told Skye.

When she left, he broke down in Leah's arms. "I couldn't stop thinking that I'd never see her again," he cried.

We all cried. The fear of losing someone we love was very real, and it was something that we all needed to figure out how to live with.

I wiped my eyes. "May I go and talk with Skye?" I asked Leah and Quinton.

"Of course." Leah led me upstairs.

We'd just stepped onto the landing when she stopped and turned to me. "Tonight was one of the scariest nights of my life," Leah said.

"Mine too."

"But the minute I saw Mom, I knew everything was going to be okay. Mothers have a way of making their children feel that way."

I nodded in agreement.

"Anyway, as I'm sure you've figured out, things aren't great between Quinton and me at the moment, which is what brought us to where we are now." Leah glanced behind her toward the bedroom doors, then back at me. "If you didn't ask to come up, I would've suggested it because, like I said, mothers have a way of giving us hope that we can't seem to find for ourselves. Skye needs that right now." Leah took my hand in hers and then led me to Skye's bedroom door.

"Thank you," I said before she turned and left.

I stood in front of Skye's door with my eyes closed. Leah's words had planted themselves in the deepest part of my soul, and from them sprouted the thickest, strongest roots of hope and love and peace. I knocked on Skye's door.

"Come in," Skye said so softly that I almost didn't hear her.

I pushed the door open and stepped inside the room. The space was bathed in a soft purple glow that came from a string of lights that were around the upper edges of the wall.

Skye sat cross-legged on her bed, hugging a pillow in front of her. "Do you hate me too?" she asked.

My heart dropped that she would even think that. "I couldn't hate you even if I tried. You did scare us, though. I don't understand why you'd do that to your dad and Teeah, and Gran. You know what they went through when I was taken."

Skye played with a loose string on her pillowcase. "I wasn't thinking about that. I know I should've been, but . . ."

"You were angry," I finished for her. "May I sit?" I asked, walking farther into the room.

Skye nodded.

"I'm sorry for what I said at Gran's." She looked at me when I sat on the side of her bed. "I don't even know why I said it. You didn't have anything to do with whatever Daddy and Teeah are going through." She narrowed her eyes. "Do you?" she asked.

"To be honest, I don't know. So much is happening, and I'm finding it hard to keep up."

"Tell me about it." Skye rolled her eyes. "I want things to be the way they used to be." She widened her eyes. "I mean, the way they used to be, and you still be here with us."

"I get it. Listen, I may not agree with the way your dad was talking to you, but I do agree with what he said. You have to think before you act. I'm sure your coach has told you that life is a lot like basketball."

"Oh my gawd, how many times have I heard that speech." Skye groaned.

"I think they all use it." I laughed. "But they're right. To win in life, like on the court, you have to think before you move, because sometimes you can make a decision that can change your whole life. Unlike that"—I pointed to her phone—"you can't go back and edit." I smiled, remembering her filming a video at Mama's house and how many times she kept redoing it until she got it right.

"I understand," Skye said. "I wish life did have an edit option. I always wondered what it would've been like if you were here."

"I do, too, but I'm here now, and I want to spend as much time with you as I can," I told her.

Skye moved her pillow, threw her legs over the bed, then sat right next to me. "I'd like that a lot." She laid her head on my shoulder.

I had no idea what heaven felt like, but I was pretty sure it had to be very close to what I was feeling in that moment.

CHAPTER 42

Leah

Leah stood in the doorway with her head leaning against the doorframe. She had no idea how long she'd been there, but she couldn't bring herself to leave. The events of the night still lingered even after everyone was gone and Skye was sleeping peacefully. She was flooded with relief. She wished it wasn't accompanied by the overwhelming exhaustion that seeped into her bones.

"You know you can't watch her sleep all night, right?" Quinton whispered, looking into the room at Skye.

"I know." Leah crossed her arms. "It's hard to believe that sweet face caused so much hell earlier."

Quinton huffed. "Tell me about it."

"It's late. We need to get some rest." Quinton left Leah standing by Skye's door and went down the hallway to their bedroom. "You coming?" he called back to her.

"In a minute." Leah walked into Skye's room, found the remote control for her purple LED lights, and turned them off.

It was the only normal thing she'd done that day, she realized as she bent down and kissed Skye. "I love you," she whispered.

"Love you too," Skye moaned.

Leah eased Skye's door closed and then walked down the hallway and stood in her own doorway. Quinton sat on the edge of the bed. The weariness he'd worn before was still etched all over his face.

"I'm spending the night because I'm too tired to think about driving across town, but I'm sleeping in the guest bedroom," Leah announced.

"What? Why?" Quinton asked, adjusting his body upright.

"Because nothing's changed between us. We still have one major issue that has to be resolved before we start living as husband and wife again."

His shoulders slumped. Quinton ran a hand over his face, then let it fall limply onto his lap. "Leah. Please," he said barely above a whisper.

Leah didn't want to hurt him, and she knew that was exactly what she was doing, but she was hurt too. She wanted to be able to bury everything that happened tonight and last night and move forward, but that wasn't possible.

"I know I hurt you, and I can't apologize enough for that," Quinton began. He steepled his hands as he spoke. "That shouldn't have been the first time you heard how I felt, but I didn't know how to tell you. I wasn't even sure if it was how I truly felt." He paused, lifted his head, then turned to her. "When Nova came back, I started thinking about things that I hadn't thought about in years. I love the memories that Nova and I were able to share with Skye since Nova's been back, but I don't love Nova. Not like that. Not like I love you."

Leah sat on the edge of the bed, feeling the mattress dip under her weight. Quinton leaned slightly toward her, his eyes intent on her face.

"How are you able to say that with certainty now when yesterday you were still confused about your feelings?" she asked, watching his expression for any signs of doubt.

"I know because of how I felt when I watched you walk out that door last night." His gaze drifted to the bedroom door as if reliving the moment. "You said I needed time to think, and that's all I did today, but the person I couldn't stop thinking about is you. I didn't want to run to Nova, and I didn't want her to run to me. I wanted you and no one else."

She felt a pinch of guarded hope tugging at her, wanting to lean into the warmth of his declaration. The words Quinton spoke echoed in the space between them. She wondered, *Is it truly possible for him to have untangled his knotted feelings in one day?*

Quinton leaned forward, his clasped hands covering his mouth. He straightened himself again and reached out for Leah, but then pulled away as if afraid of what she may do if he actually touched her. Instead, he cleared his throat and continued speaking. "And to be honest, the past few hours felt like a lifetime to me." Sincerity etched across his face and his brow furrowed. Quinton was never good at expressing his feelings verbally. This conversation had to be hard for him, but Leah sat quietly and listened while he was willing to share his thoughts with her.

"I may not know the perfect definition of love, but I do know that when you're at your lowest and everything feels like it's falling apart, that's when you need your person by your side. The only person I wanted by my side was you. Not Nova. Just you. Because you are my number one, and I'm sorry I didn't do a better job of making you feel that way, but I promise I'm going to spend the rest of our lives making sure you know that you're the most important person in my life." His shoulders relaxed as if a weight had been lifted.

Leah closed her eyes as the wall she was determined to keep between them slowly started to crumble. "You're the most important person in my life too," she admitted.

When she looked into Quinton's eyes, she saw the raw sincerity that reached deep into her heart, touching the part of her that longed to feel like someone's number one. "I do believe you. But I also believe that we should consider counseling. I don't want to move forward until we figure out how to get back to how we used to be. We need to learn how to communicate again."

"I agree. And speaking of counseling, I decided to go back."

Leah didn't think there was any more shock left inside her, but apparently there was. She didn't expect Quinton to protest marriage counseling, not now, anyway, since they were on the road to healing, but she certainly didn't expect to hear that he was going for himself.

It had taken everything for Leah to get him to go to grief counseling after Nova went missing. He went to two sessions and then decided it wasn't for him.

"What brought this on?" Leah asked, trying to stifle a yawn.

Quinton was quiet for a beat, then looked at Leah. "Last night, when I took Nova home from the school, she and I sat and talked for a while. I didn't want to leave her alone in the state that she was in, so I stuck around and tried to wait for your mom to get there." He lowered his gaze.

"It's okay," Leah said, giving him the reassurance he seemed to need to continue.

"Somehow, we got on the topic of Lance," Quinton began.

Leah listened intently as Quinton recounted his conversation with Nova. She noted how his expression changed as he spoke and how his jaw clenched briefly at the mention of his mother. It was something she hadn't noticed before. Did he always do that whenever they talked about Renee? She was sure she would've noticed if he had.

Quinton never gave her any reason to think he had any animosity toward his mom, even when he had every right to be upset, like all the visits she never made, even though they always invited her for holidays and other special occasions. "So, Nova feels like your anger toward Lance is actually for your mom?" Leah asked, trying to wrap her mind around what she'd just heard.

Quinton nodded. "But what do you think?" he asked.

Leah lifted her shoulders. "I don't know. I guess I'd need more information. It sounds like Nova knows things that I don't."

Quinton stared straight ahead as he spoke. "Only because she was around when I was dealing with my mom not being there. Nova and I hadn't talked about that since high school. I mean, before last night."

"Why didn't you tell me that you felt that way about Renee? Why did you act like you were fine with y'all's relationship?" Leah asked.

"Because I thought I was. I was used to her disappointing me, so I never expected much from her. When she never showed up or didn't call, it didn't bother me anymore because I didn't think she would anyway." Quinton exhaled. "It wasn't like I was keeping my feelings from you. I didn't realize there were feelings to discuss."

Leah understood. She'd seen it more times than she could count during her sessions. It always amazed her how powerful the mind could be. If you said it enough, eventually, you'd start to believe it. Your words became your reality, but not a true reality, just one you'd invented to cope with whatever you didn't want to deal with.

"And now?" Leah asked. "Do you think there's something to what Nova said about your misplaced anger?"

Quinton shook his head. "I don't know. But tonight, even though he had every reason not to help me, Lance did. When we got in his truck, he asked if I wanted him to pray." Quinton gave a disbelieving huff. "I've openly expressed my disdain for this man, and he still wanted to pray." He paused as if allowing his own words to settle in. "I know it was for Skye's safety and had more to do with Nova than me, but still." Quinton bit his bottom lip.

"So, what are you saying?" Leah asked, being careful not to jump to her own conclusions.

"I'm saying that maybe that little stunt Skye pulled was a blessing in disguise. I admit that I was unsure about my feelings toward Nova, but like I said, all of that changed tonight. There's not an ounce of uncertainty left, and I know that's something I'll have to prove to you through my actions and not my words. Not only that but tonight also gave me time to be alone with Lance—something I hadn't done since high school. I know Lance isn't who I made him out to be. I think I've always known it, but for some reason, it was easier to believe the worst of him than admit the truth. And the truth is, the anger I felt for him had more to do with the argument Nova and I had the night she went missing than the injury he'd caused me to have in high school. A part of me blamed him since he was the reason we'd fought in the first place."

"You did do a lot of thinking tonight," Leah said, suppressing another yawn.

"It wasn't just tonight, but tonight was when it all made sense in my mind. And I guess it was also when I gathered up the courage to actually admit it to someone other than myself."

"I'm glad you told me." Leah was starting to lose the battle with her eyelids. They felt heavier by the second. Yesterday and today had taken so much out of her.

"I know this is just the beginning of my"—Quinton snapped his fingers—"what do you call it? A healing journey?"

Leah nodded.

"But I don't think I can do this without you. I need you, Leah. But bigger than that, I want you." He picked up her hand and intertwined their fingers. "And only you for the rest of my life."

Quinton lay back on the bed and gently pulled Leah with him. Leah rested her head on his chest, and the rhythm of his heart was like a sweet lullaby that carried her right into the most peaceful sleep she'd had in a long time.

CHAPTER 43

Nova

I adjusted myself in the plush, high-backed chair in Dr. Yvonne's office. The challenge I gave myself was to start seeing Dr. Yvonne in her space instead of mine. Our first session at her office was Wednesday. I thought Halloween was the perfect day to do something a little scary.

"Before you leave, I have something for you." Dr. Yvonne smiled, then reached over to her small round table next to her chair and removed a brown-leather book. "It's a journal." She leaned forward so I could take it.

"Thank you," I said, taking the journal. I smiled as soon as I saw the words to the poem "Footprints" engraved on the front. I ran my hand over the words. "I love it."

Dr. Yvonne had this poem framed on the wall behind her. During our first session, I read the poem and couldn't believe how much it spoke to me. The two sets of footprints represented a person and God. The person noticed that during their toughest times, there was only one set of footprints. Like me, they thought God abandoned them, but God explained that those were his footprints. He was carrying the person through their trials. Ever since the whole

Skye's-missing nightmare two weeks ago, I'd vowed to make more of an effort to renew my faith.

That night in Leah and Quinton's bathroom, I felt more connected to God than I had in years. It was hard to explain, but for some reason, I knew he heard my prayer, and I knew he was going to answer it. Ever since that night, I started talking with him more. My prayers didn't look the way Mama and Daddy taught us to pray, where we'd get on our knees and bow our heads. My prayers took place where I was when I felt the need to pray. Mama said it didn't matter where it took place as long as it happened.

"You're welcome," Dr. Yvonne said, scooting back in her seat. "When I saw it, I knew I had to get it." She turned and looked at the poster on the wall behind her. "Those posters get more of your time than I do." She smiled.

"And here I thought this was an anniversary gift," I said, holding up the journal. "Today marks two months. Sixty-one days, to be exact."

"I know. Today is a special day, but like I told you, every day is a special day," Dr. Yvonne reminded me.

"I know. I know." I rolled my eyes jokingly at Dr. Yvonne.

I bought a car with Lance's help. I still wasn't sure if that was such a good idea. Financially, it was, but patience-wise, nope. Not at all. Lance could never make a decision about anything without thinking and rethinking and then rethinking some more. I found the perfect car. A red Volkswagen Beetle. We used to call it a bug, and it was the ugliest little car to me back then. I guess my taste changed over the years. Shocker.

After wrapping up my session with Dr. Yvonne, I took the elevator to the first floor where Lance was waiting, leaning against the wall with his head lowered and looking at his phone.

At some point, I knew I'd feel comfortable driving to my appointments alone, but right now the only driving I did was in Bayou, where there were fewer people on the road.

I stopped and watched him for a second. My heart skipped a beat—an involuntary reaction I wasn't quite ready to dissect. Which was what Dr. Yvonne always wanted me to do whenever I brought up a feeling about something. That was why I never told her about these feelings I had when it came to Lance. There was no need to dissect something that I was sure was nothing.

"Why are you standing there?" Lance's deep voice filled the huge lobby.

"I was about to ask you the same thing," I said, a little embarrassed that he caught me standing there in a daze.

"Are you ready for this?" Lance held the door open while I walked through.

"The question is are you ready for it?" I slid into Lance's truck.

"I don't know. Maybe if I knew what was going on," he said before closing the door.

Lance got in and started the ignition before I continued our conversation. "Leah was very vague. She asked if we could come by after my session."

"And you're sure she said we and not you?" Lance pulled out of the parking lot.

"She asked if you were bringing me to my session. I told her I wasn't sure. She said, 'If it's Lance, can the two of you stop by after your session?'" I repeated Leah's words to him for the hundredth time.

"Well, I guess we'll find out soon enough." Lance merged onto the interstate.

I'd talked with Leah every day since everything happened with Skye. She and I met for lunch a couple of days ago, and she didn't say anything about all of us getting together.

Lance turned into Leah and Quinton's driveway. Unlike the last time we were there, this time, it was in the middle of the day, so I could see how huge all the houses were in their subdivision. Leah and Quinton's house was as big, if not a little bigger, than the others.

"Why am I so nervous?" I asked Lance when he opened my door.

"I don't know. I'm the one who should be nervous. I could be walking into a setup." He narrowed his eyes. "Are you trying to set me up, woman?"

"Yes, because, of course I'd want to alienate my only friend," I joked.

Lance pushed the doorbell, and we waited. The door swung open, and Leah stood looking comfortable and beautiful. She wore a red jumpsuit that showed off her petite yet curvy frame.

"Come in." She waved us forward and stepped aside.

I leaned down, and Leah and I kissed each other's cheeks, making a "mwah" sound as we always did for some reason. I felt like it was my first time in their space instead of my second. The house was huge and beautifully decorated. Of course, I'd expected nothing less for Leah. She was the fashion queen, in my eyes. She got that from Mama.

"Quinton's on the back deck. We're going to sit out there, if that's okay." Leah looked up at me and Lance.

"Sounds good," I answered.

Lance nodded and smiled.

On the way to the back of the house, I admired the artwork along the wall. The kitchen was another space that I didn't pay much attention to during my last visit. It was all white with stainless-steel appliances. The floors were so shiny I was sure I could eat off them. Not that I would. Then, as it sometimes did, I saw a flash from the past of me eating off the floor after Adam knocked everything off the table, then demanded that I clean it up.

"No!" he shouted when I picked up the roll of paper towels. "Eat it."

My stomach lurched as Lance reached over, placed his hand on the small of my back, and guided me through the sliding glass door.

Lance's touch was what I needed to be brought back to reality. The flashes didn't come as often as they did when I first came home—but every now and then, they did, and whenever I had one, Lance would always touch me in some gentle way. If he weren't around, he'd call or text right when I'd find myself being pulled into an unhappy memory. It happened every single time, as if he just knew I needed him.

"Hey, guys." Quinton lifted the long fork-looking thing he was using to grill.

I looked over at Leah. "Why didn't you tell me we were eating? I would've brought something."

Leah squeezed my arm. "That's why I didn't tell you. We didn't want you to bring anything. Only yourselves."

Lance was still standing next to me looking even more uncomfortable than the first time.

"Have a seat. Before we eat, there's something Quinton and I want to talk with the two of you about," Leah said.

"Sounds serious," I said, pulling out a chair and sitting at the glass table. Lance sat next to me.

"It is, but not bad. Promise." Leah raised her hand and then sat across from me.

Quinton lowered the grill lid before joining us at the table. He sat next to Leah and directly across from Lance. I didn't think I'd ever see a time when Quinton and Lance would sit so close without one of them hurting the other.

"I'm sure you're wondering why you're here," Quinton said. "I asked Leah to invite you over tonight because there's something important I need to talk with you about." His voice was steady but held a tinge of nervousness.

That made me even more uneasy. The Quinton I remembered didn't get nervous—or at least he didn't show it if he did. At our wedding, I was shaking so much that Leah had to take my bouquet before all the petals fell off.

I glanced over at Lance, who was staring straight ahead at Quinton.

"This conversation is long overdue." Quinton looked at me, then at Lance.

"I won't bore you with all my problems, but the main thing you should know is that I've been holding on to feelings from my past that had nothing to do with you. I know you didn't hurt me on purpose. During what I have to imagine was one of your darkest times, I tried to make it darker. Unlike you during one of my darkest times." Quinton bit his bottom lip for a second before continuing. "I wanted to acknowledge my wrong to your face and apologize to you." Quinton paused. "I understand if you choose not to accept. Not sure if I would, either, if I were you, but I had to at least clear the air."

There was a strange flutter in my chest. I never thought I'd see the day when Quinton would apologize to Lance. I thought the hate he had for Lance would last a lifetime. I, more than anyone, knew how hard it was to admit that you were wrong and openly expose your faults for everyone, especially the person you'd wronged, to see. It took a lot to forgive and even more to ask for forgiveness.

I looked over at Lance. He nodded slowly and looked as if he was giving Quinton's words a lot of thought before he spoke. "I appreciate your honesty. It means a lot to hear you say that, and I accept your apology. If life's taught me anything, it's that we're all a work in progress. And letting go of past hurt isn't as easy as it sounds." Lance chuckled nervously.

"You can say that again," Quinton said.

"Amen to that," I added.

Quinton's words seemed to lighten a perfect November night. I had no idea how much better things would get, though. It wasn't until Quinton turned his attention to me.

"Nova, there's something else. I've been talking with Skye, and we think it'll be good if she splits her time between here and with you. She'd alternate weeks. I was concerned because our daughter isn't the most organized. I know she'll leave something she needs here or vice versa, but this means a lot to her. And I know how much it means to you too."

I was sure my heart would burst right there at that table. It felt like my birthday, Christmas, and all other holidays wrapped together.

Skye and I hadn't talked any more about her moving in because, honestly, I still didn't know if I was ready, but it wasn't like Skye was a baby. It was Mama who reminded me that I was the only one who remembered what Skye was wearing the night she was missing. "You pay attention to every detail of her. You see things others don't see. Like every other mother does," Mama said when we'd left Leah and Quinton's house that night.

Leah smiled. "We think it will be good for her—and for all of us. We're family, maybe not in the traditional sense, but family nonetheless." She looked at Lance. "Even you, Lance."

That got a laugh out of all of us when Lance pretended to be upset. We sat out on the deck, ate, drank, and talked until the sun started to set. Quinton had gone inside and grabbed two blankets for Leah and me.

Once the conversations started to die down, Leah looked over at Quinton. "Did you say you wanted to try those new cigars you bought the other day?" she asked.

Quinton furrowed his brows and stared at her for a minute. "Oh yeah, I forgot about those." He stood and looked at Lance. "Care to join me?"

Lance wasted no time moving from his seat. "Don't mind if I do."

I drank the rest of the water in my glass and then looked over at Leah. "What was that about?"

She laughed. "Was it that obvious?"

"Yeah, kinda."

"Quinton wanted some time to talk with Lance alone. You know, man to man." She stood. "I'll be right back."

Leah went inside and then came back with two wineglasses and a bottle of wine. We moved from the table over to the cushioned chairs that were around the firepit. Leah lit the pit and then poured each of us a glass of wine. We sat side by side on the sofa. Our bodies turned toward each other with one leg tucked underneath us. It was hard to believe that there was a time, not so long ago, when I couldn't be in the same room with my sister.

"So," Leah said, unfolding her cover and draping it over both of our legs. "What's the deal with you and Lance? And don't you dare say nothing because even a blind man can see that's not true." She lifted her arched brows.

My face warmed, and it had nothing to do with the fire.

"Oh wow. You're blushing." Leah laughed. "I guess I have my answer."

"No, it's not like that." I swatted Leah's leg. "But my feelings for Lance are different, I guess you can say. It feels so strange and so . . . I don't know, scary, to be honest. Lance has been there for me in ways I never expected. Like Quinton said, he had every right to turn his back on me, too, but he didn't. He's the same dependable and sweet Lance that he's always been."

"Dependable and sweet?" Leah lowered her head but aimed her gaze at me. "Is that it?"

I was confused. "What else am I supposed to say?"

"You're not attracted to him?" she asked.

I pursed my lips and dipped my head to the side. "Well, that goes without saying. Lance has always been gorgeous. Even as his friend, I knew that."

"Okay, just checking." Leah sipped her wine.

"Anyway." I rolled my eyes and chuckled. "It doesn't matter anyway because I'm not ready for anything serious. I can't jump into a relationship, not now, maybe not for a while."

"It's okay. You don't have to rush into anything. Just because your feelings are changing doesn't mean you have to act on them right away. It's okay to just be, to let things unfold at their own pace."

The back door slid open, and Leah and I both turned in that direction.

"Well, look who finally decided to come home," Leah said when Skye walked out and joined us.

Skye leaned down and kissed Leah's cheek, then mine. "How was practice?" I asked when Skye sat across from us.

"Hard. Then to make matters worse, I had to go to Ava's to work on our project that's due before we get out for Christmas. I'm over school. Can't I just drop out?" She leaned back in the chair.

"Yeah, that's a great idea. I'm sure it won't send your dad to an early grave," Leah teased.

Skye huffed. "My legs burn. Coach had us running so much today."

"Why? What happened?" I asked, remembering the days when my basketball coach made the whole team run. Usually, it was because we'd either played a bad game or had a bad practice.

"At our last game someone on our team called someone on the other team the 'R' word. The other coach heard it and told our coach. No one owned up to it even though we knew who it was. Since no one confessed, everyone had to run."

I leaned forward. "The 'R' word?" I couldn't think of any curse word that began with the letter *R*.

"The word people say about someone who has a disability," Skye explained.

I was still confused.

"Remember in school, how Mrs. Smith taught a small group of students, and the kids said that's the blank class," Leah said.

"Oh." I looked at Skye. "You didn't tell me about that word. Good thing I don't use it anyway. I'll still add it to the list just in case."

It was Leah's turn to be confused. "The list?"

"Skye's been telling me about all the words that people were discontinued for using," I explained.

Skye laughed. "Canceled, not discontinued."

"Same thing." I laughed too.

Skye stood. "I'm going to soak." She gave Leah and me another kiss before making her exit.

Leah and I had almost finished the whole bottle of wine before Lance and Quinton came back out. They sat and we all talked a while longer before Lance and I left. I'd forgotten how much fun we all used to have together. I couldn't lie and say things weren't a little awkward at times, but it was to be expected. One night wasn't going to erase everything, but it was a great start.

CHAPTER 44

Leah

The past month had been the best that Leah had felt in a long time. She and Nova were almost as close as they used to be. The only challenge they had was Skye, and that was only because they both loved her so much. Whenever Skye stayed with Nova and Martha, Leah missed her more than she thought she could. The house didn't feel right without her daughter's presence. Of course, Leah and Quinton found creative ways to pass the time. Being an empty nester wasn't going to be so bad after all, they eventually learned.

Skye was with Nova for the weekend, so Leah and Quinton took an impromptu road trip. Leah couldn't believe it herself. They woke up Saturday morning, and Leah said, "Let's take a road trip." She didn't plan it weeks in advance or anything. It was spontaneous, and she only had a mini panic attack after the words left her mouth. She had a slightly bigger one when Quinton agreed. A part of her hoped he'd suggest waiting until another weekend, which would've given her the proper time to plan, but oh well.

"Where should we go?" Quinton asked once they were both up and dressed for the day.

That was a great question. It was the first week in December and seventy-one degrees in Baton Rouge, but wherever they traveled could be colder, or warmer depending on the direction they took. Leah had a thought, but she wasn't sure how receptive Quinton would be to her suggestion. It didn't hurt to try, though. He'd surprised her once by agreeing to the road trip. There was no harm in pressing her luck for a second time, right?

"How about Houston?" she said.

"Houston?" His forehead wrinkled. "Why Houston?"

She was pretty sure he knew why that was her suggestion, but if he needed her to say it, then she would. "Well, first, because I love going to Houston, and we haven't been in a while. It'll give us a chance to shop at the Galleria."

"And?" he said, confirming that he already knew her motives.

"And we can stop by and visit with Renee for a little while."

"So, not a fun trip then?" he asked.

"Okay, we don't have to go to Houston. But you did say that you'd like to go into the new year with a fresh start. I thought this would be the perfect time for you to visit with your mom and tell her everything you've said to me."

Quinton leaned against the wall next to the walk-in closet. "I don't know if I'm ready to have that conversation with her."

Leah walked over and pressed her body against his. Quinton wrapped his arm around her waist. "Then we won't go to Houston. Or we do go and skip the visit. It's your call. I'm riding wherever you're going."

He stared away from her, then lowered his head to meet her eyes. "The truth is I don't know if I'll ever be ready. And you're right. I did say I didn't want to take any unfinished business into the new year."

"So, we're going to Houston?" Leah asked.

Quinton's deep and passionate kiss was her answer.

Leah checked the temperature and saw that it was pretty close to theirs, which made packing much easier. Leah hadn't pulled out any of her winter clothes yet because when it came to Louisiana's weather, she might need them, and she might not.

"Ready?" Quinton asked while zipping up his overnight bag.

"All ready," Leah said, zipping her last one.

Quinton shook his head at the three bags she'd packed. "We're staying two nights, Leah. That's it."

"I know." She lifted one bag and left the other two for him, since they were the heaviest.

After calling Skye to tell her they were leaving and stopping for gas and road snacks, they were finally ready for the four-hour drive. Leah loved that Quinton always insisted on driving. It was probably because he didn't trust Leah's driving. He said she had a lead foot, but it only felt that way because Quinton drove like a grandpa. Leah hated driving, especially out of town, so his insistence on it worked for her.

Leah couldn't help but laugh when Quinton found his favorite talk radio station.

"What's so funny?" He turned the volume down.

"The night of the sleepover. You remember that night, right?" Leah joked.

He narrowed his eyes and shot her a quick look. "How could I forget?"

Leah realized that she and Quinton talked about the bad part of the night, but that part seemed to erase all the fun they had before Leah dropped the bomb to Nova about their marriage. Now that things were better, she could fill him in. "Before the night was shot to hell, Nova was telling Skye about your taste in music back in the day, then Skye told Nova what you listened to now, and she was shocked."

"Really? Why?" Quinton asked, obviously not getting the humor in that statement.

"Are you serious? Nova said you listened to rap music and at one point thought you were a rapper." Leah waved her hand toward the radio as if presenting it to him for the first time. "That's a lot different from this, wouldn't you say?"

"Well, yeah, but I'm a lot different than I was at seventeen. This is an improvement, wouldn't you say?"

Leah knew her face shouted, "No, I wouldn't say," but she rearranged it before Quinton looked at her for an answer. "Um. I'm not sure if 'improvement' is the word I'd use. Maybe more mature. Yes, that's it. It's more mature."

Quinton's mouth flew open. "What? You said you liked listening to talk radio and jazz. What changed?"

"Nothing. Other than the fact that I lied. I don't like it at all, but you do, so I went along with it."

"What? You lied to me? Who are you? I don't even know you anymore," Quinton joked. "Okay, you choose. How about that?"

That was a huge change. Leah and Skye knew that the number-one rule when riding with Quinton was that the driver controlled the music. That was the only part about not driving that Leah hated. It didn't matter too much, though, because she always had an audiobook loaded on her phone for times like those.

Leah changed the station until she landed on one playing Michael Jackson's "Remember the Time." She and Quinton sang at the top of their lungs. After that was a Prince song, followed by a Whitney Houston song, all the greatest who were gone too soon. The mini concert went on for hours and helped Leah to forget about the anxiety that she'd felt ever since they left home. The visit to Renee was needed, but Leah hoped Quinton didn't feel pressured to do it. More than anything, she wanted him to be ready for whatever came from that meeting. This led Leah to conjure up a list of things that could go wrong, the main one being Renee dismissing Quinton's feelings.

A commercial came on, giving them a break from their singing and giving Leah a chance to do a quick check. She didn't want to kill the mood because it was great, and they hadn't had that much fun together in years, but it would help her if she knew Quinton was okay.

"Hey, you know just because you said you wanted to do this before next year doesn't mean you have to, right? Like I said, we can spend our time in Houston doing other stuff."

Quinton didn't respond at first, and Leah thought he was about to agree that maybe he shouldn't do it now, which she would've supported 100 percent, but he didn't say that at all. "No, I'm actually happy I'm doing this now. Having that conversation with Nova and Lance made me feel so much better. I believe the same will happen with my mom."

"But you understand that this conversation may not go the same way the one with Nova and Lance went, right? That one involved you admitting you were in the wrong. This is you telling Renee how she wronged you."

"I get that, but no matter what, I know I'll feel better when I've said it." He flashed Leah a smile, then winked. "I know you're concerned, but don't be. I'm a big boy, I'll be okay."

"I know you are, big boy," Leah said seductively, which she didn't pull off too well, and once again she and Quinton laughed, which definitely lightened the mood that Leah had temporarily dampened.

The four-hour trip took close to five hours between Quinton's cautious driving, construction, and bathroom breaks. When Quinton pulled into the driveway, he sat for a few minutes. Leah held his hand until he was ready to get out. They'd called Renee when they made it to Houston to see if she was home and up for company. As usual, Renee was excited to hear from them and said she couldn't wait to see them. That was because she didn't know what the visit would entail. Leah did, though, and that didn't make her feel any better.

Since she didn't know the history and how Quinton really felt about being sent to live with his grandparents, she didn't harbor any ill feelings toward Renee. As far as Leah knew, her mother-in-law was a wonderful, loving mother who worked odd hours day and night, and had no choice but to send Quinton to live with his grandparents so he wouldn't be home alone so much. It wasn't safe. It all made sense to Leah, and Quinton certainly benefited from his mom's hard work with all the new clothes and shoes she sent. Leah hadn't realized those clothes and shoes might have been bought out of guilt.

Quinton and Leah continued holding hands while Quinton knocked on Renee's door. He fidgeted with the keys, and Leah could tell he was nervous. Quinton looked over at her and smiled.

"We got this." Leah winked.

It wasn't long before they were greeted by a woman who looked like an older version of Quinton, including the light-brown eyes. Renee's curly hair was cut short. She'd always been a beautiful woman, but time seemed to weigh heavily on her. Her skin was pale, and her eyes were weary. Renee led Leah and Quinton into a cramped family room that was cluttered with furniture that was too big for such a small space.

As they settled in, they spent time catching up and filling Renee in on Skye and Nova. Once the pleasantries were over, Leah sensed a shift in the atmosphere. She volunteered to give them some time alone, but Quinton held Leah's hand tighter, letting Leah know that her husband needed her support, and she was more than happy to give it.

"There's something that I need to talk with you about that I should've done a long time ago," Quinton began, his gaze steady on Renee.

"Okay. This sounds serious." Renee smiled nervously, looking from Leah to Quinton. "What is it? You're scaring me."

"You don't have to be scared. It's nothing bad. Recently, I realized that I've been carrying around some unresolved issues that I needed to deal with so I can find a way to let it go and move on," Quinton explained.

"Unresolved issues? About me?" Renee touched her chest and looked genuinely surprised that Quinton could have any issues with her.

"I didn't realize how much it affected me and how much anger I was still holding on to from you sending me to live with Grandma and Grandpa." Quinton's leg bounced as he spoke. His words spilled out with a raw honesty that touched Leah as if it was her first time hearing them. "I never got over that you chose your boyfriend over me. I couldn't imagine ever doing that to Skye. I can't understand how it was so easy for you to do it to me." His voice broke slightly, and he paused, closed his eyes, and gathered himself as he often did lately whenever he talked about his feelings toward Renee.

Leah held his hand tighter, and her heart ached for Quinton. She wished more than anything that she could take his pain away, but she understood that this was something he had to go through in order to get to the other side of his healing.

Renee folded herself in two, and her body shook as she cried. The ache in Leah's heart grew as it took in Renee's hurt along with Quinton's. Quinton released Leah's hand for the first time since they arrived and sat closer to his mom. When Renee was composed and able to speak, she dropped a bombshell neither Leah nor Quinton expected.

Renee sniffed, and her voice trembled. "I didn't send you away because of my boyfriend," she admitted.

Quinton's brow furrowed in confusion. Leah imagined his expression matched her own. "What? But you said he didn't like children, so I had to go and live with Grandma and Grandpa," he reminded her.

"I know, but that wasn't true. It was easier to tell you that than the truth." Renee's admission felt heavy to Leah, so she could only imagine how it must've felt to Quinton.

"Then what was the truth?" Quinton reached for Leah once again, and she wrapped her hand around his.

"I sent you away because I was addicted to pills," Renee said, her voice barely above a whisper as she adverted her gaze away from Quinton.

Pills? Leah repeated to herself. She never expected to hear that.

Quinton's body stiffened, and the hold he had on Leah's hand tightened. Leah looked at him, and he stared at his mom, unblinking. Leah could tell he was still trying to get his mind to understand what she'd just said.

"What kind of pills? When? I never remember you taking any pills." Quinton's words were filled with disbelief.

Renee wrapped her arms around her body and rocked back and forth as if trying to soothe herself as she told them about one of the most painful times in her life. "When your dad died . . . was killed, it hit me harder than you may have known. I tried to do a good job covering it up because you were young and had just lost your dad; you didn't need a mom who was falling apart to worry about too. So, I pretended to be okay, but I could only pretend for so long. I was the reason your dad went back out that night." Renee shook her head. "I was upset because he'd stopped by the store, and I reminded him to get some eggs. Of course, he forgot because he always forgot something I asked him to get." She blinked as if a memory had stolen her attention. "Anyway, I made such a fuss over him forgetting that he went back out just to shut me up." Renee wiped a tear that rolled down her cheek. "Then, as you know, on his way back, he was hit by a drunk driver and died on the spot. I held on to so much guilt that I could barely function. The doctor gave me some pills for anxiety, but they didn't seem to work. Not the amount he prescribed, anyway. I was taking way more than I was supposed to, and I didn't want to admit it, but I was addicted. No one knew except my best friend, Farah. You may not remember Farah."

"I remember her," Quinton said.

"She knew something was wrong. She found the pills that I'd bought when the prescribed ones ran out. Farah threatened to call and take you away if I didn't get help." Renee's eyes watered. "I was sick, Quinton, and I didn't realize it. The only way to protect you and get the release I needed was to send you to your grandparents."

Leah watched as Renee's body shook with sobs. The raw pain in Renee's voice made Leah's chest tighten with empathy even as her mind raced to process everything she was hearing. Her eyes darted to Quinton, and the sight of him nearly broke Leah in two. Tears streamed silently down his face, but he remained motionless as if frozen in place.

Leah felt torn. The therapist in her wanted to step in and facilitate this crucial moment of understanding between Quinton and his mom. But the other part, the wife, knew this was Quinton's journey to navigate. Her role as his wife was to be there for emotional support, so that was what she did.

For a brief moment, Quinton's eyes met Leah's. She tried to convey her support through her gaze, offering a small, encouraging nod.

"I wish you would've told me," Quinton said softly.

"Believe me, I would've told you the truth a long time ago had I'd known you thought I chose a man over you. Quinton, baby, there's no one on earth that I'd choose over you. You were and have always been the best part of your dad and me. Sending you to your grandparents was the hardest thing I've ever had to do, but I knew you'd have a great life with them. They always spoiled you rotten." Renee's mouth slowly turned up at the edges. "I noticed that only got worse when you moved in. I saw all the clothes and shoes they'd bought you. Things I could never afford on my salary."

Quinton's head raised, and his face asked the same question Leah was thinking. "You didn't buy those things?"

"No, Mom and Dad did."

"They told me that you sent them."

"I guess they didn't want you to think I abandoned you. They tried to do whatever they could to make me look like a good mom, even though I was the worst. What kind of mother sends her child away so she can keep popping pills? You have every right to hate me, Quinton. I don't blame you if you never want to see or speak to me again. It would hurt me to my core, but it's what I deserve."

Quinton once again shifted his body toward Renee. He reached for her hand. "I don't hate you, but I wish we'd had this conversation a long time ago. Things could be a lot different now. Between us, I mean."

Renee nodded.

"There's still time, you know?" Leah spoke for the first time. "This is a good start for both of you, but this also opens up the line of communication so you can continue talking and sharing your true feelings with each other. But it's going to take commitment on both sides." She looked at both of them and then said, "Sorry. It's hard to keep the therapist quiet at times." Leah shrank back to allow them the space they needed to continue talking.

"No. Don't apologize. Sounds like a therapist is just what we need." Renee chuckled.

Ignoring everything that was just said, Quinton said, "I understand now why you made the decision that you did. You said it was the hardest thing you've ever done, but it was also the most selfless thing you could do. I couldn't imagine having to make that choice."

Renee cleared her throat, then swallowed. "Thank you for saying that."

"There is something else I need to ask, though," Quinton said. "It's clear why I was sent away, but what's kept you away? We've invited you for holidays and birthdays, but you never show."

So, it did bother him that she didn't show up. Leah knew it had to, but he'd done a great job pretending it didn't matter. All Leah knew was she'd have a fit if her mom weren't there for her. Over time, Leah chalked it up to Quinton being a man and not letting things bother him like they'd bother her.

Renee rubbed her hands together and then exhaled. "I stayed away because I never felt like you really wanted me there. It was just the vibe I felt, and I hated the thought of making you feel that way."

Quinton's eyes narrowed, and his head shook slowly in protest of Renee's words.

"Maybe I was reading too much into it, or maybe I was the one who felt awkward or out of place. I don't know. I just hate that so much time had to pass before we had this conversation."

"I do, too, because I would've told you that I loved having you around. When I invited you, it was because I wanted you there," Quinton said.

The number-one problem that Leah saw with all her couples was communication or the lack thereof. Listening to Quinton and his mom really drove home how important it was for people to open up and talk with each other, even if it was hard or uncomfortable. Assumptions had stolen so much precious time that neither of them could ever get back. To Leah, that was the saddest part of all of this.

"Well," Leah said, glancing at Quinton, then Renee. "Christmas is in a few weeks. We'd love to spend it with you."

Relief washed over Leah when Quinton smiled at her offer. After she'd asked the question, she thought that maybe she'd overstepped and should've waited to see if it was what Quinton wanted.

"That's a great idea," Quinton added. "You can ride back with us on Sunday if you want, and I'll buy you a plane ticket back."

Renee sat expressionless, and Leah held her breath, praying that Renee didn't deliver Quinton another letdown.

"I'd love that," she finally said. "It's perfect timing, too, because I'm off next week. The lady I sit with is visiting with her daughter for the holidays." Renee's smile lit up her whole face.

Leah had forgotten that Renee was a home health aide. She'd been doing it for years, and she seemed to love it. Before today, Leah used to say she wished Renee cared for Quinton as much as she cared for her patients, but of course, that was before she knew the whole story.

Leaving Renee's house that evening was like an awakening that both Leah and Quinton needed. Quinton was able to shed all those unsaid words and emotions he tried to bury but couldn't.

Quinton pulled out of Renee's subdivision and stopped at an empty lot not far from her house. Leah didn't know what was happening. Quinton got out, and Leah went to him. Quinton pulled her close and held her tight.

"I just needed some air," he explained.

"I understand. That was a lot." She rested her head on his chest.

They stayed that way until Leah lifted her head to him. "You okay?"

He nodded. "I will be." Quinton sighed, then pushed out the word, "Pills." He shook his head. "I can't believe she was addicted to pills. I used to hear Grandma and Grandpa whispering whenever she would call, but I never asked what they were talking about. Not that they would've told me anyway."

"How are you feeling about all of this?" Leah asked as Quinton leaned against the SUV and pulled her with him.

"I feel better knowing she didn't just abandon me for a man. I feel bad that she had to go through all of that, though. Holding on to guilt about my dad's accident. I wish I could've told her it wasn't her fault."

Leah arched her neck toward him. "But you realize she wouldn't have heard you, right? She needed time to come to that conclusion for herself. And time to forgive herself. The same way you needed time to forgive yourself for not being there for Nova. All this time you and your mom were carrying around similar pain and didn't know it," Leah said once that realization came to her.

"They say timing's everything. Maybe this was the right time for me to deal with the issues I had with her. At least that's what I have to believe so I won't beat myself up for not coming sooner."

Leah shook her head. "No, you won't do that because I won't let you. And I agree. Everything happens exactly when it's supposed to happen." She lifted her head more, and Quinton wasted no time pressing his lips against hers.

"Thank you for being you." He kissed her again. "And thank you for loving me through all my stuff." Another kiss.

"You don't have to thank me for doing what I want to do and would choose to do a thousand times again."

That weekend felt like a new beginning for Leah and Quinton. They both knew that they weren't the same people they'd been a few months ago. Between the couples counseling and that trip, they were learning and growing together, and they weren't bonded by grief. They were bonded by love.

CHAPTER 45
Nova

As we walked into the gym, a wave of nostalgia washed over me, so intense it felt real. The squeak of sneakers on the polished floor, the distinct smell of varnished wood mixed with the faint scent of popcorn from the concession stand—it all brought a flood of memories from my days of playing in that very gym. Back then, nothing made me feel better than looking into the stands and seeing Mama, Daddy, Leah, Quinton, and Lance cheering so loud I could've sworn I heard them over everyone else.

I was determined to be a part of Skye's cheering crew during this holiday tournament. School was out for Christmas break, and each year, as they'd done for many years, the school held a basketball fundraiser for needy families. When Skye told me she was playing, I'd made up my mind that there was no way I'd miss it.

Last time, Mama and I were alone, and my anxiety was too high for me to pass the front doors. This time, I walked through the front door and the gym doors with Mama on one side, Lance on the other, and Leah, Quinton, and Renee following behind. I was surrounded by love and protection, and anxiety had no room to break through.

A few people waved as we passed, but for the most part, no one made a big deal about me being there. I couldn't be sure, but I wouldn't have been surprised if Mama went to every house in Bayou and threatened anyone who looked too long. It sounded like something Mama would do, but I'm sure she didn't. After two months of seeing me around town, I believe everyone was used to me now. I wasn't the kidnapped lady who'd just come home. I was just Nova now, and I loved being just Nova or Skye's mom, which Skye's best friend Ava called me whenever they were on the phone, or when she visited with Skye during her weeks with Mama and me. Both worked for me.

After the game started, I completely forgot about everyone else. The whole gymnasium could've been gawking at me for all I knew, but it didn't matter because my entire attention was on that court. "Watch the baseline!" I called out, slipping into coaching mode without thinking.

"Save it for Monday, Coach," Lance teased.

When he asked me to help at the community center, I never imagined it would lead to me assisting Skye with the Little League team. Most of my time was spent at the center helping Lance plan for a two-week summer enrichment program. Since it was only December, I thought it was too early to start planning, but I quickly learned better. Securing food, teachers, supplies, and buses for field trips was a lot of work, and I enjoyed every second. I'd enjoy every second of anything as long as it was with Lance. He made the most mundane activities bearable. I had to be careful saying things like that around Leah, though. She was convinced that Lance and I were in love but that both of us were too stubborn to admit it. Leah had no idea what she was talking about.

"I'm going to grab some popcorn." Lance touched the small of my back as he spoke, and as always, my body reacted. He had to stop doing that. My body had to stop doing that. One of them had to stop doing that.

After a very close and nerve-racking game, we all walked across the court to congratulate Skye on an amazing win. She pulled it off by scoring the winning point in the last few seconds.

Skye was talking with her teammates but broke away from them and ran in our direction when she saw me. She hugged me for so long, and yet not quite long enough. She lifted her head, and I saw the moisture in her eyes.

"Oh, sweetie," I said, attempting to wipe her eye.

Skye shooed my hand away. "No, don't. I can't cry in front of these people. I'm supposed to be tough," she said, attempting a scowl that didn't quite work with the red glossy eyes.

We all laughed.

"I'm glad you came," Skye said as we made our way out of the gym.

"Me too."

Before we drove away, I looked back at the gym that used to be my comforter, which became my challenge and was now my triumph. It was a full-circle moment that would've been absolutely perfect if we weren't missing one important person. I knew that no matter how much time passed, the void Daddy left would always be felt.

I forced myself away from the dread that always came when I missed Daddy. That was a challenge since I missed him every second of every day. Tonight, I was going to focus on the people who were still here and remind myself that the rest of my life was to be about creating new memories. Which was what my family and I were about to do. The annual bonfire was about to start, and I couldn't wait to sit around the fire, roasting marshmallows and drinking Mama's homemade hot chocolate.

Mama and I went home to get more supplies and, of course, the thermoses for the hot cocoa. I didn't know how other places did their bonfires, but in Bayou, it was a big deal. It was more like a festival than a bonfire because there was live music, games, and more food stations than I cared to count. I'd forgotten how much I loved them until Mama reminded me about it a few weeks ago. Since then, it was all I could think about.

I called Lance when Mama and I made it to the field, and he and Quinton came and helped us carry the chairs and thermoses back to our spot.

"This is where we used to set up our chairs every year," I said, unfolding a chair and looking over at the huge fire that sat in the center of the field.

"Well, your father was a creature of habit. Once he found something he liked, he refused to change. I said this was the perfect spot, and we've been sitting here every year since." Mama smiled, but it didn't hide the sadness in her eyes that always came when she remembered Daddy.

"Oh my gawd." Leah rolled her eyes. "Nova, one day Mom took Daddy to Shoney's for breakfast. Do you know that every Sunday for at least six months, we had to go to Shoney's? I was so sick of that place." Leah laughed.

I used to feel so sad hearing stories about my dad of times I'd missed, but now it didn't hurt as much as it did before. There was still a tinge of jealousy, but it didn't stop me from wanting to hear more.

"Has anyone seen Skye?" I asked, looking around the field at all the people gathered in groups, laughing and talking.

"She's around here somewhere with Ava," Leah said.

Lance went to help unload more food while Mama and Quinton were engaged in some conversation. Leah and I chatted about different people who passed by. Some I remembered, but most I didn't. Even before my life was disrupted, I was horrible with names and faces.

"Hey, is that Lance?" Leah stared.

I turned my head, and sure enough, that was Lance. His back was to us, but it was definitely him, and that was definitely a woman with her arm around his waist.

"Who's that woman?" Leah asked.

"I have no idea." I tried to sound nonchalant, but I wasn't sure I was doing a good job.

A few seconds later, Lance came over and sat in the chair beside me. "Having fun?" he asked.

"Yep." I bounced my leg because I always did when I was irritated. The only problem was I had no right to feel that way.

"So, Lance." Leah leaned over me, practically resting her whole body on my lap. "Who was that woman you were just talking to?"

Lance narrowed his brows. "Who, Sierra?" He pointed to the spot they were standing in before.

"Sierra? And who is this Sierra?" She raised one brow.

"Leah," I hissed her name.

Lance laughed. "Sierra"—he turned his attention away from Leah and looked right at me—"is my cousin from Detroit."

"Why are you looking at Nova? I'm the one who asked the question," Leah said.

"Because she's the only one I need to know that information," Lance stated.

I lowered my head and tried to hide the smile of pleasure I couldn't wipe away.

"Well. I guess you told me," Leah said playfully before straightening her body and turning toward Mama and Quinton.

She wasn't the least bit interested in anything they were talking about, but I knew that was her way of giving us some privacy.

"You wanna take a walk?" Lance asked, reaching for my hand.

"We'll be back," I told Leah.

She gave me a thumbs-up, and I tried not to giggle like a silly schoolgirl.

Lance and I walked around for a while, then stopped and stared at the fire. Before then, our conversation had been light, but I had a feeling that that was about to change. Whenever he started a sentence with my name, it meant he'd turned serious.

"Nova, why did Leah really ask me about Sierra?" Lance asked.

I hunched my shoulders. "Because she's nosy."

"Oh. Well, in case she was asking on someone else's behalf, I thought it would be good for us to talk about . . . well . . . us."

"Us?" I turned to him.

He nodded. "I think we both know that things aren't the same between us, right? I mean, and maybe it's just me, but I don't have the same feelings for you that I used to have when we were in high school. And because of that, I think I need to be completely honest with you."

My heart was about to run away from my body.

"Okay?" I heard the shakiness in my voice and cleared my throat.

"After everything happened, I made a vow that I'd never put myself in that position again. The only way to do that was by making sure I never allowed anyone else to get that close to me again. I mean, yes, I've been with other women since then, but it was always clear that I wasn't looking for anything serious. I made sure that point was made by only dealing with them once, maybe twice, and that was it. I'd never see them again." He held up his hands. "I'm not saying it was right, but I felt like it was what I had to do to protect me."

"Okay," I said, trying to figure out where he was going with this.

"Anyway," he continued, "being in a serious relationship again was never something I saw for myself."

I nodded. "Okay," I said again because it was the only thing I could squeeze past the lump in my throat.

"Like I said, I just wanted to be completely honest with you."

"I understand. And we're friends. That'll never change. I just . . ."

"Wait." He held up his finger. "Let me finish."

I thought he had finished, but I stood quietly and allowed him to continue.

"I wanted to be honest with you about where my mind was at the time. My past with women wasn't the best. I'm sure I hurt a lot of them by going silent, and I have deep regrets about that. It wasn't my intention to hurt anyone. I just needed to protect me." He exhaled. "I guess I'm telling you all this because I don't want you to hear it from anyone else and because I used to think that I was trying to guard my heart, but now I think what I was doing was preserving it." He took my hand in his. "For the person I'd trust with it a thousand times."

My eyes burned and I blinked, refusing to break down. "Me?" I asked, as if I didn't know the answer.

"I know you aren't ready for a relationship, and I understand that." He chuckled. "Probably more than anyone, but I would like for both of us to try and open ourselves to trusting and loving again. And I'd really like if we did that with each other."

I closed the space between us. "I'd really like that too." My words broke into pieces, but they were clear enough to put a smile on his face.

Lance and I held each other and stared at the fire. That night, I knew, without a doubt, that my best friend had just turned into one of my greatest loves. I used to think that God didn't care for me, but I'd since learned that he cared for me so much that he gave me not one but two of his best creations. Quinton was the love of my past, and Lance was the love of my always. Once as a friend and now as much more.

EPILOGUE

Nova

One Year Later

The community center buzzed with warm, inviting energy. Conversations softly murmured, and laughter occasionally burst. The large banner hanging above the makeshift stage read, TOGETHER WE HEAL, the name of the program Leah and I started. We chose today to introduce the program to the community because it marked the one-year anniversary of my freedom.

"You look gorgeous," Leah said, scanning me from my freshly cut hair, which I now wore straight and in a bob, to my black-leather boots.

"Thank you. You look rather gorgeous yourself," I said, mimicking her movement from her curly shoulder-length hair to her brown-leather boots.

We acted as if we weren't together when we picked out our outfits. Well, when Leah picked out our outfits. I still wasn't the most fashionable one, but I never was, so that wasn't a surprise. I did have to admit that I loved the gray sweater dress she chose for me. I'd been working out every day with Lance, and my body looked even better than it did during my basketball days.

Leah chose a nude-colored fitted dress that fell right above her knees. Her body had always been perfect for fitted clothes. I, on the other hand, had to work to keep mine that way.

Lance walked past me and touched the small of my back. His touch sent a ripple of tingles across my skin and caused my heartbeat to quicken. My gaze followed him as he made his way to the front of the crowded room and up to the microphone, where he asked everyone if they could take their seats so we could get started. *Am I ready for this?* That was the question I'd been asking as the day drew closer. I still didn't know the answer, but I had no choice but to move forward, which had been the theme of my life this past year.

After Lance welcomed everyone, he called Skye up to the podium. I looked around because he was supposed to call me up. "What's going on?" I asked Leah.

"I have no idea," she whispered.

The sound system made a loud screech as Skye adjusted the microphone. She placed her hand over her chest as if the sound had startled her. Every time I saw her, I had to pinch myself because it was so hard to believe that the beautiful, tall young lady who stood so bold and demanded everyone's attention with her presence alone was my daughter.

Skye tucked her chin-length hair behind her ear. Quinton still wasn't keen on her cutting her hair, but what could he do? She was eighteen now, and in seven short months, she'd be graduating and going off to college. A thought that made me want to cry every time it came to me.

"Good evening, everyone," Skye began, her voice so clear and confident. "I'm actually not supposed to be a part of the program today, but I had to take the time to say something about the two women who brought us all here. Two women who have impacted my life in ways I can't begin to explain." Skye smiled as her eyes found Leah and me.

Leah's hand flew to her mouth and her eyes glistened. I caught a glimpse of her right before my own tears distorted her image.

"Not many young girls are blessed to say that they have two moms, but I can. Both of them have taught me different lessons that I know

I'll use for the rest of my life. Teeah taught me to never let anyone tell me who I am. My job is to show them, then demand that they treat me how I'm supposed to be treated. Even if that means walking away sometimes."

I rubbed Leah's back and bit my bottom lip before I remembered the lipstick that I rarely wore.

"Then, there's my mom, Nova." Skye exhaled loudly into the microphone. "Sorry," she chuckled. "My mom has taught me to never stop fighting. She's taught me that times may be tough, but so am I. In fact, I'm tougher." She paused again while everyone clapped. Once the applause died down, Skye continued, "So, I guess I just want to stand here, in front of everyone, and say, Teeah . . . Mom . . . I love you both so much, and I'm so proud of you." A tear rolled down her face, and Leah and I couldn't get to her fast enough.

By the time Skye was seated, there wasn't a dry eye in the room. I had no idea how I was supposed to speak after that, but I managed to do it.

"You got this," Leah whispered when she took my hand and stood beside me.

I took a minute to scan the room, which was filled with familiar faces from Bayou and a few reporters from the local newspapers and television stations. Everyone was there, from teenagers to senior citizens, and all sat and waited to hear what we had to say.

Leah stood beside me while I stared at the microphone. I was about to share something with them that I'd never shared before. Three squeezes from Leah, "I-got-you," was enough to get me started.

"Good evening, everyone." I paused and willed my voice to stop shaking.

I looked at the people in the front row: Mama, Lance, Skye, Quinton, and Dr. Yvonne. Skye gave me a little nod before I continued.

"I returned home a year ago today, but I didn't come alone. I brought with me fifteen years' worth of hurt. Had you told me last year that I'd stand here today and share my story with a room full of people, I wouldn't have believed it. In fact, it would've been more believable if you'd told me I could fly like a bird. But here I am, standing here, ready to tell my story, and that's because I wasn't alone in my journey."

The room was silent. All eyes were on me, but not in a threatening or uncomfortable way. In their eyes I saw encouragement, so I continued.

"Dr. Yvonne taught me that healing doesn't mean the damage never existed. It means the damage no longer controls me. My sister and I started this program on the foundation of healing together. It's a place for us to speak, to listen, and most important, to understand that no one needs to face their past alone. Once my family and I could open up and be honest about what we were going through, we realized that we were all healing from something." I pointed to Mama. "My mom from losing a spouse and recently a very good friend." Then I pointed to Quinton. "Quinton, from childhood trauma and overcoming the guilt he carried when I was kidnapped." Next, I pointed to Lance. "Lance, from accusations that, though proven to be false, still had a major impact on his life." Mama, Lance, and Quinton all nodded as I shared a piece of their story, with their permission, of course. "And my sister, Leah"—I turned to Leah—"who you'll hear from shortly and will tell you of her journey of healing and acceptance."

After going into more detail about my will to survive in the room and my life after that experience, I moved aside so Leah could share her story. She talked about accepting that she'd never be able to give birth and how that impacted her life.

"What I've learned," Leah said, "and my sister has learned is that when it comes to healing, there is no definitive end point. Some days, you may feel like you've made it. You've reached the end of your healing journey, but then out of nowhere, something can happen that will pull you right back in. The one thing I stress to my clients is grace. Give yourself grace during your process and know that there's no right or wrong way when it comes to healing. My process looked a lot different than Nova's. And Nova's process looked a lot different than Quinton's and Lance's and even our mom's," Leah said.

Almost all heads in the crowd, from young to old, were nodding in agreement. Some people were crying, some were smiling nervously, and some sat expressionless with their hands over their chest as if our words hit them right where they needed them the most. That was when I knew that this idea was bigger than me and bigger than Leah. It might even be bigger than Bayou itself, but that was where we had to start, because for Leah and me, Bayou was home, and healing should always begin at home.

Afterward, Leah and I were standing around talking with people who kept coming up and thanking us for doing this. Many people signed up for the group sessions that Leah, Dr. Yvonne, and other therapists and psychologists they knew wanted to be a part of. I was overwhelmed with gratitude.

"Hey, can I speak to you for a minute?" Lance asked after a couple I was talking to walked away to get some snacks.

"Sure." I followed Lance out of the building.

"We had to come out here? This must be serious," I joked, but not really.

Lance looked at me in a way I'd never seen him look at me before. There was no smile, no frown, just Lance.

"What's wrong?" I braced myself for bad news that couldn't have come at a worse time because all I wanted was to hold on to the amazing feeling I'd felt.

"Nothing's wrong. Everything's perfect." His deep voice, as it always did, soothed my soul. "I wanted you to know how incredibly proud I am of you. When I had the idea to open this place, the only people I thought about were the kids. It never crossed my mind to do something like this for anyone in Bayou, or anywhere, who needed it."

"Thank you," I said, determined not to break down any more tonight. "I couldn't have done it without you."

"That's where you're wrong. You could've done without me because that's how strong you are, but I'm glad you didn't." Lance took his finger and swept my hair away from my eye. "Have I told you how beautiful you are?" He wrapped his arm around my waist.

"Maybe once or twice, but I can hear it again?" I smiled.

Lance tilted his head. "You're the most beautiful woman I've ever seen."

"Okay, now you're stretching it." I laughed.

He didn't laugh. Not even a little bit.

There was a time I used to ask God why he hated me so much. Now, I asked what I did for him to love me so much. Ever since the night of the bonfire, which would be a year this December, Lance and I had moved way past friendship. I thought it would be strange being with him and kissing him, but there was nothing strange about it. It felt right. And the best part was that we still talked way into the night. We still made each other laugh until we cried. He was the first person I wanted to talk with every morning and the last voice I wanted to hear before I fell asleep at night.

"Where'd you go?" His deep voice drew me back to him.

I pressed my body into his. "Nowhere. I'm right here with you."

"Where I hope you plan on staying." He winked.

"Oh yeah. How long would you like for me to stay?" I teased.

He bit his bottom lip, and my body went wild. Every gesture he made aroused me. I was still trying to get used to that feeling.

"How about forever?" He released me and reached into his jacket pocket.

"What are you doing?" I asked nervously.

He didn't answer. He pulled out a box and dropped to one knee.

My mouth gaped open.

"Nova," he began, his voice soft but clear. "We've been through so much together. From scraped knees and frozen-cup summers underneath our special tree. We've always shared our deepest fears and our biggest dreams. Every special memory in my life includes you." He lowered his head as if he needed time to gather himself before he continued. "There is one moment we haven't shared yet, and there's no one else on earth I want to share the rest of my life with more than you." He released my hand and opened the box.

My eyes fell on the largest, most elegant ring I'd ever seen. It had to cost a fortune. I was about to protest that it was too much. That I didn't deserve it. But I stopped myself because I did. I deserved all the good things life had for me, but more than that, I deserved to be loved the way Lance loved me.

Through tears I said, "I love you more than I imagined I could ever love anyone again. Someone spent years tearing me down, but it only took months for you to help build me back up again. For us to build each other back up again," I corrected. "Yes, Lance. I'll marry you."

Lance slid the ring on my finger, and out of nowhere a thunderous applause came from behind me. I turned around to see that my family, and the few people who were still there, had made their way out to witness what would become one of the best events of my life.

"Oh my God." I covered my mouth with my free hand.

We were hugged and kissed by our family and friends, then Lance and I stood with our arms wrapped around each other and waved as the rest of the visitors drove away. The only people left were the five people I loved most in the world.

"Oh my God, would you look at that sky," Mama said, causing all of us to lift our heads. The sun was going down, and the sky was now a palette of vibrant oranges, deep pinks, and soft purples, all bleeding into the next like watercolor on paper.

"Mama, are you okay?" I asked when I noticed a tear sliding down her cheek.

Mama nodded. "One evening, right before your dad took a turn for the worse, he and I sat out on the front porch and talked for hours. The sky looked like it did now, and we couldn't get over how beautiful it looked. He told me if it was God's will and our prayers weren't answered the way we wanted, then whenever I saw a sky that beautiful, to remember that night and all the others we'd shared together." She looked at me, then Leah. "He's so proud of both of you." She looked around. "Of all of you. We're family, and nothing or no one will ever tear us apart."

ACKNOWLEDGMENTS

First, I can't acknowledge anyone before acknowledging God and His work through me. I firmly believe that every creative idea is a gift from Him, and I'm deeply grateful He chose me to bring this story to life.

I want to express my deepest gratitude to my incredible agent, Michelle Jackson. Thank you for believing in me and championing my vision for this novel. Your guidance and encouragement have been invaluable.

To my amazing beta readers: Shavonna Futrell, Antionette Gates, Marcena Hooks, and Chantel Rogers. Your feedback, honesty, and insights helped shape this story into what it is today. I'm so grateful for your time, attention, and love for this book.

To my sister writers: Nicole Bird-Faulkner, Keleigh Crigler Hadley, and Gina Johnson, your support, camaraderie, and words of wisdom kept me going on the toughest days. You've been my inspiration and my cheerleaders, and I'm so thankful for our connection.

A heartfelt thank-you to my editor, Megha Parekh, for believing in my story and investing in it with such care and passion. Your faith in my work means more than I can express.

To everyone at Lake Union Publishing, thank you for making this journey such a remarkable experience. To my developmental editor, Tiffany Yates Martin, your insights elevated this story in ways I couldn't have imagined. Working with you was one of the best parts of this process. To my copyeditor, Hannah Buehler, and my proofreader, Tara

Whitaker, your meticulous attention to detail ensured that every word was polished to perfection. To the entire team who worked tirelessly behind the scenes, thank you for turning my dream into a beautiful reality.

To my husband, Neil, and my children, AJ and Kirsten, thank you for your patience, understanding, and unwavering support as I poured my heart into this book. Your love means everything to me, and I couldn't have done it without you three by my side.

And finally, to my faithful readers. You are the reason I write. Thank you for your continued support and for taking this journey with me. Your love for my stories fills my heart and fuels my passion.

This novel wouldn't exist without each and every one of you. Thank you for being a part of my life story.

ABOUT THE AUTHOR

Lorna Lewis is gifted in turning characters' dreams into drama and crafting stories rich with emotion while exploring the complexities of real-life situations such as marriage, infidelity, fertility struggles, betrayal, and the power of forgiveness. In addition to being an author, Lorna is also an educator. She believes in using her creativity to inspire and teach others both in the classroom and through her writing.

A native of Varnado, Louisiana, a small town much like the ones she loves bringing to life in her stories, Lorna's southern roots influence the sense of community, culture, and warmth in her work. When she's not writing her next novel, Lorna enjoys spending quality time with her husband and their two beautiful children, finding joy in family life, and drawing inspiration from her own experiences to enrich her writing.